Getting off on
Frank
Sinatra

IMBRIFEX.

Also by
Megan Edwards

Roads from the Ashes:
An Odyssey in Real Life on the Virtual Frontier

Getting off on Frank

Sinatra

Megan Edwards

IMBRIFEX BOOKS

IMBRIFEX BOOKS
Published by Flattop Productions, Inc.
8275 S. Eastern Avenue, Suite 200
Las Vegas, NV 89123

Printed in the United States of America.

Set in Adobe Caslon, Designed by Jennifer Heuer

www.MeganEdwards.com
www.Imbrifex.com

ISBN 978–0-9972369-0-3 (trade paper)
ISBN 978–0-9972369-2-7 (e-book)
ISBN 978–0-9972369-1-0 (audiobook)

First Edition: March 2017

For Ruth

Getting off on Frank Sinatra

Chapter 1

My life in Las Vegas improved dramatically when I started getting off on Frank Sinatra. That's what I tell people. Then, while they're still trying to figure out how to react, I continue.

"I'd like to get off on Dean Martin, too, but I just can't. And in case you're interested, Mel Tormé is too short, Hugh Hefner's a dead end, and I can never remember whether Jerry Lewis goes both ways."

The truth is, I can never even remember where Jerry Lewis is exactly, but I know there's a street named after him somewhere on the west side. Hugh Hefner is really just a driveway next to the Palms casino, and Mel Tormé can claim only one block near the Fashion Show Mall. Frank Sinatra, on the other hand, really takes a girl places. When I-15 is jammed, I leave the red lights to the tourists and slip off to join the taxis and locals zipping unimpeded up the back side of the Strip. Dean Martin serves almost the same purpose on the other side of the freeway, but he didn't rate an exit. So Ol' Blue Eyes is my man. When life in the fast lane slows to a crawl, I know I can count on Frank for relief.

In fact, getting off on Frank Sinatra saved my life the time a crazed maniac in a jacked-up Ram pickup tried to push me off the freeway. If Frank hadn't been right there offering a quick getaway, bits of my DNA might still be clinging to the embankment just north of Russell Road.

Now that I think of it, Frank Sinatra also helped me out the day I found my first dead body. It was the hottest day of the millennium, and I had not only discovered the bloody corpse of a local philanthropist, but I'd spent more than three highly stressful hours with a homicide detective who was trying to decide whether I was capable of mutilating a woman's face and strangling her with a drapery cord. A traffic jam on the way home might well have turned me into a genuine psycho killer, but there was good ol' Frank waiting to fly me to the moon. Or at least get me up to Flamingo without committing a felony.

I should never have found that body, let alone recognize that it belonged to Marilyn Weaver. Yes, *that* Marilyn Weaver, the founder of the most prestigious school in Las Vegas and the city's best-loved altruist. I had met her only the day before, and I had met her son just that afternoon. How I ended up snooping in her bedroom, looking inside her closet, and entangling myself in a high-profile murder investigation is a perfect example of that plentiful Las Vegas commodity: bad luck. I'm going to call it bad luck, at least. Because if I don't call it bad luck, I'll be stuck agreeing with what I know my family and friends think: It was David's fault.

Before my rendezvous with murder, David Nussbaum and I were as perfect a pair as Barbie and Ken. Like them, we were designed to complement each other. I'm blonde, and he's dark. He's Jewish, and I'm a WASP. We do have some things in common, of course. We both come from commuter towns north of Manhattan, and we both went to Princeton. I still think it's ironic that we met in Las Vegas instead of on the East Coast, and until everything flipped upside down, it was my favorite coincidence. The day I hooked up with David was the day I smelled the roses, saw the birds, and heard the music. The morning he turned twenty-eight, I still lived in paradise.

By midnight, I'd moved to hell.

David's birthday evening started out happily enough. We hooked up after work and went to a concert at Mandalay Bay.

"Really, I thought she'd be good," David said as we walked out to the parking garage afterward.

"She was practically over the hill when you were still in diapers. Why are you such a fan?"

"Copper, don't be such an age snob. Youth isn't everything."

"She didn't suck because she's old. She just sucked. I thought you had higher standards."

I looked at David. He does have higher standards. I was shocked that a concert he had carefully selected to celebrate his twenty-eighth birthday had turned out to be such a dud. If the tickets hadn't set him back over three hundred bucks, I would've suggested we duck out at the break.

"Well, Chris Farr said he'd get me comp tickets for Tori Beaulieu at Caesars Palace next week," I said. "Maybe she'll make up for it."

That's one of the benefits of working for the arts and entertainment editor at *The Las Vegas Light*. So many free tickets come my way that I could pass them out to the entire population of my hometown in Connecticut and still have enough left over to treat my whole family. I haven't even worked at *The Light* for a whole year yet, but I've seen every production show on the Strip, most of the "just passing through" ones, and a whole slew at venues scattered all over the rest of town. If the word didn't already mean something else, I'd call myself a showgirl.

David usually came along. As a staff reporter, he was higher ranking than me, but free tickets came his way only occasionally. Since "Copper Black, Assistant Editor" found them stuffed in her mailbox daily, our dating ritual revolved around what shows looked the most appealing.

Unfortunately, I didn't score any tickets for Jamie Hixson, the slightly passé, surgically remodeled diva in platform boots whose voice gave David goose bumps. He also likes old Clint Eastwood movies, so maybe he just came of age a couple of decades too late. On the other hand, I've become a rabid Rat Pack fan since I've lived in Las Vegas, and I'm four years younger than he is. Age snob, my ass.

"So where do you want to eat?" David asked.

"We have reservations at Ciliano," I said.

"Wow!"

"Your birthday deserves it. Surprise!"

Ciliano is my favorite Las Vegas restaurant. It's at the top of the Monaco, and it has an eagle's-eye view of the whole valley. With luck, we'd even rank a table next to the windows overlooking the Strip. I don't have a lot of "juice" in this town yet, but I've learned how to drop my connection with the newspaper where it makes the loudest clang. I don't really like doing it, but David's birthday was an occasion that deserved a bit of chutzpah. He always has plenty, and I never seem to have enough. It is a quality, I reminded myself before reciting my résumé to the maître d', that I need to cultivate. Updating show times and writing blurbs about hypnotists and lounge singers is okay for the moment, but it's getting to be time to insist on a promotion.

"Damn, this is impressive," David said after the hostess seated us at the best table in the room. Champagne arrived automatically, just as the maître d' had promised. "This is really sweet, Copper. I love you!"

"I love you, too, David. Happy birthday."

If only that had been the end of the evening. When you start off with a bad concert, does it have to mean you're stuck with a bad finale? At least David waited until after the chocolate soufflé.

In fact, he waited until we got back to his place.

"We've got to talk, Copper," he said after we'd walked into his kitchen from the garage.

My heart took a swan dive to the floor. Guys never say "We've got to talk" unless they've signed on with al-Qaeda, gotten indicted for income tax evasion, or they're about to dump you.

"Haven't we been talking?" I said. "Isn't this the part where we take off all our clothes?"

"I mean it. Let's go into the living room."

Getting cozy on David's sofa held undeniable appeal, but first I needed to know just a little more about what was going to hit me.

"Got something to drink?" I said, and we ended up sitting across from each other at the kitchen table over a couple of glasses of ruby port.

"My mother's weakness," David said as he recorked the bottle and set it between us. "I never know when my parents might show up, so I always keep some on hand."

I took a sip. Not bad. I took another. I waited for the blade to fall.

"Rebecca called today," David said at last.

Damn! I was expecting a Boy Scout hatchet, but this was a double-sided Paul Bunyan axe. Rebecca is David's not-quite-ex-wife, the person who made me the one thing I have always scorned: an "other woman."

At least I am not a home wrecker. Rebecca had gone back to New York more than six months earlier, back when David was a coworker I barely knew. He swore their marriage had been dead for a year, and their divorce was "only a formality." I shouldn't have bought that line, but it just proves that love really does conquer all. I fell in love, and my so-called principles fell to the wayside.

"We've been through this before," I said. "I thought you only talked to her lawyer."

David was silent far too long.

"Copper," he said at last, "I love you."

Damn, again! I love "I love you," but don't expect me to be thrilled when it occurs in the sequence I just reported.

"Remember when I went to visit my parents?"

"Memorial Day."

David nodded as my stomach knotted.

I didn't like thinking back to the last week in May, and until now, I thought I'd never have to. David and I had one of our worst fights ever while I was driving him to the airport.

"I'm going to be seeing Rebecca," he said while we were stopped at a light on Eastern.

My pulse quickened. "Why?"

"She wants to talk. She thinks we can work things out better face to face. She might be right. The lawyers have created a lot of tension."

"You told me you were done talking to her. You *swore*." We were rolling again, my hands gripping the wheel, my heart pounding.

"Copper," David said. "It's no big deal. I'm only telling you because I don't want secrets between us."

I don't want Rebecca between us. She's supposed to be ancient history. Only a technicality.

"Where are you seeing her?"

"Her new place in Scarsdale. She invited me for dinner."

Fortunately, we were stopped at another red light when he said that. I clutched the wheel and stared straight ahead as a candlelit dining room materialized in my mind's eye. Along with music and wine and Rebecca, dressed to ensnare …

"Don't go," I said.

"Copper, I—"

"*I mean it. Don't go.*"

He didn't speak again until we were pulling up in front of the terminal.

"I'm not sure whether I'll go or not," David said. "But it's my decision."

A line in the sand.

I stopped at the curb and shifted into park. Two could play that game. "If you go, we're done."

That was the last thing I said to him. We didn't kiss, and I didn't reply when David thanked me for the ride. He waited, shrugged, turned, and walked into the terminal.

And there began the longest weekend of my life. Pride, anger, and righteous indignation kept me from calling David, but I couldn't help longing for his number to appear on my cell phone's screen. The only thing that did appear was a text message Saturday night informing me that I didn't need to pick him up at the airport on Monday. It was all I needed to know.

We were done.

And we might have stayed done if I hadn't woken up Monday morning in a cold sweat. Dreaming about life without David was horrible enough. I couldn't bear the thought of actually living without him. I grabbed my phone.

"I'm sorry," I said when he answered. "I never should have—"

"I'm sorry, too," he said. "I never should have, either."

I picked him up at the airport later that day. By the time we got to his house in Green Valley, I'd forgiven him for seeing Rebecca, and he had forgiven me for trying to stop him.

As though there had been no hiccup, life resumed.

Until now.

I watched as David took a huge swallow of ruby port. He took another, set his glass down, reached across the table, and took my hands in his.

"Copper, I love you."

I didn't say anything. If he was going to tell me he was calling off the divorce, I wasn't going to help him.

"Rebecca called today. She's pregnant."

Chapter 2

I wish I'd been born a billionaire heiress. David's announcement combined with a bottomless bank account would have sent me scurrying to any available source for mind-altering drugs. I would have enhanced their effect by ensconcing myself in the most throbbingly deafening Strip nightclub, and if I was still ambulatory in the morning, I would have cleaned out all the high-end boutiques at the Caesars Forum Shops. Instead, I was stuck with making David drive me home. I stayed up all night twisting, turning, and watching infomercials for Magic Bras and old episodes of *Cheaters*.

It was unfair. It was wrong. Worst of all, it required me to start a new life when the old one had been perfectly fine. Okay, I was dating a married man, but it's not like we could never be seen in public together or he had to worry about lipstick on his collar. His wife had vanished, and David had erased her from his house. The only thing that still linked them was a freaking piece of paper I had never even seen.

Unless, of course, he was about to become a father. That was what I couldn't get my head around. There was also the image of what an impending baby meant logistically. My mind wandered unwillingly to a bedroom in Scarsdale. The details of my mental images did not include a turkey baster.

David's snugglefest in Rebecca's boudoir had occurred three months before. When he came back to Las Vegas, there I was waiting for him with open arms and willing loins. He hadn't said a word until now, and I couldn't help thinking that if Rebecca hadn't called with her delightful news, he never would have.

Did he owe me full disclosure for the time we were officially uncoupled? I didn't know what the rules were anymore. I just felt hurt, confused, and—above all—angry.

David had wanted to talk more, but I'd told him I needed some space. He couldn't avoid providing it, because he had to go to Tonopah in the morning. A talk show host from Denver had turned up with a bullet in his head in the same motel room where Howard Hughes once got married.

Designer hallucinogens would have been more fun, but it was plain old caffeine that got me to work in the morning. At least it was Tuesday. Mondays are rough on calendar girls, but Tuesdays are generally pretty easy. My boss had editorial meetings in the morning, and I usually caught up on my personal email before attacking my long list of press releases.

There were four messages in my inbox, and three were spam. "Road Trip!" read the subject line of the fourth. I took a gulp of coffee and clicked it open.

Dear Copper,

Will you be around this week? I was going to fly to Berkeley, but I found a car I couldn't resist, and now I'm driving. I'm leaving

Austin later this week, and planning to make Vegas by Saturday afternoon. Mind if I crash with you for a night or two? It would be great to catch up.

Love,
Daniel

I set my mug down and almost smiled. This was revolving-door timing at its best. Out with Soon-to-Be-Daddy-David and in with Thought-It-Was-Over-Daniel. The only thing still connecting me to the love of my college life was his last farewell at the airport when he was in Las Vegas at Christmastime.

"Bye," I had said.

"Bye *for now*," Daniel had insisted.

Damned if he wasn't right.

Daniel,

Of course you can crash with me! I'm still living in the apartment at my brother's house. Do you need directions? What time do you think you might get here?

XO
Copper

I hesitated before I clicked "Send." Did an X and an O imply something I really didn't mean? No, I decided. I write "XO" when I write to my mother. It's just cute and friendly and totally platonic. Or at least I could claim it was.

"Copper, do you dye your hair?" The voice shattered my thoughts like a wrecking ball on old stucco. I looked up to find Mary Beth

Sweeney filling the entrance to my cubicle.

"Are you a natural blonde?" she asked.

"Yeah," I said. "Why?"

"Are you sure?" Mary Beth took a couple of steps toward me, and I couldn't help shrinking back as she reached a hand toward my hair. "I thought maybe because your name is Copper, you might really be a redhead."

"It's a family name," I said, flipping my hair over my shoulder and out of her reach.

"Crap," Mary Beth said.

"Excuse me?"

"I'm working on a story about hair dye," she said. "There's a new study linking it with depression and obesity."

Gee, thanks, Mary Beth. Not only was she insinuating that I was lying about whether I color my hair, she was also suggesting that I'm a gloomy fatso, which describes her considerably better than it does me. Mary Beth has gray roots that vanish like clockwork under a fresh coat of magenta-tinged auburn every couple of months, and she wears expand-o-matic pantsuits. She's been at *The Light* since the days of the Mob, and she knows everyone in town, along with their credit ratings, police records, political affiliations, sexual preferences, blood types, cup sizes, medical histories, grade point averages, and mothers' maiden names. It was difficult to believe she didn't know that my first name had nothing to do with my hair color.

"I wanted to ask you if you'd be worried enough about the study to stop using hair dye."

"Maybe you should ask Alexandra Leonard," I said. "She told me she's been dyeing her hair since she was in eighth grade."

"I don't want to quote her. She has a byline. I need a nobody."

I bit my tongue. Someday I'd show her who was a nobody.

"You'd be perfect, Copper. You're slim and perky. Would you risk losing that for golden hair?"

"I guess I don't have to," I said, feeling a little mollified. "Sorry I can't help you."

"Oh, well," she said, waving her hand dismissively. "Never mind. I'll come back when I need something about boyfriends or tattoos." I sighed, almost glad that I had more serious things to think about. Although I couldn't help wondering how she knew about my tattoos.

Mary Beth's chunky heels were still clopping down the hall when my cell phone buzzed.

"Hi, Copper."

It was Sierra. Ordinarily, I don't particularly like it when my sister-in-law calls me at work, but her next words made me forgive her instantly. "Dinner tonight? I'm making pizza."

Sierra's not terrible. It's just that she and my brother are also my landlords. I swore I'd move out of the studio apartment over their garage right after Christmas, but somehow August arrived, and we all still shared an address. Their landlord skills have improved slightly since I moved in a year ago, but they're still guilty of a little too much *in loco parentis*. Michael, who's an Episcopal priest and twelve years older than me, has always felt obligated to act as Dad *pro tem*, and ever since he and Sierra adopted a toddler last December, I've had an extra mom, too.

For Sierra, motherhood is a sacred vocation that has inducted her into a divinely sanctioned sisterhood headed up by the Virgin Mary. All that saintliness can be a little hard to take, especially considering that Sierra once made her living as an exotic dancer. Fortunately, there's an adorable little boy in the picture who howls with delight every time he sees me. Nicky is just learning how to talk. If it didn't make people uneasy, I'd howl with delight every time I saw him, too.

Sierra is also the best cook I know, and tonight a family dinner at the vicarage—that's what I call their house—was just the sort of R and R I needed. I loved the thought of forgetting about boyfriends and sinking my teeth into a big fat slice of homemade pizza with the fabulous *linguica* she gets at the International Marketplace. Sierra, bless her heart, even makes her own dough.

"Want to go to a fund-raiser for the Neon Museum tomorrow night?" Michael asked as I was finishing my second slice. "Sierra can't make it."

"Will it be at the Boneyard?" I asked.

"The party's downtown at the El Sereno," Michael said, "but there'll be buses to the Boneyard all evening."

"Count me in," I said as I failed to remove a big spot of tomato sauce from the front of my white tank top. "I've been dying to get inside that place ever since I found out it existed."

The Boneyard is where neon signs go when they die. It's at the north end of Las Vegas Boulevard, and you can see the tops of rusted neon wonders sticking up over coils of razor wire when you drive by. I don't know what it is about bulb-studded arrows, crumbling genies, oversized slippers, and other relics from bygone bingo parlors, motels, casinos, and trailer parks, but I'd been eager to take a closer look ever since David explained why the signs from businesses with many different owners all ended up in one gaudy cemetery.

"It's because the company that's made most of the signs on the Strip over the years has always preferred to lease them rather than sell them outright," he'd told me. "When old buildings die, the obsolete glitz goes to the Boneyard."

And now, at last, I was going to the Boneyard, too. It didn't make me forget about David, but it was definitely a nice distraction.

"Fancy clothes?" I asked.

"Not black tie," Michael said. "But don't dress like a tourist."

"I'll meet you at the El Sereno," I said. "I'll be coming straight from work."

Then Nicky grabbed my leg and dragged me into the living room to play with his pirate ship.

Chapter 3

As I walked from the parking garage into the El Sereno the next evening, I realized Michael hadn't told me exactly where to find the party. In any other city, I would have asked at the desk, but in Vegas, baby, you just look for the showgirl. Sure enough, there she was, filling an archway with a peacock headdress and displaying a few miles of fishnet-encased leg. She handed me a glow-in-the-dark necklace as she told me to head up the escalator. When I got to the top, another sequined babe pointed the way to the Special Moments Room. A crowd had formed in front of a check-in table. I spotted Michael in the huddle, ensconced in a conversation with a woman I recognized. Jenna Bartolo, whose juice flows from her May-December marriage to a local casino mogul, serves with Michael on the board of the Alliance for the Homeless. She was decked out in a floor-length strapless scarlet dress studded with rhinestones. Bracing myself for a wordless but scathing appraisal of my cotton slacks and knit top, I took a step toward them. Fortunately, my brother saw me before I got any farther. He excused himself and crossed the floor to meet me.

"Hey! I thought you said this wasn't black tie!" I said. My brother was wearing a tux.

"It isn't. The suit I wanted to wear is at the cleaners."

"Jenna Bartolo—"

"Jenna always dresses to kill. You know that."

I glanced around the rest of the crowd. Only a few guys were wearing monkey suits, and there were plenty of people in outfits more like mine. Jenna really did stand out.

After Michael had procured our name badges, we headed into the Special Moments Room, which looked like it also served as a wedding chapel. One wall was covered in a mural featuring chubby cupids flitting past puffy clouds and floating rosebuds. I was still checking out the gazebo covered in plastic ivy when Michael handed me an orange card.

"Your Boneyard bus pass," he said. "I've got some schmoozing to do up here, but they're running shuttles every few minutes. Why don't you go on over there while it's still light?"

Sounded good to me. Old signs are photogenic any time of the day, but a desert sunset makes them positively enchanting. I immediately made my way back past the two feathered females and out to the curb. Joining a line of partygoers, I boarded a shiny black shuttle bus. When I stepped inside, there was exactly one seat left, on a four-person banquette facing the door. I plopped down next to a sixtyish blonde woman in a black silk shell and matching capris. She was balancing a Prada purse on her knees. My little backpack—even though it was made of leather—looked impossibly plebeian sitting next to it on my own knees, so I leaned forward and stuffed it behind my feet. As I straightened back up, I caught sight of my seatmate's nametag.

Marilyn Weaver.

I knew that name. Taking another look at her face, I recognized the strong jawline and high forehead I'd seen in newspaper pictures. Marilyn Weaver was the founder of the Anna Roberts Parks Academy. A private prep school, it generated news stories whenever one of its students won an award, a celebrity gave it a big donation, or someone picked on it for being snobby. I always thought the allegations of elitism were slightly unfair because the school was known for giving full scholarships to students who couldn't afford the tuition. On the other hand, the children of several Strip performers and high-end casino magnates, including Jenna Bartolo's stepdaughter, went to school there. The campus—at least what you could see of it from the street—looked like a resort.

"I like your backpack," Marilyn said.

"I like your purse," I said.

"Birthday present," she said with a sigh. "I've got a closet full of them. My husband doesn't have much imagination in that department, and I seem to have birthdays every couple of months these days."

The bus pulled out.

"Ever been to the Boneyard before?" Marilyn asked.

"My first time," I said. "How about you?"

Marilyn laughed. "The signs are old, old friends. My husband's on the board of the Neon Museum."

"Oops," I said as I connected a couple of mental dots. "I think I should have known that."

"I don't see why," Marilyn said. "It's not like he's the mayor."

"He's Curtis Weaver, though, isn't he?" I asked. "The architect who's working on the new service center for the Alliance for the Homeless?" I knew about Curtis Weaver because my claim to volunteer fame is that I write the Alliance's newsletter. I just never thought about who Mr. Weaver might be married to.

"Yes, that's right," Marilyn said. "Curt's best intern has been working on their new building nonstop for the last six months. That site of theirs next to the wastewater treatment plant has been a real baptism by fire for the poor boy." She turned to the young woman sitting next to her.

"This is my niece," she said. "Charlene's visiting from Montana."

From her hat to her boots, Charlene looked like an ad for a dude ranch. She responded to my "Nice to meet you" with a husky "Howdy." If I'd had only her voice to go by, I might well have assumed she was a guy. Charlene was definitely female, however. Her long dark hair flowed over her shoulders, and she was wearing bright red lipstick.

"Charlene's in town for the cutting horse trials at the Silverado," Marilyn said.

What the hell is a cutting horse? I wondered, but there was no way I'd ask. That's what Google is for.

"Charlene's the defending national champion."

Charlene shot her aunt a disapproving look over the top of her glasses. "Don't boast about me," she said.

Marilyn chuckled and patted her knee. "Be proud of your accomplishments, honey," she said. "I certainly am."

Charlene looked away, and Marilyn turned toward me. "What do you do?"

"I work for the newspaper."

Whether that registered with Charlene, I couldn't tell, but it really got Marilyn's attention. By the time we reached the corner of Las Vegas Boulevard and McWilliams Avenue, she knew all about my gig at *The Light*. At first, I'd given her the "assistant editor" line, but she didn't stop grilling me until she knew the truth about my lowly role.

"I'm serious about journalism, though," I said as we climbed off the bus. "Right now I'm looking for a good topic for a freelance piece I can sell to a national magazine. It's one of the reasons I came tonight."

"The Boneyard's definitely popular for that sort of thing," Marilyn said as we crunched through the gravel along the chain link fence to the entrance, "but that's why you might have trouble selling an article about it. Half a dozen photographers show up here every week, and all of them are writers or working with writers. You need a topic with less competition."

As we walked past the first cluster of old signs, a tall string bean of a guy wearing a Neon Museum name badge rushed up.

"Marilyn! Is Curtis here?"

"No. He had a late meeting. He's going directly to the El Sereno. If he doesn't make it, I'm set to give his after-dinner remarks. He gave me his notes."

"Okay," the guy said. "Let me know if you need anything."

"Thanks, Brad."

Marilyn, Charlene, and I were standing in front of a twelve-foot yellow sign with the words "Gambling Hall" spelled out in red Western-style letters studded with empty lightbulb sockets. Rusty only around the edges, it looked more serviceable than some of the other signs standing and leaning nearby. "Mobil Park" read a faded blue one, and another touted a bygone all-you-can-eat buffet.

"I gotta go." Charlene's abrupt announcement broke the silence.

"Oh, honey, are you sure?" Marilyn said. "I thought you said you could stay for dinner."

"Sorry. I've gotta get back for tonight's exhibition round."

Marilyn put her arm around Charlene's shoulders. "See you tomorrow, then. I'll be there at nine—for the semifinals."

Charlene sauntered off toward the shuttle bus, her long dark hair concealing most of the artwork on the back of her black leather jacket. All I could make out was the bottom half of a big eagle with outstretched wings.

"Charlene's the head wrangler at the Lazy B Ranch, which has been in our family for three generations. She's a fabulous horsewoman, but she's—well, she had a tough childhood." She paused. I pulled out my camera.

"Hey, I've got an idea for you," Marilyn said.

I snapped a picture.

"For a story," she continued. "Do you know about the Anna Roberts Parks Academy?"

"Your school," I said. "Yes. It sounds wonderful."

"Yes, my school," she said, "but I avoid calling it that because too many people think I own it. I don't own it. It's a nonprofit corporation. It owns itself."

I took another picture, this time of a high-heeled shoe covered in peeling silver paint and burnt-out lightbulbs.

"That's from the old Silver Slipper," Marilyn said. "The story is that the slipper kept Howard Hughes awake at night in his rooms across the street at the Desert Inn, so he bought the place and took it down."

"Nice to have the funds to solve all your problems," I said.

"It would be even nicer if money really did fix everything."

I snapped another frame and looked at Marilyn. I'd known her for less than half an hour, but it was easy to see that something was troubling her. Whatever it was, she shook it off.

"So, anyway, I was thinking you might like to do a story about the Parks Academy. This is our seventh year, and we'll be graduating our first senior class. Twenty-six students. Three painters, one sculptor, six singers, four dancers, five musicians, four actors, one novelist, one filmmaker, and one poet-songwriter."

She rattled it off so smoothly I had the feeling she could easily have gone on to provide me with complete résumés for each one.

"Several have a good shot at Juilliard," she continued, "and some already have agents. One is doing ads for the Monaco—"

"Dressed as Marie Antoinette?" I'd just seen the Monaco's new billboard near the airport.

"Yes, that's Michaela Parrish. It's a good contract for her. It's already opened a few more doors."

Marilyn pointed at a large rusty sculpture of a man holding a pool cue. "When he was at the Granada he had a sword and a Zorro mask," she said. "Then he got moved to Lotsa Slots on Boulder Highway and turned into a pool hustler."

I laughed, happy that I had a knowledgeable tour guide on my first visit to the Boneyard. Every sign had to have a story, and Marilyn probably knew them all. But even though the forest of aging neon was enthralling, I couldn't help pausing to consider her suggestion. I'd driven by the Parks Academy several times. Surrounded by an ornate but impenetrable wrought iron fence, it wasn't the sort of institution you could stroll through uninvited.

"Could I interview a few of your students?" I asked. "Maybe at several points during their senior year?" I could think of at least three local publications that might jump at a story about hometown kids shooting for the stars, and if I could latch onto a bigger angle, maybe I could get a major magazine interested.

"I'd be happy to arrange it," Marilyn said. "With your background, you'll understand what they'll be going through."

Along with my job description, Marilyn had elicited my academic credentials during the bus ride. I wasn't sure that applying to Princeton was the same as trying to make it in Hollywood or Nashville, but if my Ivy League experience was getting me inside her citadel, I wasn't going to argue.

"Why don't you come to campus tomorrow afternoon? I'll be there until four thirty or so. I've got a plane to catch."

"I could probably make it by three thirty," I said, hoping my boss wouldn't mind if I left early. "Would that be too late?"

"Not at all," Marilyn said. "I can give you a quick tour. And even though it's still summer vacation, you might meet a student or two."

Back at the El Sereno, Michael spotted Marilyn and me as soon as we stepped inside the Special Moments Room.

"Marilyn!" he said, rushing to join us. "I'm so glad you've met Copper."

"Not half as glad as I am," Marilyn said. "She's going to catapult the Parks Academy into national headlines."

Michael arched an eyebrow at me, and I felt my ears warm.

"Marilyn's invited me to interview members of the first graduating class at the Parks Academy," I said. "It should make a wonderful story."

"Have you seen Curtis?" Marilyn said, as a tall slender man in a linen jacket slipped out of the crowd and moved behind her. He smiled and winked at Michael, then put a finger to his lips. Then he snaked his hands around the sides of Marilyn's head and covered her eyes. Marilyn yipped and jumped.

"Curt! You know how I hate that!" she said. But she was smiling as she turned to him, and he pecked her on the cheek.

"I'm glad you're here, darling," Marilyn said, smoothing her hair. "I wasn't looking forward to being your understudy."

"My meeting finished early, and I dropped by Kayla's on my way over here."

"Oh, God. You mean the old Nash house?" Marilyn said with a visible shudder. "Is it habitable?"

"Yup, Kayla moved in just before she left for Singapore last week," Curtis said. "Michael, nice to see you." They shook hands, and Curtis turned to me.

"Curt, this is Copper Black," Marilyn said, preempting my brother. "Michael's sister. She's a journalist."

"A privilege to meet a member of the press," Curtis said as he bowed and brushed his lips across the back of my hand. I blushed. God, I love being called "the press."

"It's great to meet you," I said. "And thanks for all your work on the Neon Museum."

"It's been a long haul," Curtis said, "and there've been times I thought we'd never make it. But here we still are, and fortunately, so are the signs. Are you sticking around for the rubber chicken?"

"Wouldn't miss it," I said. "I'm looking forward to your talk."

Curtis beamed. He had a happy round face and a full head of sandy hair. His wire-rimmed glasses gave him the air of a jolly college professor.

Michael and I had scored seats at the head table because he was giving the invocation, and I silently thanked Charlene for cutting out early. Her empty chair meant that I could sit next to Curtis and continue our conversation.

As we waded through our overdressed salads and toyed with our *coq au Michelin*, he told me all about how he had grown up in western Massachusetts, gone to school in Los Angeles, worked in San Diego, and come to Las Vegas for a six-week project twelve years ago.

"I fell in love," he said. "With a woman and a city." It sounded like a well-rehearsed line, but Curtis seemed sincere.

"Enough about me," he said. "Tell me all about you."

And that began the conversation that made an already pleasant evening a truly smashing success. Not only did I visit the Boneyard and get an invitation to tour the Parks Academy, but by the time I had finished my last bite of polyethylene cheesecake, Curtis Weaver had set me up with a new place to live.

Chapter 4

I woke up an hour earlier than usual the next morning, my mind racing. *I've got to send Daniel my new address,* I thought, *before I forget.* More sleep would have been nice, especially after the three glasses of *Chateau Mal de Tête* I'd had at the Neon Museum party, but with a school tour and a new home looming on a near horizon, I was way too exhilarated to doze.

While my coffeemaker gurgled, I logged on and sent a message to the guy who once called me "babe."

> *Dear Daniel,*
>
> *Amazing news! I'm going to be house sitting while you're here. My new address is 425 Vista Miranda Street (see attached map). I haven't seen the place yet, but it's a huge house (with a swimming pool!) that was built for a mobster's girlfriend and later lived in for years by a family that owns a mortuary. The current owner had to go to Singapore to rescue her daughter from the aftermath of a whirlwind romance with a Canadian diplomat, and her original house sitter unexpectedly bagged out to go into rehab. In exchange for free rent, all I have to do is take care of her houseplants and let some workers in who are doing some remodeling. And get this—in addition to free*

rent, she's going to pay me. I didn't let on that I would have gladly paid her.

Looking forward to seeing you on Saturday. I just might throw a party!

XXOO,
Copper

At work, I was extra happy to have the Parks Academy and moving plans to think about, especially when David showed up at my desk. My heart stopped briefly when I looked up. Damn those eyes of his. They're these dark pools of wisdom and emotion, and when he's upset, they smolder all the more. They burn straight through to my core. The guy melts me faster than Vegas sun on butter.

"Can we talk?"

His voice was even, but I could still hear a plaintive note. Combined with the look in his eyes, it very nearly made me stand up and hug him. Instead, mustering the anger I also felt, I continued leafing casually through my mail. David didn't seem to notice that my hands were shaking.

"I've got news," I said. "I'm moving."

Silently, I thanked Curtis Weaver once again for setting me up with a house-sitting gig. Talking about my new home was a great tension reliever.

"You're going to live in the old Nash house?" David asked when I finished telling him. "The love nest Nylons DeLuca built for Lollipop Lassiter?"

I wasn't surprised that David recognized the house. I'd done a little Web research on it earlier and already knew that Lollipop's real name was Betty.

"I thought the guy's name was Vincent."

"Yeah," David said, "but strangulation by panty hose was his sig-nature murder method."

"Oh," I said, regretting that I hadn't looked beyond Wikipedia. "Well, somebody named Kayla Lord just bought the place. She's a real estate broker."

"I've heard of her."

I am always amazed at what a small town Las Vegas really is.

"She made headlines a couple years back when she bought some land the airport sold off," David said. "She was accused of being in cahoots with the appraiser because she got a real sweetheart of a deal."

"She's crooked?"

"Nothing was ever proved. It's possible she was just lucky."

"Anyway, I'm her house sitter for a month. I'm moving in tomorrow after work."

"Need some help?"

I hesitated. I'd filled the last two days with as many distractions as I could find, but now that David was standing in front of me—damn it. I couldn't deny I missed him. Why had he gone and wrecked a beautiful thing?

I looked at him and heaved an inaudible sigh. Maybe we could morph into those mythological creatures known as "just friends."

"Well, could you bring takeout to the Nash place tomorrow?" I asked. "Around seven?"

"I'll stop at Lotus of Shanghai," David said, brightening up consid-erably. "And maybe I'll pick up some incense and a Bible on my way."

"What are you talking about?"

"You may not be safe there without an exorcism."

I shrugged off the small wave of uneasiness that David's last com-ment left me with. Who cared if the Nash house was built by a mobster? Living in a Las Vegas landmark was going to be fun, I told myself. Something to dine out on. Something to shock my parents with, which suddenly made me remember that I actually *could* show the place off to my dad.

He was going to be in town the next week for something called the LifePower Convention. It was exactly the sort of New-Age-find-your-bliss-self-help thing that my father used to laugh at. That all changed when he announced he was gay last winter and started listening to Bette Midler CDs and spiking his hair with sculpting gel. And then, along came the boyfriend who's a "life coach." I wasn't sure how I'd feel hanging out with them, but inviting them over for dinner seemed like a good way to get used to the new dynamic.

And in addition … a swimming pool all to myself! The mercury had climbed to 110 yesterday, and today was ripening into an even hotter scorcher. I closed my eyes and imagined myself floating at midnight under the stars. If the backyard was as private as Curtis had told me, there'd be no need for a bathing suit.

"Good morning, Copper."

Oh, brother. Mary Beth Sweeney was back. At least she was smiling this time.

"How are you?"

"Fine, thanks," I said warily.

"I hear you're going to be staying in the old Nash place," she said.

Damn! News travels fast around *The Light*. But I guess I hadn't told David it was a secret.

"Yeah. I'm house sitting for the new owner."

"So I heard, and your experiences there would make a great column. Nobody but a Nash has been inside that place for thirty years, but the stories from back when Lollipop Lassiter lived there—"

"Why was she called Lollipop?" I asked.

Mary Beth smirked. "Well, the story is that she had a talent. Think

Monica Lewinsky."

"Oh," I said, hoping I wasn't blushing too obviously. But it's not like Mary Beth had embarrassed me. I'm just programmed to turn fuchsia whenever I'll look the silliest.

"You write a column now?" I said. Had I missed the latest round of new assignments?

"Not quite," she said. "Greg's put out the word that he wants a new human interest column. He's been rearranging the editorial lineup ever since Ed Bramlett died and Lorraine Baxter moved to Seattle." She shifted her weight, reached inside her blouse, and hitched up her bra strap. "He's says the field's open, so I'm working on a few spec pieces to convince him to pick me."

I managed to ease Mary Beth out of my cube without making an actual agreement to let her write about me. As the sound of her clodhoppers died off down the aisle, I called Chris Farr. He's my boss, but he's very collegial. If our editor-in-chief was making new assignments, I could count on Chris to tell me all about them.

"Yes, that's right, Copper," he said when I reported what Mary Beth had told me. "He wants a new Art Braverman. Art was before your time. His 'man about town' column ran three days a week for over twenty years. Nobody's ever really replaced him, and Greg thinks the time is right."

I took a breath and let it out slowly. I wasn't sure what I was about to say was politically advantageous. I took another breath. What the heck?

"I'd like to try for it."

Chris was silent longer than I liked.

"I know I'm inexperienced, but—"

"It's not that."

"Well, what, then?"

"First, I don't want to lose you. Second, you probably won't get the job. Third, you'll make enemies if you do."

We talked a bit longer. In spite of his concerns, Chris thought it was remotely possible that Greg Langenfeld would like the idea of a "fresh young voice." He agreed that writing about living in the Nash house and visiting the Parks Academy would make good spec pieces. By the time I hung up, I was very nearly convinced it would be worth risking the wrath of people like Mary Beth Sweeney to try for the new gig. Even if I didn't land the job, I told myself, I'd be building my portfolio. I swore to Chris I'd do it all on my own time. I'm not sure he believed that was possible, especially when I followed my declaration with a request to leave early.

"Of course," he said. "You know our deal."

"Our deal" is that I'm willing to work nights and weekends on a moment's notice in exchange for a few hours off here and there. It usually works to my advantage, because emergencies are rare in arts and entertainment. I've had to work at night only twice: once when a comedy magician keeled over dead on stage, and once when a Chinese acrobatic troupe had visa difficulties.

Really, Chris Farr is the best boss anyone could ever have. His only flaw is that he keeps his private life private. I don't know where he lives, where he went to school, or even his sexual preference. The only tidbit he's ever let slip is that some of his past occurred in Huntsville, Alabama. As for the rest, he might as well become a shadow as soon as he steps outside *The Light*.

I'll talk this whole column thing over with David tomorrow night, I decided as I turned back to my inbox full of press releases. It will be perfect for keeping us off the subject of babies.

Curtis Weaver surprised me by dropping by after lunch. I walked out to the front desk to meet him.

"Slight change of plans. I've got to go out of town," he said, handing me a set of keys. "Sorry I can't give you a personal grand tour of the Nash house, but everything's pretty straightforward. Call me on my cell if you need anything."

I took the keys, which were dangling from a brass keychain with a tag that said "Lady Luck."

"Oh, and I almost forgot. Never use the front door. The big key goes to the door on the side that's under the grape arbor."

"What's wrong with the front door?" I asked.

"Hasn't been used since Lollipop Lassiter's day."

"What's this little key for?"

"Oh, that's for the basement. Colby's studio."

"Colby?"

"Colby Nash—didn't I mention him?"

Even though the property now belonged to Kayla Lord, it turned out there was still a Nash attached to it. The youngest of three brothers who had grown up in the house, Colby was the family's black sheep. Instead of following tradition and becoming an undertaker, Colby had decided his calling in life was making movies. The basement had been his studio since he was in high school, and he'd made a deal with Kayla to rent it for a few months while he found new space.

"He really does make movies," Curtis told me. "Sci-fi, horror, that kind of thing. You won't ever see them in theaters—they go straight to video and supposedly sell well in Thailand. You can find them online if you're interested."

I was more interested in whether I really wanted to share a house with a stranger. I mentioned my concern to Curtis.

"Colby only has a key to the basement," he said. "And you can't get into the house from down there. It has a separate door outside."

"That's what the little key opens?"

"Yeah. It also opens the gate to the yard behind the swimming pool, but I left that gate open for the guy who's building the tortoise burrow."

The tortoise burrow?

It was just one more thing Curtis had forgotten to mention. Besides the Steven Spielberg wannabe living in the basement, there would be a fifty-year-old desert tortoise named Oscar living in the backyard. Kayla Lord had recently adopted Oscar from the Las Vegas chapter of the Tortoise Protection Society. Somehow, Curtis's assurances that "Old Oscar will be no trouble at all" did little to calm my nerves. Besides a tragically short-lived guinea pig I was given when I was ten, the only animal I've ever called my own was a stray cat that decided to move in with me last winter. I still considered Sekhmet mine, but she had quickly realized that my sister-in-law was a much better kitty mother than I could ever hope to be. Sierra and I have negotiated a "joint custody" arrangement, which at least makes it easy for me to be away for a month without having to take the cat away from her regular haunts.

"The guy who's building the burrow is keeping Oscar at his place until it's done," Curtis said. "You won't have to worry about him for another few days, but I left Oscar's manual on the dining room table."

His manual?

"Look, I've got to run," Curtis said, "but call me if you need anything."

"Thanks, Curtis," I said.

"Thank *you*, Copper. Kayla really didn't want to have to fly back from Singapore to take care of Oscar. She definitely owes you one."

Chapter 5

"A great place to call home." That's the all-American slogan of Henderson, the city south of Las Vegas that used to be an island in the sand. Then, like rising bread dough, both Henderson and Las Vegas expanded to the point where the two cities bumped up against each other.

Because David lives in Henderson, I'm more familiar with the place than I would be otherwise. He'd pointed the Parks Academy out to me a couple of times when we were first dating, but just to make sure I'd find it on my own, I printed out directions and a map.

I already knew from my earlier drive-bys that the Anna Roberts Parks Academy was surrounded by a formidable fence, so I wasn't completely surprised that the entrance gate had a guard. He set down his oversized Coke cup when I pulled up to his kiosk.

"I'm Copper Black, here to see Marilyn Weaver," I said.

"Oho! Just who I was a-waitin' for," he said as he scribbled something on his clipboard. Then he turned off his television and did something to make the gate in front of me begin to swing open. "Wait just a sec, please."

He pulled a baseball cap over his bald dome and popped out the side of his booth. Wedging himself behind the wheel of a golf cart, he pulled in front of my minivan and waved at me to follow.

Just past the kiosk a landscaped traffic island featured a carved stone sign. "Anna Roberts Parks Academy," it read in large chiseled letters. Underneath, a delicate italic script spelled out "Reach for the stars."

Zipping into a parking lot, the guard pulled up near a space next to a white pickup truck and pointed. He waited while I pulled into it, then I stepped out into the afternoon furnace and locked my door.

"Where—?"

"Hop in, miss," he said before I could finish. He patted the seat next to him and smiled. "I'm driving you. Nobody's getting heatstroke on my watch."

The campus seemed deserted as we rolled down a tree-shaded lane and pulled up in front of a tan two-story building with big letters over the door that spelled out "Beeman Hall."

"Ms. Carpenter'll help you," my chauffeur said. "Her desk is just inside the door." He offered me a return trip to my car when I was ready to leave, but I assured him I could manage on my own. Tipping his baseball cap, he rolled off.

I stood at the door of Beeman Hall for a moment, surveying my surroundings. Except for the sound of a distant lawn mower, the place was utterly quiet. It seemed more like a retirement community than a high school, but maybe that was the golf cart influence.

Inside, it took a second for my eyes to adjust from the bright glare of afternoon sunlight, even though I found myself in a two-story atrium with a skylight. A serious-looking gray-haired woman was sitting on a high chair behind an elevated desk. A name placard read, "ANASTASIA CARPENTER, REGISTRAR." Turning from her computer monitor, she peered at me over her half-glasses.

"You're here for Sean," she said. It wasn't a question.

"Um, no," I said. "I'm here to see Ms. Weaver."

"Oh," the woman said, staring at me as if she didn't believe what I'd just told her. "Of course. One moment."

Just then Marilyn appeared in a hallway I could just see from my spot in front of Ms. Carpenter's desk. Someone was behind her, and as they drew nearer, I recognized Charlene, Marilyn's cowgirl niece whom I'd met at the Boneyard.

"Copper!" Marilyn called as soon as she saw me. "I'm so glad you could come!"

"Thanks for inviting me," I said as they reached Ms. Carpenter's desk. "Hi, Charlene."

Charlene looked exactly as she had the night before, except this time she wasn't wearing earrings, and she had slung her leather jacket over her shoulder. Understandable, I thought, given how hot it was outside.

"Charlene made it to the finals today," Marilyn said. "We're so thrilled." She squeezed Charlene's shoulder and tried to pull her close, but the cowgirl resisted.

"Oh, come on, honey," Marilyn said. "It's perfectly okay to be proud."

Charlene caught my eye before she hid her face under her cowboy hat, but I couldn't read her expression.

"Congratulations," I said.

"I only wish I were going to be in town on Sunday for the finals," Marilyn said, trying the hug thing again. "Would you like to go, Copper? I'd be happy to get tickets for you and a friend."

"Well—"

Why not? Daniel might like to go, and a little online research had revealed that cutting horses are actually pretty interesting. The trials were all about how well the horses could separate one cow from a whole herd. In addition, attending the finals might just give me another topic for a column.

"Thanks," I said. "I'd love to."

"Great! Two tickets will be waiting for you at the box office,"

Marilyn said. She turned to Charlene. "And I'll be there in spirit, honey. Just like your mom."

Charlene's cheeks reddened, but I couldn't tell whether it was because she was pleased, embarrassed, or something else.

"I need to show Copper around," Marilyn said. "You want to come along, or—?"

"I'll wait in your office," Charlene said, "but I do have to head back to the Silverado pretty soon. Gotta take care of Scarlett."

"I'll be back in a few minutes, honey," Marilyn said. "I'm just giving Copper a quick tour."

"See you on Sunday—" I began, but Charlene was already heading back down the hall.

"Scarlett's her horse," Marilyn said as she moved toward the registrar's desk. "You're going to love seeing the two of them in action." She laid her hand on Ms. Carpenter's shoulder. "Annie, this is Copper Black," she said. "She's a journalist—here to make us famous."

Ms. Carpenter looked at me, but she didn't smile. In fact, I could almost swear she sniffed.

"How nice," she said.

"This school couldn't operate without Ms. Carpenter," Marilyn said. "The students all call her "The Hard Drive," because she remembers absolutely everything. She never forgets a face or a name, and she even remembers all their birthdays."

I glanced at Ms. Carpenter as we moved down the hall, and our eyes met for an instant. Memorizing me, I couldn't help thinking. Maybe I'd get a birthday card next March.

"Lucky for us, Kelly Baskin and Chanel Torres are on campus today. They're seniors, and both of them have entered a singing competition in Los Angeles. They've been coming in to work with Mr. Rice, our voice coach."

I was about to say something when a guy stepped out from around a corner in front of us. He was about my age, I guessed, and he was wearing a pressed white shirt and tie.

"Sean!" Marilyn said. "I thought you were heading out to meet with Larry."

"He canceled," Sean said. "I'll reschedule for later next week."

A look of doubt crossed Marilyn's face, but she banished it with a smile. "I'd like you to meet Copper Black."

"It's a pleasure," Sean said, grasping my hand and flashing a friendly grin. "I've heard so much about you."

Marilyn rolled her eyes.

"This is my son Sean," she said. "He's our director of development."

"Money scavenger, she means," Sean said with another grin. "Keep an eye on your purse."

As his mother rolled her eyes again, I couldn't help noticing Sean's resemblance to her. In addition to being similarly blonde, he was fit and tan. A tennis player, I was willing to bet.

"So you're going to write about us," Sean said. "*Fast Times at the Anna Roberts Parks Academy.*" He shook his head, still smiling. "Well, okay, maybe not."

"I'm no screenwriter," I said. "I'm a nonfiction sort."

"Is there really any difference between fiction and nonfiction?" Sean said. "Maybe we should get together over some absinthe and discuss story theory sometime."

I couldn't help smiling as Marilyn heaved another heavy sigh.

"I'm introducing Copper to Kelly and Chanel," she said, "but—"

She glanced at her watch. "Goodness, it's getting late, and I still have to run home before I go to the airport. Sean—my office, please. I need to touch base with you on a couple of things."

"Yes, Ms. W," Sean said, snapping his hand to his brow in a military salute. "I hear and obey."

Just then, a door opened down at the end of the hall. Two girls and a young black man in a workout suit stepped out.

"Just who we were looking for!" Marilyn said. "Kelly, Chanel, and Mr. Rice." She started walking toward them.

I turned back to Sean, but he was gone.

"Mr. Rice!" Marilyn called. "There's someone I'd like you to meet!"

She introduced us, then excused herself and headed toward her office. For the next twenty minutes, I learned all about how Kelly and Chanel had both made it through cattle-call auditions for a reality show called *Rising Stars* in Hollywood the week before. Kelly looked like an updated Spice Girl, and Chanel had obviously modeled herself on Beyoncé. I didn't hear them sing, but if the judges could be swayed by looks, both of them should continue to do well.

Mr. Rice was eager to recite all his credentials. He seemed most proud of his stint as "Ooey Tophat" in a Broadway musical called *The Dalai Lama Goes to Washington*. I'd never heard of it, but I emitted an obviously expected "Oooh."

"So, what brought you to Las Vegas?" I asked after the girls had left to change their clothes. Marilyn reappeared just in time to hear my question.

"A gig with *The Boys from Bali*," he said. "It was a bit of a shock going from Broadway to rip-away pants, but *Dalai* had just ended, and I needed to eat. Fortunately, I met Ms. W."

Marilyn smiled. "I was the fortunate one. To have someone with Mr. Rice's abilities and background at a high school is simply amazing. I'm always afraid we're going to lose him to someplace with more prestige."

"This is where it happens," Mr. Rice said. "To be able to work with young talent is a privilege beyond anything else I've ever done." He looked at Marilyn. "Even Ooey."

"We're so lucky," Marilyn said, putting her arm around Mr. Rice's shoulders. "So, so lucky."

I looked at both of them, wishing I had a camera. The two of them looked so sincere, so dedicated. I hoped I could stage such a shot in the future, when a photographer would be with me. It would be the perfect complement to the story I was already outlining in my mind.

"Thanks so much for visiting, Copper," Marilyn said before she headed out to catch her plane. "I'm so glad our paths crossed last night. I have a feeling this is the beginning of an exciting relationship." I watched her as she said good-bye to Ms. Carpenter and move toward the door. When she opened it, intense afternoon sunlight instantly turned her into a black silhouette.

"She's amazing," Mr. Rice said, looking after her. "And that's an understatement."

Soon I had made plans to meet Mr. Rice, Kelly, and Chanel the following Tuesday afternoon. All three seemed eager to talk and to be included in my story, and Chanel even promised to talk to another senior named Margot Tanner.

"She's a writer," Chanel told me. "And she's published. Two poems in *Southwest Magazine*, and her screenplay came in third in the Nevada Film Office's screenwriting contest."

It put my high school to shame, I couldn't help thinking. At New Canaan High, all we worried about was whether we'd look good to the admissions officers at Ivy League schools. These kids were out testing their mettle in the real world—and they were obviously succeeding. While it made me feel a little inadequate, it also made me feel as though I'd struck gold. This was going to be a great story.

After Mr. Rice showed me the rest of Beeman Hall, I steeled myself for the hot trek back to my car. I figured I'd go home, peel off my clothes, pour myself a—

"I meant it about the absinthe," a voice behind me said. I turned to find Sean smiling at me. "Ever tried it?"

"Doesn't it make you crazy?"

"Maybe the kind van Gogh drank," Sean said, "but the new stuff's okay. Can I prove it? Like right now?"

Was he actually asking me out? God. The universe was throwing guys at me.

"I'm sorry, but—"

"How about a quick beer?"

"Well—" I said, intending to decline.

"I can tell you all the school's dirty secrets."

Damn! How could I resist an offer like that?

"Okay," I said, mopping my brow.

"Let's go to the V. It's the closest place, and you're in dire need of refrigeration."

Chapter 6

The V Resort's most distinctive feature is a blue glass tower rising near the corner of St. Rose Parkway and Las Vegas Boulevard. The only high-rise for miles around, it's a major landmark, but I'd never been inside.

Sean glanced at his watch. "The bar on the eighteenth floor opens in five minutes. How about we meet there? Fabulous view and great martinis."

Hmmm. A bit of a shift from a quick beer.

"I've got to swing by my office," Sean said, "but I'll be right behind you."

We exchanged telephone numbers just in case, and I headed out the Parks Academy gate.

After finding a parking space in the V's garage and getting lost in the casino, I finally discovered the elevator to the bar in the tower. At the top, a friendly hostess pointed me in the right direction, toward a long narrow room with huge glass windows overlooking the city. Sean hadn't been exaggerating when he called the view fabulous.

I looked for him at the tables next to the windows, and when I didn't see him, I moved to the other side of the bar, where a long shelf of wine bottles behind glass covered one wall.

"Welcome to Tempo," the bartender called. "Is this your first time here?"

"Yes," I said, glancing around for Sean.

"Do you know about our Enomatic system?"

I shook my head, and he smiled. Moving from behind the bar, he explained how, with a "wine card," I could serve myself a "one-ounce, three-ounce, or five-ounce pour" from any of the thirty or so bottles lined up behind the glass. While he was talking, a guy in a loud Hawaiian shirt walked up, stuck a plastic card in a slot, pressed a button, and filled a glass half full with something clear.

"Sake," the bartender said. "We've got several kinds."

I looked around again, but Sean still hadn't shown up.

"Would you like your own wine card?" the bartender asked.

"Sounds like fun." A few moments later, I was the proud owner of a slick white card configured to allow me to serve myself twenty dollars' worth of whatever I liked from the Enomatic's lineup.

I started with a "one-ounce pour" of a Napa Valley gewürztraminer. Sean still hadn't shown up by the time I finished it, so I headed back to the wine wall. I had just settled on a New Zealand sauvignon blanc when he materialized at my side.

"Want to try some wine?" I asked.

"Thanks, but I'd rather sit down and enjoy the view," he said, dropping his eyes to my chest.

I blushed, damn it, but I managed to wave a hand toward the windows and say, "Me, too."

"I'm still new in town," Sean said as we took chairs across from each other at one of the bird's-eye-view tables. "Don't know all the bars yet. My mother and stepfather brought me here my first night in Las Vegas."

New in town. Interesting. So was *stepfather.* For that matter, so was the Manhattan area code I'd noticed in front of his telephone number. *Where had he gone to college?* I wondered. Since I'd moved to Las Vegas, I hadn't met many people my age from the East Coast. David was an exception, and his apparent departure from my life made Sean all the more interesting.

"So, what's with the 212 phone number?" I said. "You just visiting?"

"Ooh, straight to the interrogation," he said. "Mind if I rustle up some drinks first?"

Conveniently, a waitress had just arrived at our table. Sean ordered a martini, and I opted for the white wine I had been about to serve myself.

"I moved here from New York six months ago," Sean said when the waitress had left. "I could get a new number, but I'm not sure I'm really a 702 kind of guy."

"You might leave?"

"Oh, probably not. I've gotten kind of used to being a Vegas big shot. Between the two of them, my mother and Curtis have plenty of juice, and it all seems to transfer to me. I get invited to all the clubs and openings—way better than any treatment I ever got in New York. And my mother's pretty good at encouraging me to stay in other ways, too—like employing me."

"Your mom's really something," I said. "I've been reading up on her."

"How far into her past have you dug?"

"Well, I know she's lived in Las Vegas for eighteen years."

"Sounds believable," Sean said.

His response caught me by surprise.

"Don't you know?" I asked.

"I met my mother for the first time six months ago, when she picked me up at the airport."

By the time he was on his second martini, I had learned even more surprising facts about Marilyn Weaver's only child. The result of a brief relationship with a violin maker in Chappaqua, New York, Sean had grown up with his father and a series of girlfriends, most of them opera singers or violinists.

"I didn't even know my mother was alive until my junior year at Columbia," he said. "And I might never have found out if my father hadn't needed a bill of sale for a rare violin when he was in Europe on business. He told me where to find the key to a safe-deposit box, but he had forgotten what was in it besides the piece of paper he needed."

Sean chuckled, but he didn't sound very happy.

"If only he had asked his latest girlfriend. I could have lived out my life in blissful ignorance."

"What was in it? Your birth certificate?"

"No," Sean said. "A packet of letters. Letters to me that my father had never shown me. Marilyn started writing the day she left: April 16, 1982. I was nine months old."

Sean picked up his glass and took a long drink.

"I grew up believing my mother had died giving birth to me. When I found out she was alive, I decided to find her. Didn't take long."

What did the letters say? Why did she leave? I wanted to ask. But it seemed too prying, so I just took another sip of wine.

"My mother's always on the run," Sean said, "in case you haven't already noticed."

"Busy, you mean?" I said. "Yeah, she's got enough energy for three—"

"No," Sean said. "I mean on the run. On the lam. Running away. But she'll never make it."

Now I was completely baffled.

"After I found out she existed, my father filled in a few gaps, and I did some research on my own," Sean went on. "Her maiden name was Canaday, and she grew up in Seattle. But her mother's family was from Montana, and Marilyn spent every summer on her uncle's ranch near Flathead Lake. The Lazy B. Her uncle, a guy named Chuck Beeman, was pretty famous for his rodeo stock."

"Beeman—as in Beeman Hall at the school?"

"Yeah, it's named for—well, the whole family."

"So, Charlene's a Beeman?"

"Her mother was," Sean said. "At least I think that's how the connection works." He shook his head. "I sure never dreamed I'd wake up one day and find out I'm related to a bunch of cowpokes."

I smiled. "Sounds like Charlene's a really good cowpoke, at least. She's doing really well in the cutting horse trials."

"I don't doubt it," Sean said. "She's had a lot of—support."

He paused and looked at me, thoughts moving behind his eyes. I thought he might launch into a longer story, but instead he smiled.

The only other fact I'd learned about Sean by the time we stepped back out into the evening heat was that his last name was DuBois.

"Just like Blanche," he said, "and I've always depended on the kindness of strangers."

It was still oppressively hot as Sean walked me to my minivan. It's at moments like these that I wish my parents had chosen something slightly more hip as a college graduation gift. Tapered at both ends and painted white, the van immediately inspired my best friend to christen it "The Maxi Pad." I still call it "The Max," but only because nobody in Las Vegas knows why.

But if Sean thought my wheels were less than cool, he didn't let on.

"Do you have to be anywhere right away?" he asked. I told him about my house-sitting gig. I had packing to do.

"I have a house to babysit this weekend, too," he said. "My mother's. She's going to a meeting in Carson City, and Curtis is off entertaining clients in Palm Springs. I'm their designated cockatiel nanny."

"Good luck—"

"Here's an idea," Sean said, leaning in between me and my car door. "Why don't you follow me to Marilyn's? It's near here, and we can order a pizza. You've got to eat, don't you?"

"Well—"

"We can go swimming, too, if you've got a suit."

How could I say no? My well-stocked gym bag was riding shotgun in my van.

Chapter 7

Marilyn Weaver's house was in San Ramon, a gated community just east of Las Vegas Boulevard. I followed Sean through the main gate, which swung open magically in front of his BMW. The houses inside the enclave were all large, and many of them were huge. Each one occupied its own oasis of manicured landscaping. I followed Sean around a traffic island and pulled up next to him in a wide driveway in front of a three-car garage.

I slung my backpack over my shoulder and grabbed my gym bag. Crossing the front yard, an artful collage of lawn, gravel, and exotic-looking shrubs, I joined Sean at the ornate front door. He was staring at a blinking light on a panel just inside.

"We're lucky," he said. "They didn't set the alarm when they left. I know the code, but I'm always afraid I'll call the police instead of disarming it."

"Brrr," I said as he shut the front door behind us. "This is serious air conditioning."

"Marilyn likes to freeze," Sean said. "I'll turn the thermostat up."

I followed him through the entry hall into an enormous

high-ceilinged living room with an entire wall of plate glass windows. The hardwood floors were covered with oriental carpets, and floor-to-ceiling bookcases flanked a carved stone fireplace. Leather furniture and plenty of mahogany made the room sumptuous, but it was also warm and inviting.

"Want something to drink?" Sean asked as we headed through a spacious dining room to the kitchen. "I only wish I had picked up some absinthe."

I laughed. "I've got to drive. Water would be nice."

"Sure I can't tempt you with some champagne?" Sean said, pulling a bottle of Mumm out of the refrigerator. "Goes great with pizza."

I declined, and Sean didn't push. I looked around the kitchen while he filled a glass with ice water for me and opened himself a beer. Like the living room, the kitchen was huge and opulent but also pleasant and homey.

"I love this house," I said, hoping the Nash place might be just a little like it.

"Curtis and Marilyn bought it ten or so years ago when they got married," Sean said. "I love it when they're gone."

After Sean showed me the family room and introduced me to Frank Lloyd the cockatiel, he opened a glass door that led outside. Soon we were standing on the edge of a long rectangular swimming pool with a fountain and waterfall at one end. The whole yard looked particularly inviting in the raking rays of sunset.

"Why don't you change into your suit while I order a pizza?" Sean said, and I had to admit it was an enticing idea. I followed him back inside, where he led me to the bedroom wing.

"Here you go," he said, opening the door to a large bathroom tiled in pale peach. "Towels in the cabinet."

He shut the door behind him, and I surveyed the room. It was messier than I expected after what I'd seen in the rest of the house. The countertop next to one of the sinks was littered with hairbrushes, a couple of cosmetic bags, and a clutter of hair clips, jars, tubes, and bottles. Some were tipped over. I pushed enough of the jumble aside to set my bags down. While I was extracting my bathing suit and beach towel, I noticed a wet washcloth in the sink. She must have been in a hurry, I thought, which would also explain the half-open drawer in the vanity and the towel on the floor next to the shower stall.

Another door across the room from where I had entered stood ajar. It must lead to the master bedroom, I guessed, and an irresistible nosiness seized me. Was there any reason not to take a quick look?

I pulled the door open further and peeked inside. Like the living room, the bedroom had an entire wall of glass looking out onto a forest of palm trees, shrubs, and flowers.

My eyes fell on something I couldn't make sense of. Was it a pole? I pushed the door even further open, letting more light into the room.

It wasn't a pole. It was a thick braided cord, stretched taut from the leg of the king-size four-poster bed. My eyes followed the cord to the top edge of a door that stood ajar on the other side of the room. Curious, I stepped into the room and crossed the carpet. I stumbled twice, first over an open suitcase and then on a high-heeled shoe. I think I knew before I laid my hand on the closet door that something was terribly wrong.

Hanging from the other side of the door, her neck cinched in a loop of cord and her face bloody, was Marilyn Weaver. Her legs were buckled under her, and one was sticking out at an odd angle, the foot shoeless. Something made of metal jutted from Marilyn's mouth. What was it? My mind struggled to make sense of it, though it hardly mattered.

How long I stared at her, I don't know. My heart crashing against my rib cage, I gasped for breath. A big part of me wanted to run away, but some other force—shock, maybe, or disbelief?—kept me glued in place.

I should touch her, I told myself. She looks dead, but what if she isn't? My heart still thudding, I forced myself to lay a couple of fingers on her arm. Cool but not stone cold. What if she could be revived? It looked impossible, but—

"Sean!" I screamed, hoping he'd hear me. "Sean! Oh, my God! Come here!"

I kept staring at Marilyn for the eternity—or was it five seconds?—that it took Sean to join me. Blood from her face had puddled on the floor, but it looked as though it had begun to dry. I couldn't bear to look at the scene for another moment, and I also couldn't tear my eyes away. Suddenly I recognized the object in Marilyn's mouth. It was a slide bolt—the sort of thing you see on an old shed—

"Copper! What's the—?"

Sean emerged from the bathroom to join me at the closet door. He gasped as the horrible scene in the closet came into his view, but he didn't say anything. I clutched his arm and looked at him. His face had turned paper white, and his eyes were riveted on Marilyn's body.

"Do you think there's a chance she's still alive?" I said. "Shouldn't we do something?"

"She's dead," Sean said. "There's nothing you can do about dead."

Even though he was obviously right, his words shocked me. I stared at him, but he still didn't return my gaze.

911, was all I could think. *We've got to call 911.* Releasing my hold on Sean's arm, I turned to look for a telephone by the bed. I couldn't see one on either nightstand, so I raced back into the bathroom and dumped out my backpack on the counter. I grabbed my phone out of the heap. I sucked air as I unlocked the screen.

In an instant, Sean was at my side. He snatched the phone from my hand.

"What are you doing?" I said, gaping at him stupidly. As he moved away from me a barrage of terrifying thoughts rushed into my head. *Why was he preventing me from calling 911? Had he killed his mother and brought me here to find her? Was he going to kill me, too?*

"Hold on a second, Copper."

"What?"

"You don't have to be part of this."

Our eyes met.

"What do you mean?" I said. "We've got to call."

"She's dead," Sean said. "There's no rush."

"Sean, please," I said. I looked toward the door to the hall. There had to be a phone out there somewhere.

"Take your stuff and go," Sean said. "After you leave, I'll call the cops. You can forget this ever happened."

"What? I can't do that."

"You can't do it after you call, that's for sure. It's an option you have only right now."

I stared at him, my mind whirling with conflicting thoughts. Was he really trying to spare me the stress of dealing with a murder investigation? Or did he have some other, less altruistic motive? All I could be sure of was that I couldn't undo what had just happened. I couldn't drive away and play dumb for the rest of my life, even if I could get away with it.

"I'm staying, Sean," I said, surprised at the calm conviction in my voice, "and if you don't call 911 right this second, I'll go find a way to do it myself."

"Okay, Copper, okay," Sean said, shaking his head. "I just wish—I mean I'm just sorry I got you into this."

"Call 911," I said. "Now."

Chapter 8

Silently, Sean tapped the numbers into my phone. Our eyes met as he waited for an operator to answer, but I couldn't read his expression.

"I want to report a death," he said, still looking at me. "A murder."

That's it, I thought, the news is out. And the call was being made on my cell phone, connecting me indelibly with the whole gruesome situation. For a fleeting moment, I wished I had acted on Sean's suggestion. I could have been on my way to the Nash house instead of stuck in the middle of a crime scene.

While Sean talked to the 911 operator, I glanced at the pile I had left sitting on the bathroom counter. I should get that stuff out of here, I thought. Who knew what might happen to it if I didn't. It wasn't evidence, but it could easily get mixed up with some. By the time Sean handed me my phone, I had crammed all my belongings back into my bags.

"I'm going to put this stuff in my car," I said. I left Sean standing in the bathroom and headed to the front door.

The evening heat hit me like a blowtorch as I stepped outside, and with the jolt came a new realization of what had happened. Marilyn Weaver had been killed, and the only thing I knew for certain was that I hadn't done it.

Sean was standing motionless in the living room when I returned.

"They'll be here any minute," he said. As if on cue, sirens sounded in the distance. The wail grew into an ululating chorus, and just as I was wondering how cops get inside gated communities, the sirens got even louder. A moment later, a sharp rap on the front door made it clear that electronic gates are no barrier to law enforcement. I stood next to Sean as he admitted two police officers, one male and one female.

As though they had planned it before they arrived, the man attached himself to Sean and the woman began talking to me. As Sean disappeared down the hall to the bedroom wing, I found myself being escorted to the living room and seated at one end of a long brown leather sofa. The policewoman pulled up a footstool and sat down facing me.

"I'm Officer Mendoza," she said. "I need you to tell me what happened."

I took a breath and began describing the path that had led me to Marilyn Weaver's closet door.

"I met her yesterday," I said. "At a fund-raiser for the Neon Museum." God, it sounded strange! Two days ago I hadn't even known the woman, and today I was snooping in her closet. But if my story seemed odd, the policewoman didn't let on. She just kept prompting me to keep talking while she took notes.

As I related how I had met Sean at the Anna Roberts Parks Academy, had a drink with him at the V, and ended up following him to his mother's house, a swarm of public servants gathered. Half a dozen more policemen showed up, along with a squad of paramedics. I guessed the three guys carrying cameras and toolboxes were crime scene investigators, and several others looked like detectives or coroners. The scene looked oddly familiar, like a police movie in slow motion with the dialogue muted. Surreal, I thought. Even the body in the bedroom began to seem like a dream as activity swirled around me.

"May I go now?" I said at last. More than an hour had passed since Officer Mendoza had parked me on the long couch, and I'd answered all her questions, many of them more than once.

"I need you to stay," she said. "Detective Booth needs to talk with you."

Detective Booth. I had no idea which member of the swarm he was. I also wasn't sure I wanted to hang around and find out. Could I leave even if Officer Mendoza "needed" me to stay? She wasn't treating me like a suspect, but—

Suddenly I thought about Sean. Was he a suspect? It didn't seem likely that he'd killed his mother, or even possible. On the other hand, all I knew about Sean was two martinis' worth of self-description. Not a great knowledge base from which to draw conclusions.

Thanks to my clear view of the front door, I knew Sean was still in the house somewhere. For that matter, so was Marilyn. Paramedics had rolled a gurney down the hall, but they hadn't returned with a body on board.

What was going on outside? I wondered. I couldn't see much even when the door opened, but the sounds of hubbub suggested that a good-sized block party had erupted. Oh, God—and television cameras. The media would probably have no more trouble getting through those gates than the cops had.

"Would you like some water?" Officer Mendoza asked. I nodded, and she called to another cop to hand her a bottle. As she unscrewed the top, it dawned on me that she was my babysitter. She hadn't strayed more than five feet from me since she'd arrived. Damn. I probably *was* a suspect.

"Detective Booth will be here in a minute," Officer Mendoza said. "Is there anything else you need?"

I need to rewind back to three o'clock, I wanted to say. Or better yet, back to last week, when I was blissfully unaware of an unborn baby. "Boring" had never seemed so appealing.

"No," I said. "Thanks for the water."

It was more like an hour before Detective Booth relieved Officer Mendoza of her spot in front of me. He lowered himself onto the footstool, his long legs forming an A-frame in front of me. He was about forty, I guessed, and he was wearing cowboy boots, khaki slacks, and a short-sleeved seersucker shirt. When he arrived on the scene, I'd lumped him together with the crime scene investigators, though he hadn't been carrying a camera.

"How you doing?" he said after introducing himself. It's the sort of question that usually doesn't require a serious answer, but Detective Booth stopped talking and waited.

"Just terrific," I said, regretting my sarcasm as our eyes met. Damn! The guy looked like my uncle. My father's younger brother has the same square face and tall, flat forehead. Detective Booth's eyes were like Uncle Jeff's, too—a steely blue-gray. He even had the same bristly five o'clock shadow.

"Tell me what happened."

I sighed, realizing that once again I would have to recite the events that had led me to this spot. I knew without asking that "I already told Officer Mendoza" was not going to satisfy Detective Booth.

"What was in the street when you got here?" Booth asked when I got to the part about following Sean from the V. "Did you notice any vehicles?"

"Only Sean's BMW," I said. "I can't remember any others, but there might have been a car parked across the street." I racked my brain for more details but came up empty. "Let me know if you remember anything," Booth said. He jotted some notes, then nodded at me to continue my story.

"I was curious," I said when I got to the part about why I had entered Marilyn's bedroom. "Especially after I saw the cord."

I met Detective Booth's gaze, and his similarity to my uncle vanished. Uncle Jeff is always friendly and warm. This guy had icicles in his stare.

"I know I had no business being in Ms. Weaver's bedroom," I continued. "But the cord was too weird to ignore. I think anyone in my position would have looked inside that closet."

Booth smiled at me in a way that was anything but friendly. "We're not talking about anyone, Ms. Black. We're talking about you."

I gulped. I'd stayed pretty calm the whole time I was talking to Officer Mendoza, but this guy was making me feel like I had something to hide.

"Did you touch or move anything?"

"I touched Ms. Weaver's arm," I said, "to see if maybe she was still alive."

"What else?"

"Nothing," I said.

"Think," Booth said.

"No," I said, meeting his laser-beam gaze as defiantly as I could. "I touched her arm. Then I called Sean. Then we called 911."

Booth kept staring at me. I looked away as unpleasant thoughts flooded my brain. What had Sean told him? Did it match what I had said? Should I tell him what Sean had done when I first tried calling 911? I looked at the detective again. He was still staring at me.

"Do I need a lawyer?" I said.

Booth snorted as a mean smile revealed his teeth. "I don't know. Do you?"

Damn. I was only making things worse.

"Tell me the whole story again," Booth said. "Beginning to end. No detail is unimportant."

It was almost a relief to have to start over, and for the bazillionth time, I recounted events beginning with the fund-raiser for the Neon

Museum. If Booth wanted the unabridged version, well, he was going to get it. By the time I was finished, he knew about everything from Marilyn's Prada purse to Curtis's revelations about Oscar the tortoise. He knew about Colby Nash and my brother's building project. He even knew that Sean had wanted to introduce me to absinthe. If I had failed to tell him about Sean's weird behavior with my cell phone— well, too bad. I wasn't about to make Sean look suspicious without doing a little investigation of my own.

"So that's it," I said triumphantly when I reached the end of my narrative. "Now you know what I know."

Booth scratched his head with the end of his ballpoint pen and shook his head. Then he flipped back through some notes. Then he scratched his head again and squinted at me.

"I must have missed something," he said. His whole tone had changed, and he seemed genuinely confused. He shook his head again.

"That really is all I know," I said. "I've told you everything, I swear." But prickles of sweat were popping out on my forehead. What had Sean told this guy?

"Would you mind starting over?" Booth said.

I stared at my hands. Yes, I wanted to say, I do mind. I've already told you everything, and I'm sure you heard every word. I didn't kill Marilyn, and I have no idea who did. My only sin is nosiness, and last I heard nosiness isn't a crime.

I sneaked a peek at Booth. He was still looking at me, and when he caught my eye, he winked.

Flustered, I looked down again. The guy was downright creepy. I wished I had the nerve to get up and walk out, but Detective Booth had me far too tangled in his net of innuendos.

I sighed. "Where do you want me to start?"

Before I left the Weavers' house, Detective Booth had made me repeat my story at least three more times. Somewhere in the midst of one of my soliloquies, Officer Mendoza brought me a slice of pepperoni pizza, and I wondered if Sean had actually managed to call in an order before Marilyn's body took center stage. As I imagined an unsuspecting pizza delivery boy arriving on a murder scene, I realized how narrow my view of everything was. I was telling Booth more and more, but I felt as though I knew less and less.

I liked the detective less and less, too, though I kept telling myself he was only doing his job. Or was he? Shouldn't he be out looking for the murderer instead of sitting around making me squirm? I had almost corralled enough nerve to confront him with this question when he abruptly rose to his feet.

"We're done here," he said.

"Done?" I said. "You mean I can leave?"

"Just don't go too far," he said, handing me his card. "And call me if you remember anything—anything at all." He went on to explain that I could seriously damage his investigation if I talked about the crime, especially around *The Light*.

"Keep your mouth shut," he said. "Let the police department do the talking."

I was wondering how I could possibly avoid instant celebrity as I walked out the front door, but I needn't have worried. The police had set up barricades at both ends of the Weavers' block, and the television cameras and reporters hadn't been allowed past them. The only people near the house were cops and a few neighbors from homes nearby. Marilyn's body had still not been removed from the house when I left, and Sean's BMW was still parked next to the Max.

I climbed behind the wheel, drove to the traffic island, and waited while two policemen moved a barricade. A television reporter with a microphone in her hand was moving toward me as I stepped on the gas and pulled away.

Chapter 9

Driving through the gate at the entrance to San Ramon, I felt I'd left a little of the horror behind me. I checked my cell phone while I waited for a light to change at Silverado Ranch Boulevard. God, it was after ten. I'd been stuck to that leather couch for over three hours.

Hoping my brother and his wife would be home and awake, I drove directly to the vicarage. This was one of those times when family might be a wonderful thing, especially with everything that was going on between David and me. I couldn't help thinking about how different things would be if he hadn't screwed things up. The high point of my evening would have been beating him at backgammon—a far cry from finding a fresh corpse.

Lights were on in the living room when I pulled into the driveway next to Michael's Jetta. I rang the bell.

"Copper!" my brother said when he opened the front door. "Is something wrong?"

Sierra was stretched out on the sofa, and the television was on. "Come on in," Michael said. "We're waiting for the eleven o'clock news, to see what—"

"You already know?" I said. "You've heard?"

"Know what?" Sierra said, and Michael looked just as baffled.

"About the murder," I said. "Isn't that—?"

"*Murder?*" Michael said. Sierra jumped up and crossed the room to join us.

"Who got killed?" she asked. "What happened? Are you all right?"

"Come on, Copper," Michael said, putting his arm around my shoulders. "Come sit down."

For the second time that day, I was escorted to a sofa and seated at one end. For the forty millionth time, I told the story of how I came upon a body in a closet.

"Copper, are you sure you're all right?" Michael asked when he had recovered from the shock of learning what had happened to Marilyn. "I'm willing to bet this is the first time you've ever seen the aftermath of a murder."

I nodded. "You'd win that wager."

"You're still in shock," Michael said.

"I'm fine. Just a little dazed."

"Exactly. I can arrange for counseling—"

"Thanks, bro," I said. "But I think Curtis might need it more than I do."

"Holy cats!" Michael blurted. "Does Curtis know?"

"I have no idea. He's in Palm Springs."

"Really?" Michael said. "When I talked to him around seven, he said he was in Henderson."

I shrugged. "All I know is what Sean told me."

"If you're positive you're okay, I'd like to call Curtis," Michael said. He looked at his watch. "Where's my cell phone?"

"You left it in the kitchen," Sierra said, and Michael headed through the dining room.

"Are you sure you're all right, Copper?" Sierra asked. "Do you need anything?" She was making a real effort to be nice.

"I'm getting there," I said. "Still in 'I can't believe this is happening' mode."

"Well, I guess now we have two reasons to watch the eleven o'clock news," she said. "Although the murder might mean Michael's problem doesn't get mentioned at all."

"Michael's problem?"

Just then, my brother returned from the kitchen.

"I can't raise Curtis," he said. "Voice mail everywhere. I'm heading down to the South Central police station—it's the nearest one to the Weavers' house."

"Are you sure you can't wait until morning?" Sierra said. "It's pretty late."

"I've got to go," Michael said, "Cutis is a good friend, and he's just lost his wife. Given how things work with murder investigations, it's possible he's being held."

Oh, my God. Maybe Sean was "being held," too.

"I'll check on him," Michael said when I mentioned my concern. "I'm going to change."

"A local philanthropist has been found dead in her home." The eleven o'clock news had just begun.

Sierra and I watched as a young female reporter described the scene from the end of the Weavers' block.

"Police aren't saying whether it was an accident or foul play, but Marilyn Weaver, founder of the Anna Roberts Parks Academy, has died. Her body was found by her son this evening in her home here in the San Ramon development just south of Silverado Ranch."

Interesting, I thought. Untrue, but I liked it. I had been dreading hearing my name. An unexpected wave of relief washed over me. I was anonymous. With luck, my connection to Marilyn's murder would still be a secret when I went back to work tomorrow.

"Human remains have been discovered at the construction site of the new downtown homeless service center."

With no more details to reveal about Marilyn's death, the newscasters had moved on to their second story.

"Oh, my God," I said. "Michael found a body, too?"

"Just bones," Sierra said. "Old ones. A couple of laborers found them when they were digging a trench this morning. At first they thought they might be an animal's, but then they found a human skull."

"It's a mess," Michael said. He had reappeared, clad in his clerical shirt and collar. "We've had to suspend construction while a forensic anthropologist checks everything out."

"Maybe it's Jimmy Hoffa," Sierra said, but Michael did not smile.

"I don't know how long I'll be," he said. "Don't wait up."

"Sean's last name is DuBois," I said, suddenly remembering I hadn't told him.

Michael grabbed his briefcase, and as he headed out the door, I felt a rush of gratitude that I had a brother whose calling in life was providing kindness to strangers.

"I'll be right back," Sierra said after Michael left. "I've got to check on Nicky."

I was trying to pay attention to the rest of the eleven o'clock news when she returned with a glass in each hand.

"Thought you could use this," she said, handing me one. "I know I can."

I took a sip of something sweet and minty.

"It's a *mojito*," Sierra said. "Good medicine on a hot summer night."

She was right, and I forced myself not to drain my glass in two swallows.

Michael had still not returned by the time I thanked Sierra for taking care of me and headed to bed. With luck, I'd even be able to sleep.

"I'm making breakfast early, if you'd like to join us," Sierra said. "*Pain perdu.*"

God bless my sister-in-law. She could be a thorn in my side when she wanted to be, but she could also whip up the best breakfasts this side of New Orleans.

Chapter 10

After stopping by the Max to grab my gym bag and backpack, I headed up the stairs to my apartment over the garage. The interior was not only as hot as a toaster oven, it was stuffy. Because the outside temperature had finally dipped below 90, I bypassed the old air conditioner and opened the window over my bed. A breeze that was almost cool instantly freshened the whole room. I kicked off my sandals, sat down on the bed, and sighed.

Here I was, back in my old apartment as though nothing at all had happened in the last forty-eight hours. The calm before the storm, I couldn't help thinking. What would happen when everybody found out that I—not Sean—was the one who had discovered Marilyn's body? It didn't seem possible that it would stay a secret forever, and—did I even want it to?

I stretched out with my clothes still on. I was certain I'd never fall asleep, having just lived through one of the most shocking days of my life. My mind whirled as I stared at the ceiling. Who would want to kill a person as generous and lovely as Marilyn Weaver? There had to be some dark secrets under that sweet philanthropic façade.

God, I wished I could talk the whole nightmare over with David. My brother's offer of counseling was thoughtful, but what I really longed for was the comfort of David's bear-like embrace while we analyzed everything.

Too bad, Copper. You're on your own now, a star player in a celebrity murder investigation.

Damn. Yesterday, writing about kids at the Parks Academy had seemed like a big journalistic break. But now—with a dead body in the picture—

Shut up, Copper! Marilyn Weaver is still on a morgue table, and here you are thinking about how her death might catapult you to fame.

The self-admonishment didn't do any good. As I lay there, phantom footage rolled in my head.

"Our guest tonight is Copper Black, the investigative journalist who solved the murder of Las Vegas philanthropist Marilyn Weaver. Her best-selling book ... "

The camera panned over the audience. There, in the front row ...

Daniel! Oh, my God! He'd be here in less than two days.

Seeing Daniel again would be challenging enough without throwing a murder into the mix. When he and I last parted right before New Year's, we'd just had the huge fight that dealt our relationship a mortal blow. I'd been investigating a story I hoped would get me taken seriously as a journalist. It involved prostitutes and a family in distress, but he thought I was just being nosy. He couldn't—or wouldn't—understand that it's a reporter's job to find things out, even when it means a little invasion of privacy. He steadfastly refused to acknowledge that I have a professional obligation to poke into other people's lives.

And now you're invading their closets! I could almost hear Daniel say it. I really didn't have a good excuse for snooping in Marilyn's bedroom. I couldn't claim I was working on a story. Nothing more than plain old curiosity had led me to her body.

I sighed. If Daniel can't accept me for what I am, I told myself, he can just get back in his car and keep driving to Berkeley. We aren't a couple anymore, even if we have never formally broken up.

That thought made David pop into my head again. We aren't a couple anymore, either, even though, once again, our relationship has not been formally terminated. God! That's weird! What am I? Some sort of crazy person who can't say good-bye?

My mind kept spinning. I'll never sleep, I thought. Never, never, never …

And then it was morning.

A cat was curled up next to me, and a slight breeze was blowing in the window. Sekhmet stretched and yawned along with me, and she showed no sign of wanting to leave after I got up.

"Nothing to eat here, my darling," I said, stroking her. "We both need Sierra for that." I showered quickly, threw on my clothes, and headed into the vicarage. With work and moving day ahead of me, I didn't want to miss Sierra's *pain perdu*.

Nicky was bawling at the top of his lungs from his high chair next to the kitchen table when Sekhmet and I walked through the back door. He stopped mid-wail when he saw me.

"Copper! Copper! Copper!" he cried, dropping a spoon and holding his arms out. I crossed the room and hugged him. He was even better than a cat for making me feel wanted.

"You're truly amazing," Sierra said. She was slicing strawberries next to the sink. "He's been trying to convince me to let him play with a steak knife for the last fifteen minutes, and nothing I could think of would distract him. Then you walk in, and—"

"More fun than a steak knife," I said, ruffling his hair. "I'm flattered, Nick!"

Sierra brought him some strawberries. "There's coffee," she said. "Oh, and the newspaper. Your story's on the front page. Michael only made the local section."

I was still looking at the file photo of Marilyn Weaver, looking considerably younger than when I met her at the Boneyard, when Michael walked into the room. He was dressed for ministerial activity, but his hair was still damp.

"Hi, Copper," he said. "I never did find Curtis last night."

"Copper! Copper!" Nicky yelled. I lifted him out of his high chair and sat down at the table with him in my lap.

"Sean wasn't arrested. I did learn that much."

"That's good news, at least," I said, although it reminded me that I still had some investigating to do. I didn't know much about Sean, other than what he had told me himself. He seemed fine, but what if he wasn't what he appeared to be?

"The situation with Curtis is a little more complicated," Michael continued. "The police were still searching for him when I left the station last night. I'm going to do a little looking of my own later on."

"I hope you talk to the shaman dude first," Sierra said as she set the table.

"Shaman dude?" I said.

"Front page, section B," Michael said, lifting a squirming Nicky off my lap. "A Paiute medicine man is claiming the bones we found are from an Indian burial ground. He's gearing up to hold a ceremony of some sort this weekend, and he could generate some serious media interest."

"Give him his fifteen minutes," Sierra said, "Maybe it'll blow over."

"We can hope," Michael said. Nicky tugged at Michael's collar. "Word is that Willie Morningthunder is coming."

"Who's Willie Morningthunder?" I asked. The name seemed vaguely familiar.

"A Lakota chief from South Dakota," Michael said, "and former congressman."

"That does put a different spin on things," Sierra said.

Michael sighed. "I'm bracing myself for a very long weekend."

"Speaking of which, you want to have dinner here tomorrow night, Copper?" Sierra asked. "Hans and Dustin are coming over. Dustin's making *crêpes suzette*, and I'll try to hold my end up with *coq au vin*."

Oooh. Scratch the thought of a party at the Nash house.

Hans and Dustin are my favorite neighbors, a gay couple who bought a wedding chapel in downtown Las Vegas as a retirement project. Dustin used to be a pastry chef at the Tropicana.

"Daniel's arriving tomorrow afternoon," I said, which prompted Sierra to drop a spatula. She recovered quickly.

"Daniel? You can bring him along, but I thought you two had—"

"Yeah, we did," I said. "He's on his way to graduate school in Berkeley. I told him he could crash at the Nash place for a night or two."

"Are you sure you really want to move into that creepy house?"

"It's not that bad," Michael said. "Curtis says it's 'architecturally significant.'"

Sierra shrugged. "It's significant, all right, but it has nothing to do with architecture."

Once again, I wondered what I was getting myself into, but the thought shrank to nothing when I compared it to all the other things I could allow inside my brain. Speculating about the Nash house was a whole lot more enjoyable than letting my thoughts drift to a dead body at the end of a tasseled drapery cord.

"I'm excited about it," I said, "I think it's going to be fun."

Which was more than I could say about the prospect of going to work. Had my coworkers learned that it was one of their own who had found Marilyn's body? All the news I had heard and read suggested they wouldn't have, but there was only one way to find out for sure. I thanked Sierra, promised Nicky I'd be back soon to play pirates, and headed back upstairs to prepare myself for the gauntlet that might await me at *The Light*. If I hurried, I would have time to pack some basics to take with me to the Nash house.

Figuring I could cram all my toiletries into my gym bag, I unzipped it and pulled out my beach towel. As it unfurled, a hairbrush clattered to the floor.

But that wasn't all.

Bending down, I picked up a tiny bottle of Shalimar perfume. Next to it lay a small tube of something called Next Generation Wrinkle Eraser.

Damn!

They had to be Marilyn's. I must have grabbed them by accident when I cleared my stuff off her countertop. And I'd inadvertently carried off three more objects, too, I realized as I dumped out the rest of my gym bag's contents.

A lipstick, a packet of tissues, and a slim black case.

I picked the case up and snapped it open. A pair of expensive-looking aviator sunglasses lay folded inside. I snapped the case shut, and that's when I noticed the initials "CW" engraved into a small gold oval stuck to the top.

Holy crap.

In addition to everything else, I'd managed to steal Curtis's sunglasses. I thought back to those surreal moments right after I found Marilyn's body. I must have been in shock, and I'd definitely been in a hurry.

And now—*double crap!*—I should probably call Detective Booth. I'd sworn to him that I hadn't touched or moved anything, and I hadn't changed my story when Booth told me a cop needed to check my car. That was when I realized I should have mentioned that I'd had my bags with me when I was in Marilyn's bathroom, but the last thing I wanted to do was to give Booth reason to think I was less than truthful. He might have kept me stuck to that sofa all night, and the only important thing was that I was innocent. That's all the cops needed to know.

But now …

I looked at the small pile of objects I'd unintentionally lifted from the crime scene. What if they held clues to the killer's identity? I didn't see how a bottle of Shalimar could help, and Curtis's sunglasses were hardly a smoking gun. It was his bathroom, too, after all.

Opening the case again, I removed the glasses and unfolded the temples. Super-strong prescription, I noticed as I peered through the lenses. Especially the right lens. With a sigh, I put them back in the case and closed it. Curtis will definitely wonder what happened to them, I thought. Maybe I could find a way to return them.

But not right now, I told myself. I've got too many other things to think about.

Oh, my God, like getting to work before it got any later.

Grabbing only my backpack, I left everything else in a pile on the floor and motored off to *The Light*.

Chapter 11

My day felt like a decade. Every time my phone rang or someone stuck a head into my cube, I braced myself for questions about the murder. The only questions I got, however, were about the Nash house. Everyone seemed fascinated that I was willing to call the place home for a month, and no one said a word about Marilyn Weaver. Even so, I never really relaxed until I was on my way home. And once I got there, the pile I'd left on the floor sent my stomach back into a knot. What was I going to do about Curtis Weaver's sunglasses?

One more day, I told myself. Waiting one more day can't do any harm. Right now, I've got a notorious new home to deal with.

After I loaded all the stuff I thought I might need for the next month into the Max, I followed the map I'd printed out at *The Light* and headed down past the airport to Sunset Road. It was nearly six, but the summer sun was still high in the sky as I made my way through a labyrinth of short streets to Vista Miranda. Most of the houses in the neighborhood were hidden on huge lots surrounded by high walls and tall gates. The only defense the Nash estate boasted, however, was a dense forest of overgrown oleanders. The house wasn't visible from the street, but a sun-bleached mailbox labeled NASH stood to the left of the driveway. A path of crumbling blacktop just barely wide enough for the Max led through the tangled jungle.

I inched along as my eyes adjusted to the deep shade inside the enclosure. The driveway split as I approached the house, a faded gold stucco two-story with an aging wood-shingle roof. The left fork led to a porte cochere and, I assumed, the nonfunctioning front door. I continued straight, looking for the back door.

The side of the house was studded with a row of round windows. The glass bulged, as if each window were a huge fish eye. I inched along, trying to peer inside, but the glass was dusty, and the room beyond was dark. Just past the porthole windows, I slowed to a stop under the arbor Curtis had mentioned. Festooned with several surprisingly healthy-looking grapevines, it spanned the driveway right in front of an ordinary-looking screen door that was capped by an aluminum awning.

Despite the shade, triple-digit heat blasted me as I opened my car door, and I realized I hadn't asked Curtis whether the house was air conditioned. The thought of broiling in a creepy stucco oven gave me serious second thoughts about my new abode. I couldn't help thinking back to what I'd discovered yesterday, when I'd opened a door far nicer than any door this house could offer. On the other hand, I noticed as I moved toward the back door, there were bunches of plump green grapes hanging off the arbor, and they looked ready to eat.

As I fumbled in my pants pocket in search of the keys, my eyes took in a detail that made me hesitate. The door was not locked. The door was not even totally closed. It had been pulled almost shut, but the latch hadn't quite engaged. Ordinarily, that wouldn't have bothered me in the least, but fewer than twenty-four hours had elapsed since I'd peeked behind another strange door that was slightly ajar. Call it paranoia, but I wasn't in the mood for discovering another dead body. And what if a violent prowler was inside? I wasn't in the mood to become a dead body, either.

I glanced down the driveway. Was there another car out of view behind the house? I decided to take a look.

The stretch of wall beyond the back door had louvered windows and a large terra cotta wall sculpture of a grinning mermaid with gigantic protruding breasts. It had been left a natural clay color except for her oversized lips and nipples, which had been painted an unapologetic shade of hot pink. I reached the end of the house and peeked around the corner. Attached to the back wall was a structure with glass-paned walls. A greenhouse, I decided, or maybe a solarium. Like the bulging windows I had already seen, the glass was dusty on the outside. The light inside was too dim for me to make out anything specific, but a forest of shadows suggested it was far from empty. For a second I thought a couple of them were moving, but I shrugged it off as post-traumatic stress.

Beyond the greenhouse—the lot seemed to go on forever—I could just see the end of a swimming pool. My heart sank. The water was not murky green as I had begun to fear it might be. It was black.

I wiped my brow while I pondered what to do. The house seemed quiet enough, and the likelihood someone dangerous was lurking inside seemed low. After taking one last glance over each shoulder, I cracked the door. Mercifully, cool air hit my face. Pulling the door open, I stepped inside. As my eyes adjusted to the dim light, I realized I was standing in a laundry room. The brand-new washer and dryer against the left wall looked decidedly out of place, but their presence heartened me. It's just an old house, I told myself. It'll probably look great once Kayla Lord finishes fixing it up. The house didn't smell bad, either. In fact, it smelled pretty good, as though someone had recently baked an apple pie. Gaining confidence, I moved farther inside.

I could see that the next room was the kitchen even before I found a light switch and flipped it on. Again, it was encouraging to see a brand-new blender and coffeemaker sitting on the counter next to the sink, and the rest of the kitchen wasn't scary. In fact, the decor reminded me of my aunt's house in Rhode Island. She'd remodeled it into her dream home after she dumped her husband in the seventies and got her hands on half of his retirement fund and all of their real estate.

"The year I bought that refrigerator and picked out this Formica is the year I became my own person," she always says if anybody asks her if she's considering replacing the old avocado and gold. "The symbols of my independence will never go out of style."

Maybe she has a point, I thought as I looked from the Aztec-inspired wallpaper to the vintage double oven. It was all in reasonably good shape, and none of it could have been cheap when it was new. Really, it was almost cute. I wondered whether Kayla was going to preserve it. I should take pictures, I told myself, and send them to Auntie Melanie …

Bam!

The kitchen floor shook. Holy crap! Was it a gunshot?

Bam!

I wasn't about to stick around to find out. Frantically groping for my keys, I careened back through the laundry room, slammed the door behind me, and jumped into my minivan. I backed down through the tunnel of oleanders and crashed into a birdbath while doing a three-point turn in the driveway fork.

I should call the police, I told myself as I zoomed away. If I'd caught a burglar in the act, it was the only responsible thing to do. Even so, I really didn't want to, because what if it was somebody with a perfectly legitimate reason to be crashing around in the basement? Then I'd just look like an idiot, or maybe even suspicious myself. I'd have to mention Curtis Weaver, and then—who knew where the line of questioning might lead?

It wasn't until I pulled into a drugstore parking lot up on Sunset that I remembered.

Colby Nash.

The movie dude who had the key to the basement. Of course. No call for hysteria, and no need for reinforcements.

Even so, I couldn't bring myself to head back to Vista Miranda Street. Colby might well be a whack job.

I pulled my phone from my backpack. I didn't resist as my fingers punched up David's number.

Chapter 12

"I'm sure it's nothing too dangerous," David said when I called him and asked him to forget about Chinese takeout and get to the Nash house as fast as he could. "But what if the place is possessed? I'll fill a jerry can with holy water, and my pistol's already loaded with silver bullets."

Yeah, he was making fun of me, but I couldn't help smiling.

"Wish I had a crucifix," I said. "At least I've had a lot of practice making the sign of the cross."

"Between us, no fiend shall stand," David said. "I can be there in twenty minutes."

Just to be on the safe side, I waited half an hour before heading back to Vista Miranda Street. I was relieved to see David had already parked in the porte cochere when I pulled into the Nash driveway. His Jeep is a genuine desert assault vehicle, and he really does carry jerry cans on the back.

David met me under the grape arbor, his face etched with concern.

"Copper, why didn't you tell me?"

Our eyes met.

"What happened last night? Why were you there? Are you all right?"

"How did you find out?"

"Greg Langenfeld called me ten minutes ago."

Whoa. The big boss. News had definitely spread about my evening at the Weavers' house.

"Long story with a sad ending," I said. I looked at David again. He patted my arm, which only reminded me how screwed up everything was between us. Soul mates do not pat each other's arms when something hideous happens.

"Well, if there's anything I can do—"

Soul mates don't say that, either. I sighed.

"Right now, I've got a haunted house to explore."

David opened his mouth to say something, but then closed it again. He forced a smile. "Ghoul buster, at your service."

I opened the door and waved him inside. We walked through the laundry room into the kitchen, where everything looked exactly as it had earlier.

"Cool decor," David said, looking around. "The Brady Bunch goes to Mexico."

He opened the upper oven. "No severed heads," he said, peering inside. "Always a good sign."

"I don't really feel like joking about what happened last night," I said.

"Sorry. Thoughtless of me."

"It's okay," I said. "It's just that—"

"I just hope you're all right, Copper, and if you want to talk—if you need anything—"

"Let's look around," I said. "I've got to find out if I can actually live here."

Together we moved through an archway, and a whiff of paint thinner drifted into my nostrils as I flipped another switch. A chandelier made of deer antlers lit up a high-ceilinged room. The smell was coming from several large cans that were standing on a canvas drop cloth spread on the floor in front of a huge, ornately carved mahogany bar. Someone was obviously in the process of refinishing it—the surface was scattered with sandpaper, sponges, and rags. The only other things in the room were a fireplace constructed out of massive rough-hewn stones and a mounted buffalo head hanging over it.

"Those gangster molls sure knew how to party," David said.

"Morticians, too, apparently. Who would have guessed?"

The switch beyond the next archway brought another chandelier to life, this one a gaudy creation with iridescent red roses intertwined with dangling crystals. The long rectangular room was empty except for a bare wood dining table in the center. Lying on it was a fat black three-ring binder labeled "OSCAR."

"Your filmmaker must have aspirations," David said when he joined me.

"Oscar's a tortoise," I said, and I explained that houseplants weren't the only living creatures I was supposed to keep alive for the next four weeks. "I better put this on the top of my bedtime reading stack."

"Talk to Mary Beth Sweeney, too," David said as he headed through a double door at the far end of the dining room. "She's got a pair of tortoises who are always hatching out babies, so she must know what she's doing."

I'll stick with the book, I thought. Way preferable to asking my about-to-be rival for advice. The thought of babies wasn't appealing to me at the moment, anyway, even reptilian ones. Suddenly I wished I lived on a planet where reproduction didn't take two creatures and love was an alien concept.

I leafed through the pages of Oscar's manual, pausing to wonder how I would procure "two freshly picked hibiscus flowers" to feed him every day for breakfast. I was moving on to a detailed recipe for tortoise-pleasing bok choi when I heard David yell.

Oh, my God! There was a burglar, after all!

I ran after him, desperately looking for something heavier than Oscar's manual to grab along the way. But I was still armed with nothing more than a three-ring binder when I caught sight of David standing calmly in front of a sliding glass door. I moved through a hallway lined with empty wine racks to join him.

"Why'd you scream?" I said, willing my heart to slow down. "I was expecting Freddy Krueger."

"You didn't recognize my Tarzan yell?" David said, sounding almost offended. "Take a look."

He pointed through the glass, and I slowly realized that I was looking into the glass-walled greenhouse I had seen earlier from the outside.

"Into the heart of darkness," David said, sliding the door open. "Hear the sound of distant drums?"

Moist heat slapped us in the face as we stepped into at least a thousand square feet of the kind of ecosystem that automatically puts you on the alert for anacondas and poison dart frogs. The temperature was twenty degrees warmer than the rest of the house, and all around us, dense shiny greenness dripped with condensed moisture. Even though the structure was all glass, the plants cast a deep shade.

I looked for a light switch and finally found a whole row of switches back in the hall with the wine racks. I flipped them all, lighting up several strings of white Christmas tree lights hanging in scallops from the ceiling.

When I stepped back into the greenhouse, the light drew my eyes to a shrub covered with bright red flowers. At least that was one problem solved. Oscar would get his hibiscus for breakfast.

"Check this out," David called from the other side of a lattice festooned with a vine that looked like a green intestine. I moved past the lattice to see a pool lit by an underwater light I must have turned on when I flipped the switches by the door. David bent down and scooped up some water. "Warm," he said. "Almost like a hot tub." He stood up. "And look. You can swim under that wall."

He flipped the latch on another sliding glass door, and slid it open. We stepped outside.

"Whoa! Welcome to Bali Hai."

I stared at the pool. A waterfall I must have also brought to life when I flipped all the switches crashed over a black lava wall. More black boulders created lounging grottoes, a bar, and the channel that connected the outdoor pool with the section inside the greenhouse.

"Nothing says Vegas like a swim-up bar," David said. "You're going to need a good daiquiri recipe."

"I caught a glimpse of this when I was here earlier," I said. "I thought it was full of slime."

It didn't look slimy now, though. It was an inviting shade of dark blue.

"Black plaster," David said. "The ultimate in seventies pool styling—popular not only because it looked sophisticated, but also because it's a natural solar heater when the sun beats on it all day."

I looked more closely as David bent down and stuck his hand into the water. "See? Perfectly clear." He shook his arm. "And a perfect temperature. Wish I'd brought my swimsuit."

And I wish we didn't have to talk about swimsuits, I thought. It was just my luck to score a private oasis in the middle of a Vegas summer and then find out I had no boyfriend to go skinny-dipping with.

Back inside the house, we made our way toward the front door, which involved a walk through a large room that featured the row of fish-eye windows I'd seen from the outside. Even unfurnished, there was no disguising the fact that it was yet another party room. A sunken zone at one end had a built-in sofa that wrapped around a circular fireplace, and a bar stood in front of a rock-faced wall with a huge built-in television screen and an equally large aquarium. The aquarium was empty, thank God. No piranhas or electric eels to worry about, at least.

"This clinches it," David said.

"Clinches what?"

"You have to throw a party."

"Maybe." I was glad I was far enough away from David that I didn't have to meet his gaze. The house would be so much more fun if he and I were still a couple.

But we weren't, were we? We hadn't really broken up, but his impending fatherhood had to have the same effect, didn't it? I'd never really adapted to "other woman" status. How could I possibly adjust to being "not-quite stepmother" of a child conceived by what I considered cheating? Maybe nobody else would see it that way. Maybe they'd all shake their heads and say, "Well, she *is* his wife. What did you expect?" Even if I decided David hadn't really cheated because we were momentarily separated, it still didn't match with my idea of good behavior. What had the guy been thinking?

All of which had no bearing on the fact that I couldn't imagine my life without David. And I couldn't imagine being "just friends," either. He was like cream to my coffee. Once poured in, there was no taking him out. All I could do was dump the whole cup down the drain.

Fortunately, one look at the living room was all it took to change the subject. It didn't take much investigation to understand why the front door had been permanently sealed shut.

"It's a *Star Trek* door," David said, examining it. The opening for the door was round, and two sliding panels met in the middle. "I think it's supposed to whoosh open when you push this." He pressed a button on the wall next to the door, but nothing happened.

"According to Curtis Weaver, it hasn't worked since Lollipop Lassiter's day," I said.

"This looks like it dates from Lollipop's day, too," David said. He had moved away from the door to peer behind a wall panel that had been partially destroyed. "Check this out."

I peeked into the ragged hole to see a mural covering the wall behind the panel. It was difficult to see the whole thing because of the narrow space and the lack of light, but the subject matter was still easy to discern. Larger than life and reclining seductively on a brocade sofa was a voluptuous woman wearing nothing more than a ruby-lipped smile and a mane of red hair.

"Is it Lollipop?" I asked. "I thought she was blonde."

"I don't know," David said, "but whoever it is certainly must have made an impression on guests when the sci-fi door whooshed open."

"I can see why the Nashes covered her up," I said, "but I'm sort of fascinated that they also preserved her."

We spiraled our way up the corkscrew metal staircase that rose at the back end of the living room.

"Looks like something out of a Victorian London Underground station," David said. "Definitely not for the fat or infirm."

"Or those susceptible to contact highs," I said. As we ascended, the unmistakable odor of burning cannabis engulfed us. I lowered my voice. "It smells like someone's smoking right now."

A large carpeted landing at the top of the staircase was ringed with five doors. The dope miasma was even stronger now, and I was half tempted to head right back down the stairs. Looking in strange bedrooms hadn't worked out well the last time I tried it, after all.

David, however, headed straight to the door that was standing open. I hung back, but when he failed to shriek again, I joined him.

My whole apartment would have fit inside the room we found ourselves in. It had been freshly painted an oddly pleasant shade of pumpkin orange, and the dark green carpet and deep purple drapes looked brand-new. A king-size bed covered with a puffy black comforter and oversized pillows was flanked with two bed-side tables, each with a reading lamp. The only evidence of habitation was a large ceramic ashtray that was far from empty. David held his hand over it.

"It's cold, but somebody was smoking in here recently," he said.

"Excellent deductive work, Sherlock," I said.

"Maybe your underground filmmaker has been making himself at home in his old bedroom," David said.

"He doesn't have a key," I said. "I bet it was the house sitter I replaced, who bagged out to go into rehab." But even though I said that, I couldn't help wondering whether the house was really as secure as Curtis had promised.

I flipped the light on in the bathroom. Covered floor to ceiling in little white hexagonal tiles, the room featured double sinks, a walk-in enclosure with two showerheads, a Jacuzzi tub easily large enough for a couple, and a throne-like toilet with matching bidet. None of it was new, but it was in impressively good shape.

David didn't comment on the bathroom, nor did he seem to want to linger there. I felt the same way about all the fixtures designed for two as I had about the swimming pool. What evil deity had arranged to give me a honeymoon suite right after stealing the honey I'd want to moon with?

Together, David and I explored the rest of the upstairs bedrooms. I think we both assumed that the first one we had entered was a master suite, and that the others would be more modest. They were not. All four were equally spacious, and all four had cavern-ous bathrooms with Jacuzzis, oversized shower enclosures, double sinks, and matching toilet-and-bidet combos. The only thing that set the first bedroom apart was that it had been painted, carpeted, and furnished with a bed. The other three rooms were devoid of furniture and in varying stages of remodeling. One of them had a big hole in its back wall.

"And I thought the rooms downstairs made this a party house," David said as we descended a staircase on the other side of the landing. A more ordinary structure than the iron corkscrew we had ascended, this stairway deposited us in a hallway that connected to another bedroom and the wine cellar between the dining room and the greenhouse.

"The maid's quarters," David said, and I think he was right. This bedroom was much smaller, and its bathroom didn't have a bathtub, only an ordinary shower stall big enough for one. Oh, and no bidet.

"There's definitely more to this house than meets the eye," David said when we had returned to the kitchen.

"You mean like more murals of naked ladies hidden behind false walls?"

"I don't doubt it, but I was thinking along the lines of secret storage places. You know, like in *Hitman's Holiday*."

The film's most famous line instantly sprang to my lips.

"'*The head! The arms! The whole goddamn torso!*'" I said it with Joe Piscatello's signature mobster accent, and as soon as I finished—

"Oh, my God!"

I looked at David. He was staring right back at me.

"Is *that* why you checked for severed heads in the oven?" I asked.

"Copper—I thought you knew."

"This is the *Hitman's Holiday* house?" I shook my head. "I had no idea."

Under other circumstances, I'm sure David would have hugged me. As it was, I just stared down at the Aztec gold tiled counter and wondered how I had failed to find out that Nylons DeLuca was the inspiration for the role that had earned Joe Piscatello his first

Academy Award. I'd known the story was based on real events, but—

"There can't be any body parts decaying in the walls. The Nash family lived here for more than thirty years. They would have noticed, right?"

"You'd think so. They're morticians, after all."

"David, you're really creeping me out."

"I thought you knew this was the *Hitman's Holiday* house. Really, Copper, I never would have—"

"It's okay, David," I said. "I should have known." I sighed and ran both hands through my hair. "At least it explains why Curtis was so grateful and why everybody at *The Light* was so interested."

"And why I was joking around about exorcisms," David said. "Copper—I had no idea, and—I'm really sorry."

I looked up, and our eyes locked. Instantly, I knew David wasn't just talking about the dismembered extremities of old hitman targets. He was sorry I'd found a body in a strange closet, and he was sorry we couldn't talk about it. He was sorry about Rebecca, and sorry about a baby who had no name.

But what good was "sorry"? How could I "kiss and make up" with a man who'd casually impregnated his supposedly alienated not-quite-former wife? Didn't that trump a thousand games of backgammon, endless nights of talking, and sex so divine the gods on Olympus were probably sneaking a peek?

I couldn't tear my eyes from David's. For a minute—or maybe ten—we just looked at each other. His eyes were bright with unshed tears. Mine escaped and crept down my cheeks.

"I'm sorry, too," I said, mostly for lack of anything better to say.

I looked away, and we fell silent again. At last, David opened his mouth to speak, but I beat him to it.

"What I mean is," I said, "I'm really sorry I ever told Curtis I'd stay in this house. With everything else that's going on—"

There was no way I'd come right out and admit I was scared, but suddenly my stuffy little pad at the vicarage held irresistible appeal.

"It's just a vintage Vegas party house with a colorful history," David said. "There's nothing haunted about it, and I'm sure the resident filmmaker is perfectly harmless."

Easy for you to say, I thought. I squared my shoulders and took a breath.

"As you know, I found a dead body yesterday," I said. "Perhaps such things are old hat to a seasoned newsman like you, but frankly, I'm not in the mood to spend a month wondering whether there's a desiccated rib cage lurking around every corner."

"You won't. It's mostly legend."

"Mostly. How comforting."

"The movie exaggerated the story. The only thing Nylons was ever really suspected of doing in this house was storing a bowling ball carrier somewhere."

"You mean—a head?"

He nodded. "Yeah. Only the head. Not the arms. Not 'the whole goddamn torso.'"

"Why am I not reassured?"

David sighed and wiped a hand across his eyes. "I can understand if you're not, Pepper—" He stopped. "I can understand if you're not, Copper."

Pepper. His pet name for me.

I wrapped my arms around myself, wishing more than ever that I could erase a few bits of recent history. I missed David's hugs more than I'd ever admit.

"Where did Nylons store the head?" I asked. "Is it still here?"

"It was never found, but old timers at *The Light* doubt it," David said. "Joe Corrigan, Duane Garcia, Mary Beth—they were all around then, and they think the head joined the rest of the body in Lake

Mead. But it's ancient history."

"The sixties?"

"1973, actually."

"Hardly ancient."

"Time moves quickly in the shifting sands."

And things change quickly, too. A week ago, I had a relationship with a future. Now all I had was a house with a past.

Chapter 13

By the time we finished exploring the rest of the Nash house, I had begun to entertain the possibility that David and I might be able to talk about our relationship. A phone call shot that idea to hell. Late-breaking events in a Vegas-related fraud case meant that David would have to catch an early-morning flight to San Diego.

"I'll call you as soon as I get back," he said, and it felt like a dart straight to my heart. Since we'd been together, we'd always talked at least once a day, and usually more.

"Need a ride to the airport?" I asked. Until now, such things had been unquestioned between us, assumptions built upon the convenience of getting out of bed together.

"Car service'll get me," David said, and right then it hit me. He was going back to his wife. How could I have thought otherwise with a baby in the picture? His life was none of my business anymore. My heart had to toughen up and move on.

The temperature was still over 100 when I left the Nash house. When I stepped into my stuffy garage apartment, I couldn't help thinking about the central air conditioning I'd left behind on Vista Miranda Street. I could have been stretching out on that big cool bed after a soak in the Jacuzzi or a midnight swim under the stars.

Okay, the bedroom reeked of dope, but wasn't that easier to ignore than the wheezing death rattle of an ancient window-mounted air conditioner? Suddenly, even the chance that Colby Nash was a predator or that Nylons DeLuca had parked a severed head behind a wallboard a few decades ago seemed unimportant. The house was a palace compared to my stifling one-room pad, and it was blissfully—not to mention silently—cool.

Tomorrow night, I promised myself, I'd overcome my chicken-hearted uneasiness, pack up my toothbrush, and sleep in my new home. It was far preferable to adding to Curtis's problems, and there was also the fact that Daniel was arriving. Given the uncertain nature of our relationship, I preferred the flexibility of multiple bedrooms over the one-room intimacy of my apartment. And we could swim—with or without bathing suits. As I lay sweating on top of my covers and tried to sleep, that black-bottomed swimming pool kept drifting into my mind's eye. Plants, tortoise, subterranean housemate—I could handle them all. As for heads in bowling ball carriers, I'd avoid the attic and resist the temptation to peek behind wallboards. Superficial living is actually quite appealing, I told myself, and it was only for a month. Maybe I really should throw a party.

When I pulled into the Nash driveway the next morning, I immediately saw that I had company. A red van with a rack on top was parked under the grape arbor, and Shania Twain was blasting from the open side door. Definitely not Daniel.

The sound of a hammer led me to the far end of the backyard, beyond the swimming pool. A skinny guy with a scraggly ponytail hanging out from under a straw hat was pounding a stake into the ground while a boy of about ten played with a remote-controlled car on the pool deck. Neither one of them noticed me.

"Hello!" I yelled over the music, the hammering, and the buzz of the toy car. The man stopped pounding and sauntered over. His T-shirt had a big black tarantula on the front, and his jeans rode so low on his hipless torso, I was afraid they might fall right down. Hoisting them up with his left hand, he stretched his right out toward me.

"You must be Copper," he said. "I'm Thor, and that's my son Micah."

I shook his callused hand.

"I'm finishing up the burrow," Thor said. "Should be able to get Oscar over here in a day or two." He squinted at me. "You ready to take care of a tortoise?"

"I'm reading his manual," I said.

"Oscar's been mistreated in the past," Thor said. "Some asshole painted him and drilled a hole in his shell. If you ain't gonna give him proper care—"

"I will," I said. "I promise." How difficult could it be?

Just then, the sound of another vehicle joined the noise. Thor followed me back to the side of the house, where a pickup truck had joined the lineup in the driveway.

"Howdy y'all! We're just unloading! Won't take but a minute!" shouted a young guy with a beer belly and a mullet. He trotted around to the back of his truck and let down the tailgate. The bed was stacked with boxes.

"What are those?" I asked, failing to sound like I was in charge.

"Tile," the mullet said. "*¡Joaquín! ¡Póngalos allá!*" He pointed to the porte cochere, and a young Hispanic guy climbed out of the passenger side of the pickup and pulled a dolly out from beside the boxes. Before I could say anything, a stack began rising in front of the nonfunctioning front door. The sound of hammering told me Thor was back at work on the tortoise burrow. It was obvious that none of these people considered me their boss. I should call Curtis,

I thought.

Oh, right.

The whole world was probably trying to call Curtis, and if they were reaching him, he had far more important things to think about than whether a tile delivery was supposed to occur at the Nash house.

I was about to unlock the door under the grape arbor when another vehicle turned into the driveway, a blue Toyota FJ Cruiser with a white roof.

Jesus. Two vans, a truck, an SUV, and there was still room for more. That's what I call a long driveway.

I watched as a dark-haired man in a yellow polo shirt and cargo shorts climbed out of the driver's seat. As he came closer, I saw that he was younger than I had first thought. Even younger than me, maybe.

"Hi," he said when he reached the door. "I'm Colby Nash."

The subterranean movie maker! And he didn't look like he slept in a coffin!

"Oh!" I said. "I'm pleased to meet you! I'm Copper Black, Kayla's new house sitter."

"Curtis Weaver told me," Colby said. "I wanted to come by and introduce myself."

"By any chance, did you fire a gun in the basement yesterday?" I asked.

"You were here?" Colby looked shocked. "I had no idea. I'm sorry—and—they were blanks."

I arched an eyebrow at him.

"It won't happen again."

"I didn't know anyone was here," I said. "There were no cars—"

"Oh, I usually park in the alley out back so I don't block the driveway—"

Just then, another car pulled in. That made five, and now that the porte cochere was full of tile boxes, there was no way for anyone to get out without backing all the way out to the street.

This new arrival was an old, green sedan I didn't recognize, but as soon as the door opened and a tanned leg with a sandal on the foot hit the asphalt, I started running.

"Daniel!" I called. "You got here!"

Chapter 14

Few things feel as wonderful as a bear hug from a friend when you're surrounded by strangers.

"I'm so glad you're here, Daniel," I said when he finally released me. "I've got a lot to tell you."

"First tell me what you think of my car," Daniel said. "My '*turn it on, wind it up, blow it out GTO.*'" He sang the words, but whatever song they were from was not in my repertoire.

"Um, well, it's kind of old," I said.

"It's a classic, Copper! This is a '74!"

Goes well with the house, I was thinking, but it was clearly a source of macho pride for Daniel, so I thought up something else to say.

"I like the color."

"Original paint job," Daniel said. "This baby's virgin to the core."

"Goes fast?" I said tentatively.

Daniel laughed. "I'll take you for a ride. No place like Nevada to hammer down."

By this time, Colby had joined us.

"Nice ride," he said, after I introduced him to Daniel. "I'd love to use it in a film."

Daniel looked at me, a question in his eyes. But before Colby or I could open our mouths to explain, yet another car pulled into the driveway. I recognized this one immediately. It was Sean's dark blue BMW. There was just enough room left for him to pull it off the street.

"Oh, my God, it's Sean," I said.

"Who's Sean?" Daniel asked, but before I could answer, Thor ambled up.

"I need to get out," he said, looking at Daniel. I looked at Daniel, too, wishing I'd had a chance to explain.

"Can y'all move y'all's *vee*-hicles?" The tile dude was calling from the door of his pickup.

I'd have preferred to do it myself, but Daniel immediately took command. Within five minutes, all of us had joined in the musical cars game he orchestrated, and within seven, the tile dude and his muscled Mexican sidekick had vanished down Vista Miranda Street. The tortoise-burrow builder and the kid with the radio-controlled car were right behind them. My only remaining problem was the three perspiring guys left over. All they had in common was me.

"I'll be in the basement for an hour or so," Colby said. "I promise I'll be quiet."

Daniel shot me another bewildered look as Colby walked to the side of the house, unlocked the padlock on a small door, and disappeared down the steps inside. Daniel deserved an explanation, but he was going to have to wait.

"Are you all right?" I asked Sean. He was dressed as he had been the first time I saw him—in suit pants, a white shirt, and tie. Sweat was pouring down his forehead behind his sunglasses. "Maybe we should go inside."

The two guys followed me into the kitchen, where I found some glasses and discovered with relief that the ice water dispenser in the refrigerator's door was functioning. I introduced Daniel and Sean to each other as I handed them each a glass.

"Curtis is at the police station now," Sean said. "I've been meeting with the mortuary people."

I was about to say something when Daniel interrupted. "How about I go get my stuff and bring it in?" he said.

He was outside before I could answer.

"Who is that?" Sean asked.

"A friend," I said.

"Oh."

"From college," I said. "He's on his way to Berkeley. He's staying here a night or two."

Sean took off his sunglasses, but I still couldn't read his look.

"I don't know when the police will release the body," he said. "Makes it hard to tell the mortuary what to do."

Isn't that Curtis's job? I wanted to ask. Or—*oh, my God.* Was Sean telling me that Marilyn had been murdered by her own husband?

"Curtis didn't kill her," Sean said, as if he had read my mind. "But the police are still talking to him."

I couldn't bring myself to ask why Sean was so sure about Curtis's innocence. I struggled to think of something to fill the awkward silence.

"Are you okay?" Sean asked.

"I'm fine," I said. "I hope you are, too."

"All I wanted was a date with you, you know."

As luck would have it, Daniel reappeared just as Sean said that.

"Where should I put this?" he said, failing to conceal the frown in his voice.

"The bedrooms are upstairs," I said. "You'll find the stairway through there, and you can have your pick. You can even take the one with the bed if you want."

"I have an air bed," he said, heading off through the dining room.

"I'm sorry," Sean said, looking after him. "I don't want to cause trouble. I just wanted to make sure you're okay. Have the police called you?"

"No," I said, "but I know they probably will." I shrugged. "Not that I can add anything to what they already know."

"The school's in shock," Sean said. "I've been on the phone all morning."

The school?

Oh, of course. The Parks Academy.

"Marilyn's family has been calling nonstop. The Montana cousins, her mother in Seattle." He shrugged. "I guess I should call them *my* family, but I've never met any of them except Charlene." Sean heaved a heavy sigh. "I've been taking all the calls. Curtis couldn't, even if he wanted to. He's a mess."

I'd wait to ask more questions about Curtis, I decided. I also wanted to talk to Sean about why he had tried to keep me from calling 911. It couldn't matter too much, though. Sean didn't kill his mother. He'd either been at the Parks Academy or with me at the V when it happened. I should do more checking, of course, but I was pretty sure already that Sean was exactly what he seemed—a nice guy who had tragically lost the mother he had so recently discovered.

"What will happen to the school?" I asked.

"The board's meeting right now to figure things out," Sean said. "It's going to be tough for a while. The dean of the school—who would normally take Marilyn's place—is in Vienna. He's an organist, and he can't come back without breaking a contract. It's something he worked out with Marilyn. He does it every summer, and he always gets back the week after school starts. I don't know what the board will figure out, but—oh, Christ—"

Sean wiped his brow with the back of his hand, and a wave of sympathy rolled over me. I took the glass from his hand and set it on the counter. Moving back toward him, I reached out my arms.

"You look like you could use a hug."

Immediately, Sean's arms were around me like a python, and I hugged him hard right back.

"Thanks for coming by," I said. "You have a lot on your mind, and it means a lot to me."

Sean's shoulders heaved, and I hugged him harder. He was sobbing audibly when Daniel reappeared.

"Excuse me," he said as he stalked through the kitchen. "Sorry to interrupt." The door slammed as Sean released me.

"God, I'm sorry, Copper," he said, wiping his eyes.

"You have nothing to apologize for," I said. "Is there anything I can do to help?"

"The hug was a huge help," he said. "Thanks."

When Sean and I walked back outside, we passed Daniel carrying a duffel bag and a computer case.

"Nice to meet you, Dan," Sean said, and Daniel mumbled something unintelligible in reply.

"He doesn't know about yesterday," I said. "He just got here, and I haven't had a chance—"

"I hope he's understanding," Sean said. "It's not your fault."

"It's not your fault, either," I said as Sean opened his car door. "And really, let me know if there's anything I can do."

"You can still do your story at the school," Sean said. "It's going to need all the good publicity it can get."

My story. It was the last thing on my mind.

As Sean backed out of the driveway, my cell phone buzzed. I pulled it out of my pocket and looked at its screen. Whoever was calling me had blocked caller ID, but when you're in the news biz, you have to get used to things like that.

When I stepped back inside the kitchen, Daniel was leaning against the counter. Our eyes met as I said hello to my mystery caller.

"Ms. Black?"

Oh, my God, not now. It was Detective Booth.

"I have a few questions."

My heart sped up, and I took a breath. I felt my face flush and hoped my voice wouldn't betray me.

"I'm happy to cooperate, but this is not a good time."

"When *would* be a good time, Ms. Black?" His sarcasm was heavy. Hell, I didn't deserve that.

"Business hours," I said. "Monday."

Booth snorted.

"*Gesundheit,*" I said, even though I knew he hadn't sneezed.

Booth was silent for a beat.

"Business hours don't apply to murder investigations, Ms. Black. I'll be in touch soon."

He hung up before I could do it first.

What a jerk.

Daniel remained silent even after I slipped my phone back into my pocket.

"Are you hungry?" I said, in a lame attempt to lighten the mood.

Expecting it to be empty, I opened the refrigerator. Although utterly devoid of food, all three shelves were completely filled with cans of beer. They were all Coors Light, but it was still a gift from God. Or—it immediately occurred to me—more probably the gift of whoever had been smoking dope in the bedroom upstairs. But I wasn't in a mood to nitpick.

Cold beers in hand, Daniel and I headed into the party room with the sunken sofa.

"This is some house," Daniel said as we sank down into the cool cushions. "I'm sure it's got an amazing story." He took a long drink of beer. "But somehow I'm getting the feeling it pales in comparison to the one you're about to tell me."

Chapter 15

It was a good thing the Coors was "light." By the time I'd finished filling Daniel in about everything that had occurred over the last few days, we'd polished off two cans apiece, and Daniel was working on a third. We'd moved upstairs, where Daniel had chosen a bedroom furnished with nothing more than a gold shag carpet.

I offered him the bed again, but he insisted on blowing up his air bed. I sat down on the floor and chatted with him while the motor pumped it up.

"I'm really very sorry you're wrapped up in a murder investigation," he said. "But what concerns me even more is your new boyfriend. That guy's got a dark cloud over him."

"Sean is not my boyfriend," I said. "And if he has a 'dark cloud,' he's got a pretty good excuse. His mother was murdered, for God's sake. I thought it was nice of him to come over and check on me."

"You just met him, right?"

"A few days ago."

"Did you invite him over today?"

"No, but—" I was about to make an excuse for Sean when I suddenly realized I had never told him where I was living. He must have found out from Curtis, but—damn. That *was* just a little unnerving.

"You don't know enough about him."

"What difference does it make?" I said. "All I did was accept his invitation to go over to his mother's house for a swim. Who knew that one spur-of-the-moment decision would tie me to him forever?"

Daniel's look was enough to answer my question and send a shiver through my body.

Damn. I *did* need to find out more about Sean.

"Want a tour of the rest of the house?" I asked when Daniel's inflatable bed was sufficiently plump. "You're going to die when you see the swimming pool."

But the pool wasn't what made Daniel breathe hard. It was the greenhouse. I knew his field was botany, of course, and I knew he had just spent a year in Costa Rica on a Wilberforce Fellowship studying tropical mistletoes. Even so, I was completely unprepared for the whoops of incredulous delight the peculiar green jungle evoked.

"Do you have any idea what these are, Copper?" Daniel asked. I had to admit that I was as clueless about them as I had been about his classic car. I hadn't had a chance to read the notebook labeled "Plant Care" that I'd found in the kitchen.

"This one's a pitcher plant, probably from Borneo, and these are sundews. I've never seen so many healthy-looking bladderworts in a greenhouse and—damn! This is better than Berkeley's collection. Hell, it's as good as Atlanta's, and they've got the best one in the country."

While he was going on and on, I was growing more and more nervous. If these things were so rare and so valuable and so hard to cultivate, how was I ever going to keep them alive? I was lucky they hadn't all shriveled up already. I hadn't watered them. I didn't even know *how* to water them.

"I sure never expected to find a world-class collection of carnivorous plants in Las Vegas," Daniel said.

"Wait," I said, staring at him. "Did you say *carnivorous*? These things eat *meat*?

"Yeah," Daniel said. "Nobody told you?"

"All I heard was 'houseplants,'" I said. "I was expecting a potted cactus or two."

"Who brought them here?" Daniel asked. "It's a fantastic lineup."

"I have no idea," I said. "The current owner's only had the place for a month or so."

Nylons DeLuca popped into my head, along with the family of morticians who had just vacated the place.

"Um, Daniel?"

"Yeah?"

"How much meat can one of these things eat?"

"That one probably needs a cricket or two a month," he said, pointing to one of the biggest ones. "I've read about pitcher plants large enough to eat a rat, but I don't see anything here you'd want to give more than a pinch of hamburger."

The minute I heard "hamburger," my mind instantly created an image of a guy in a pin-striped suit slicing bits of flesh off a severed leg with a switchblade and dropping them one by one into the hungry orifices that surrounded us. It might look like a serene solarium, but was it really a well-fed corpse disposal method?

"This may sound silly, Daniel," I said, "but could you get rid of a body by feeding it to plants like these?"

"*What?*"

I gave him a quick overview of the Nash house's sordid history.

Daniel listened quietly, his face taking on a more disgusted look with every revelation.

"Good God, Copper, I don't know how you pick them."

I wasn't sure whether he was referring to the house or the people connected with it, but I had no intention of getting into a fight.

"Could they do it?" I asked. "Could they digest a body?"

Daniel rolled his eyes, but he gave me a straight answer. "Technically, I guess you actually could dispose of a human body by feeding it to carnivorous plants," he said. "But it would probably take years, and you'd still have the bones to deal with. Nothing here is anywhere near large enough to digest a femur, never mind a skull."

It did seem preposterous, I told myself, but even so, the plants made me shudder. Before I knew about their dietary requirements, they'd been odd little Dr. Jekylls. Now that I knew about their flesh-eating habits, they were suddenly creepy Mr. Hydes. Maybe Daniel had a point when he said I knew how to pick them.

"I think what you're seeing here is someone's hobby," Daniel said, "and it looks like they're really serious about it. These plants are in great shape, and I can help you keep them that way without murdering anything more than a few crickets."

"I'm really glad you're here, Daniel," I said.

Daniel looked at me, a half-sad smile on his lips.

"I'm glad I'm here, too, Copper," he said. "Even if it's just to feed your plants."

On the way over to the vicarage for Sierra's dinner party, Daniel gave me a crash course in the physiology of flesh-eating flora. It made me think differently about Sierra's *coq au vin*, but her cooking was too good to let Daniel's description of vegetative gastric processes get in the way. By the time we got back to the Nash place, I was feeling a lot more confident that I could keep the green-mawed monsters alive for a month. Daniel even promised he'd take care of procuring the required insects and depositing them in the appropriate orifices before he left.

"I'll leave you enough bugs for one more meal, which is all they should need in a month. After you watch me feed them, you'll see how easy it is."

When we were back inside the house, Daniel explained the greenhouse's automated climate control system.

"It's as good as they get," he said. "This house may need work, but the greenhouse is top of the line. I still can't believe it."

I couldn't believe my good luck in having Daniel around to educate me. I might still have a murder to worry about, but at least I wouldn't have the corpses of neglected flytraps on my conscience.

"Want to go for a moonlight swim?" I asked. "I haven't had a chance to try the pool yet, and it's still plenty hot outside." Even though it was after ten, the temperature hadn't dropped below 100.

"Sure!" Daniel said.

As tempted as I was to suggest that we forgo bathing suits, we were each wearing one when we stepped outside ten minutes later. Bathing suits come off easily, I had decided. Might as well start out on the safe side.

"What's that light?" Daniel asked, pointing to a ground-level window at the back end of the house. "Is your basement tenant still here?"

"I don't think so," I said. "He must have forgotten to turn the lights off. I guess I better do it."

Together, Daniel and I walked around to the small basement door. It was padlocked shut.

"You're right," Daniel said. "He couldn't have locked himself inside."

After I returned with the key, I opened the padlock, slid back the bolt, and pulled the door open.

"This is good," Daniel said. "A chance to see what this guy is really up to."

"And you call *me* nosy," I said, preceding him down the stairs. "I'm just going to turn the lights off."

The section of the room into which I stepped was nearly pitch black, but I could see a light burning at the far end of the basement.

"Maybe I better get a flashlight," Daniel said as I tripped on something at the bottom of the stairs.

"I think I can see okay—" My eyes had adjusted just enough for me to see what I had stumbled over. I screamed before I could stop myself.

Daniel was right behind me. "What's the—oh, my God!"

The darkness could not completely conceal the fact that I had tripped over a human arm.

"I'm out of here," I shrieked, shoving my way past Daniel and staggering up the stairs. "I'm out of this whole freaking house!"

"Copper! Wait!"

"What? You're sticking around? Come on!"

"No—come here. I think it's okay."

Amputated arms are never "okay," but even so, I turned around. Daniel stood in the doorway, holding the arm.

"Daniel! Oh, my God!" I was screaming again. "Put that thing down!"

"It's okay! It's fake!"

I shut my mouth.

"Are you sure?"

I inched closer, my heart still racing. Even in the dim light, I could see that Daniel was right. The arm was decidedly unnatural when you got a closer look—nothing more than a stuffed shirtsleeve spattered with red paint with a rubber hand attached to one end. Slowly, my pulse returned to normal.

"He must be making a slasher flick," Daniel said.

Together, we headed back down the stairs into the basement. As our eyes adjusted to the light, I realized that the arm had company.

An entire body was lying there in pieces.

"*The head! The arms! The whole goddamn torso!*" Daniel said. "I guess it's true after all."

"Different movie," I said. "This one must feature a mad scientist."

I had just discovered a table covered with glass beakers, a Bunsen burner, and a rack of test tubes.

Behind it was a wall of orange crates stacked up to make a bookcase. The crates were crammed with books, videos, stacks of paper, newspapers, magazines, and boxes. We moved past it on our way to the light source.

In the room created by the wall of crates, a lighted ceiling fan turned slowly overhead. Against the far wall, under the window we'd seen from outside, an elaborate array of computers, monitors, and speakers stood on a row of tables.

"His editing suite, I bet," Daniel said. "I don't know much about this stuff, but it all looks new."

"He's supposed to be a serious filmmaker," I said.

"These look serious, anyway." Daniel was pointing to a gun rack mounted on the wall under the window. Wooden dowels supported a couple of rifles, a musket, and a shotgun.

"Here are some more," he said, opening a cabinet with glass doors.

"Careful," I said. "I don't want him to know we were poking around down here."

"How's he ever going to know?" Daniel said. "Hey, check these out."

The gun cabinet held at least a dozen pistols, some of which looked like the sort of thing a pirate or Paul Revere might use. Others looked like hitman guns, and there were also a couple of Wild Bill six-shooters.

"Probably for films, too, don't you think?"

"Hope so," Daniel said. He closed the cabinet's doors and headed back toward the other room. "There's got to be another light in here somewhere."

After he'd flipped a switch near the stairs, I turned off the fan and the light in Colby's editing suite. I headed for the door, but as I crossed the room, I tripped over a power cord and hit a cardboard box sitting on a stack of newspapers.

Damn! Styrofoam packing peanuts flew everywhere.

It took Daniel and me at least twenty minutes to pick them all up. While we were doing it, we got an even closer look at the amazing variety of books, knickknacks, costumes, gadgets, and junk Colby had collected in his subterranean hideaway.

"He might actually be a pretty interesting guy," Daniel said as we emerged from the basement and padlocked the door. "That's a pretty cool setup he's got down there."

"I'm not exactly thrilled about the guns," I said, "but you're right. Seeing his lair actually makes me kind of like him."

"The guns are probably just props," Daniel said.

The pool was pleasantly warm, and as we slid into the water, I suddenly realized that one of my daydreams had almost come true. I was alone in a tropical lagoon with a hunky guy. Aside from the fact that we weren't a couple anymore and we were wearing bathing suits, it was wonderful. I paddled over near the waterfall, flipped over, and floated on my back. The sky was studded with stars, and the palm trees swayed gently. Yep, pretty damn close to perfection.

I felt hands under my back. Turning my head, I was face to face with Daniel.

"This is great, Copper," he said. He planted a wet kiss on my forehead.

"You're starting to like Las Vegas in spite of yourself?"

"Well, I have to admit that this house is pretty amazing."

"It's the plants," I said.

"No," Daniel said. His arms were still under me, not quite cradling me. "It's not the plants."

"The antique guns, then?" I said. "The naked lady in the living room? The *Star Trek* door? The real severed head that might be lurking—"

Daniel kissed me. This time it was on the lips, and his arms tightened around me. The kiss lasted a long time.

"I've missed you, Copper," he said at last. "The last six months have been the longest of my life. I want you back."

Still holding me, he swam us both over to the basking ledge near the swim-up bar. He set me on the ledge and floated in front of me.

"We're good together," he said. "Really good."

I looked at him, my mind awhirl. This was the guy I'd been so sure I would marry, the guy I thought I'd spend my life with. But then, when he came to Las Vegas last Christmas, everything had fallen apart.

"We belong together," Daniel said. Our eyes stayed locked as my mind started spinning again. Here we were, two former lovers alone in an idyllic pool under a starry sky. Should I give him another chance? Could I forget how fiercely he'd tried to convince me that Las Vegas was awful, my friends were losers, and my job was a joke? Had he changed?

I kept gazing into those enchanting hazel eyes. Maybe he really was ready to take me seriously, and if David was out of the picture—

Both of us heard the gate creak at the same moment. We turned to see a dark form enter the pool enclosure.

My heart skipped a beat as I sucked in a breath. Who could it be, at eleven o'clock at night?

The form stepped into the light shining from the surface of the pool.

Damn! It was Sean! As he walked toward us, I saw that he was carrying a huge bouquet of red roses.

"Hi," Sean said when he reached the edge of the pool.

"Hi," I managed, my heart still pounding. Daniel didn't say anything, but he moved in front of me.

"Hope I'm not interrupting anything," Sean said. Daniel moved closer to me, shielding me with his body.

"It's nearly midnight," Daniel said. "Hardly an appropriate time to show up unannounced."

Sean took a few steps closer, and I felt Daniel's body tense.

"I just wanted to make sure you're okay, Copper," Sean said. "I'm really sorry—"

That's when I saw the bottle in Sean's right hand. What was going on with this guy? "I'm sorry" just didn't match up with a couple dozen long stems and a bottle of wine.

"You should have called," I said. I couldn't prevent the quaver in my voice.

"You're frightening Copper," Daniel said. "You better go."

"Sorry, *Dan*," Sean said. "Good-bye, Copper."

I watched him as he bent down and laid the roses on the pool deck. Setting the wine bottle next to them, he straightened up. He raised both hands as if in surrender. Then he let them fall to his sides. His shoulders drooped, and he hung his head.

My fear dissolved as I watched him. I pulled away from Daniel.

"Copper, don't—" he said, but I hoisted myself out of the pool and walked over to Sean. Still dripping, I stood in front of him. When he raised his head, I looked into his eyes. They were red. From crying, it was easy to see. I couldn't help feeling a stab of sympathy.

"You really should have called," I said. "You can't just drop in on people in the middle of the night."

"The police are going to arrest Curtis," Sean said. "They think he killed Marilyn."

"Oh, no!"

"These flowers came to the house this afternoon, and I thought you'd like them. And I had a crazy idea you might have a glass of wine with me—"

"Sean—"

"It was a bad idea. Everything's just so weird."

By then, Daniel had joined us. He towered a head taller than Sean, and he looked like he was ready to lunge. I laid my hand on his arm.

"I'm sorry," Sean said, and I looked at him again. Maybe those red eyes weren't entirely the result of tears.

"Have you been drinking?"

"No."

"Are you sure?"

"Well—"

"Look. I'm going to make you some coffee, and then you have to go."

"He doesn't need coffee," Daniel said. "He needs to leave." His voice vibrated with anger.

I glared at him, then turned back to Sean. I opened my mouth, but Sean spoke first. "He's right. I'm leaving."

Sean turned and headed back out the gate. I listened as his footsteps crunched down the driveway at the side of the house. A minute or two later, I heard a car start in the distance.

"The guy parked on the street, Copper," Daniel said. "He snuck up on us."

I didn't say anything.

"I'm sure glad I was here," Daniel said.

I turned to face him. "Why? To protect me?"

"There's something wrong with that guy."

"There'd be something wrong with you, too, if you found out your stepfather murdered your mother and you hadn't lived here long enough to have any friends. Show a little sympathy."

"Copper, he turned up with flowers and wine in the middle of the goddamn night. He wasn't looking for sympathy."

I couldn't totally disagree with Daniel, but I was still angry that he'd contradicted me in front of Sean and assumed I needed a guy around to keep me out of trouble. How could I have ever thought there was a chance we could get back together again?

I walked over to the flowers. As I leaned over to pick them up, I couldn't help thinking that bringing someone second-hand condolence flowers was more than a little disturbing.

On the other hand, I told myself, it could just prove how upset Sean is. I couldn't swear I might not do something equally peculiar if I were in his shoes. I picked up the wine bottle, too.

"I'm taking these inside."

I thought he might stay out by the pool, but Daniel followed me into the kitchen. I found a plastic pitcher large enough to hold the roses and filled it with water.

"Want some wine?" I asked.

"No, thanks."

"Look, Daniel, I—"

"The guy could be dangerous."

"Oh, come on. He left."

"You really don't get what I'm talking about?"

"I think he's a little strange, but it's not like he showed up with a gun or anything."

Daniel shot me a "How can you be so sure?" look.

"You scared him off, Daniel. If you hadn't been here, I would have done it myself."

"You were going to invite him in and make him coffee."

He had me there, damn it. Even so, I didn't feel grateful. All he had really succeeded in doing was to remind me of why we hadn't been in touch for the last six months.

"Look," I said. "Why don't we get some sleep? Then tomorrow—"

Daniel looked up and our eyes connected.

Yeah, that's right, Daniel, I almost felt like adding. *We're going to sleep separately. Until I've straightened a few things out, what sane choice do I have but celibacy?*

I straightened the roses in the pitcher, and a thorn caught my thumb.

"God damn it," I said.

"You okay?"

"I'm fine," I said. "Except my life's too complicated."

"Doesn't have to be," Daniel said. "I could be your highwayman, here to whisk you away in my mighty GTO."

There was a time when a comment like that would have tractor-beamed me into Daniel's arms, but now it was just more evidence that he still saw me as a damsel in distress.

"These aren't complications I can run away from," I said.

"Well, maybe you could use a little break," Daniel said. "Want to go for a drive tomorrow? We could shop for crickets, then head out into the desert and let 'er rip."

I sighed. This was the good Daniel talking again, and getting away from everything in town, even for just an hour or two, actually did sound appealing.

"I'll make a picnic," I said, and we headed upstairs to our separate rooms.

Chapter 16

I can't say I didn't feel a longing to creep into the room with the gold shag carpet and slip in beside Daniel on his air bed. I'd loved the guy ever since he sat down next to me in biology and asked to borrow a pen. Daniel was impossible *not* to love, and I wasn't the only person who found him irresistible. Everybody loved Daniel, including all my dorm mates, both my parents, and even my brother and sister-in-law. We'd had a great time at Sierra's dinner party that evening, and Nicky screamed when we left. This time, it was not because I was leaving. It was because Daniel was leaving.

Staring at the ceiling, I thought back to the first nights we spent together, crammed into a single bed in his dorm room. We'd crawled in on a Friday, and we didn't come up for air until Sunday night.

Daniel was right. We were really good together—had been from the start. And we still were, so long as nothing happened that called my judgment into question, or my instincts, or my choice of cities to live in …

Daniel was already in the kitchen when I headed downstairs in the morning, and he had already fired up the coffeemaker.

"Nothing much here for breakfast, I see," he said, handing me a mug. "Want to go out?"

I was about to say yes when my phone buzzed. I checked the screen, but no number appeared. Another mystery caller.

"Ms. Black?" a raspy voice said.

Detective Booth. Crap.

"I've got a couple quick questions," he said. "I could really use your help."

His cordial tone caught me off guard.

"Okay … " Daniel was shooting me a questioning look. I rolled my eyes at him and shrugged.

"When did you get together with Sean DuBois on Thursday?"

"A little after five," I said. "At the V. The bar at the top of the tower."

As I had already told him at least a hundred times.

"You're sure about the time?"

"Not to the minute. But the bar opens at five, so it couldn't have been before."

"And you got to the Weavers' house—when?"

"Six thirty or so."

"Do you recall what kind of shoes Sean was wearing?"

His shoes? That was a new question. I tried to remember.

"Dress shoes, I think," I said. "Maybe brown. Can't swear to it."

"Okay, thanks," Booth said. "I appreciate your cooperation."

"No problem," I said.

"Oh—Ms. Black? One other thing—"

With this dude, there was *always* one other thing.

"Are you sure you didn't move or touch anything in Mrs. Weaver's bathroom?"

Bingo. The real reason for the fishing expedition. I felt my cheeks warm as I decided this fish was going to put up a fight. He'd asked me variations of that question at least fifty times already, which essentially meant he was calling me a liar by reprising it yet again. The fact that I *was* a liar didn't mean he wasn't a pain in the ass.

"As I've already told you," I said, trying to keep my voice steady, "I didn't compromise your crime scene."

"Did Sean move anything?"

"I didn't notice," I said. "But he could have when I wasn't there."

"You left while he was still in the room?"

Oops. I'd left to go put my stuff in my car, but I couldn't tell him *that.*

"I don't remember."

"And let me get this straight—Sean used *your* cell phone to call 911?"

"Yes." *As I've told you seventy million times.*

"Is there anything else you'd like to tell me?"

"No." But there was plenty I wanted *him* to tell *me.* Did he know Sean had tried to stop me from calling the police? Only Sean could have told him that. And why had the detective asked about his shoes? There was way too much I still needed to find out, but I couldn't do any real research until I got back to *The Light.* Could I put Booth off for another couple of days? I had to try.

"I was too upset to call 911, so Sean did it."

"Tell me about that."

"That's it," I said. "I was freaked out. I'd never seen a dead body before."

Okay, that was technically another lie. I had seen my grandfather after the poor old guy had been plumped up and painted by some very skilled morticians. He looked better than he had in a decade—nothing like Marilyn Weaver with a noose around her neck and a piece of hardware sticking out of her mouth.

Detective Booth didn't say anything.

"I've got another call," I said. "I've got to go—"

Booth didn't protest. After he hung up, I slumped into a chair. Somehow, I didn't need coffee anymore to feel wide awake.

"Who was that?" Daniel asked, but I was in no mood to try to explain why I had lied to a police detective. Daniel would never understand. I wasn't even sure I understood myself.

I shook off my angst as well as I could and tried to add a breezy tone to my voice.

"Oh, it was just the detective who's investigating Sean's mother's death. Want to go have breakfast?"

"Sounded like he was kind of grilling you. Is everything okay?"

"Everything's fine."

"I worry about you."

"I know. You should stop. It's not your job."

Daniel seemed to acknowledge the steel in my tone. He shrugged.

"Know a good breakfast place?" he asked.

The sky was gray and overcast when we stepped outside, adding humidity to the already oppressive heat.

"Looks like rain," Daniel said.

"Maybe," I said. "But don't be surprised if the clouds just move on through without leaving a single drop."

Even though I was new to the neighborhood surrounding the Nash house, I had lived in Las Vegas long enough to know that you are never far from good food, no matter what time of day it is. We climbed into Daniel's GTO, and I guided him up to Sunset Road.

"There," I said, pointing toward a stucco building with cosmetic half timbering and a fake thatched roof. "Pull into the lot."

"It's a bar," Daniel said. "I'm really not in the mood for beer, video poker, and second-hand smoke."

"Trust me," I said.

Daniel was forced to admit that Patrick's Irish Pub is actually an excellent, if windowless, breakfast spot.

"How'd you know?" he asked as he dug into a good-looking Denver omelet.

I shrugged. "It's just one of those basic Vegas facts," I said. "Kitchens are open twenty-four hours wherever you turn. Very civilized, and smoking's not allowed anywhere food is served."

I was about to try my Belgian waffle when my phone buzzed. Dreading another call from Detective Booth, I looked at the screen before I answered. *Phew.* It was Sierra.

"Hey," I said. "Great dinner last night."

"Copper, we've got a problem. Michael got the deacon to cover for him at St. Andrew's, but he's still got too much to handle."

I looked at Daniel, rolling my eyes as Sierra explained further. There was no longer any need to pick up picnic supplies.

"We've got to go to the homeless center construction site," I said when she hung up. "Sierra says there's a media circus going on, and Michael needs our help."

Daniel smiled. "I've got to give it to you, Copper," he said. "You really know how to show a guy an interesting time." He ticked things off on his fingers. "That house, those plants, a murder investigation, and now an Indian uprising—"

"Michael told you about Willie Morningthunder?"

"Yeah, last night," Daniel said. "Don't know what I can do to help, but I'm happy to go find out."

Sierra has a tendency toward hyperbole, so when she said "media circus" I imagined a couple of news vans and a reporter or two. But when Daniel and I had to park six blocks away from the construction site, I began to realize that this time she was guilty of understatement. We joined a human herd on the sidewalk and moved with it toward the corner of Clinton Avenue and J Street.

"I can't believe this," I said as the crowd grew denser. "There are ten times as many people here than there were for the Helldorado Days Parade."

As we neared the chain-link fence surrounding the construction site, we could see that the center of attention was at one corner. A man in a full feather headdress was standing on the back of a flatbed truck. Three news vans were parked near it, each with a mast cranked up. I couldn't see any musicians, but steady drumbeats and chanting rose above the noise of the crowd.

"Willie Morningthunder, I presume," Daniel said. "Looks like he's getting ready to speak."

We wriggled our way to the fence. Security guards were patrolling the perimeter of the building site, keeping the crowd at bay. One end of a trench was ringed with yellow caution tape and covered with a white tarp. Two more security guards stood like sentinels on either side. The fence itself was festooned with feathers, strings of beads, photographs and drawings attached with clothespins and paperclips, little bouquets of lavender and sage, bigger bouquets of flowers, ribbons, handwritten notes, wooden carvings, cloth dolls, dream catchers, candles, coins, woven scarves, crosses, ankhs, peace symbols, and any number of other tokens and offerings. Right in front of me was a hot pink rabbit's foot, a handmade arrow, and a plastic statuette of the Virgin Mary.

"How are we going to find Michael?" I asked. "Do you see him?"

Daniel, at more than a head taller than me, could easily see over the crowd.

"There he is," he said, pointing toward the news vans. "Looks like he's being interviewed."

A few fat raindrops hit my arms as we wormed our way toward Michael. I squinted upward, and a few more spattered my face. Even though they were steamy, they felt a little refreshing.

Just then, Willie Morningthunder launched into his speech.

"Peoples of the world," he began. *"All you who have heard the call of the Great Father."*

"He's got a great preacher-man vibrato," Daniel whispered over his shoulder, and I had to agree. Willie Morningthunder had the sort of voice that could accompany tablets down from Mount Sinai.

"We stand on holy ground."

And a powerful sound system, too. If it hadn't been for the ripe whiff from the sewage plant across the street wafting over us, I might have actually been in a mood to be moved by his oratory. We inched forward. I tried not to seem too sacrilegious as I nudged my way through the crowd.

Willie paused. The drummers pounded more fiercely, and an undulating chorus rose above the throng. The crowd swayed, and many of them crooned along. Who were all these people? I wondered. They didn't belong to any one ethnic group, although lots of them were wearing outfits that might plausibly be described as "Native American."

When we finally reached the Channel 8 news van, Michael had just finished answering the questions posed by a smartly dressed young Asian woman whose heavy stage makeup was showing signs of slippage. She immediately ducked into the front seat of the van. I couldn't blame her. The temperature was well over 100, and a few more raindrops were falling. I was grateful I'd remembered my oversized sun hat. My poor brother had obviously not been as lucky. His hair was plastered to his scalp.

"Lordy," he said, mopping his brow. "Am I ever glad you're here."

"We have gathered today to reconsecrate this place," Willie Morningthunder boomed above us, *"but in a real sense we cannot hallow this ground further."*

"Where are we, Gettysburg?" Daniel said, a little too loud.

"Shh." I elbowed him. "Michael's got enough to deal with."

"Channel 3 wants to do a live remote in ten minutes," Michael said, "and somebody from KNPR is on the way over, too."

"How can I help?" I asked.

"Can you do the interviews for me?" Michael asked. "The Alliance's point of view needs to be heard, but I really want to go see Curtis. He's about to be arrested. I'm hoping I can get to him before the police do."

Oh, God. Sean hadn't been kidding.

"Did he really do it?" I asked. "Did he actually kill his wife?"

Michael sighed and wiped his forehead. "I don't know, and I can't think about it," he said. "I just want to be there for him. Even if he did, he needs a friend."

"Okay," I said, trying to shift into media mode. "But do I know enough?" I racked my brain for every shred of information I knew about the Alliance for the Homeless. Fortunately, it was quite a bit. I'd been writing the Alliance's newsletter for the last four months.

"You'll do a lot better than Jenna," Michael said.

Jenna Bartolo, the Alliance board member whose casino-owner husband had donated a couple of kings' ransoms to the building project, never missed a chance to be on camera. She had "given up her acting career" when she got married, but she had retained her love of center stage.

"Is she here?"

"She's supposedly on her way."

"Get going, and let me know how Curtis is doing," I said. "Call me."

"Oh, that reminds me," Michael said. "Can you call Sierra? She needs someone to watch Nicky this afternoon. Ordinarily, I'd do it, but—"

"Just go," I said. "I'll take care of everything."

"Thanks, Copper."

Leaving me a couple of damp business cards belonging to reporters, Michael disappeared into the crowd.

"I wish I were better dressed for this assignment," I said to Daniel, "and not dripping."

"You look fine," Daniel said. "Except it's too bad you aren't wearing a headdress."

"*Shut up!*" I looked from side to side to see if anyone had heard. "We're here to make things better, not worse."

"Okay, okay," Daniel said. "Trust me. I know all about political correctness."

"Prove it," I said. "My brother's career is at stake."

"Hi, Copper." The voice came from behind me, and even in the heat, it sent a chill down my spine.

I whipped around. Even though our eyes were hidden behind sunglasses, the connection was instantaneous. My heart sped up.

"David!"

Daniel cleared his throat in a not-very-subtle fashion.

"Oh!" I said, jarred from my spinning thoughts. "David—remember Daniel?"

The two guys grunted and shook hands. I knew they remembered each other all too well. They'd met when Daniel visited me at Christmastime, when David and I had just begun to click, and Daniel and I had just begun to crack.

"I—I thought you were—"

"Still in San Diego. I thought I would be, too, but things wrapped up more quickly than planned, and I lucked out getting an earlier flight."

"So, you're covering—this?" I waved my arms.

"No," David said. "I didn't even know about it. I just needed to swing by *The Light* on my way home from the airport. I caught sight of the hullaballoo while I was driving up J Street, and I decided to check it out."

"It's crazy," I said, "and I'm doing a remote with Channel 3 in five minutes."

David didn't reply, and I was about to fill the silence when he spoke abruptly.

"Have lunch with me tomorrow." His tone was more commanding than friendly.

My heart skipped a beat, and I felt Daniel stiffen beside me.

"What?" I said, even though I had heard him clearly.

"Have lunch with me. I need to talk to you. It's important." Still an order, but at least he'd given me a reason.

"Okay," I said. "Noon in the lunchroom. I won't have time to go off campus."

David nodded his agreement. "I've got to run," he said. "Nice to see you again, Dan."

"Same here," Daniel mumbled, and David moved off into the crowd.

Willie Morningthunder was introducing people now: a chief from Idaho, a roadman from Arizona, a shaman from Florida. How had they all gotten here so fast? I wondered.

Willie had just invited a woman in a fringed leather dress and feathered headband to join him on the flatbed when a blinding flash of lightning zapped across the sky. Before he could say another word, a thunderclap exploded above us. The noise was still hanging in the air when the clouds let loose.

Within ten seconds, we were all drenched to the skin. Puddles rose around our feet, and the building site took on the look of a muddy lagoon.

"We have gathered here from across the land—" Willie boomed, but that was all we heard even though his lips kept moving.

"The rainstorm must've taken out his sound system," Daniel said.

The crowd thinned a little as some people ran for shelter or cars. The awnings on the stores across the street attracted huddles of refugees, but many more people stayed where they were, chanting and swaying in the downpour. Willie's helpers scurried to restore his sound system, and the news crews retreated to their vans.

"Let's get out of here," Daniel said. "It looks like the media's calling it a day."

"Do you see Channel 3?" I asked, straining to see over the crowd. "I really shouldn't leave until I'm sure they don't want to do the remote."

The rain began to let up as Daniel and I slogged through the puddles toward the remaining news vans.

"I see it!" Daniel said, peering over the crowd. "This way."

As we moved closer, I recognized the peacock logo of Channel 3 on the side of a white van. By the time we reached it, the rain had stopped completely, and sunshine had broken through the cloud cover. We walked around to the other side, and—

"Oh, my God!" I whispered to Daniel. "That's Jenna Bartolo!"

Jenna, dazzling in a magenta shell and matching miniskirt, held a bright tartan umbrella over her sleek sable bob. As usual, she was encrusted with enough gemstones and gold to finance an army, and her makeup was flawless. Erin Murdock, Channel 3's news reporter, held a microphone to Jenna's exquisite carmine lips.

"Yes, that's right," I heard Jenna say. "There's such a thing as 'too much empowerment.' The natives have been given ample territory to do with as they please. If they were truly as noble as they would like us all to believe, they would realize that the Alliance for the Homeless is doing God's work here. Many Indians are homeless alcoholics, after all, and they'll all benefit from the new service center."

Shocked, I glanced around. Had anyone else just heard that? But the only person listening besides Daniel and me was the reporter. My heart crashed to my feet as I watched Erin's smile widen into a sly grin. Jesus. Why was I worrying about a few people standing within earshot? A few hours from now, the whole planet would be hearing what Jenna had just said. And to make it all a hundred times worse, she spoke with a clipped pseudo-British accent that made "Indian" sound far too much like "Injun." Michael was going to kill me, and I deserved it. Unless—

Erin signed off and started moving toward her van. I rushed to catch up with her.

"Just a second," I said. "I'm here to represent the Alliance—"

"Oh! Thanks, but I've already got what I need," Erin said. She smiled a little too happily. "And I've got another appointment."

"Please don't air that," I begged. "It'll be devastating—"

"Copper!" Jenna had just joined us. "Your brother told me you'd be doing the interview, but you weren't here! Lucky for you, I was!"

Still smiling, Erin climbed into the van. I watched it pull slowly away.

Damn! Should I follow her to the station and keep pleading for mercy? But I already knew it was hopeless. If I were Erin, I'd be just as gleeful. The footage she'd just captured was the kind of thing reporters get prizes for.

"You poor thing," Jenna said, clucking. "You're absolutely soaked."

"I didn't know where the van was," I said. "And then the rain—"

"I'm so glad I was here!" Jenna said. "And that I had the foresight to bring an umbrella. We wouldn't want the Alliance to look bad on television."

I stared at her and bit my tongue.

We wouldn't want the Alliance to look bad. What an idiot!

But I knew better than to try to explain how much damage she'd just done. "Loose cannon" didn't come close to describing Jenna Bartolo, and I certainly didn't want to make things worse.

As my mind grappled with the disaster the five o'clock news would bring, I watched Jenna sashay off in search of more microphones. I couldn't stop her, but I did manage to head off another nightmare by calling the program manager at KNPR and rescheduling the interview.

"Michael will have to go to the radio station at some point," I told Daniel. "Or maybe he can do the interview by phone. Either way, he's got a mushroom cloud to deal with after Jenna's little performance." I shuddered as I thought about Jenna's hot pink suit and racist commentary blasted all over the Web. She'd probably be a YouTube all-star.

"Talk about shit hitting the fan," Daniel said. "Worse than this place with a breeze."

Willie's microphone blasted back into service, and the sky was nearly clear again. Should we stay? No, I decided. The damage Jenna had done was going to take planning to overcome, and Sierra needed a babysitter.

"Let's get out of here," I said to Daniel, and he offered no resistance.

Chapter 17

"I'm sorry, Copper."

"It's not your fault."

"I could have been quicker finding Channel 3."

"Jenna Bartolo is not your fault."

Daniel apparently didn't have an easy comeback for that, and we were both silent for a minute or two.

"Turn left at the next light," I said, and soon Daniel was pulling in next to Sierra's SUV in the vicarage's driveway.

As we approached the front door, it sprang open. Nicky, clad in a barely hip-hugging diaper, burst out as though he'd been shot from a cannon. Sierra was right behind him, but it was Daniel who caught him.

"My man!" Daniel said, tossing Nicky above his head and catching him like a football. "How you been?"

Nicky shrieked in delight while Sierra and I rolled our eyes at each other.

"He's been a handful all day," Sierra said. "Are you sure you want to take him on? I can skip my Stay-at-Home-Moms Meetup."

The "Stay-at-Home Moms" meet at a brewpub in Henderson, which always makes me think they should call themselves the "Go-to-Barroom-Moms." I could have taken Sierra up on her offer, but I knew how much she loved hanging out with her friends. Besides, I'd just let Michael down so badly he might never recover.

"It's fine, Sierra. Go on. Take as much time as you need."

Sierra looked at me. I don't know what she saw in my face, but I watched her lips compress and her forehead wrinkle.

"Are you okay, Copper?"

"Other than damp, yeah. We really got nailed by the storm."

"Is Michael okay?" she asked.

"He's soaked, but he's fine. He went to be with Curtis."

Sierra shot me a dubious look, but then she shrugged.

"Okay. I'll be back in a couple of hours. There's some chocolate mousse in the refrigerator if you feel like it. And stuff to make sandwiches." She paused as though she was about to say something else.

"Really, Sierra, we're fine," I said, cutting her off. "Actually, I've been looking forward to it. I never get to spend enough time with Nicky."

Sierra drove off, and I followed Daniel into the living room. As soon as Nicky's feet hit the floor, he dragged Daniel over to his pirate ship.

"I've got to call Michael," I said, but they were already too involved in a mock naval battle to notice. I pulled out my cell phone, sat down on the sofa, and forced myself to punch up my brother's number. The last thing I felt like doing was informing him of the impending disaster, but the thought of Michael finding out by watching the five o'clock news was even worse.

"Hey, Copper," Michael said after only one ring. "Can you hold on a minute? I'm just finishing something up … "

"Sure," I said. Daniel was flat on his back on the floor now, holding Nicky up on his feet.

"You're an F-15!" Daniel said.

"Effifteeeee!" Nicky screamed. "Effifteeeeeee!"

I couldn't help smiling as I watched them, and I couldn't banish a pang of regret that Daniel and I would never start the family we'd once imagined. "I want a dozen kids," he'd told me. "Or one. One is the important number."

He'll make a fabulous father, I thought, and that made my thoughts shift to David. He'd make a good father, too. I hated the fact that Rebecca was the mother, but was it fair to hold that against a baby?

"Copper?" My brother was back on the phone.

"I've got some bad news," I said. What was the point of dragging it out?

"What?"

"Jenna Bartolo got to Erin Murdock before I did."

The silence lasted way too long, and I could hear Michael breathing.

"You're joking, right?" he said at last.

"No." I quoted Jenna as well as I could, and I could almost hear the color drain from Michael's face.

"Hold on," he said at last. "Curtis is here. Let me see—"

"He wasn't arrested?"

"No. A detective just bullied him a little."

"Detective Booth?"

"That's the one. Just a second."

Interesting, I thought. Curtis seemed to be getting the same treatment I was from Detective Booth. At least I hadn't been threatened with arrest.

"Curt's going to call Jeremy," Michael said.

"Who's Jeremy?"

"Jeremy Fitch. Station manager at Channel 3. Curt says Jeremy owes him one."

"I hope it works."

"Me, too."

As I pocketed my phone, I noticed that Daniel's was in his hand.

"Wow! That's what I call multitasking!" I said. Daniel was playing horse now, but he was still managing to hold a text conversation in between trips around the room.

"So … is your brother sending a hitman?" Daniel asked.

"Nope. He's using some juice to get the story axed. But we won't know for sure until five o'clock."

An hour later, Daniel and I sat facing each other at the kitchen table. Daniel had managed to wear Nicky out enough that he hadn't complained when we tucked him in for a nap. I made some ham sandwiches, and we polished off the chocolate mousse.

"Not quite the picnic we had in mind," I said. "Thanks for playing with Nick."

"It was fun," Daniel said.

"To show my gratitude, I'll take you out to dinner," I said. "Someplace on the Strip, like—"

"Thanks, Copper," Daniel said without meeting my gaze. "But I can't. I'm leaving today."

"But I thought—"

"I know. I've had a change of plans."

So that was what all the texting was about.

"A—friend invited me to stay overnight in L.A., but I've got to be in Berkeley Tuesday morning. If I leave today—"

That little pause between "a" and "friend" answered the question I hadn't asked. The friend was female. Not that I should have expected anything else.

"Okay, okay," I said. "As soon as Sierra gets back, we can go back to the Nash house, and you can get your stuff—"

"We're still friends, right?"

That word again.

I looked at him, and this time his eyes met mine. I half expected to fight back tears, but none appeared. I sighed. What did I expect? We both had to get on with our lives.

"You mean we'll send each other Christmas cards?" I said. "Sure."

"I mean I love you," Daniel said, rising from the table and taking our dishes to the sink. He didn't see it, but this time, a couple of tears really did spring to my eyes.

We stopped at a pet store on our way back to the Nash house, and Daniel bought food for my carnivorous garden. As we pulled in under the grape arbor, I saw that the lights were on in Colby's lair. As I unlocked the door to the house, I noticed that the padlock was gone from the hasp on the basement door, and faint sounds of marching band music wafted up from below. The sound was oddly comforting, now that I'd be spending my first night alone in the big weird house.

After Daniel fed the plants and showed me how to feed them next time, he went upstairs to pack. I scanned my email on my laptop in the kitchen. Mostly junk, but two items jumped out—one from Mom and one from Dad. They could wait, I told myself, only—

Oh, my God. I'd totally forgotten that this was the week my father was coming to town with what's-his-name.

I clicked his message open. *Damn.* With everything else that was happening, there had been no space left in my brain for remembering their visit.

> *Graham and I will be arriving on Wednesday, and we'll be staying at Cal's Town. On Boulder Highway, I think? I'm not familiar with it. We want to see you, and even with Graham's packed schedule, we'll make sure it happens. Love you, Dad*

Graham. I knew my dad had a boyfriend, but this would be our first face-to-face meeting. My father had revealed his true sexual preference only last December, and I was still grappling with ideas that my mind just couldn't seem to stretch around. Like—had he ever really loved my mother? If he'd been gay his whole life, how had he managed to have enough sex with her to produce two kids and live with her—apparently happily—for over thirty years?

Oddly, my mother seemed to have less trouble dealing with the whole paradigm shift than I did. She never complained—just went out and had an affair of her own with Mr. Cluff, a retired insurance actuary and my old Sunday school teacher.

Suddenly, it seemed as though both my parents had been playing an elaborate game of charades my whole life. They were strangers to me now, and they even looked different. My dad, once a poster child for Dockers and seersucker shirts, now had a Sting haircut and wore designer jeans. My mother had lost thirty pounds and made herself over in every way possible short of knife and needle, unless you count the tiny tattoo on her right shoulder.

Yes! My mother, charter member of the pantsuit brigade, dedicated vestrywoman at St. Mark's Episcopal Church, former president of the Whittier School PTA, and devoted Friend of the Library, got herself inked on the boardwalk in Atlantic City.

Sheesh, Mom! If you'd had the class to come to Vegas, I could have reduced your likelihood of exposure to hepatitis by at least ninety percent.

Weirdest of all, my parents hadn't gotten a divorce. Last Christmas, they'd made it sound like an official schism was all but complete, and I could swear I heard my dad talk about moving to Key West. But here it was, eight months later, and they were both still calling the family abode in Connecticut home. The big old empty nest offered plenty of room for them to cohabit and still go for days at a time without seeing each other. Really! I was there for a weekend in March, and they were less in touch with each other than I was with my boss.

I was still trying to decide whether to host a barbecue for my father and Graham when Daniel materialized in the doorway.

"I guess I'm ready," he said.

"You're headed for L.A., right?"

"Yeah. Four hours?"

"It depends," I said. "What part?"

"Venice," he said.

Venice. I tried to resist it, but a suntanned surfer girl barged in front of my mind's eye.

"It could take longer," I said. "Sunday's the day Californians go home, and Venice is on the far side."

"Five, then?"

"Maybe. Could be six. Could be more, even, if there's an accident." I wasn't really trying to talk him out of leaving. I was just being honest, but whether Daniel thought so, I wasn't sure.

"Guess I better hit it, then," he said, and I could tell he wasn't looking forward to the good-bye scenario.

"Guess so," I said, feeling the same way.

Out next to Daniel's car, we didn't kiss. We only sort of hugged. Then I stood there on the hot asphalt in the raking rays of the descending sun and watched the green GTO disappear around the corner with a manly *vroom.* Daniel Garside, once the lord of my universe and king of my fantasies, was disappearing from my life forever.

Or at least until it was time to exchange Christmas cards.

The weird thing was that I didn't feel forlorn. I didn't even feel sad. The only emotion that rolled over me was a giant tsunami of relief. It lasted until I went back inside and noticed the clock on the kitchen wall.

Seven minutes to five! Grabbing my cell phone, I rushed to the party room and clicked on the big television. Sinking into the sofa, I called Michael.

"Are you home?" I asked. "Are you watching?"

"Yeah, and praying," Michael said. "I'll call you back after the show."

The newscast began with a teaser about the gathering at the building site, complete with aerial footage of the crowd and a booming bit of Willie Morningthunder's rhetoric. No lady in hot pink, though. Had they cut Jenna out completely? I sat there wondering through stories about the price of hotel rooms on the Strip, a drive-by shooting near the university, and—*damn!* The cutting horse finals at the Silverado. I had totally forgotten about the tickets that Marilyn Weaver had arranged for me.

It was a short segment, but it was easy to recognize Charlene and her long dark hair on the winners' podium. A pang of sadness shot through me as I realized that Marilyn had missed Charlene's moment of glory. Her own mother couldn't have been prouder than Marilyn would have been.

At last, the camera turned to Erin Murdock again, and this time a hot pink suit and plaid umbrella did fill the screen. I held my breath as Jenna Bartolo began to speak.

"Yes, that's right," she said. *"They … realize that the Alliance for the Homeless is doing God's work here. We will all benefit from the new service center."*

And that was it! Hooray for talented video editors, Michael's prayers, and Curtis Weaver's juice! Jenna hadn't made a lot of sense in her edited appearance, but she also wouldn't make any waves.

My phone rang almost immediately.

"We still have to worry about Jenna," Michael said. "She may not like her censored interview, and she may try to do something about it."

"Keep praying, then," I said. "But in the meantime, at least she's been temporarily defanged."

"I'm going to call Curtis," Michael said. "With all that's going on, it was really nice of him to step in."

"How's he doing?" I asked.

"He's holding up pretty well, all things considered," Michael said. "Family members are beginning to arrive. The house is still a crime scene, so his stepson rented a suite at the Silverado where they can all hang out."

"Sean?"

"Yeah. Marilyn's niece is helping out, too."

"Charlene? The cowgirl?"

"Yeah, poor kid. She's really suffering."

"Does anybody know who killed Marilyn?"

"Nope. Marilyn didn't have any enemies, and it wasn't a burglary—nothing was taken," Michael said.

Not quite true, I thought. Curtis must not have noticed that his sunglasses were missing.

"By the way, did you know Marilyn was married before?"

"I guess—to Sean's father?"

"Before that—when she was just out of college. I was talking with one of her cousins from Montana. She married a guy the day she graduated, and he died when they were on their honeymoon. Looked the wrong way on a corner in front of Harrods. Stepped out, and got hit by a London cab."

"That's awful!"

"Yeah, but evidently not financially. The guy was loaded, and it all went to Marilyn."

My mind snapped back to my conversation with Sean at the bar at the V, back before I'd stumbled into Marilyn's closet. He'd hinted that her past held some secrets, but at the time I hadn't pressed. Tomorrow, I told myself, I'd finally get the chance to put the high-powered research tools at *The Light* to work and do a little digging.

"Detective Booth is still bullying Curtis," Michael went on. "Even though he swears he was in Henderson at the time of the murder."

"What? He was supposed to be in Palm Springs. That's why Sean was house sitting."

"Strange."

"Why?"

"When I talked to Sean, he seemed to know Curtis was in Henderson."

He'd lied to me? Or maybe he'd just made a mistake. Or maybe Curtis was supposed to leave for Palm Springs later, and then never got the chance.

My mind was spinning again. Things'll be clearer tomorrow, I told myself. I'll find out more about both Marilyn and Sean, and I could talk it over with David at lunch. Even though our relationship was probably toast, my heart sped up at the thought of seeing him. Would I ever get over the guy?

I spent the rest of the evening answering email and playing online backgammon. Before I climbed into bed, I slipped into my bathing suit and headed out to the pool. The lights were off in the basement, and the door was once again padlocked. At last, I thought. I could live another one of my fondest fantasies. I peeled off my suit, slipped into the water, and floated alone under gently rustling palms.

Chapter 18

My phone buzzed before my alarm went off.

"Good morning," an unfamiliar masculine voice said.

"Um—who is this?" I asked, shaking myself awake.

"Thor," the voice said. "The tortoise guy."

Had I given him my phone number? I guess I must have.

"I'm going to be finishing up the burrow today. I'm bringing Oscar."

"Okay," I said. "I'll be at work all day, but I'll check on him when I get home."

"You've read the book, right? You know he's got to fatten up to be ready to hibernate through the winter?"

I hadn't actually read that far, but I swore to Thor that I was committed to Oscar's well-being.

As I walked downstairs to the kitchen, I realized that there was still no food in the house, unless you counted the remaining cans of Coors Light in the refrigerator. Somehow, I had to find time to do some grocery shopping today. In addition to food for myself, I needed to stock up on bok choi for Oscar.

After stopping at Starbucks to pick up a *latte* for my boss and a bagel for me, I headed to *The Light*. What was awaiting me there? I wondered. Had I achieved celebrity status by snooping in a bedroom? Would I be walking into a horde of interrogators? I practiced my one answer as I drove.

The police have asked me not to talk about that while the case is still open.

But when I walked into the building, everything was dead normal. I collected my mail at the grid of pigeonholes in the hall near my cube, but no one said anything more than good morning. Maybe everyone already knows I can't talk about Marilyn, I thought. Or maybe a murder is just not that big a deal around here. But whatever was keeping everyone mute on the subject was okay with me. A big relief, in fact. I was almost smiling until I rounded the corner into my cube.

Mary Beth Sweeney was sitting in my chair.

"Hi!" she said brightly. "I was waiting for you! I want to hear all about it."

Well, I thought, I guess I shouldn't be too surprised. *Somebody* had to be curious. But I played dumb anyway.

"About what?"

"Marilyn Weaver," she said in a tone that added an unspoken, *"What else, stupid?"*

"I can't," I said. "The police have asked me not to talk about that while the case is still open." It poured out even more smoothly than when I rehearsed it.

"You can tell me how you knew her—and what you were doing in her house."

"Mary Beth, I'm not going to do anything that might jeopardize the case. The cops'll talk when they can. Why do you want to know, anyway?"

She shrugged. "It'd make a great spec column, that's all. I would think you'd want to make sure I got my facts straight."

By the time I managed to get Mary Beth off my chair and out of my cube, she had decided to switch her focus to Marilyn's personal history.

"But it's a shame," she said before clumping down the hall. "An interview with the girl who found the body would make a much better story."

Mary Beth did have a nose for news, I had to admit. But if anyone was going to write about finding Marilyn's body, it was going to be me.

Before Chris Farr's *latte* could cool off any further, I headed for his office. He wasn't there, so I left it on his desk.

Bracing myself for the stack of press releases I knew awaited me, I headed back to my cubicle. I swung around the partition and found myself face to face with—and I'm sure my mouth dropped open—Detective Booth.

My heart stopped midbeat. What was he doing here? How had he gotten past the gatekeeper?

Oh, yeah. He was a cop.

"Good morning, Ms. Black," he said politely.

I finally found my voice. "Uh, yeah—good morning."

"I have a few more questions," he said, "now that it's *business hours.*"

Blood rushed to my cheeks. I forced myself to look at him.

Damn it! My face was screaming.

"How can I help you?" I said, trying my best to sound calm and professional.

"Well—" Booth dragged it out. Then he rubbed his chin. "It comes down to this. You've got to talk to me."

I stared at him as I willed my cheeks to cool down.

"Tell me what you know that you've been keeping from me." He paused, his icy eyes holding mine captive.

Weird. How could he know I had left a few things out if he didn't know what they were? Had Sean told him that I'd taken my stuff out to my car? Maybe that was it.

"I've told you everything I remember."

Booth's eyes narrowed. "It's time your memory improved."

Was he threatening me?

Sweat prickled on my forehead, and I prayed it didn't show. But even though I felt the pressure the detective was applying so effectively, I also felt a rising tide of anger. I didn't deserve the treatment this bully was giving me. Well, okay, maybe I did, but it still pissed me off.

"I've told you everything I remember," I repeated, surprised at how steady my voice sounded. I paused, my eyes still locked with his. "More than once."

We both kept staring as my mind whirled. Was I digging myself in too deep?

"Okay, Ms. Black. You win." He turned both palms toward me in a classic sign of surrender. I held my breath as I watched him turn to leave. I was about to exhale when he stopped and turned back.

"If you remember anything, give me a call," he said. "Here's my card."

"I have one," I said.

"Oh, I *forgot*," he said with another dose of sarcasm. "But here's something you might want to remember. If I don't start getting a little more cooperation from you, I'm going to be looking into charges."

Charges? For what? I'm sure my face asked the questions that I didn't ask aloud.

"For obstruction of justice," Booth continued. "It won't be pleasant."

He waited, but I didn't respond. My mind was spinning, and I had no idea what to say.

"Have it your way, Ms. Black," he said. "Hope to hear from you."

I stood there as Booth's footsteps faded down the hall. What did he think I was concealing? He couldn't possibly know that I'd accidentally removed a few toiletries from Marilyn's countertop. Even Sean didn't know that. I didn't know myself until hours later when

I emptied my bags. And if Sean had mentioned that I'd taken my stuff out to my car, why hadn't Booth asked about that specifically? It didn't make sense. He had to be fishing, but why? Time was running out. Somehow—and fast—I had to find out the truth about Sean.

I glanced at my desk. The last thing I wanted to think about was work, but it was Monday. If I wanted to have time to investigate, not to mention time for a decent talk with David over lunch, I had to get my calendar updates finished in double time.

Fortunately, there are two things I like about my job. One is that my Monday morning updates don't take much brainpower. The other is my boss. He called a minute or so after Booth left.

"Hey, Copper, thanks for the *latte*. Don't know how you knew I needed a *grande*."

"Well, it's Monday—"

"Are you doing okay?"

"I'm fine, thanks, Chris."

"Tough weekend, though, right?"

"Yeah."

"If you need some time—"

"Thanks, Chris. I think what I really need is normalcy."

"You'll get it back someday. In the meantime, let me know if I can help."

"Well—if I get all these updates done, could I take a little extra time at lunch?"

"Sure. If you're back in time for the editorial meeting, that'll be fine."

"Thanks, Chris."

See what I mean? He's a great, great boss. Now that I didn't have to be back until three, I'd be able to go someplace private with David. *The Light*'s lunchroom seemed like a terrible place to discuss unplanned babies and strategies for dealing with homicide detectives.

Not only did the walls have ears, so did every table. And afterward, I should still have some time to delve into the private life of Sean DuBois.

Tuning my iPod to some soul-soothing New Age massage music, I tried to focus on changes in the Strip's lounge singer lineup. But as soon as I began reading that Jose Jaramillo was moving from the Excalibur to Harrah's, my cell phone vibrated. I was tempted to ignore it, but I pulled out my earbuds and answered.

"Copper! Are you all right, darling?"

Oh, God.

"I'm fine, Mom. How are you?"

"Why didn't you call me?"

"I was about to."

"Goodness gracious, sweetheart! Sierra just told me what happened. Are you sure you're all right? Should I catch a plane?"

"Really, Mom, I'm fine."

Twenty minutes of reassurance later, I finally convinced her that while finding a body was awful, it wasn't an emergency. No, she didn't need to cancel her plans to go to the Adirondacks with my old Sunday school teacher. It helped that she knew my dad was coming to town.

"You let Ted know if you need anything, darling," she said. "And call or email me, okay? I'll have my cell phone with me at Lake George, and Patrick's bringing his computer."

Okay, Mom. But no matter how much time passed, Ted was still Dad, and Patrick would forever be Mr. Cluff.

My phone buzzed again as soon as Mom hung up. At this rate, I'd never finish in time for lunch.

"Copper! It's Dad! How are you?"

Sierra had definitely done a good job of spreading the word. Fortunately, my father doesn't like talking on the phone, and our conversation lasted only long enough for me to assure him I was still alive and to invite him and Graham to the Nash house for a barbecue on Thursday.

"That'll be great, Copper," he said. "I'm really looking forward to introducing Graham to everyone."

As I hung up, I wished I could feel the same. At least the house would provide plenty of topics for conversation, and if Sierra, Michael, and Nicky came, too …

So then I had to make another call to invite them, and by the time I got back to my game of musical lounge singers, a whole hour had gone by. And now I had a dinner party to plan.

Fortunately, nothing else interrupted me until noon.

"Hi, Copper."

The voice sliced right though Enya and zinged straight to my heart.

I yanked out my earbuds and swiveled my chair around.

"Hi, David."

We just looked at each other for a minute.

A quarter of an hour later, we were looking at each other from across a table in the café at the Palace Station casino. People from *The Light* didn't go there unless they had to, and we melted easily into the anonymous casino crowd.

"Thanks for agreeing to have lunch with me, Copper. I was afraid you wouldn't."

"You practically commanded me. What choice did I have?"

"You had a choice."

Our eyes met again, and I knew what he was going to say before I heard the words. Regret was written all over him.

"I'm sorry."

I didn't say anything. I just stared into those deep dark eyes.

"I wanted to talk to you about it in person, Copper. I don't expect you to forgive me."

Then the waitress appeared, and we had to pretend we were

interested in eating something.

After we'd put in our orders for iced tea and sandwiches, I looked at David again. He was staring at his silverware and fiddling with his napkin. Getting ready to say something else, I figured. Maybe I should have planned something myself. But I'd been too busy worrying about Detective Booth and Sean DuBois.

"The baby's due in February," he said at last, still looking down. He paused, then added, "It's a boy."

"You know already?" *Wow. That was fast.*

"She had to have a special test because of her family history."

It's a boy. I've always loved how that sentence transforms a blob of tissue into a human being. "It" was now "a boy." A real person.

We both just sat there for a minute or maybe five.

"I'm sorry, too," I said at last. A storm of feelings surged through me. Most of the storm was anger, but a couple of lesser whirlwinds circled with the vortex. Sadness and jealousy.

Somehow, sadness won out.

"I've missed you so terribly I can't begin to tell you." I looked straight at him. "I believe you when you say you're sorry, but I can't just—I can't just—"

David looked down. I struggled for words.

"I don't know what this means for you or for—your family, and that's for you to figure out. But for me—for us—" I dropped my eyes to the keno card stuck between the salt and pepper shakers.

Shut up, Copper. There's nothing you can say that will set things right.

"God damn it, David. I love you." I looked up, my heart hammering. Had I really just said that?

Tears stood in David's eyes, and I watched two of them roll down his cheeks. Tears welled in my own eyes.

"I love you, Pepper," he said. "And I'm sorry. I made a terrible mistake."

"It's not a mistake anymore," I said. "It's a baby."

"I know. I'm sorry—and I'm terrified."

"You'll have to get past that." I couldn't quite believe the conviction in my voice. "Your son deserves better. If you decide to, you'll make a great dad."

"If I get the chance, I'd like to try." He fiddled with his napkin, then looked at me again. "Rebecca and I aren't getting back together. There's no way. I think I knew it even the night I was with her. But I was hurt and angry, and I thought I'd lost you."

He reached across the table and took both of my hands in his. "I'll understand if you don't want me back. I don't think I'd want me back—"

"I want to be with you." The words burst out as though my heart had spoken without permission from my head. Was I crazy? Could I really love and trust this man? My heart didn't seem to care. I pulled my hands from his and wrapped my arms around myself. "I'm also angry. I'm also hurt."

The waitress appeared with our food. I stared at my tuna sandwich as my mind came to grips with what had just happened. Were David and I getting back together? Could love really conquer all, even the consequences of an unintended baby? Right now, just being with David again was all that mattered. But what if resentment returned full force? How would I feel when other people found out my boyfriend had fathered someone else's child? What would I feel about the kid, if I ever met him? I sighed. The only thing I knew right then was that I was open to finding out. I looked at David. He was staring at his plate.

"I hope he has your eyes, dude," I said. Looking up, he met my gaze.

"I wish he were going to have yours, Pepper."

Fortunately, tuna sandwiches taste okay when moistened with tears.

David was holding my hand when the waitress reappeared. She set down an order of strawberry shortcake and two forks.

"On the house," she said before either of us could protest. "You two look like you could use a little extra sweetness today."

Chapter 19

"You're the world's worst liar."

David didn't say it as an accusation. He was just stating a simple fact that would be ridiculous for me to deny. When I say something that's even only a slightly modified version of the truth, my ears flame and my cheeks blaze. It's as bad a poker tell as an auto-enlarging nose.

"You really think that's all it is? You don't think he knows I accidentally stole Marilyn's mini-bottle of Shalimar?"

David and I were curled up on the sofa in his living room. He'd invited me over for spaghetti after work, but dinner was the furthest thing from our minds once we got inside the door. We didn't even make it upstairs.

"You should have told him about the stuff you took as soon as you found it," David said. "You really are guilty of something, you know."

"I know, I know," I said. "Do you think he'll really arrest me?"

I felt David shrug underneath me. "I think it'll depend on whether he catches the killer. He doesn't think you did it. He just thinks you know something about who did."

Oh, my God. That was it.

We were both assuming that Detective Booth didn't think I was the murderer. But what if he *did* think I had killed Marilyn? What if he was biding his time—collecting enough tidbits of evidence to arrest me?

I had no way of knowing what Sean had told him or what else Booth had uncovered, but there was no solid reason to believe I was safe from suspicion. If I didn't find some things out right away, I could easily find myself accused of something far worse than obstruction of justice.

"You should give the detective the stuff you accidentally took, explain what happened, and then let him do his work."

David's suggestion sounded reasonable, but all it did was galvanize my resolve to do some digging on my own. I was in a better position than Booth to get Sean to talk, and maybe I could find out why Curtis turned up in Henderson after Sean told me he was in Palm Springs. In fact, I was uniquely positioned to investigate without arousing any suspicion. I could save myself from undeserved accusations, and I could help solve a heinous crime. It was all so clear now. It was not only in my best interest, it was my moral duty to pursue the truth with every ounce of energy I possessed. Justice—not to mention self-preservation—demanded it.

"I'll take care of everything tomorrow," I said.

Fortunately, David didn't press for specifics. I settled back down into his arms, and—

"Oh, my God!" I sat bolt upright. "I forgot about Oscar!"

"The tortoise?"

"Yes. He arrived today. I've got to get to a grocery store."

So much for David's plan to make spaghetti. Instead, after stopping at a supermarket on the way, we arrived at the Nash house with a big bag of vegetables and a frozen pizza. Setting everything on the kitchen counter, I pulled out some of the more tempting-looking greens and grabbed the flashlight I'd parked next to the door.

"Your resident filmmaker?" David asked as we passed the ground-level window on the way to the pool. Light was pouring from it, along with the strains of Judy Garland singing "Easter Parade."

"Yeah," I said. "He creeped me out at first, but he really is just making movies down there, and I'm glad to have him around. This place can feel awfully isolated."

We walked past the pool and through the gate to the rear yard. I switched on my flashlight.

"There he is!" David said as the beam came to rest on the faded peace symbol painted on Oscar's shell. The tortoise was hard at work digging in the rocky soil next to the back fence. We walked closer.

"I guess he doesn't like his burrow," David said.

"I hope he can't dig out," I said. "If Oscar disappears, the tortoise guy will hold me responsible."

I turned my flashlight on the entrance to the burrow. Thor had left a big bowl of water and a plate full of something that looked like hay and twigs.

Moving closer to Oscar, I saw the hole Thor had told me about. It was the diameter of a quarter, right over his tail. "Asshole" was right. The painted peace symbol was bad enough. Only a sadist could have drilled a hole through the carapace of a living creature.

Poor old guy.

I bent over and laid a couple of leaves of Swiss chard in front of him. Oscar ignored them and kept digging.

"He's not making much progress," David said.

It was true. Even though Oscar's claws were long and sharp-looking, he hadn't made much of a depression in the rock-like desert crust. Making his efforts even more futile, the fence was a balustrade of heavy wrought iron anchored in a course of cinder blocks. The bars were fairly close together, and Thor had beefed up their tortoise resistance with a run of chicken wire. Oscar could get a lot of aerobic exercise trying, but unless he suddenly mutated into a Ninja Turtle, he wasn't going anywhere.

Watercress wasn't any more tempting to him than chard, so David and I finally left him to his determined excavation efforts. After pizza, we checked on him again. He was still digging. He was still getting nowhere.

I had just arrived at my desk the next morning when my phone buzzed.

My heart stopped, then started again as I reassured myself that if it was Booth, at least he hadn't arrived in person with handcuffs.

But it wasn't the detective. It was my brother.

"How are you?" I asked. "How are things at the building site?"

"Still a standoff," he said. "That's why I'm calling. That full-page ad in *The Light* this morning—"

"Ad?" I grabbed my copy of the paper. I hadn't even glanced at it. "What ad?"

"Section one, page six," Michael said. I flipped the pages until the headline jumped out at me.

"THE ALLIANCE FOR THE HOMELESS IS A COALITION OF HATE," it read. "Don't be fooled!" the line below continued. "The organization that so piously solicits your donations to 'help the homeless' is nothing more than a tax shelter for the wealthy." The rant went on to name Michael and the other board members as self-serving, tax-evading promulgators of racism and elitism.

"A donation to the Alliance for the Homeless is a tax-deductible gift to the Tyranny of the Privileged." The text wound up with a call to shut down the Alliance's building project and to return the property to "the original owners whose ancestral lands have been systematically appropriated through the unjust hegemony of an unfairly advantaged aristocracy."

"Oh, brother," I said. "Who did it?"

"That's what I want to know," Michael said. "It's easy to assume Willie Morningthunder's behind it, but I'm not so sure. Can you find out?"

"I think so," I said. Too bad David wasn't around. He'd gotten a call early that morning that had sent him to the airport in search of a last-minute flight to Reno. He wouldn't appreciate my pestering him with questions I could answer myself with a trip downstairs to talk with the people who handle display advertising. "I'll go down to the ad department as soon as I can and ask."

"Thanks."

"Any word from the forensic anthropologists about who those bones belonged to?"

Michael sighed. "Not yet. But the way things are going, it almost doesn't matter."

After I hung up, I decided to spend a few minutes finding out what I could about Sean DuBois on the Web. I had just clicked my way to his Facebook page when Mary Beth swung around the corner.

"Oh, good," she said. "You're here. Have you heard the latest on the Weaver murder?"

"I'm not sure," I said, wondering what Mary Beth knew that I didn't.

"The husband is off the hook."

"*What?*"

She smiled triumphantly. "Yep. He's come clean. Or his alibi did, anyway."

"His *alibi?*"

"His girlfriend. Jenna Bartolo."

My jaw dropped before I could stop it. She had to be joking.

"She'll be all over the news tonight. She claims she was with Curtis at the time of the murder. In a hotel room at the Fiesta in Henderson."

My mind was still grappling with the image of Curtis Weaver canoodling with an airhead while his wife was being strangled when Mary Beth started talking again.

"I've been doing some research on Marilyn Weaver," she said. "That lady had quite a history."

"Her first marriage was a sad story," I said, trying to sound knowledgeable.

"Yeah, heartbreaking," Mary Beth said. "Although seven million dollars for a two-day marriage could be considered a pretty good silver lining." She waved her hand at me. "But that's not what I'm talking about. I'm talking about the three deaths she was involved with when she was a kid."

What? I didn't voice the word, but my face said it anyway.

Mary Beth smiled again. "I thought you might not know about the family tragedy. I found out only after some real digging."

I stayed mute.

"Lucky for Marilyn, she grew up pre-Internet." Mary Beth handed me a photocopied newspaper story. "But she didn't grow up pre-microfiche."

I looked at the headline on the article in front of me.

"DEADLY FIRE AT THE LAZY B RANCH."

I couldn't tear my eyes from the story. On a Saturday morning in the summer of 1962, all three of Marjorie and Richard Beeman's young children—Marilyn's cousins—perished when they couldn't escape from a burning chicken house.

"It sounds like a terrible accident," I said.

"It does, doesn't it?" She handed me several more pages. "Keep reading."

But Mary Beth filled in the details of the story before I had the chance.

"Marilyn and her cousin Anita locked the little kids in a chicken house and set it on fire."

"Looks like Anita was the mastermind," I said, skimming ahead. "And she was 14. Marilyn was only 10."

"The kids who died were 7, 6, and 4," Mary Beth said.

"She tried to rescue them," I said, and I read aloud. "'Marilyn

Canaday ran back to the chicken house, but she was unable to open the door before flames engulfed the structure. The girl suffered second-degree burns on her hands, arms, and chest."

"Yeah, I saw," Mary Beth said. "She got a lot of credit for that."

I kept reading. "Anita set the fire," I said. "She admitted it."

"Yeah, and she paid the price. Spent the next four years in a juvenile facility in Billings."

I looked at the photographs that accompanied the articles. Three adorable, curly-haired children smiled from pictures taken at what looked like a family picnic. Next to them was a photo of a pretty little fair-haired girl wearing a white cowboy hat: "Marilyn Canaday, 10, of Bellevue, Washington." The last photo was a little blurry and not nearly as charming. Anita Whitmore, even at age 14, was built like a fullback, and she was scowling from behind a pair of unflattering batwing glasses. The ugly evil cousin, I couldn't help thinking. The bad seed.

"My column about Marilyn is turning out a lot more interesting than I ever dreamed it would," Mary Beth said, "but it would be even better if I could convince you to go on the record with a tidbit or two."

So *that* was it. Mary Beth was being helpful and friendly because—as usual—she wanted something. I sighed.

"You know I can't talk to you, Mary Beth."

"Being a good girl isn't always the best move for a journalist."

Her words rankled. Too bad I couldn't tell her just how bad I really was. I gathered up the photocopies and held them out to her.

"Sorry, but I'm not talking until the cops say it's okay."

"Oh, keep them," Mary Beth said. She heaved an exasperated sigh and spun around to leave, but before she disappeared, she turned back.

"If you want to make it in this business, you're going to have to stop being such a freaking Goody Two-shoes."

She didn't stick around for a reply, which was a good thing. I might not have been able to stop myself from setting her straight.

I leafed through a few of the other stories Mary Beth had copied from old Montana and Washington newspapers. As time went by, it seemed, Marilyn was portrayed more and more as a brave heroine, while Anita was more and more frequently labeled a child-killer.

What happened to Anita? I wondered. According to the last story Mary Beth had given me, she was released from the juvenile facility in Billings when she turned 18. She'd be in her sixties now, four years older than Marilyn. It might be worth doing a little checking of my own, or—wait a second! Could she be among the family members gathering for Marilyn's memorial service?

Just then, my phone buzzed. Without bothering to check caller ID, I braced myself for Booth's voice on the other end.

"Ms. Black?" The voice was male, but it was definitely not the detective's.

"Yes."

"This is Evan Rice."

Who? I searched my brain.

"From the Parks Academy. We met last Thursday—when you visited."

Oh, yeah. The voice coach.

"Yes," I said. "How are you? I'm so sorry about—"

"Thanks," he said. "We're all still in shock." He paused, and I had no idea what to say to fill the silence.

"I'm calling to find out if you're still coming to campus today," Mr. Rice finally continued.

Oh, my God. I had completely forgotten.

"Kelly Baskin and Chanel Torres—the two girls you met when you were here last week—will be here at five thirty," Mr. Rice said. "I can tell them not to come, but—"

"I'll be there."

Mr. Rice let out a breath. "Thank you, Ms. Black. Thank you." His words kept tumbling out. "These kids are devastated by what's happened. You have no idea how reassuring it will be for them to talk to you. They need their faith in the future restored."

I didn't feel capable of restoring anybody's faith. "I'll definitely be there at five thirty," I said anyway.

"We'll meet you at the entrance to Beeman Hall. Thank you again."

Just after noon, I checked my mailbox and found a yellow envelope addressed in hand-written block letters to "Copper Black." Inside was a card with a picture of a smiling sun on the front. I opened it and read the message.

Sending a little sunshine your way to brighten up your day.

Underneath, in ultra-neat cursive handwriting, were the words, "You're in my thoughts. Sean."

When I finally made it down to the advertising department, I learned that a group called the Seminole Political Action Committee had paid for the full-page ad in today's newspaper.

Seminoles. Don't they live in Florida?

As I drove over to the Parks Academy from work, I struggled to force my mind into journalist mode. While I was hardly the seasoned reporter David was, I had interviewed several dozen people since I'd worked at *The Light*, mostly in conjunction with my role as calendar girl. The trouble was, they'd all been old hands at dealing with the media. I hadn't had a serious conversation with a high school girl since I was one myself. Suddenly I felt ancient—would they really open up to someone old enough to be their teacher? And I also felt too young—maybe they wouldn't take me seriously.

Then I remembered something David had told me.

"When I have the luxury of plenty of time," he'd said, "I never push things. All I do is sort of ease the cork out, and when their souls finally come gushing forth—they'll tell you more than you ever wanted to know."

With their whole senior year ahead to "ease the cork out," I didn't need a specific agenda for today's meeting. By the time I turned onto Academy Lane, I was actually looking forward to chatting with Kelly and Chanel.

I pulled up to the main entrance a little after five. The security kiosk was deserted, but the gate was standing open. I drove through, headed to the lot where I'd parked on my last visit, and pulled in next to the only other car, a white sedan.

The door to Beeman Hall was unlocked, but no one was in sight when I stepped inside. Looking down the hallway past the registrar's desk, I could see that the door to Marilyn's office was standing open. Light poured out into the hallway, and I thought I could hear voices. I hesitated a moment, then headed toward it. Maybe whoever was in there could call Mr. Rice for me.

I peeked around the door.

Standing in the middle of the room, his back toward me, was Sean. Facing him was Chanel, the beautiful olive-skinned girl I was here to interview. As her eyes met mine over Sean's shoulder, she let out a startled, "Oh!"

Sean whipped around, and I caught the look of shock on his face before he had a chance to erase it.

"Copper!"

"Hello, Sean."

Without a word, Chanel brushed past me and rushed out of the room.

"Excuse me," I said. "I didn't mean to—"

"Oh, it's okay," Sean said, draping his arm around my shoulders and pulling me into the room. "Things are just in turmoil around here—I've had to put on my counselor's hat."

What? Sean was "counseling" teenage girls? Didn't the school have real counselors for that? I pulled away from him and edged back toward the door.

As I moved, I couldn't help noticing the shredder sitting next to Marilyn's desk. Next to it stood a tall wastebasket, filled to the top with paper spaghetti. Stacks of manila file folders covered her desk, and more were piled on the credenza behind it. The drawers of two large filing cabinets were pulled out, and more file folders lay scattered on the floor.

"Mr. Rice is expecting me," I said. "I better get going—"

But Sean was too quick for me. He slid past me and blocked my way through the door.

"Have dinner with me," he said.

"What?" I stared at him. "No, thanks. I have other plans."

"Okay, then, a beer," he said. "Odds are it'll turn out better than last time." He barked a laugh that instantly tied my stomach in a knot.

"Let's see what time it is when I'm finished with my interviews," I said, hoping it would make him move.

Sean stood his ground in front of the door.

"I've been giving that some thought," he said. "And I really think it would be better for the school if you didn't do those interviews—or write that story."

"Really? That's not what you said before." Our eyes met, and my heart sped up. "And it's not what Mr. Rice thinks."

"Teachers don't always know what's best for institutions as a whole," Sean said. "I can make apologies for you—"

"I'll make my own apologies if I need to," I said. Sean took a step to the left, and I seized the opportunity to push past him into the hall. I could feel his eyes on me as I retraced my steps toward the main door. I didn't look back, even when the door slammed.

"Hello, Ms. Black." Ms. Carpenter had materialized in her spot at the registrar's desk, where she was putting away papers and obviously getting ready to leave. "May I help you?" she asked as she put on a pair of sunglasses and slung her purse over her shoulder.

Her voice was formal but reassuring. My heart rate slowed down.

"I'm here to see Mr. Rice," I said. "I'm a little early."

"You're here to interview Kelly and Chanel, right?"

"Yes," I said, remembering how Marilyn had told me her nickname was "The Hard Drive."

"We're all very glad you're still going to write your story," she went on. "It's just the kind of thing the school—and the students—need to pull through. I'm sure Ms. Weaver—bless her sweet soul—would agree."

"Ms. Carpenter—" I looked at her. "I'm so sorry."

"Thanks."

I couldn't let that be the end of our conversation.

"Do you know why Sean is shredding Ms. Weaver's files?"

Ms. Carpenter stared at me, her face careworn behind the glasses. "That's what he's doing in there?"

I nodded.

She dropped her eyes and shook her head. "There's nothing I can do about it. The board's named him acting principal. He's in charge for three weeks—until Mr. St. John gets back from Vienna."

"Do you have any idea why he'd want to destroy her records?"

When she looked back up at me, I could almost hear The Hard Drive whirring.

"If Sean's doing something that will harm the school, he should be stopped," I said.

She stared at me.

"I can help," I said.

Just then, Mr. Rice popped out of a door at the end of the hall.

"Ms. Black!" he called as he jogged toward us. His well-tended dreadlocks were pulled back in a ponytail. He wore another designer warm-up suit and running shoes so new they glowed. I looked at Ms. Carpenter. She had removed her sunglasses.

"Don't forget to say good-bye before you leave," she said as Mr. Rice arrived at my side. "We're all so glad you're here."

Mr. Rice led me down a hallway to an auditorium I hadn't seen before, talking all the way.

"I thought you might like to see both girls perform first," he said as he ushered me to a third-row center seat. "And then—how much time do you have?"

"I've got plenty," I said, glad that I had already decided that I didn't need to manage the situation. I was curious to see what Mr. Rice and his two protégées had cooked up for me, and if I was lucky, Sean would get tired of waiting and leave.

I could hope, anyway.

Chapter 20

Mr. Rice disappeared into the light booth, and the houselights dimmed. A spotlight followed a dark-haired girl in a red evening dress as she entered from stage right. Taking the microphone off the stand, she spoke directly to me.

"We're so glad you're here, Ms. Black. I'm Kelly Baskin, and I'm going to be singing 'Over the Rainbow' for you today."

What followed was a sweet rendition that showed off Kelly's lovely soprano voice perfectly. At the end, she bowed, and I tried my best to fill the auditorium with the sound of only my two hands clapping. I wished I had a photographer with me. The little digital camera I carried in my backpack wasn't even worth pulling out. On the other hand, Kelly probably had stills to give me, if not video footage. The girl was already an experienced performer.

"And now I'd like to introduce Chanel Torres," Kelly said. Chanel, who had changed into sleek black capris and a sparkly tank top, took the mike.

"I'm staying with the theme," she said with a brilliant smile, and when the music started, I smiled, too. She'd chosen "Indigo Dreams," a song I'd loved ever since Auntie Melanie took me to see *Captive in Elysium* for my twelfth birthday.

"You promised me the rainbow's end. You took my hand and smiled ... "

I heard a door open behind me, and the light from the hallway washed over the stage. As the door closed, I watched Chanel struggle to keep singing.

"I don't need broken promises. Keep your pot of gold ... "

Her voice cracked as she sang the words, and an anguished look seized control of her eyes.

I couldn't resist. I turned around. Five or so rows behind me, Sean had taken a seat. When my eyes met his, he smiled. To any onlooker, it would have seemed like a friendly gesture, but the same uneasy feeling I'd had in his mother's office crawled over me.

"Now I dream in indigo, indigo blue ... " Chanel sang.

I turned back. She'd regained her composure, and her voice was strong again. I kept my eyes on her as she continued singing. A few lines later, I heard the door open, and the hallway light once again bathed the stage.

Gone for good, I hoped, when the door clicked shut.

I applauded as loudly as I could when Chanel finished. Kelly joined her, and both bowed.

"That was wonderful!" I called as I stood up and moved to the edge of the stage. "And those are two of my favorite songs. You really know how to wow your audience." Both girls were still beaming as Mr. Rice joined us.

"Sorry about the interruption," he said. "I could have manned the door, but there are so few people on campus, I didn't think I needed to."

"It's okay," Chanel said, but a troubled look clouded her face again.

"You did really well," I said. "If it had been me, something like that would have totally thrown me."

"I should have done better," Chanel said, shaking her mass of brown curls. "We're supposed to be ready for everything."

"I'll leave you three here to chat," Mr. Rice said after he'd led us to the auditorium's greenroom. "If you need me, I'll be in my office."

As the door swung closed behind him, we all took seats around a table in the center of the room.

"Mr. Rice seems like a really great teacher," I said, pulling my notebook and pen from my backpack.

"Oh, he is," both girls answered in unison.

"We're really lucky," Kelly added.

The girls fell silent. They smiled at me expectantly, and I flipped my notebook open. I looked at the questions I had jotted down. How long have you been singing? What are your career goals? What are your plans for next year?

I looked at Chanel. What I really wanted to ask was what she and Sean had been talking about in Marilyn's office. Why had he interrupted her performance? Maybe someday I could find out, but right now, I knew questions like that would probably make both girls clam up completely.

"I'm sorry your senior year is getting off to such a rough start," I said. "Ms. Weaver's death was such a shock."

Even though it was an unpleasant topic, it turned out to be a good one to begin with. By the time we were heading toward Mr. Rice's office an hour later, both girls had relaxed enough to tell me about their dreams of becoming recording sensations, and they'd even begun telling me which teachers and boys they liked. Neither one mentioned Sean, though, and as tempted as I was to bring him up, I didn't. Wait till next time, I told myself. Right now, it's more important to get them to trust me.

Back in Mr. Rice's office after the girls had left, I thanked him for calling me and reminding me about the appointment.

"I told them I'd be back during the school year," I said. Mr. Rice handed me a calendar of the school year and a list of all twenty-six members of the graduating class and their creative accomplishments.

"Of course, the school will have a memorial for Ms. Weaver," he said, "but the details haven't been worked out yet. I can let you know."

"Oh, please do," I said. "I'd like to come."

My eyes caught Mr. Rice's as I said that, and I saw the sorrow there.

"It will be the show of my life," he said quietly. "She deserves nothing less. Marilyn—Ms. Weaver—brought my own dreams back to life, and she inspired all these kids to dream. It's what she did—what she was. It's almost like she couldn't help it. Just her presence—"

He broke off, and my mind jumped back to the conversation I'd had with Marilyn at the Boneyard.

"I only knew her for a few hours," I said, "and even in that short time, she inspired me to reach higher than I thought I could."

"You're very fortunate to have met her, Ms. Black," Mr. Rice said. "And it makes it all the more important that you be the one to write about her—about us—about the school. The media will pounce, but all those other reporters will only know Marilyn—" He didn't correct himself to say "Ms. Weaver" this time, I noticed. "Those other reporters will only know Marilyn from hearsay."

I assured him I'd attend the memorial, and I also promised to attend the school's opening assembly on September 2.

"I'll have a photographer with me then," I said, hoping David would have time to play the role. Or maybe I could get Sierra to do it in exchange for some extra babysitting. She'd just invested in a fancy new camera, and she has a good eye. Whatever else happened, I was going to make sure Marilyn's legacy was captured to the best of my ability while her influence was still so palpable.

After saying good-bye to Mr. Rice, I headed back to the registrar's desk in the front lobby of Beeman Hall. Ms. Carpenter stole a glance in the direction of Marilyn's office before speaking.

"Here's the information about the school you asked for, Ms. Black," she said. With both hands, she held out a fat manila folder held shut with a rubber band. "If you have any other questions—" She nodded toward the front of the folder, where a telephone number had been written in pencil in the top corner. "Don't hesitate to call."

"Thanks so much," I said. I fished a business card and a pen out of my backpack, and added my cell number to the information already printed on it. I handed it to her, we nodded at each other, and I made it all the way out to my car without seeing another person.

It wasn't until I had climbed into the driver's seat that I allowed myself to entertain the delightful possibility that I wouldn't have to deal with Sean again. But as I slid my key into the ignition, a face appeared at my window.

Fortunately, it was Kelly. I lowered the window.

"I need to talk to you," she said, glancing over her shoulder. "Okay?"

"Sure," I said. "Why don't you get in? I'll turn the air conditioning on, and it'll be cool in a second."

Walking around to the passenger door, Kelly climbed in beside me.

"I hope this is okay," she said nervously. "I'm—I'm—"

"What's wrong?" I said. "Are you all right?"

"Oh, *I'm* fine," Kelly said. "It's not about me. It's about—" she hesitated. "It's about Chanel."

Surprised as I had been by Kelly's sudden appearance, I was not astonished at all to hear her mention Chanel. I waited while she chewed the end of her thumbnail off.

"She needs help," the girl said at last. "I don't know what to do, and I thought maybe you might—"

"Does it have something to do with Mr. DuBois?" I asked. Kelly jerked her head up and gaped at me.

"How did you know?"

"Let's just say I had a feeling," I said.

"Sean's been hitting on girls ever since he got here," Kelly said. I knew the minute she said "Sean" and not "Mr. DuBois" that whatever she said next would not make him look good. "At first, it seemed kind of—well, kind of exciting, you know?" She looked at me, and I nodded. "A bunch of us went out with him."

"Chanel?" I asked, already knowing what the answer would be.

"Yeah, but—" Kelly paused. "With her it's different." She bit her thumbnail again. "The rest of us were—I don't know—just having fun. I mean, like, nobody took him seriously. We just went out with him and then gossiped about it afterward. It was like a big joke. But Chanel—she's really innocent, you know?" Kelly paused again and looked down at her hands. "She was a virgin."

Damn! All the while he had been hitting on me, Sean DuBois had been seducing high school girls.

"Chanel's Catholic—her mom's from El Salvador," Kelly went on. "This other girl helped her get birth control pills, and—I don't think Chanel really wanted to do it, but she was in love. And she thinks—thought—Sean was going to marry her."

"What about her singing career?" I asked. What Kelly was telling me didn't seem to fit with what Chanel had shared about her dreams during our interview.

"Sean told her he'd make her a star," Kelly said. "Said he has connections on Broadway. We all told her it's a load of crap, but Chanel believed it." She shook her head. "And now—oh, my God." She balled both of her hands into fists and pressed them tightly under her jawbone.

"Something's happened?"

"Well, when Ms. Weaver was around, somehow it seemed like, well, kind of a game. I mean—oh, I don't know—we sort of used her as an excuse. It was like—we *had* to go along with Sean or he'd tell his mother, and then we'd be in trouble. I know it was backwards, but I think we all figured we'd tell her if things really got bad." Kelly paused and shook her head. "And now they are. Oh, my God. I can't believe she's actually dead. I was just talking to her *last week*."

"Me, too," I said.

Kelly shot me a doubtful look. "Chanel made me promise not to tell anyone, but—"

"Whatever it is, I'll do everything I can to help," I said.

Kelly exhaled, took a deep breath, and looked me square in the face. "I hope you will," she said. "Chanel thinks she might be pregnant."

We both just sat there for a moment, the news hanging in the air between us.

"I'm glad you told me," I said at last. "You did the right thing."

"I don't know," Kelly said. "If Chanel knew about it, she'd kill me."

"You're just being a good friend, Kelly," I said. "People don't always recognize that they need help."

"There's more," Kelly said. "She told Sean about it today, and he said that if she really is pregnant, she has to have an abortion. It's horrible for Chanel, because like I said, she's Catholic. But just before you got here today, he told her that if she won't get rid of the baby—or if she tells anybody about their relationship—he'll cancel her scholarship, wreck her chances for college, and maybe even get her mother deported. God, if it had been me, I never would have been able to sing."

As Kelly gnawed off another chunk of fingernail, my mind wrestled with everything she had just told me. I'd already come to the conclusion that Sean was a serious creep, but a sexual predator? That landed him in a whole new hideous category.

I thought back to the scene I'd interrupted in Marilyn's office. Sean had been destroying her files. Had Marilyn known about Chanel? Maybe that was what Ms. Carpenter's fat folder would reveal. Although I couldn't believe she'd keep quiet if she knew Sean was taking advantage of—

"I gotta go," Kelly said.

"Look, give me your phone number," I said. I grabbed my backpack from behind my seat and dug out a notebook and a pen. "I'll call you later." I paused, choosing my words carefully. "In the meantime, I think it would be best—"

"I know, I know. Act like nothing happened. That'll be easy. I've been doing that ever since Sean got here."

That bastard.

As I watched Kelly walk back toward Beeman Hall, David suddenly popped into my head. "Ease the cork out," he'd said. I just wish he'd given me some pointers about what to do when you succeed.

And then another thought hit me. In addition to everything else, I was now mixed up in *two* inconvenient pregnancies.

Chapter 21

Trying hard to shift my brain into neutral as quickly as I threw the Max into reverse, I backed out of my parking place and drove toward the main gate. As soon as I got off campus, I'd call Detective Booth. Sean was a sexual predator. He had to be stopped.

And—what if Marilyn had found out about his bad behavior? A guy like Sean wouldn't need a better motive to kill someone.

I thought back to how Sean had tried to get me to leave the crime scene before he called the police. That was strange, but was it incriminating? There was no way he could have murdered his mother. I'd been with him when—

My mind jumped back to our rendezvous at the V. I'd managed to park at the farthest possible point from where I wanted to go, get lost on the way, chat with the bartender, buy a wine card, and drink an ounce of gewürztraminer before Sean showed up. Had that given him enough time to drive to San Ramon, kill his mother, wash up, and get to the Tempo bar in time to stop me from buying an ounce of sauvignon blanc? It didn't seem likely, but I sure as hell couldn't rule it out.

And if I couldn't rule it out—*oh, my God.* Neither could Booth. He probably thought I had been covering for Sean all this time. I really couldn't blame him. Sean had set things up perfectly.

That goddamn bastard. The sooner Booth led him away in handcuffs, the better.

As I rounded the traffic island, the security kiosk came into view. In the exit lane next to it was a dark blue BMW.

Damn.

It was Sean's car, and as I pulled nearer, I realized it wasn't moving. To make matters worse, the gate in the entrance lane on the other side of the kiosk—which had been open when I arrived—was now closed. Unless I was willing to ram it, Sean had effectively trapped me.

Before I could decide what to do, the BMW's door opened, and Sean emerged. A moment later, he was at my window. Reluctantly, I lowered it.

"Talk about lucky!" Sean said, pulling off his sunglasses. "I just stopped here to call you and let you know I was leaving, and then— here you are."

Right. As though I couldn't recognize "lying in wait" when I saw it. But even so, I knew I'd better practice what I'd preached to Kelly— act as though nothing had happened.

"Yeah, that *is* lucky," I said, forcing a smile. "But listen. Can I have a rain check? Like I said before, I've got—"

"So what did the budding prima donnas tell you?" Sean asked. "You're going to have a hard time separating fact from fiction with those two."

God, I wished I were a better liar! I felt my cheeks warm up, and my ears were blazing. I could only hope Sean couldn't see.

"Oh, we just chatted a bit about their hopes and dreams," I said. "And I'm a thorough fact-checker, so if they told me anything that isn't accurate, I'll definitely find out—"

"What were you talking to Kelly about in your car?"

Damn. He'd seen us.

Sean wasn't smiling anymore. I felt sweat form on my palms and hoped nothing visible was popping out on my forehead.

"Just more of the same," I said, struggling to make up vague but plausible details. "Kelly's a real go-getter. I think she sees me as some-one who can help her get auditions or something." My eyes locked with Sean's.

Who did I think I was fooling?

"Look, I really have to get going," I said. "I have an appointment." I stared straight ahead, gripped my steering wheel, and willed him to move, but he just stood there peering in through the window. I couldn't banish the feeling that he was about to reach in and grab me.

"I'm already late," I said.

He still didn't move.

"Call me later, okay?" It was the last thing I wanted to say, but amazingly, it worked.

"Yeah, yeah, okay," Sean said. "I'll catch you tonight."

I watched him warily as he walked back to his car, got inside, and pulled forward far enough to let me by. Relieved to have him in my rearview mirror at last, I waved as I turned onto Academy Lane. His reflection waved back.

As soon as I escaped onto Bruner Street, I hightailed it up to St. Rose Parkway and then headed north on Las Vegas Boulevard. I didn't stop until I saw a shopping center with a big Food 4 Less. Pulling into a parking space between a delivery van and a pickup truck, I hoped that if Sean happened to drive by, he wouldn't notice the Max. Digging into my backpack, I found my cell phone, scrolled down through the saved numbers, took a deep breath, and called Detective Booth.

After three rings, I heard a click.

"You've reached Detective Michael Booth, Las Vegas Metro Homicide. I'm unavailable at the moment, but please leave your name and number, and I'll call you back. If this is an emergency, hang up and dial 911."

Damn. The last thing I expected was to get Booth's voice mail. I'd been so busy trying to avoid him, I never imagined he wouldn't be instantly available when I changed my mind.

I left my name and number after the beep, adding, "Please call me as soon as you can." I sat there for a moment after I hung up. Nobody was bleeding, but reporting a sexual predator might easily be considered an emergency.

I looked at the fat file Ms. Carpenter had given me. Maybe it contained evidence that would incriminate Sean of—what? I didn't know, but whatever it was, it would strengthen what I had to say about our rendezvous at the V. But I couldn't explain all that to some anonymous 911 operator.

Please, Detective Booth. Call me back.

Opening my door, I climbed out and scanned the parking lot. It was fairly crowded, but I didn't see a single dark blue BMW.

I'll run into the market, I told myself, grab some things for dinner, and head home. If Booth hasn't called me by then—well, I'd just have to come up with another plan.

The produce department was near the door, and all the shiny piles of fruit instantly made me remember Oscar. The poor old tortoise still hadn't eaten anything, and he was expending far too much energy trying to escape. In addition to a submarine sandwich for myself, I decided on a container of tropical fruit salad for my reptilian friend. Watercress and chard hadn't worked, but maybe I could win him over with papaya, kiwi, and mango. I grabbed a banana, too.

The sun was dropping behind the palm trees when I pulled into the driveway at the Nash house. Stopping under the grape arbor, I got out, unlocked the back door, and carried my bag of food into the kitchen. Deciding I better feed Oscar before it got dark, I fished out the fruit salad I'd splurged on and headed for his enclosure.

As I walked past the basement door, I noticed it was standing ajar, the padlock dangling from the hasp on the open latch. Colby was here. I wouldn't bother him, but I was glad I wasn't alone.

When I reached Oscar's enclosure, however, Colby's FJ Cruiser was not occupying its spot in the back alley. Was he running an errand? I wondered. Or maybe he'd just forgotten to lock the door when he left.

Oscar was scratching away next to the back wall of his enclosure, but he still hadn't made a measurable dent in the rocky soil.

"Hey, old man," I said, stepping over the burrow's fence and moving close to him. "I brought you a treat."

Oscar ignored me. I moved closer and squatted down next to him. He still seemed oblivious to my presence, so I pried the lid off the plastic container. I fished out a chunk of mango and set it on the ground near his face.

At last I'd made an impression. Oscar twisted his head and looked at the fruit with one eye, blinking slowly. Then he opened his mouth, stretched his neck out, and bit into it.

As he chewed, I realized I had never seen a tortoise's tongue before. In fact, I had never even thought about a tortoise's tongue before. And if I had, I certainly never would have imagined a big soft pink one. But there it was, a decidedly humanoid appendage moving in and out of a scaly reptilian maw. I watched as Oscar slowly finished off the mango and started in on some papaya.

"See, it's not so bad here, after all," I said. "You've been hurting my feelings with all your escape attempts."

Watching Oscar eat was amazingly calming, and I sat there in a state of mesmerized meditation as he lazily munched his way through three chunks of pineapple, several slices of kiwi, and another round of mango and papaya. Only when the carton was empty did I stand up to leave.

"Good night, old man," I said as I stepped back out of his enclosure. "I promise I'll be back in the morning with something just as good."

I half expected the tortoise to head immediately back to the wall he'd been so determined to dig under, but he didn't move. He just watched me, neck stretched out, as I walked back toward the house. If I were a little more prone to anthropomorphism, I might have believed he was actually sorry to see me go.

As I passed the ground-level window to Colby's lair, I noticed in the gathering darkness that the lights were on. Was he down there?

"Colby!" I called.

No answer. I pulled the door further open.

"Are you there?"

Silence. He must have forgotten to lock up again.

Deciding I might as well turn off the lights and lock the door so I wouldn't have to come outside again later, I climbed down the stairs.

I braced myself for artificial body parts, but I needn't have. Instead of a fake arm, I found a replica of Stonehenge in the middle of the room. Whatever else you might say about Colby, his work was definitely eclectic. Sidestepping the Styrofoam monoliths, I made my way back to his editing suite and turned off the overhead light. As I walked back into the main room, I heard a car pull up in the driveway. A moment later, footsteps crunched on the gravel.

"Colby?" I called. "Is that you? I just came down here to—"

But as I stepped on the first stair and looked up, I saw immediately that the legs looming above me in the doorway did not belong to my movie-making housemate. Colby always wore cargo shorts and Birkenstocks. These legs were wearing gray slacks and loafers.

Oh, my God. My heart missed a beat as I realized it was Sean.

"Hello, Copper."

I couldn't speak. My mind was too busy racing. What was he doing here? How could I make him leave?

"Glad I caught you," Sean said.

Caught me? Trapped was more like it.

"We've got to talk."

As threatened as I felt, I almost laughed when I heard that.

We've got to talk. That's what David said just before he dropped his baby news on me.

Damn. This wasn't funny. Sean had baby news of his own.

"You should have called first."

"What did Kelly tell you?" Sean said. His voice was rock hard.

"Please move," I said, hoping my own voice sounded firm.

Sean didn't budge.

"Copper, you've got to help me out here. Those girls have already done me a lot of damage, and it's really not what I need right now."

My mind raced back over the afternoon's events. Was it possible that Kelly had made up her story about Sean? I had only her word for it, after all. No other evidence, except—no, that wasn't right. I had definitely interrupted a serious exchange between Sean and Chanel. And there was no denying her distress when he interrupted her performance. Okay, maybe I didn't have proof that would stand up in court, but Kelly's explanation of events was pretty damned compelling.

"Please move," I said again. "This is no way to hold a conversation."

"I asked you a question. I want an answer."

My heart rate sped up, but I struggled to sound unconcerned.

"I'm coming up, Sean. We can go inside and—"

"What did Kelly tell you?"

"Come on, Sean. This is ridiculous. Let me—"

"Let you what? Tell the cops on me?"

Oh, God. I suddenly remembered that I had left my backpack in the Max. My cell phone was in it.

"Is that what you've done?" Sean demanded. "Did you actually believe them?"

Yes, I do believe them, I wanted to scream. *You pervert! How could you?*

But there he was, looming over me, blocking my only escape route. He'd never seemed like the physically violent type, but I'd never seen him so angry. And there was the undeniable possibility that he was the monster who'd strangled his mother.

Think, Copper! Tell him whatever you need to, so long as it gets you out of here.

"I haven't told anybody anything, Sean." I said. "I'm a journalist, remember? I get my information verified."

"You're no journalist. You're just a fucking wannabe."

Damn! He'd never spoken to me like that before. I was only making him madder! I racked my brain for something else to say—something convincing, something calming.

"I'm telling you the truth, Sean," I said. "Come on! Don't you think I know better than to believe everything a high school girl tells me? I used to be one myself!"

My attempt at humor elicited no response from above, and Sean's legs didn't move. I had no idea what he planned to do next, but my attempts at breaking the impasse were obviously failing miserably.

"Look, Sean," I said, struggling to keep my voice even. "Think about it. If I'd called the cops, you'd know about it by now."

Sean didn't respond, but I could almost hear the wheels turning inside his head. As I waited, the wheels began turning inside my head, too. Telling Sean that I hadn't called the police might have been a big mistake.

"Sean," I said. "We're getting very worked up about something that's really not that big a deal. Do you think I even care if you're dating Chanel? That's between you and her!"

Still no response. My heart was racing again. I was talking too much, but I didn't seem to be able to stop myself.

"You've got to believe me! I'm telling the truth!"

Silence.

"Oh, I believe you," Sean said at last. "At least about the cops."

God damn it! Why had I told him that? Now I was scared *and* angry.

"Let me out," I shouted. *"Now!"*

Moving up one step, I leaned forward and looked up. I caught sight of Sean's contorted face one second before his shoe connected with my face.

The next thing I knew, I was lying flat on my back amid the wreckage of the Styrofoam Stonehenge, my whole body throbbing. Had Sean really kicked me? I staggered to my feet and lurched up the steps to the door. I turned the handle, but when I pushed the door outward—

Locked!

Panic rushing over me, I pounded on the door.

"Sean! Let me out!"

Silence. Oh, my God! How long had I been unconscious? Then I heard the back door of the house slam.

"Let me out!" I screamed as loud as I could.

"I'm sorry, Copper."

Sean was right outside the door.

"Open the door this second!"

"Can't do that," Sean said. "Can't let you—" he interrupted himself with a chuckle. "This is pretty ironic, if you think about it."

"What are you talking about?"

"I'm not the first person in my family to lock somebody up in a confined space. Guess I take after my mother more than I knew."

"What are you talking about? Unlock the goddamn door!"

No response.

"I'm calling the police!"

"The fire department might be a better choice."

Chapter 22

The fire department? Oh, my God! That could only mean—

Lurching back through the Stonehenge rubble, I scanned the room for a telephone. No luck. Making my way toward the editing suite, I flipped the light back on. I looked up to the ground-level window above Colby's computer. Could I squeeze through it? It'd be a tight fit, but—

I heard a car start and drive away. Was this really happening? Had Sean really locked me in the basement and torched the house?

But I couldn't waste any time wondering. I kept searching, even though I knew my chances of finding a hard-wired telephone in Colby's high-tech rat's nest were slim.

Wait! The computers!

I careened back to Colby's desk, where a thousand electronic ants were marching across one of the monitors in elaborate patterns.

Hooray! It was turned on! Grabbing the mouse, I succeeded in waking the machine up, but—

Enter your password.

Damn!

Okay, okay, I told myself. One quick look for a phone, and then—

I heard a noise from above, something popping. Then a muffled crash. The sounds of a fire? I had no way of knowing for sure, but one more minute of searching, and then I'd have to find a way out.

Dashing back into the main room, I scanned the shelves. Books, knickknacks, props—and then I saw it!

An old black rotary-dial telephone.

I held my breath as I picked up the receiver. It was probably a prop, but—

Never have I heard a more welcome sound than that dial tone!

I dialed 911, hoping that the series of little clicks that ensued would actually connect me with a human being.

"911. What is the nature of your emergency?"

Relief surged over me like a tidal wave.

"It's a fire," I said, hoping against hope I was wrong. Maybe Sean had just been trying to scare me.

After I had given the operator my name and whereabouts, she told me to stay on the line. But how could I just sit there when an inferno might be exploding above me?

I set the receiver down and headed back to the window over Colby's computer. I had no choice but to try to squeeze through.

I climbed up onto his desk, and—*oh, no! It couldn't be!*

The window wasn't merely latched. It was nailed shut. Looking around for something capable of smashing glass, my eyes fell on the gun rack on the far wall. Jumping off the desk, I rushed toward it. As I grabbed a rifle from the bottom rung, my eyes took in the lettering on the top of a big cardboard box underneath it.

"DANG ..."

I pulled a frayed blanket off to reveal the rest.

"DANGER! EXPLOSIVES!"

I peeked under a flap. The box was full of plastic jars. I pulled one out. *Gunpowder!*

Then I noticed that the box was only one of five equally large, identical containers.

Jesus Christ! I was trapped in a basement full of explosives underneath a burning house.

Scrambling back up onto Colby's desk, I smacked the rifle's butt tentatively against the glass.

Not even a crack.

I tried again, harder. The window was tougher than I expected.

The third time, I threw everything I had into my swing.

Whack!

Thank God! A satisfying cascade of broken glass. Sharp shards still jutted out from the window frame, but a few more smacks with the rifle broke off the biggest ones. With luck, I just might be able to slip through without severing any major arteries.

I was still gauging my chances when the smell of smoke met my nostrils.

Oh, my God! He really had done it!

I had to get out. Who knew how long it might take the firefighters to arrive? The smoke smell was getting stronger by the second.

Bending down, I grabbed a beach towel draped over Colby's desk chair. It might not be enough to protect me completely from the broken glass, but it would help. I spread it over the bottom half of the window. Then I boosted myself up, and—

This will never work. The window might have been big enough if I'd been able to open it, but the frame made it way too small.

All the same, I managed to get my arms and head through the opening. Even in the deepening darkness, I could see smoke, and the smell was overpowering. I inched forward, clenching my teeth as gravel scraped my arms and broken glass cut through my shirt. Would my hips fit through? If only I didn't like Sierra's cooking quite so much.

I'd made a few more inches of progress when I heard the first siren. Soon it was joined by a second. It was reassuring to hear them grow louder and louder until—*thank God!*—I heard the sound of men's voices.

A power I never knew I possessed took charge. I screamed so loud I couldn't believe my lungs were generating the noise, and I didn't stop until two firefighters had found me.

"It's okay, it's okay," one of them said. He knelt down by my face. "We'll get you out of here."

"It's going to blow up," I said, but neither one seemed to notice. I tried again. "It's going to blow up—*ow!*"

The two firemen were pulling me through the window, whether I fit or not. Fortunately, they were stuffing something soft between me and the broken glass, and when they finally yanked me free, I didn't seem to be bleeding too badly.

A minute later, I was lying on a stretcher.

"The house is going to explode," I tried again.

"Everything's okay, sweetie," a fireman said. "We've got it under control."

Just then, a giant plume of black smoke erupted from the roof of the house. Flames leaped at least seventy-five feet in the air, lighting up the sky in every direction. I heard shouts.

I sat up.

"Hey!" I yelled as loudly as I could. "Listen up! The house is going to blow! The basement is full of gunpowder, ammunition, and dynamite!"

Okay, I exaggerated, but at last I had their attention. A different, high-pitched siren began shrieking, and I heard men yelling at the top of their lungs.

"Evacuate!"

"Clear the area!"

"Go! Go! Go!"

Suddenly, I was lying down again, bouncing along under the power of four guys in yellow fire jackets. A moment later, I was inside an ambulance. Siren blaring, it began rolling. I was about to ask where we were headed when—

Kaboom!

Chapter 23

"Holy crap!"

"Jesus!"

"*Shee–it!*"

The simultaneous exclamations of the three other people inside the ambulance drowned out my own feeble "Oh, my God."

"What the fuck was in that house?" I heard the driver ask, but I decided to let him wonder. There had been a lot of things inside that house that nobody would ever know about now. The blast had surely pulverized any lingering body parts, not to mention—

"Oh, my God!"

"It's okay, honey." The paramedic sitting next to me patted my arm. "Everything's okay."

"Not Oscar," I said. "I've got to go back—"

"Someone was in the house?" Now I had her attention.

"No. Out back," I said.

"The fire crew's still there," she said. "They'll check the whole area. Is Oscar your husband?"

That almost made me smile.

"Oscar's a desert tortoise," I said. "Fifty years old. I was taking care of him for a friend."

"If he's there, they'll find him," the paramedic said. But I could tell she thought Oscar was a goner. For that matter, so did I. How could any creature survive a blast that sounded like a nuclear attack?

And what about the plants? Not only had I brought on the destruction of an arguably historic property, I'd wiped out a whole greenhouse full of rare flora.

"What's your name, honey?" the paramedic said.

"Copper," I replied automatically. "Copper Black."

"Address?" the paramedic was asking, and while the autopilot part of my brain was reciting the number and street of my brother's house, I suddenly thought of—

Sean! He'd tried to kill me! He had to be caught! I sat bolt upright.

Or I would have if there hadn't been nylon straps tying me to the gurney and some kind of vise gripping my head. I was flat on my back, whether I liked it or not.

"It's okay, honey," the paramedic said.

"No!" I said, still struggling. "I've got to call the police! The fire's connected to a murder!"

"The police have already rolled to the site," she said. "Standard procedure. The arson unit'll be there, too."

"But I know who did this!" I said. "Sean DuBois! He was trying to kill me!"

The other two guys stopped chattering for a second, and I thought they might actually do something. I was wrong.

"We'll get you to the hospital—get you checked out," my attendant said. The driver started talking into his radio.

"But he should be arrested—"

"We'll take care of everything at the hospital, honey," the paramedic said. "You just stay calm—"

I couldn't believe it! I could identify the guy who had just locked me in a basement and torched the house—a guy who had probably also murdered his mother—and a by-the-book paramedic wasn't going to do anything except call me honey.

"Come on!" I protested. "I've got to speak with Detective Michael Booth—*please!*"

Just then, the ambulance made a quick right turn. We screeched to a halt, the back doors flew open, and I found myself sliding outside, bouncing as the paramedics lowered the gurney. A few seconds later, I was blinking under the bright lights of an emergency room, a bevy of scrubs-clad medicos hovering over me.

"I'm fine," I said. "I just need to talk to the police—"

But nobody seemed to listen. Someone shined a light into my eyes, somebody else took my pulse, and I could feel pokes and prods up and down my legs and arms. Was that a needle poking into the back of my hand? An ice pack behind my neck? My whole head throbbed.

Five minutes or three hours later—really, I have no idea—I was alone again, tucked into a hospital bed inside a pseudo-private space defined by a curtain hanging from the ceiling on a track.

"Relax," a nurse had told me. "I'll be back to check on you in a minute."

As if I could relax when Sean DuBois was still loose! Tentatively, I lifted my head. Not too painful, although it felt like it had gained thirty pounds. I couldn't see a telephone, though.

Damn! Somehow, I had to find a way to—

The curtain zipped on its track. I turned back to find a policeman standing next to my bed.

"Hello, Ms. Black," he said. "I'm Sergeant Cavalleri, Las Vegas Metro Police. If you're feeling up to it, I'd like to ask you a few questions."

"I'm fine," I said, noting the doubtful look on the cop's face. "And I'm glad you're here. Although, actually, I really need to talk to—"

Just then, another face appeared around the edge of the curtain.

"Detective Booth!"

"You're full of surprises, Ms. Black," Booth said, joining the sergeant at my bedside. "How are you feeling?"

"I'm fine," I said again. Booth looked just as doubtful as the other guy.

"Sounds like you're one lucky lady," he said, "although it's going to take some serious makeup to hide those shiners."

Shiners?

My look must have spoken volumes. Without a word, Booth pushed the rolling bed table toward me. My face peered back at me as I looked into the mirror.

Oh, my God! I could star in a zombie flick, no makeup necessary.

Slumping back onto my pillow, I stared at Detective Booth.

"Sean did it," I said. "He kicked me down the basement stairs, locked me in, set the place on fire, and took off."

"We've picked him up," Booth said.

"You have? *Really?*"

Booth nodded.

The guy was off the streets. Thank God.

"But how did you know—?"

"Just tell me everything that happened," he said. "From the beginning."

My mind jumped to the folder Ms. Carpenter had given me. It was gone, along with—holy crap! Everything else I owned! Except for the few belongings still in the apartment at my brother's house, I didn't have anything left. Even the Max must be toast. That meant a whole lot of other stuff was gone—my driver's license, my laptop, my cell phone, my credit cards, at least two twenty-dollar bills, and—

The stuff I'd unintentionally swiped from Marilyn's bathroom. Oh, well. It hadn't mattered, anyway. I knew enough to make sure Sean got locked up for a long, long time, and Ms. Carpenter could help.

I looked at the two policemen and rubbed my shoulder. My back was beginning to ache, too. They both flipped notebooks open.

"It all started at the Anna Roberts Parks Academy," I said.

Over the next half hour, I did my best to paint an accurate picture of the events that had brought me to the emergency room at Desert Springs Hospital. While I talked and the cops took notes, a steady stream of medical professionals came and went.

By the time I finished my tale, a doctor had decided that my body and brain were basically intact. My worst injury was a broken nose, but even that had required no more repair than a splint and some adhesive tape. My face was going to terrify small children and ward off romantic advances for a month, but I figured I could reduce the impact with oversized sunglasses and industrial-strength makeup.

Sergeant Cavalleri had departed, and I'd just finished signing several dozen forms presented by a bean counter from the hospital's business office when my brother arrived. He was wearing his clerical collar, his usual outfit when visiting a hospital. It gave him near-super powers to go through whatever doors he wanted.

"Holy cow, baby sister!" Michael said when he got a look at my face. "You look worse than I did that time I wrestled the lawn mower."

"Thanks," I said. "You're doing wonders for my self-confidence." Michael had given up his one and only attempt at entrepreneurship back in high school when his first gardening job resulted in a concussion, a broken arm, and a ticket for operating a substandard vehicle on a public roadway.

"Detective Mike Booth," Booth said, extending his right hand. "Metro Homicide."

"Michael Black," my brother said. "Man of God."

Mike and Mike, I thought. Good thing the only attribute they shared was a name. I'd rather be related to a klutz than a bloodhound. On the other hand, the bloodhound had arrested Sean DuBois.

"Jackie's on her way," my brother said.

"*Mom?*" I said. Michael called our parents by their first names, and I was still having trouble getting used to it. "What for?"

"Sierra called her as soon as we heard what happened to you," Michael said. "She and Patrick are both getting into McCarran tomorrow around two. Almost the same time as Ted and Graham."

Mom and Patrick and Dad and Graham. It sounded like a premise for a really bad movie.

"Jackie said she was kicking herself for not coming out here after you found Marilyn's body, and '*By golly, nothing's going to keep me from being at my baby's side now.*'"

I had to smile at Michael's perfect imitation of Mom, but then I looked at Booth. Damn him! He was smiling, too. Made me feel like I was six years old.

And my back ached, my face hurt, and all the cuts on my arms and legs were beginning to make themselves known.

"I'm fine," I said anyway. Tentatively, I pulled myself up into a sitting position. My head still felt like a bag of concrete, but at least I wasn't dizzy. Slowly, I moved one leg, then the other. Not too bad. As I sat up on the edge of the bed, it dawned on me that I was clad in nothing more than a hospital gown.

Weird. I'd totally forgotten that someone had removed my clothes. I tugged on the skimpy gown, hoping I was covered in back. *Yikes.* Had Detective Booth seen the tattoo on my—

"Have you got the time?" Michael asked Booth.

He glanced at his watch. "Eleven."

Eleven! I'd been at the hospital for at least three hours.

"I brought you some clothes," Michael said, adding quickly, "Sierra picked them out." He held up a canvas shopping bag. "Once you're dressed, I'll take you home. You're staying with us tonight."

"We'll talk tomorrow," Booth said. "You've got my number. Call me if anything else happens." As he vanished behind the curtain, a nurse appeared with a plastic bag.

"Your belongings," she said, handing it to me. Inside were the clothes and sandals I had been wearing when I arrived. A quick look made me extra grateful Sierra had sent some replacements. The only other thing in the bag was the set of keys that had been in my pants pocket.

Great. Perfectly serviceable keys to a house and minivan that probably no longer existed. At least the keys to my apartment and the vicarage would still come in handy.

Using Michael's cell phone, I called David as soon as we were on the way to the vicarage.

"Copper! I've been trying to call you! Are you okay?"

"I think so," I said, "and I'm definitely in better shape than the Nash house."

"What are you talking about?"

I spent the rest of the trip to the vicarage describing the evening's events and persuading David that there was no reason for him to fly back from Reno immediately.

"Okay, sweetheart, I'll be there in the morning," he agreed at last. "I love you."

An hour later, after a big dish of Sierra's homemade peach ice cream, I was tucked into the fold-out sofa bed in Michael's study at the vicarage. I was perfectly willing to climb up the stairs to my apartment, but Sierra wouldn't hear of it.

"Maybe tomorrow night, Copper," she said, "but tonight I'm your Florence Nightingale, like it or not. I'm used to getting up in the middle of the night, anyway, so if you need anything, just use Nicky's technique and cry."

That's Sierra for you. Down deep she's sweet, but she refuses to sound like it.

"Thanks again for sending the clothes," I said. "The T-shirt and workout pants were a perfect choice."

My own bed would have been more comfortable than the slightly lumpy fold-out, but I had to admit that I liked knowing Michael and Sierra were in the room next door. Even though my injuries were far from life-threatening, they'd been caused when someone tried to kill me. The thought that Sean had actually wanted me dead disturbed me far more than two black eyes and a broken nose. The term "mortal enemy," a phrase I'd tossed around so casually when I was young, now took on new meaning.

When I was young. That was yesterday! Today was the day I woke up young and went to bed old.

I must have drifted off at last, because—

I was Cinderella dancing with my prince, spinning and turning until—

"Halt! Who goes there?"

"The black knight, my lady! None can save you now!"

My prince vanished as the black knight slashed my dress away. I stood naked and alone, and then—the magic mirror!

I'm cut and bruised and—old! I'm hideous! A withered hag—

I woke up. Had I screamed aloud? But the house was quiet.

And so the night crept by, disturbing dreams waking me every time I managed to fall asleep. It helped that I found Sekhmet curled up next to me after one nightmare, and she stayed till morning. I couldn't really claim her as my cat anymore but, like my family, she'd shown up when I needed her.

It also helped to remember that David would be back in the morning. That was a comfort, even if tomorrow also brought both my parents and their boyfriends.

And at least I could take a sick day without feeling guilty.

Chapter 24

Sometime before dawn, I fell sound asleep from sheer exhaustion, and when I awoke, bright shafts of sunlight were streaming through the blinds. The clock on Michael's desk read 8:45. Oh, no! I needed to call my boss and let him know I wouldn't be at work today.

Easing myself vertical, I reached for the phone. As I punched in *The Light*'s number, I scrambled for the right words to explain to Chris why he'd have to do without me today.

Someone nearly killed me yesterday.

No, that sounded melodramatic.

I have two black eyes, a broken nose, and more cuts and scratches than I can count.

"Copper! Are you all right?"

I might have known. Chris already knew about my brush with annihilation.

"Mostly, I think," I said. "I wish I could come to work, but—"

"Just take care of yourself," Chris said. "I don't want to see your face around here until you're fine."

"No one wants to see my face right now," I said. "I'm afraid to look at it myself."

Chris chuckled. "Glad your sense of humor is still intact."

Very slowly, I managed to outfit myself in the T-shirt and workout pants Sierra had loaned me. Stiff in every joint and sore in all the spots in between, I creaked into the bathroom and braced myself on the sink before looking into the mirror.

The face that stared back at me was so alien I almost felt I was looking at a movie poster instead of my reflection. Deep purple bruises ringed both my eyes, darkening to solid black underneath. Mottled splotches of magenta, mustard yellow, and brown covered my cheeks. I'm sure my nose was similarly discolored, but it was still encased in adhesive tape. The only upside to the whole nightmare was that my eyes were only a tiny bit swollen. In fact, I tried to convince myself, if it weren't for my *Dawn of the Dead* color scheme, I'd look almost normal. Maybe Sierra could help me in the makeup department, but in the meantime, everyone was just going to have to get used to the family monster.

Concerned that I might scare Nicky, I grabbed a baseball cap Michael had left on top of his computer monitor and pulled the bill down as far as it would go. But when I walked into the kitchen, Michael was alone at the table.

"Hi, Copper," he said, without looking up from the newspaper. "How are you feeling?"

"I'm feeling pretty good, all things considered," I said. "Thanks for taking care of me."

"Oh, hell," Michael said.

"What?" For my brother, those were serious swearwords.

"This story about Frank," Michael said.

"Frank who?" I asked. The only Frank I ever think of in connection with Las Vegas is Frank Sinatra, but he's not exactly newsworthy these days.

"Frank Bartolo," Michael said.

Jenna's husband. The owner of the Monaco, not to mention a string of pleasure palaces in Mississippi, Florida, and, most recently, Macau.

"What's it say?"

"He's obviously angry about her affair with Curtis Weaver. He's filing for divorce, and he called a press conference to announce it."

"Without even telling Jenna?" I asked.

"Can't tell from the article," Michael said. "But what he did say is that all her bleeding-heart causes are history as far as his money is concerned."

"Oh, my God," I said. "That means—"

"Yeah. It's bad. Jenna guaranteed our construction loan." He sighed. "I really don't know whether we can pull this thing off now without a *deus ex machina*. The Indian situation was difficult enough, and now—oh, hey, I'm sorry. There's coffee and oatmeal and cantaloupe—"

Michael pushed his chair back and stood up. "Sit down. Let me bring you breakfast."

"Where are Sierra and Nicky?" I asked, taking a seat at the table and removing my baseball cap.

"Doctor's appointment," Michael said. "They'll be back in an hour or so. You want milk and brown sugar on your oatmeal?"

"Sure," I said. "Thanks."

"I've got a meeting this morning, and then I'm picking Jackie and Patrick up at the airport at two."

Mom and her beau. How could I forget?

"Fortunately, Ted and Graham are renting a car, so they're on their own."

Dad and his boyfriend. Too bad I had to meet Graham looking like I'd just lost a prizefight.

"Sierra's planning a big dinner for everybody here this evening," Michael went on. "Hope you'll feel up to it."

What choice did I have? I was the reason the impromptu family reunion was taking place. And it was nice to have a replacement for the party I could never host at the Nash house.

"Sure," I said, "but Michael—I—"

"What?" Michael said, setting coffee and oatmeal in front of me. "Are you okay?"

"Yeah," I said. "I'm fine. I just really need to go back to the Nash place."

"Why?"

"The tortoise I was taking care of," I said. "It's a long shot, but if he survived, I've got to rescue him. What if he's alive and injured?"

"Copper—" Michael began, but then he stopped. His face softened as he looked at me. "Okay, Copper. If we go right now. I've got some time before my meeting with Willie Morningthunder at the construction site."

"Smoking a peace pipe?"

"I don't have any beef with Willie," Michael said. "He wants to know the truth about those bones, but a lot of the hangers-on have already made up their minds. What worries him is that the number of militants is growing on a daily basis, and he can't figure out who's whipping them into a frenzy. It's getting scary. Three guys were arrested yesterday after a knife fight."

He shook his head and let out a long sigh. "But look. Let's get going so we'll have plenty of time to look for your tortoise."

He's a good guy, my brother, and I'm not saying it because he passes out bread and wine. Anyone who'd carve time out of an impossibly busy day to take his sister on a turtle hunt is a true saint in my book.

I hobbled up to my apartment, where I managed to wriggle into some jeans and a long-sleeved T-shirt. Oversized sunglasses and a floppy hat covered most of my bruised face. I was overdressed for a hot day, but at least I was less likely to frighten anybody.

Vista Miranda Street looked completely normal as we turned onto it from Pecos Road. The large houses stood serenely on their huge lots, none of them looking like anything out of the ordinary had happened the evening before. Even the Nash property looked normal from a block away, except for the row of cars and trucks lining the street in front of it. But as we passed the driveway looking for a place to park, I caught my first glimpse behind the surprisingly undamaged oleander hedge.

Michael and I both sucked in breaths as the wreckage came into view behind festoons of yellow caution tape.

"Holy guacamole, Copper!" my brother said. "You really are lucky to be alive!"

In spite of the heat, an icy shiver rippled down my spine.

What if—?

"Thank God for old telephones," I said. "And firemen, and a window that wasn't half an inch narrower—" I shuddered again as Michael parked behind a van with official license plates.

Michael thoughtfully slowed his pace as we walked back to the driveway. *I shouldn't be out here,* I couldn't help thinking as I limped along. But that thought only made me more determined. If the fire and explosion hadn't killed Oscar, he'd die anyway if I didn't rescue him.

Yellow tape stretched across the end of the driveway, making it clear we weren't supposed to go any farther.

"I don't care," I said. "I've got to find Oscar. Come on."

Michael didn't object, and I was glad he was wearing his collar. Considering the miracles it could work in hospitals, it might be an asset at a crime scene, too. Ducking the tape, Michael and I headed toward the heap of debris that used to be a two-story house.

As we drew nearer, I tried to make sense of the jumbled wreckage in front of me. Half-charred beams stuck up at odd angles, leaning on each other and against broken walls. The birdbath stood untouched above a pile of broken glass and tile, and everything was still wet.

Judging from the curls of steam, much of it was still hot, too. The smell that rolled off the mess would have reminded me of a barbecue if it weren't for the strong chemical odor mixed in with it.

"Don't breathe deep," I said to Michael. "No need to get vaporized attic insulation in your lungs, and God knows what else—hey! There's the refrigerator!" I pointed to the Aztec gold monster lying on its side. "And there's the comforter from the bed upstairs! It's wet, but it's not burned!"

By now, we had reached a damp jumble of blown-up house parts that blocked the driveway. Beyond it, an even bigger pile of blackened lumber looked almost like a structure, a weird lean-to held up by the remains of the wall with the fish-eye windows.

"That's about where I parked the Max," I said. "Where the back door used to be—"

"Mother of *pearl!*" Michael said. He'd moved a few steps ahead of me and was peering between the beams forming the lean-to. "You aren't going to believe this!"

Picking my way over chunks of cinder block and—whoa!—half a toilet, an oven door, and the kitchen sink—I joined Michael and squinted into the dark space.

As my eyes adjusted to the light, I realized my brother was right. I couldn't believe what stood before me.

The Max! In one piece! I couldn't tell whether it was drivable, but considering the condition of its surroundings, it looked pretty damned unscathed.

This was as good an opportunity as any to thank God, but the grape arbor was the real hero. The old wood framework, coupled with for-tuitous flotsam landings had—amazingly—created a weirdly effective bomb shelter for my minivan. I peered through the passenger-side window.

Hooray! I could just see my cell phone lying on the seat, and it looked perfectly fine. That meant my laptop was probably okay, too, and I wouldn't have to replace my credit cards or my driver's license—

"You're going to have to leave the area."

I turned to find myself face to face with a woman wearing khaki slacks, a Stetson, and aviator sunglasses.

"This is a crime scene," she said.

"I know," I said, "I'm—"

"We're authorized," my brother interjected. "May I speak with the officer in charge?"

"That would be—*me*," the woman said. She sounded insulted. I looked at Michael, wondering what he'd say next. Apparently, his priest costume wasn't working.

"I'm the Reverend Michael Black, and this is—"

"Copper Black!" We turned again to find that Detective Booth had appeared on the scene. "It's okay, Denise," he said. "I can handle it from here."

The woman straightened her hat, shot a severe frown at Michael, and headed to the back of the lot.

"Impressive," Booth said. "I was sure you'd be down for a longer count. How're those shiners doing?"

"Better, thanks," I said, even though I was actually feeling worse. I was stiff all over and my nose ached. "I'm only here because I need to find out if my tortoise is okay."

"Your—*tortoise?*"

"Well, he's not mine, exactly. He's part of my house-sitting deal."

Booth narrowed his eyes at me, and I watched the corners of his mouth turn up. Damn the guy! I could never tell what he was thinking.

"We know it's a long shot that he survived," Michael said. "We just want to take a look in the back and see."

"Incredible about your car, isn't it?" Booth said, ignoring Michael.

As he squinted at me, I thought about the stuff I took from Marilyn's bathroom. It still existed, and so did Ms. Carpenter's file folder! Unless someone had already taken action, it was all there, less than ten feet from where we stood. I stole a glance at the Max. It sure didn't look like anyone had touched it yet.

"The arson investigators have established that the accelerant used to start the fire was paint thinner," Booth said. "Make sense to you?"

So that was how Sean had done it so fast!

"Yes," I said. "There were at least three gallons of paint thinner in the big room next to the kitchen. Some guys were refinishing the bar in there."

"A big room with—a buffalo head?" Booth asked.

"Yeah," I said, wondering how he could possibly know. "Why?"

"Another lucky survivor," Booth said with a smile. "It's out next to the pool. Or what used to be the pool."

"Can we go look for Oscar?" I asked. "He could have survived, too, and if he's hurt—"

"Come on," Booth said. "Follow me, be careful, and don't touch anything without asking me first."

He had a point about being careful, and I was glad I was wearing closed-toe shoes as I climbed over a pile of broken glass just beyond the lean-to. Things looked even more ominous when we neared the shattered remains of the greenhouse.

Three guys in jeans and jackets that read "CSI" in big letters on the back were taking pictures, writing on clipboards, and poking debris with long tongs. Denise, the "officer in charge," had ensconced herself in a command station consisting of a folding chair with a clip-on beach umbrella. She was talking into a cell phone.

I could see what Booth meant about "what used to be the pool." If I hadn't swum in it myself, I might never have guessed it had been there. It was so full of wreckage we could have walked across it.

"The explosion pretty much sent the top half of the house in this direction," Booth said. "The roof literally blasted off and headed north."

"Oh, there's the buffalo head," Michael said. "Not in bad shape, considering."

We picked our way forward, checking out the jumble of artifacts as we went.

"Oh, my God! This is my hairbrush!" I said, almost stepping on it. "And this used to be my hair dryer!" The plastic housing had burst apart, but I could still recognize it.

"Do you bowl, Ms. Black?" Booth asked suddenly.

"Occasionally," I said. "Why?"

I followed his gaze. When I saw what he was looking at, the hairs on the back of my neck stood up.

A bowling bag. In perfect shape. Nicely zipped up, and obviously not empty.

"That's not mine."

Booth looked at me, and I could feel his scrutiny even through two pairs of sunglasses. I don't know how he did it, but he always seemed to know when I wasn't telling him everything.

"Really," I said. "I only bowl at, like—birthday parties. I've never owned my own ball."

I just didn't want to tell him about Nylons DeLuca and the apocryphal body parts that might have been hidden in the Nash house's walls. It was just an old story, and it had nothing to do with me. And the bowling bag was probably just what it appeared to be—

Oh, my God! Booth was bending down. Was he actually going to open the bag up? I squeezed my eyes shut, which hurt. I opened them again to see Booth squatting in front of the bag.

"Hmm," he said. "There's a monogram—an 'L.'"

Lollipop Lassiter? Nylons DeLuca? Either way—I closed my eyes again. As I stood there, baking under a rising sun, I wondered whether the next thing I'd lay my eyes on would be a dried-out severed head.

Booth shouted, and I had to look.

One of the CSI guys was walking toward him. As I watched, he poked the bag with his long tongs.

"Okay," I could just hear him say. "We'll process it."

Thank God! I'd probably be long gone when somebody unzipped the bag. I looked toward Michael. Fortunately, he hadn't realized the horror an old bowling ball bag from the Nash house might contain.

"Where did your tortoise live?" Booth called.

Good, we were back on our mission.

"Between the pool and the back fence," I called back, but as I looked in that direction, my heart sank. A huge chunk of roof, cedar shakes still attached, rested squarely on the site of Oscar's burrow. Could a slow-moving creature—even one with a shell—have the slightest chance of surviving the impact of such an enormous and fast-moving threat?

I looked at Michael. As he wiped sweat from his brow and pressed forward, I couldn't help feeling guilty that I'd brought him on a fool's errand. Especially since he had so many other things on his mind. I felt sorry for myself, too. I needed ice water and a bed, not a disaster area reminiscent of an inner circle of Hell.

Still, here we were, and it was silly not to at least take a closer look, even if it meant laying my eyes on a crushed reptilian corpse.

"Why was there gunpowder in the basement?" Booth asked when we reached the edge of Oscar's erstwhile burrow.

"Didn't I tell you last night?" I said. "It was Colby's. Colby Nash."

I bent down to peer under the wreckage lying on top of Oscar's lair.

"Colby Nash," Booth repeated. "The owner of the house?"

I straightened up. We'd covered all this stuff already. Booth was back to his old trick of asking me the same questions over and over.

Well, okay, Mr. Detective. Have it your way.

"Colby rented the basement. He's a filmmaker."

"Did you know about the gunpowder, Ms. Black?" Booth asked.

A new question!

"No," I said, looking squarely at Booth. "I had no idea I was living on top of a powder keg. I only discovered it when I was trying to escape—"

"So—let me get this straight—Sean forced you into the basement?"

"No," I said. "I went down there to turn off the lights, and—"

"So—you had a key?"

"Well, yeah, but—"

Damn him! Once again, he was making me feel like a criminal, even though I had the black eyes and Band-Aids to prove I was a victim. What did it take with this guy?

"Okay, here's what happened," I said. "Colby had left the door unlocked and the lights on. When I went down there to turn them off, Sean showed up, and—"

"Aaaaaa!" I turned just quickly enough to see Michael's legs disappear up to the knees through a hole in a deceptively sturdy-looking stretch of roof shingles.

"Oh, my God! Are you all right?" I moved toward him as quickly as I could, which was not as fast as Detective Booth.

"Yeah—just glad I wore long pants," my brother said.

"Now you know one of the reasons we're liberal with the yellow tape," Booth said, as he grabbed Michael's arm and helped him onto solid ground.

"Yeah, well, I usually find a way to be a klutz anyway," Michael said, brushing himself off. "Just ask Copper."

No! Don't ask me one more question, Detective Booth. On any subject.

Booth looked over the back fence while Michael and I skirted

Oscar's pen, scanning the wreckage. I spotted fragments of his water bowl, but that was the only evidence that a sweet old tortoise with a peace symbol on his back had ever been there.

"He could be under that," Michael said, pointing to the caved-in remains of an air conditioning unit. "Or that." Next to it lay a pile of rocks that looked like they might have come from the fireplace. "I'm sorry, Copper. I just don't see how he could have survived."

"Me, either," I said, taking off my hat and wiping sweat off my forehead. "And it's too sad to think about anymore. I feel like I killed him."

The second I said that, Booth was back at my side.

"Killed who?" he said.

I sighed and pulled my hat back on. What a guy. Now he was insinuating that I was a murderer.

"I'm talking about Oscar," I said. "Sean may not have succeeded with me, but he did manage to kill a defenseless animal."

"He's still in custody," Booth said, which actually made me feel less secure than I did before.

"He could have been *released*?" I said. "After what he did?"

"He should be in the detention center at least until tomorrow," Booth said. "Then—we'll just have to see how things go with the prosecutor, the judge, and Sean's lawyer. I'll keep you posted. But right now, I need to know more about the Nash fellow."

My head pounded. I did my best to ignore it.

"I also want to go over everything you told me yesterday at the hospital about the two girls at the Parks Academy." He flipped through his notebook. "Kelly and Chanel."

An encouraging sign. I couldn't provide hard evidence, but it sounded like Booth would follow up. He asked about Mr. Rice, too. I waited until he clicked his ballpoint pen closed and tucked it behind his ear.

"There's something else I've realized—" I paused and looked at him. Why hadn't I figured this out sooner? "Sean could have killed his mother." I tried to read the look on Booth's face. "I tried to call you yesterday before—"

"I got your message. I called you back a little too late."

"Sean and I didn't go to the V together on the day of the murder."

Booth already knew that, of course, but he could tell I had more to say.

"I got there first. I had a hard time finding a place to park, and I got lost in the casino. Then, when I finally got up to the bar, Sean wasn't there yet. I had time to talk to the bartender and buy a wine card and have a taste, and I—"

"Slow down, Copper. No rush."

Copper. Up to now, I'd always been Ms. Black.

"Afterward, we went to Marilyn's house. I followed Sean in my car, and it only took us about three minutes to get there. I haven't gone back to check, but I think the house might be even closer than that to the Parks Academy."

Booth wrote something in his little notebook.

"I just assumed Sean came to the V directly from the school," I said. "But now I think he made a detour. He had time."

Booth didn't say anything as he jotted down a few more notes.

"There's something else."

Booth glanced up.

"I'm not sure what. It's in my car. I didn't get a chance to look at it before—the big bang."

We both looked toward the Max in its blackened cage. "Your car obviously has a guardian angel."

Too bad Oscar didn't, I thought. I would have traded the Max for him in a New York second.

I told Booth about the file The Hard Drive had given me.

"I'm sure it's evidence of wrongdoing," I added. "Something that made Sean shred his mother's files."

"We'll check it out when we process the car."

Booth made a few more notes.

"Let's head back this way," Michael said, pointing. "Less debris, I think."

The path he pointed to did look slightly more navigable than the route we had taken on our way to Oscar's burrow, even though it was littered with broken glass from the greenhouse.

The three of us, heads down watching for hazards, slowly picked our way back toward the house. My head was throbbing now, and I could feel my eyes swelling. I hoped Michael would have time to stop for a cold drink on our way back to the vicarage.

"Jeepers," Michael said. "That's like—a miracle."

Michael had stopped short, and he was looking down. In front of him lay—what was it? I moved closer.

A wine bottle! Unopened and unbroken. I bent down for a closer look, and—too weird! It was the wine Sean had brought the night he showed up with funeral flowers and almost picked a fight with Daniel. It didn't seem possible, but somehow a bottle of pinot noir had flown out of an exploding house and landed twenty yards away on a concrete pool deck without breaking.

What was this, an evil joke?

Of the few things in the house to survive unscathed, one of them had to belong to the freak who'd tried to kill me. Next thing you know, I'd find a pristine bunch of long-stem roses ...

"I've seen things like that before," Booth said. "Roaring blazes that somehow miss a paper bag. Babies alive in the wreckage of a bomb blast."

While he was talking, my eyes fell on the remains of the east end of the greenhouse. The metal framework, only slightly twisted, still made it clear where the glass walls had been. The space that had held a forest of flesh-eating plants was now occupied only by piles of glittering glass shards. Except—I squinted, then moved closer. Could it be?

"What are you doing?" Michael asked.

Carefully, I crunched across the glass wreckage.

"Look at this!" I called back. "Could be another miracle!"

Not as unscathed as the bottle of wine but quite possibly still alive, a plant with a purple throat was still standing upright amid the debris.

"It won't last long in the sun," I said. "It's already wilting."

"Look," Michael said. "Here's another one."

"That's one of the pitcher plants from Borneo!" I said. "It might still be alive, too!"

I turned back to Booth, who was talking to the "officer in charge."

"We've got to take these plants with us," I called. "They'll die if they're left here."

Booth's body language looked less than sympathetic as he and the lady cop walked toward us. They both peered down at the plants.

"I think we can save them," I said. "But they need shade and water—now."

Amazingly, both cops agreed that there was no good reason to let the surviving meat-eating foliage suffer the same sad end as their greenhouse.

"I've got to let Willie know I'll be late," Michael said when the cops had left us to the task of extricating the plants from the surrounding wreckage. He pulled out his cell phone.

"Thanks, bro," I said. "You really are a saint."

In the end, however, his saintliness was unnecessary. We were making our first trip out to his car with a pitcher plant and a tray of flytraps we uncovered next to it when—

I squinted at the figure ducking under the yellow tape at the end of the driveway. Could it be—?

"David!" I yelled, trying to hold the pitcher plant steady. In my mind, I ran to meet him and threw myself into his arms. In reality, it was David who ran, and he stopped short of grabbing me when he saw what I was holding. Good thing, too. As much as I longed for one of David's bear hugs, that sort of thing would have to wait until my bumps and bruises were a little less fresh.

"Copper! I'm glad I finally found you!"

"Me, too, David. Oh, me, too."

Chapter 25

"Darling, we're going shopping tomorrow," Mom said, patting my knee. David had dropped me off at the vicarage on his way back to work. I felt like Queen Victoria, reigning over the household from the sofa in the living room. Two large pillows propped up my head, and Sekhmet had stretched out next to me. Every five minutes, somebody arrived with lemonade, an ice pack, or a magazine. Nicky even brought me the top half of an Oreo. Even though he'd licked off all the frosting, I've rarely felt more loved.

"We'll have to see, Mom," I said. "I really need to get back to work."

"Surely your boss would understand if you needed another day," Mr. Cluff said, crossing the room from the kitchen. Getting used to thinking of him as my mother's boyfriend had been easier than I'd thought. He was a polite old guy, and he treated my mother like a rare treasure.

"He would," I said. "He's a great boss, which is why I want to get back in there and keep things caught up." I shifted my body. Still sore, but my head felt a lot better. I could definitely sit at my desk for at least a few hours.

Just then, a car pulled into the driveway. Nicky whooped and headed across the living room.

"Hello, everybody!" Michael called from the doorway. "I've brought a friend!"

As soon as Michael stepped inside, Nicky tackled him around the ankles.

"Dad! Dad!" he yelled. Michael scooped him up. He stepped aside to allow his companion to enter the room. My mother stood up, and Mr. Cluff moved to her side. Sierra emerged from the kitchen.

Michael's friend was a short, stocky man wearing a plaid sport shirt and blue jeans. He stepped inside, took off his baseball cap, and removed his wire-rimmed sunglasses.

"Everyone, I'd like to introduce Willie Morningthunder," Michael said. "He's been kind enough to accept my invitation to join us for dinner."

Willie Morningthunder! But he looked nothing like the orator in a headdress I'd seen from a distance at the building site. This guy looked more like a retired school bus driver.

After shaking hands with everyone else, Willie moved toward my sofa. Squatting down on his heels, he took my hand.

"Your brother told me about your adventure," he said. I looked at Willie, and his gaze transfixed me. His eyes bored into mine, flashing in vivid contrast to his tanned and wrinkled face. Was it just the light, or were his eyes actually blue? As his hand enfolded mine, it felt like warm, soft leather. Grandfatherly, I guess I could call his presence. But he also reminded me of my high school biology teacher and the crafts counselor at Camp Wawassett. They had those piercing eyes, too, and an aura that drew you in whether you liked it or not.

"You lost your life," Willie said.

What? No! I wanted to say. *I'm here, aren't I? I survived!* But Willie was already talking again.

"When I was thirteen years old, a puma attacked me," he said. "I was alone. I should have died."

He spoke in short sentences, his deep voice rising and falling in an almost musical cadence. Everyone in the room was listening. Even Nicky was quiet.

"The puma bit my shoulder." Willie pulled the collar of his shirt open, and I could see the end of a ragged scar on his collarbone. "She was hungry. She wanted to eat me."

Willie squeezed my hand. "You know what that's like, don't you?"

My mind jumped back to the basement at the Nash house, to the moment I realized Sean really was trying to kill me. I nodded.

"The puma dropped me on the trail. She ran off."

"Why?" I said.

"I don't know," Willie said. "What I do know is that I lost my life that day." Releasing my hand, he stood up and looked down at me. "I got a new one."

The conversation hardly seemed finished, but Willie turned away. I stared at the long gray braid hanging down his back. A feather dangled from the end.

Wait! I wanted to say. Tell me more! But Sierra was already offering him a glass of lemonade, and Michael was cantering around the living room with Nicky on his back. Maybe later.

A little later, David arrived with a box of chocolates for me, a bouquet of tiger lilies for Sierra, a pirate eye patch for Nicky, and a bottle of red wine. He had just brought me a glass when the moment we'd all been waiting for—or was it dreading?—arrived. The doorbell rang. Daddy-o was here at last.

Sierra made it to the door before Michael.

"Hi, Ted!" she said, hugging my dad. "Oh, and you must be Graham!"

My father looked handsome in a sage green silk shirt and expensive-looking Bermudas. Graham wore a form-fitting red cycling shirt and black Lycra shorts that allowed everything underneath to stand out in detailed relief. His skin was a perfect shade of tanning-bed caramel, and his carefully cropped hair had been lightened by processes far more expensive than the sun. What was he—35 at the most?

"Oh, you poor, sweet *darling*," Graham said, rushing over to the sofa and squatting down next to me. I couldn't help thinking Austin Powers when I heard his accent. "I heard all about your *ghastly* accident. Ted and I have been simply *sick* with concern."

Dad joined him. He leaned down and kissed my forehead.

"How are you doing, Copper?" he asked. "You really had us worried."

"Oh, I'm fine, Dad, really. Everyone's been taking excellent care of me." I looked at him. "How are *you*?"

"Oh, Graham and I are fine," Dad said. "Yesterday was Graham's birthday, and we're still celebrating!"

Graham held his wrist up. The watch he was wearing was big enough to hold a door open, and it sparkled with a nice-sized pair of what looked to be diamonds. *How much did that thing cost?* I wondered. It looked nicer than anything he'd ever bought for my mother.

"My birthday present," Graham said, squeezing Dad's hand. "Thanks again, Teddy."

Teddy. And I was still having trouble calling him Ted.

Graham greeted everyone else with double-sided air kisses, and Dad followed up with hugs. I hadn't been able to imagine the Mom-and-Patrick-and-Dad-and-Graham dynamic, but they were obviously long past any feelings of awkwardness. Time for me to get past them also, I figured. And if Mom wasn't jealous of Graham's birthday watch, well, I'd try to ignore that, too.

The party soon shifted to the backyard, where Sierra had fired up the grill. The migration would have left me all alone, but David joined me on the sofa with his own glass of wine.

"My family may be dysfunctional, but nobody can ever accuse us of bad manners," I said.

"Here's to etiquette," David said, clinking his glass against mine. "Even better when combined with denial."

"What do you mean?" I asked. It sounded just a tiny bit insulting.

"I'm talking about myself," David said. "I was just wondering what your family would think if they knew about—"

"Your baby?"

David nodded.

"Maybe we should call him 'our baby.' It takes a village." I patted David's arm. "This is a family reunion, something this family doesn't do very often. There will never be a better time to let everybody know about a new addition."

David shot me a doubtful look, and I couldn't help smiling. Yeah, maybe I was crazy, but if my mom could get sexy with my Sunday school teacher, and my dad could show off his boy toy, why should I keep a secret as mundane as a normal pregnancy? Now that David and I were a couple again, there was no good reason to hold back our news. They would find out soon enough anyway, and this way, they'd all know at the same exciting moment.

"Nicky will love finding out he's going to have a cousin. He won't care whether he's 'up to code.'"

David was silent for a moment, and I just waited. At last he looked up, and our eyes met.

"I don't know," he said. "I wish I weren't worried about approval, but—"

"Well, I'm not," I said, and at that moment, Willie Morningthunder's face popped into my head. A day ago, before I went down into a basement, I would have been concerned about other people's opinions, too, especially my parents'. But somehow, those worries seemed to have blown up along with the Nash house. Was that what Willie had meant about a "new life"? Whether it was or not, I felt more than ready to tell my family it was about to expand in a slightly unorthodox manner.

"Let's make the announcement after dinner," I said. "We can propose a toast."

David didn't say anything for a minute. At last he squeezed my hand.

"I keep thinking about last night." He looked at me. "I can't help it. Life's just so damn fragile."

"So let's celebrate the new one. This'll be a perfect opportunity."

David was silent a moment longer.

"Okay," he said at last, "but right now, I'm celebrating the fact that you're still around to convince me."

David leaned over and planted a kiss on my lips that proved beyond a doubt that certain parts of me were definitely in working order. Then he went out to the backyard and set up the chaise longue so Queen Copper could preside over the barbecue.

Sierra, whose grilling skills could earn her a trophy, reluctantly relinquished her tongs to Graham when he announced that he was the world's best outdoor chef. Mr. Cluff, Michael, and Willie sat down in chairs near my chaise, and Nicky enlisted David to help him invade his sandbox with an army of plastic soldiers.

As I watched Mom and Dad set the table, it almost seemed like they were a couple again. No, I told myself. Don't engage in wishful thinking.

"I'm so glad you could join us tonight," Michael said to Willie. "You do my family a great honor."

Willie smiled. "You do me the honor," he said.

"I've heard from all the church leaders," Michael went on. "All of them have said they'll attend."

My ears perked up. Church leaders? What was going on? Mr. Cluff was curious, too, and we both listened as Michael explained that the Alliance for the Homeless had decided to create a "peace park" on the spot where the bones had been discovered. The identity of the bones remained a mystery, but Michael had convinced his fellow board members that creating an outdoor gathering place dedicated to world peace would be a major improvement to the building plans. A dedication ceremony had been planned for Saturday afternoon.

"The gathering will be healing for those of us who have come in peace," Willie said, "but for those who've come to fight—" He shook his head.

"I wish we knew who they really are," Michael said. "And who sent them."

Just then, Graham let out a shriek that stopped all conversation and froze all action. A giant wall of flames erupted from the grill. Dad, Mom, Michael, Willie, and Mr. Cluff rocketed across the yard, David rushed over from the sandbox, and Sierra burst through the back door.

"It's okay!" I heard Graham shout from the center of the huddle. "I'm all right!"

As the flames subsided and the crowd dispersed, I saw the can in Graham's hand. Had he actually squirted lighter fluid directly onto burning charcoal? So much for the "world's greatest outdoor chef."

"I'm glad you didn't kill yourself," Sierra said, barely covering her exasperation.

"I'm with you on that, love," Graham said, and as he turned, I tried to remember whether he had been sporting eyebrows when he arrived. Before anyone could say another word, Graham made a bee-line for the back door. He vanished into the house, my father in close pursuit.

After Graham's disappearance, my mother moved to my side.

"How are you feeling, darling?" she said. "I hope you know that nobody expects you to come to the table—"

"I'm fine, Mom," I said, easing myself up. If I really did plan to go to work tomorrow, I needed to see if I could function in vertical mode. "I'm not an invalid. I walked out here on my own, remember?"

Once she realized I wasn't going to let her be my waitress, Mom helped me to my feet. Moving like a rusty tin man, I managed to join everyone else around the picnic table. By then, Dad and Graham had rejoined the party.

Sierra, drawing on skills she learned from her Greek father, had assembled a splendid Hellenic feast: *moussaka*, *spanakopita*, *tzatziki*, three kinds of salad, olives, bread, and a big platter of—something black? Oh, yeah, the chicken.

While we were still standing, Michael reached a hand out to Sierra and my mom. Soon, we were all holding hands. Nicky stood on the bench, one hand in mine and one hand in David's. Michael asked Willie to say grace.

"I have been to the end of the earth," Willie began. "I have been to the end of the waters. I have been to the end of the sky. I have been to the end of the mountains. I have found none that are not my friends. We are all one. *Mitakuye oyasin*."

It wasn't really a grace, I thought. It was something better. If ever there was a family that needed to be reminded it was "all one," it was ours. And the restless horde over at the building site could use a reminder, too. I hoped Willie's prayer had a wide radius.

Halfway through my *moussaka*, I noticed that the platter of inedible black chicken had mysteriously vanished from the table. No one commented on Graham's failure as a barbecue wizard and, thanks to Sierra's tradition of preparing enough food for the whole Greek army, we all had plenty to eat. I was feeling better, too, I realized. My shoulders had loosened up, and if I could sit on a bench, I'd definitely be able to work at my desk at *The Light* for at least a few hours tomorrow.

The sun had set by the time we finished dinner. Michael lit the candles on the table while Sierra made coffee and served dessert. Right around the time we were finishing our *baklava*, I remembered my big announcement.

I glanced at David. One look was all it took to know that he had remembered, too. My heart pounding, I picked up my fork. Before I lost my nerve, I clinked it against my water glass. Everyone immediately stopped talking and looked at me expectantly.

"I—David and I—have an announcement," I said. My words were still hanging in the air as I saw smiles appear on most of the faces around me.

Oh, my God. They think I'm going to tell them we're getting married. My heart beat even faster. *Damn! I should have planned this out!*

"I'm happy to announce that Nicky is going to have a cousin."

The smiles faded. In their place—

Oh, my God! They think I'm pregnant!

"No!" I said. "I mean, I'm going to be a stepmother. David—"

This was a really bad idea.

"David's having a baby—it's a boy."

Nobody said anything. Afraid to look at David, I stared at the table. How could I have thought this was a good idea? All I had succeeded in doing was embarrassing him.

The awkward silence deepened. God, I had to say something else. Something—*anything*—to make things better. I took a breath and opened my mouth, hoping against hope the right words would pop out—

"The blessing of a baby." Willie's deep melodious voice filled the silence before I could speak. I looked up to see that he had stood up. "May his feet be to the east. May his right hand be to the south. May his head be to the west. May his left hand be to the north."

It was almost like a song.

"May he walk and dwell on Mother Earth peacefully. May he be blessed with respectful relatives and friends. May he be blessed with the source of happiness and beauty." Willie paused, then raised both hands. "We ask all these blessings with reverence and holiness. My Mother the Earth, my Father the Sky, my Sister the Sun. All is Peace. All is Beauty. All is Happiness. All is Harmony."

And somehow, like magic, everything was okay. I looked from face to face, each one bathed in the soft light of flickering candles. We each had our secrets, each our flaws. As David had pointed out so accurately, etiquette and denial are fabulous tools for maintaining familial bonds. Or are they? If we really love each other, can't we tell the truth at least once in a while?

On the other hand, etiquette and denial had worked great on the big plate of carbonized chicken.

Chapter 26

Willie Morningthunder's prayer saved dinner, but I knew it was only a matter of time and opportunity before my family pressed me for the full story behind the family's "new addition." Fortunately, nobody got the chance that night. We had barely finished dessert when Graham announced he had "a late-night session" at the LifePower conference that he "absolutely couldn't miss." I think my father wanted to hang around with the family a little longer, and I also had the feeling that Graham was fibbing. In any case, the two of them left while the rest of us were still sitting around the picnic table.

"Are you really planning to go to work tomorrow?" David asked me. "Are you sure you're going to feel up to it?"

I looked at my mother. I could tell she was bursting with questions about how I had managed to become an expectant stepmother. Her compressed lips reminded me of a New Orleans levee in hurricane season. Best to get away before the dam burst.

"Yes," I said. "But I could sure use some extra sleep."

"Promise you'll join us all for dinner at Caesars Palace tomorrow night," Mr. Cluff said. "I've heard the seafood buffet is wonderful."

"Wouldn't miss it," I said. I bid everyone a quick farewell, and David whisked me away to his house.

Later, as I burrowed my bruised and achy body into the covers and drifted off to sleep, a riddle I'd learned in seventh grade bubbled back into my awareness.

Q. How do porcupines make love?

A. Very carefully.

I checked my face in the mirror for the jillionth time as David pulled into *The Light*'s parking lot the next morning. I'd spent nearly an hour applying makeup.

"You look fine," David said.

"I look like the Joker," I said.

David laughed.

"Great," I said. "Nice to know I'm right."

"I'm afraid you do kind of look like you should be battling Batman," he said. "But, hey! You can cut a couple of holes in my lunch bag, and—"

"Wait! Are you calling me *coyote* ugly?"

"Don't flatter yourself," David said. "You're nowhere near scary enough to make a guy gnaw off his arm."

I sighed while he walked around the Jeep and opened the door for me. Before I could move, David kissed me.

"You're spectacular, Pepper," he said. "Come on. Get in there and turn some heads."

It took me nearly twenty minutes to navigate the hall to my cube.

"How *are* you?"

"So glad you're going to be okay!"

"Wow! I'm impressed you're back at work!"

"How *are* you?"

"How *are* you?"

"How *are* you?"

Everyone was more than kind, but all the expressions of concern were nothing compared to what awaited me on my desk.

A huge arrangement of pink roses stood next to a basket full of over-the-top girlie gifts, including a pink satin pillow and a bottle of lavender bubble bath. On top of the pile was a pink teddy bear holding a purple heart. A card was tucked behind the heart. I opened it up.

"Glad you're back!" it read. "Hope you're all well soon." Chris Farr's signature topped dozens of others. Mary Beth Sweeney had signed the card, and so had Greg Langenfeld, *The Light*'s editor-in-chief.

When I sat down, I saw the *caffe latte*. Still hot.

That had to be Chris Farr's work, I thought. I reached for my phone to call him and thank him, but it rang before I could punch up the number.

"Copper! How *are* you?" It was Dad.

"Not too bad, thanks," I said. "Trying to make some headway at work."

"How about if I pick you up at noon and we catch Graham in between sessions for a bite to eat?"

Unable to think of a good reason not to, I told my dad I'd meet him in the parking lot.

Less than a minute later, I heard familiar footsteps approach my cube. No mistaking Mary Beth's clodhoppers.

"Copper! How *are* you?"

"I'm fine, thanks," I said as she peered at my face. "Or better, any-way. Thanks for the basket and card."

"Black eyes can take a while," she said in a tone that spoke of expe-rience. I couldn't help wondering what had given Mary Beth personal knowledge of black eyes, but I also needed to get some work done. I turned back to my press release.

"I hope your brother's watching out for himself," Mary Beth said. "Wouldn't want him to get hurt, too."

What? I looked back up at her. "Did something happen?"

"Oh! I assumed you knew!" Mary Beth said, looking genuinely surprised. "Willie Morningthunder was shot this morning at the homeless center building site. He's in surgery at UMC."

Her news hit me like a bullet. I slumped in my chair.

"He should pull through," Mary Beth said. "The slug went through his shoulder."

His shoulder. The same one the puma had bitten?

"Do you know who did it?"

"No." Mary Beth shrugged. "All I know is that he isn't expected to die."

I stared at Mary Beth, unable to say anything coherent.

"Is there anything I can do?" she asked. She reached over and squeezed the pink teddy bear. It let out a little squeak.

"Thanks for the offer, but I'm mostly okay."

"Ice," Mary Beth said, pointing two fingers at her own eyes. "While you're flat on your back. When you get a chance, it'll really help."

As soon as she left, I called David.

"Did you hear about Willie?" I asked.

"I was going to call you as soon as I found out more about the guy police have in custody," David said.

"You know who did it? And why?"

"No name yet," David said. "No motive, either, other than the generally riotous state of things over at the building site."

"Call me when you know more, okay?" I said.

"You'll be the first to know, Copper."

My phone buzzed as I was about to set it down.

"Is this Copper Black?" asked a voice I felt I should recognize.

"Yes. Who's this?"

"Jenna Bartolo."

No wonder the voice was familiar.

"I need to talk to you." The voice was hoarse, too, or maybe she just felt like whispering. "As soon as possible."

As busy as I was, and as much as I dreaded limping all the way downstairs, my curiosity got the better of me. Soon I'd agreed to meet Jenna in the public parking lot on the east side of the building.

"What are you driving?" I asked.

"Um—let me see—a Ford, I think," she said. "Yeah, a Ford Escort."

A Ford Escort? That was a far cry from the Maseratis and Jaguars Jenna usually drove.

"It's silver. I'm parked next to the fence."

I found the car easily, and Jenna rolled down her window as soon as she saw me. She was wearing a broad-brimmed sun hat and huge dark glasses. If I hadn't been looking for a silver Escort, I never would have recognized her.

"Oh, Copper!" she said when she got a look at my face. "I heard about what happened to you! Come inside here where it's cool!"

I walked around to the passenger door while she reached over and unlocked it. I eased myself in next to her. *Whew.* Much better than standing on hot asphalt.

"Are you okay?" Jenna asked. "Need some water?"

"I'm fine," I said. "Or at least getting there." I watched her as she rummaged in a canvas shopping bag.

Jenna's outfit was as surprising as her car. Instead of the designer duds she usually wore, she had on a baggy T-shirt, faded jeans, and dollar-store flip-flops.

She pulled a bottle of Evian water from her bag and held it out to me. At last, a brand name. She was still Jenna.

Rummaging in her bag again, Jenna pulled out a tissue. Removing her sunglasses, she wiped her eyes.

She'd been crying, I realized with surprise. Her eyes, while not black and blue, were puffier than mine.

"Are you all right?" I asked.

"Yeah—I mean—sort of—I mean—no."

"I heard about Willie Morningthunder," I said, wondering if that might be what was troubling her.

"The Indian chief?" *In-jun. There it was again, the accent that could start a riot.* "What about him?"

"You haven't heard? He was shot this morning. At the building site."

One look at Jenna's horrified face was all it took to know that she'd heard nothing about the incident. As I stared at her, shock gave way to anguish. Her shoulders started shaking, and tears streamed down her cheeks.

"Holy Mother of God," she managed to say. "I can't believe it's come to this." She wiped her eyes again. "Did he—die?"

"No. Sounds like he'll be okay."

"It's all my fault." Fresh tears rolled down her face.

"*Your* fault? What are you talking about?" *And what's with the plain Jane disguise and tin-can car?* I stopped myself from adding.

"Frank's divorcing me."

That was a huge non sequitur, but maybe if I could keep her talking, she'd start to make sense.

"I'm so sorry," I said. But really, what did she expect after announcing her affair with Curtis Weaver on the evening news?

"It's not what you think," Jenna said. "It's not like Frank ever loved me." She heaved a deep shuddering sigh and went on. "I gave up on that fantasy ages ago. I thought I was marrying my soul mate, but we were barely home from our honeymoon when I found out I'm just a smoke screen. Frank's had a girlfriend for decades—an awful old hag who's married and won't leave her husband. It's like I'm Diana and she's Camilla, and—"

Jenna broke down into another round of gasping sobs. I waited until the grief subsided. She blew her nose, shook her head, and went on.

"Frank's known about Curtis for months. When I told him, he said—" Jenna paused to stifle a sob. "He said he was glad I'd finally figured out how the world really works."

Lifestyles of the über-rich, I thought. They look so good from the outside, but inside—totally different story.

"When I found out Curt was being accused of killing Marilyn," Jenna went on, "I didn't even think twice. I just called the police and told the detective Curt couldn't have done it. I told him he could check with the room service waiter, too, if he wanted another witness. And the maid who brought us extra towels."

Jenna paused and sniffled. A fresh cascade of tears washed down her cheeks. "It never crossed my mind to tell Frank before I told the police. He told me a thousand times he didn't give a damn what I did so long as I was there when he needed me." She wiped her nose. "Which isn't very often. I swear, I see my dentist more often than my husband."

She struggled to speak between sobs. "Oh, God, I've never seen him so angry."

As her voice dissolved into a moan, I tried to make sense of what she was telling me—and why. What did any of it have to do with Willie and the Alliance's building project? Jenna needed a good lawyer and a shrink, not a wounded calendar girl.

"Jenna, I'm really sorry, but—"

"Whoever shot Willie probably works for Frank."

What? Now she had my attention.

Jenna looked me square in the face and took a deep breath. When she spoke, her voice was almost steady.

"When I was at the building site on Sunday, I recognized a group of guys in the crowd. At first, I wasn't sure why they seemed familiar, but then it hit me. They all work security at the Costa del Sol casino in Florida." She paused.

"The casino Frank owns jointly with the Seminoles."

Chapter 27

Seminoles. I was still trying to wrap my head around Jenna's revelation when she started talking again.

"You've got to stop him, Copper."

Me? I just stared at her.

"The media's what caused all this. The media's got to fix it."

For someone who had been a blubbering mess just a minute before, she sounded remarkably calm.

"Why haven't you called the police?" I asked.

"Are you crazy?" Jenna said.

Like I was the one with a mental problem.

Even though what I really wanted to do was get back to my cube, I twisted the cap off the bottle of Evian water and sipped while Jenna poured out her whole story. At least the car was cool.

"Frank has always hated the idea of a downtown homeless center because he thinks it will just attract more homeless people to Las Vegas. He was willing to stay out of it to keep me happy, but when the news broke about Curtis and me—God, he turned into a raging monster! He decided to destroy the Alliance to punish both of us, and he doesn't care who he takes out along the way."

Jenna paused to check her face in the rearview mirror. "If he thinks I'm fighting back, or getting help from anybody he recognizes, he won't bother divorcing me. He'll kill me." She paused again, and it wasn't the air conditioning that sent a chill through my body. It was the realization that Jenna wasn't exaggerating. She was married to a guy who really could kill people without worrying about repercussions.

Jenna took a breath and continued. "So that's why I thought of you."

Copper Black, professional nobody. Hardly flattering, but I couldn't deny it was true. To Frank Bartolo, I was as high-profile as a homeless person.

"I don't see what I can do—"

"Get out your best little black dress. You're going to a party tonight."

As I sat there listening to Jenna roll out her whole crazy plan, I couldn't help getting the idea that she had figured this whole scenario out before she called me. Probably planned the tears, even. But although her scheme to "out" her husband seemed like a plot development from a bad movie, I still let her talk me into going to a party at the Monaco. Offered the right bait, I turn into a total pushover, and scheming people like Jenna seem to sense that personality flaw immediately. She didn't care that my face looked like the aftermath of a street fight. She didn't listen when I told her I was busy with work and a dysfunctional-family reunion. She just turned my own curiosity and inability to say no against me.

Within minutes, I had agreed to dig out my one awesome cocktail dress which, fortuitously, I'd had no reason to take to the Nash house. I would be joining the A-listers getting a sneak preview of the Strip's newest attraction, an upscale nightspot at the Monaco called—I'm not joking—Lick Me.

Even the obstacle that my car was stuck in a charred cage at a crime scene didn't faze Jenna.

"I'll send a limo," she said. "Be ready at six."

She handed me a business card—a black shiny number with one

word embossed on the front in silver: LIQMI.

Oh, so that was how you spelled it.

"Call me if you need anything," she said, adding her own pale pink card to the black one. "Use the cell number."

A few minutes later, I hiked painfully back up to my cube. *Damn!* Had I really just agreed to confront the sixth-richest man in the world on his own turf about issues that were getting people shot? That was the centerpiece of Jenna's plan. Posing as an ordinary member of the gossip column gang, and with plenty of other reporters and cameras nearby, I was supposed to say, "Mr. Bartolo, is it true that the violent demonstrators at the homeless center building site are on your payroll?"

Yeah! That's what Jenna succeeded in negotiating for nothing more than a bottle of warm Evian water.

And I call *her* crazy.

Dad was right on time and, fortunately, so was I. I had just emerged through the main door when he pulled up in his rented sedan.

"Copper, sweetheart," he said as I eased myself into the passenger seat. "Are you sure you should be back at work?"

"Not entirely," I said. I hadn't accomplished much after my little *tête-à-tête* with Jenna, and a peek in the restroom mirror had not boosted my confidence. "But I'm hanging in there. Where are we headed?"

"Cal's Town," my dad said, as though he were pronouncing the name of a strange land. "You ever been there?"

"No." But I knew it was a casino. David had once described it as a theme park for people who like dead animals. Or maybe it was fake animals. I couldn't remember, but either way, I can't say I was thrilled to be heading down Boulder Highway to hook up with my father's boyfriend in an ersatz zoo. On the other hand, the rendezvous felt almost mundane compared with my appointment at Liqmi later. Especially when all I really wanted to do was crawl into bed and watch reruns of *Charmed*.

The big marquee towering in front of Cal's Town identified the place as a "Hotel and Gambling Hall." Kind of refreshing, actually, in a city that had long ago dropped two letters to refine itself into the "gaming" capital of the world.

I was staring at a fake coyote perched on top of a fake mountain in the fake twilight of a giant atrium when Graham appeared. A bit more formally attired than he had been at Sierra's barbecue, he was wearing a harlequin-patterned jacket and tight black leather pants. His hair was spiked into a hedgehog do, and I could swear he was wearing eye makeup.

I was still cataloguing his outfit when Graham wrapped my father in his arms and forced me to witness something I realized I'd been dreading: my father engaged in a full-on, open-mouthed lip-lock with another man. Don't get me wrong. It's not that I disapprove on a rational level. It's just that I could happily live my whole life without ever observing Dad's sexual preferences in action.

My mind jumped back to a Saturday night when I was a senior in high school. Mom was at her sister's in Rhode Island for the weekend, and Dad was playing poker with some friends across town. That meant I had no reason not to invite Kyle Cosgrove in when he brought me home after the final performance of *The King and I* at New Canaan High. We helped ourselves to a couple of beers and got comfy on the sofa in the living room. It was only ten o'clock, after all. Dad never got home from a poker night until after two. And even if he came home early, the garage door made a great alarm. Once I heard it rumble, I had a good ninety seconds to transform myself back into the picture of innocence.

That night, however—for reasons that remain a mystery—Dad

came in the front door. I'll never forget the moment our eyes met. Mine were looking over the shoulder of a horizontal halfback.

Dad didn't say anything. Instead, he just backed out the door and closed it. A moment later, the garage door rumbled. Ninety seconds later, Kyle and I looked like the picture of virtue, if you ignored our flushed faces. Dad reentered the room, and life went on as though nothing had happened.

Except something *had* happened. My father had witnessed something he really hadn't wanted to see. Sex creates families, but families—or at least families like mine—are much more comfortable when they pretend otherwise.

So I guess you could say I deserved my front-row center view of my father and Graham enjoying an extended French kiss. I'm not sure the chubby family in matching Nebraska T-shirts standing nearby felt the same way. On the other hand, they didn't look away until the kiss ended with an audible slurp.

As Dad and Graham parted, my father's eyes met mine. I don't know what I expected, but it certainly wasn't the look of embarrassed regret so obviously written there. Where did that come from? He knew I was standing right there. If he wasn't trying to rub my nose in his new life, then why … ?

"Copper, love!" Graham draped his arm around me. "How's my darling?"

"Fine," I said for the millionth time in four hours. If only it had been true.

As the three of us made our way across the atrium on circuitous paths lined with artificial wildlife, the coyote atop the fiberglass mountain let out a long howl. That seemed to wake up all the other heretofore inert birds and beasts lurking around us. By the time we were heading into the relative calm of the casino, a flashing laser display and illuminated water jets had added gaudy visual effects to the electronic animal hullabaloo.

A hostess showed us to a table in a dark café. Just before my dad sat down, Graham leaned over for another kiss. This time, Dad shrank back, and once again, our eyes met.

"Aw, Teddy," Graham said, a clear pout in his voice.

"I'm really hungry," I said, even though I wasn't. It was just all I could think of to change the subject.

As I munched the edges of a BLT and Dad downed a glass of Mexican beer, Graham talked. Somehow he sucked down three margaritas, too, flirting ostentatiously with the young waiter every time he requested another. I half expected him to pat the boy on the bottom every time he turned around.

"That ghastly Martha Dilsaver is such a crashing bore," he said, reporting on his experiences on a panel at the LifePower convention that morning. "She's as idiotic in person as she is on her *asinine* television show. I don't see how you Americans can stand that screech owl voice of hers—and those *clothes!*"

He paused to suck down some more frozen cocktail, glanced around to see if he had an audience beyond Dad and me, and went on. "She *really* got her knickers in a twist when the news reporter interviewed *me* afterward instead of *her*. If looks could bloody well kill, I *swear* I'd be lying gutted on the carpet upstairs." Graham waved his hand theatrically as he said that, accidentally—maybe—hitting the waiter.

"Oh, I'm so sorry, love!" he said, touching the young man again on the arm. "When you get a chance, I'd love another one of these brilliant concoctions." He held up his glass and drained it.

So make that four margaritas.

My father had ordered coffee when Graham lurched to his feet and announced he was headed "to the loo."

A bit unsteadily, he banged his way among the tables in the direction the young waiter indicated.

"Copper, I—"

"Dad, I—"

We both spoke at once.

"How are you doing?" My dad asked the question, but it was exactly what I wanted to know about him. Was he actually happy as the court jester's sidekick? Did Graham really care about him, or was it my father's credit limit that interested him?

I couldn't ask those questions, of course. It wasn't—well, it just wasn't right. My dad could date whoever he wanted, and it was none of my business. Once again, I thought back to the night he'd caught me *in flagrante* with Kyle Cosgrove. We got a "do over," not a lecture, and I was still a kid. My father is sixty-two years old. He didn't deserve a lecture from his twenty-four-year-old daughter. But if not me, who? Was anybody looking out for him? My mother certainly wasn't.

My internal debate was cut short when my phone rang.

"Oh, my God, I'm sorry!" I said. "I meant to turn off the ringer."

"It's okay, sweetheart," Dad said, even though he despises cell phones.

"Maybe it's Michael," I said, and it was—but not the one I meant. It was Detective Mike Booth.

"You're free to pick up your car, Ms. Black," he informed me, "and I'd recommend making it a priority. Once the investigation closes, there won't be any security on the scene. The car and everything inside it will be an easy target for looters."

"Looters?" I hadn't thought of that possibility.

"Like flies to—" he paused. "Manure. Get over there by five if it's at all possible."

God, when was I going to have a chance to go to the Nash house, given everything else I had to do today? I thanked Booth and took a breath to ask him about Sean.

"I've got to run," he said. "Maybe I'll see you later." He clicked off.

All I could do was hope that Sean wasn't out on the street.

My dad was glancing at his watch when I slipped my phone back into my backpack. *Where was Graham?* I wondered. He'd certainly been gone long enough to offload four margaritas. Had he gotten lost? The waiter refilled our coffee cups, and Dad asked for the check.

"Have you heard from Michael?" I asked. "Have things settled down at the building site?"

"I talked to him earlier. He was at the hospital with Mr. Morningthunder. Your mom and Patrick were there, too. I've just been—here."

Damn. The sadness in his voice was unmistakable. I wished I could hug him, but I just took a sip of coffee.

Ten minutes later, Graham still hadn't returned. Dad signed the credit card slip.

"Do you think he's okay?" I asked.

Dad heaved a big sigh. "Yeah," he said. "He probably just ran into somebody from the conference."

We waited a few more minutes. The more morose my father looked, the angrier I felt. How could Graham treat him like this? The self-centered clown! If my father had fallen in love with him, I kept telling myself, there had to be aspects of Graham's personality I hadn't seen yet.

"Um, Dad?" I said at last. "I'm really pressed for time." I told him about the Max.

"Copper, sweetheart, why didn't you tell me immediately? Let's go get it before it's too late!"

On the way over to the site formerly occupied by the Nash house we both avoided the topic of Graham. Instead, Dad told me that if my car wasn't in perfect condition, he'd buy me a new one.

I wish I could get *you* a new one, I thought as we drove along Flamingo Road. And as for Graham, I wished I could *rip* him a new one.

Chapter 28

As we headed down Pecos Road on the way to the Nash house, I realized Dad was avoiding another topic, too—the baby news I'd dropped last night. He had to be at least as worried about my impending stepmotherhood as I was about his relationship with Graham. But just as I had decided to keep my mouth shut about my fears that he was being victimized by a gold digger, he'd chosen to suppress his curiosity about how I was connected to another woman's unborn baby.

God, what a family! Silence is a powerful policy, but maybe there is something to be said for the approach David's family takes. Not only do they all talk in tones better suited to street fights, no subject is ever off limits. I dreaded the next time I'd be in a room with Mimi and Harry Nussbaum, even though most of their salvos would be lobbed at David.

"You *slept* with Rebecca even though you two are *breaking up?*" Mimi would say in a voice that could lead cheers without a megaphone. "What were you *thinking?*"

Okay, I'm guessing at the exact phrasing, but one thing I know for sure. She'd hammer the topic right on the head and demand a no-nonsense answer. And then Harry would interrupt, and then everybody would talk even louder. By the time David reeled off a response or two, all the neighbors in a three-house radius would be enjoying the juicy details.

If a conversation like that ever took place in my family—well, it couldn't. It would be World War III, and the next day there'd be nothing left but radioactive desolation. And silence. David's family, on the other hand, survives such cataclysms daily. No matter what topic is broached—Menopause! Diarrhea! Republicans!—nobody ever storms out of the room. They just get louder and louder until Mimi puts dinner on the table. Even then, things don't get exactly quiet, but mashed potatoes do have a muffling effect.

Following my directions, Dad pulled to a stop on Vista Miranda. We crossed the street, and as he caught sight of the wreckage behind the oleander hedge, Dad stopped in his tracks. He sucked in a breath and grabbed my hand.

"I love you, sweetheart."

"I love you, Dad."

That's as good as it gets in the Black family.

The charred framework had vanished, but the Max was still sitting in the space it had occupied.

"Can you believe it was less than five feet from an exploding house?" I said.

"What I can't believe is that you were *in* the house," Dad said.

"Well, here's something to believe," a familiar raspy voice said. "Sean DuBois is still in the detention center. I forgot to mention it earlier."

"Detective Booth! I'm so—"

But he was already introducing himself to my father.

"Your daughter's one lucky young lady," he said. "And it looks like her car made it through pretty well, too."

"And the folder," I said. "From the Parks Academy. It has

information about Sean—"

"Got it," Booth said.

I wanted to ask what was in it, but I could sense he wouldn't tell me even if he knew. Too bad I'd never had a chance to look through it myself. All I could do was hope that The Hard Drive had managed to assemble some truly damning evidence against Sean.

"My car—you think I can drive it?" I asked.

Booth shrugged. "One way to find out."

Dad and I walked slowly around the Max, kicking the tires as we went. They all seemed intact.

"Let me try it, sweetheart," he said, peering into the driver's side window. I fished my keys out of my pocket and handed them over, glad that I had escaped with them. Dad climbed behind the wheel. I couldn't help smiling when the engine started right up. Dad's offer of new wheels was generous, but the Max was a good old friend.

"We better get it checked out, though," Dad said. "There might be damage to things we can't see."

"I need to talk with you," Detective Booth said. "I've got a few more questions."

"Can it wait?" my father said. "We need to get this car to a mechanic, and it would be better to get there before closing time."

Reluctantly, Booth said he'd call me. Dad gave me the keys to his rental car, and I led the way to a gas station up on Sunset Road. We paused there long enough to decide that we could probably make it all the way to the Chrysler dealership in Henderson. That turned out to be an excellent decision, because my father not only used his credit card to pay for any work the Max might need, he also scored me a loaner.

"See you for the family dinner at Caesars Palace," he said after we'd transferred my belongings into a large new black sedan. "I'm heading back to Cal's Town first."

He exhaled a shuddering sigh.

Damn that Graham.

"I love you, Dad." It was all our family rules permitted. Well, except maybe a kiss. I hugged him and planted one on his cheek.

"Love you, too, kiddo."

As I pulled onto the freeway behind him in my shiny black barge, it dawned on me that I might actually look like an A-lister at the Monaco. I'd definitely use the valet parking.

Happy to have a compelling reason to skip going back to work, I left a message on my boss's voice mail and headed to the vicarage. Nobody was home, so I left a note on the kitchen table explaining what a strange Chrysler was doing in the driveway. After leaving a message for Jenna that I no longer needed a limo ride, I hiked up to my apartment.

God, please let me own one intact pair of panty hose. If I was going to remodel myself into a creature who looked liked she belonged in a fancy nightspot, I had no time for a trip to Walgreens.

With forty-five minutes to get to the Monaco, I creaked down my staircase. As I reached the bottom, Sierra stepped through the front door of the house.

"What's going on?" she called. "What's with the playgirl dress and sugar daddy car? If you're skipping out on the family gathering at Caesars, I'll kill you."

She moved closer, appraising me from head to toe.

"I'll be there," I said. "Unless I die first. I just have to make a quick appearance at a club opening at the Monaco." I hesitated, considering whether to tell her the real reason I had crammed my dented body into a strapless bronze cocktail dress and high heels. "For work."

"I've gotta give it to you—you sure are dedicated," Sierra said. "Turn around."

I obeyed. Sierra knows what she's talking about when it comes to making an entrance, and she's brutally honest.

"You don't look half bad," she said when I finished my slow pirouette. "The dark panty hose cover up the bandages on your legs pretty well. And nobody—no guy, at least—will be looking at your legs, anyway."

I couldn't resist hitching the front of my dress up. I *was* showing an awful lot of cleavage.

"No! Flaunt it," Sierra said. "Your face could still stop a train."

As I headed over to the Strip, I seriously wondered whether I should go through with Jenna's plan. If I'd told Sierra, she would've called me insane. My brother might have chosen a slightly milder adjective—crazy, probably. And David? He would have spoken his mind at a hundred decibels.

"You don't believe Frank will admit anything useful, do you?" he'd say in the voice he inherited from his mother. "Copper, you're *nuts!*"

Insane. Crazy. Nuts.

Damn! Maybe my brain *had* been damaged along with my outer shell. Then again, given the job ahead of me, being out of my mind could be considered an asset.

At least I could rely on the fact that Sean wouldn't be there. The Liqmi opening was just the sort of event he would use his mother's juice to attend. Silently, I thanked Booth for telling me he was still in the slammer.

My phone lit up with the theme from *The Good, the Bad and the Ugly* while I was stopped at a traffic light at Paradise Road. David's ring.

"How are you?" he asked, sounding sincerely concerned. "Chris said you'd left for the day, and—"

"I'm okay, thanks. Just—um—"

"What? Copper, are you all right?"

I don't even remember what lame story I came up with to avoid telling David about my real mission, but he agreed to join me later at Caesars Palace for the family rendezvous.

"Oh, I almost forgot," he said. "A guy named Felipe O'Sullivan shot Willie Morningthunder. Or at least that's what the cops are saying."

Felipe O'Sullivan. A melting-pot name if there ever was one.

"A Hispanic-Irish guy?"

"I don't know. What difference does it make?"

Well, none, I had to admit. "He's—still in jail?"

"Yes, and so are two other guys, but I only got one other name. Keith Fleming."

Keith Fleming. No melting pot there.

"Have you heard how Willie's doing?"

"Yeah. He's apparently going to be fine."

"Thank God."

"I just hope you're really all right, Copper."

"I'll be fine so long as you don't stand me up at tonight's clan supper."

"I'll be there."

After I hung up, it dawned on me that I'd be joining my family in a low-cut strapless dress, spike heels, and enough pancake makeup to spackle a wall. I had an explanation, of course, but I knew I'd stop all conversation when I appeared on the scene decked out as a tart. I'll probably make Graham jealous, I was thinking as I pulled under the Monaco's porte cochere. He seemed like the type who'd pout unless he was the center of attention. The jerk. How could my dad have fallen for a guy like that?

As I eased myself out of my loaner-mobile, I tried not to look as though I needed a walker. The parking valet grabbed my arm as I teetered my way vertical, proving beyond a doubt that I wasn't fooling anyone.

"Thanks," I said, handing him my keys. He sneaked a look at my face and failed to erase a slightly stunned look from his own.

"Have a nice evening, ma'am," he said.

Ma'am. Not a good sign. I should still be a "miss" to a guy who had at least ten years on me. I sighed and thanked him again.

Garnering a couple more surreptitious stares, I checked in at the press table.

"You can pick up a media kit on your way out," a perky redhead said. "The DVD is *super* awesome."

I heard her repeat herself twice by the time I had hobbled to the elevator at the bottom of the Mont Blanc tower. Why hadn't I been sensible and worn flats? And for that matter, why hadn't I worn a bag on my head? Despite Sierra's prediction, nobody was looking at my chest.

"Copper!"

I had just stepped into the elevator when a familiar voice boomed behind me. Mary Beth Sweeney! What was *she* doing here? I turned as she pressed in next to me, accompanied by a chubby short guy with an unlit cigar between his teeth.

"What are *you* doing here?" Mary Beth said. "Shouldn't you be home with a couple of ice packs?"

Damn. I hadn't thought I'd need a backstory.

"Copper was practically murdered the other day," Mary Beth said to her portly companion. "Nobody can believe she's already back on the job. If it had been me, I'd—"

"I'm fine," I said, which was less of a lie that moment than it was the next.

When the elevator doors parted, I stepped forward, but my heel caught in the door frame. S*mack.* I was flat on my belly on a granite floor. My purse skittered off among a forest of legs, and the crowd emitted a collective "Ooh!"

"Copper! Are you all right?"

Suddenly I was very glad that Mary Beth had come to the party.

"Hey!" she called. "You there—bouncer guy! We need some help here!"

I was pulling myself up as the crowd parted to allow a large Polynesian-looking bruiser in a black suit to make his way toward me. He was quickly joined by two more black-suited no-neck dudes. I found myself hoisted to my feet, which didn't actually touch the floor until the bouncer brigade had transported me through a pair of double doors, whisked me down a hallway, and deposited me on a sofa in a room that looked like the antechamber of an über-fancy hotel suite.

"Let me in! She's diabetic! I've got her medication! She could die!"

Mary Beth's voice carried easily through the closed door, and her fabrications had the desired effect. The door burst open, and she was immediately at my side.

"How're you doing?" she asked. "Anything broken?"

"Just a couple new bruises, I think."

Plopping down next to me, Mary Beth set my purse on my lap.

"Thanks for saving it," I said. "And—I'm really glad you're here."

The biggest bouncer appeared with a glass of water. A really nice glass, I couldn't help noticing. Cut crystal.

"Take your meds, honey," Mary Beth said, winking surreptitiously and jostling my purse under the bouncer's suspicious glare. "You'll feel so much better."

Rooting around in my purse, I managed to extract a couple of breath mints without pulling out the tell-tale container. I washed them down, grateful that they were the tiny kind.

"Give her a few minutes," Mary Beth said to the dude in black with a dismissive wave. "I'll let you know if we need anything."

I had to give it to Mary Beth. The same attributes I had found so pushy and annoying back at *The Light* were nothing short of awe-inspiring out in real Vegasland. *Could I ever be that commanding?* I wondered. She ought to be the one demanding information from Frank Bartolo, not me. I couldn't even exit an elevator properly.

"I only came to this shindig because of my friend," Mary Beth said. "He's visiting from Cincinnati. I better go find him pretty soon."

"I'm okay, now," I said. "I really appreciate—"

A door on the far side of the room swung open. A middle-aged man in a black tuxedo with a gold cummerbund stepped into the room.

"I gotta go!" he barked into a cell phone. "Call me back about Keith and Felipe."

Keith and Felipe—weren't those the two guys David told me about? What were their last names ... ?

"Send Archie over to find out what's going on with—"

Just then, the man glanced up. His eyebrows shot up as he realized there were two strange women parked on the sofa. The look of surprise was instantly replaced with a glare. "I gotta go!" he barked again. He snapped his phone shut and stuffed it inside his jacket.

"Who the hell—?"

Mary Beth was already on her feet. She strode across the carpet, her right hand outstretched.

"Mr. Bartolo," she said. "Mary Beth Sweeney with *The Light*. We've met."

Frank Bartolo! So that's what he looked like. Somehow I'd expected someone taller.

"Caleb!" Bartolo bellowed, ignoring Mary Beth's hand. "Where are you? What the hell is the press doing here?"

"Your elevator caused my colleague serious injury," Mary Beth said without missing a beat. She pulled her own cell phone from her jacket pocket. "And your staff's negligence very nearly turned the situation life-threatening. I'm calling—"

She poised her finger over the keypad.

"Oh, that won't be necessary, Ms. Sweeney." Bartolo was immediately at her side. He draped his arm around her shoulders, and his voice melted into honey.

"Please sit down. Is there anything I can get you? How are you feeling, Miss—?"

"Black," I said, placing my hand into his. "Copper Black."

Suddenly, my damaged face was a major asset. I watched the wheels turning behind Bartolo's eyes, his bushy eyebrows working up and down. *Did all that wreckage really just occur in my elevator?* I could almost hear him wonder. His eyes traveled over the rest of my body. He had to find it mysterious that I had bandages *under* my panty hose.

While Bartolo was still trying to make sense of my condition, my own brain was hard at work. Here was my chance! I had the guy at a disadvantage, and Mary Beth was a terrific witness. And it was, after all, why I had come.

Bartolo opened his mouth, but I was the one who started talking.

"Keith Fleming and Felipe O'Sullivan," I said, successfully retrieving their last names from my short-term memory.

Bartolo leapt to his feet as though he'd suddenly found out I had avian flu. Mary Beth looked almost as surprised.

"Who are they?" she asked.

"I think that's what Mr. Bartolo needs to tell us," I said, amazed to find my confidence growing. I looked him square in the eyes. "But first off, which one shot Willie Morningthunder?"

Mary Beth flashed me a look of startled awe. Then she pulled a tiny voice recorder from her jacket pocket, switched it on, and held it toward Bartolo.

"Do tell," she said. "For the record."

Bartolo's face went white, and his eyebrows flattened like the ears on a threatened pit bull. His jaw worked up and down a few times as he stared at the little recorder.

"Look, we know they work security at the Costa del Sol in Florida," I said.

Mary Beth looked at me again, and I watched her face as she searched her mental filing cabinets.

"Yeah, the Seminole casino," she said, looking at Bartolo again.

Bartolo's right hand moved to his trousers pocket. Oh, my God! I thought. What if he has a gun? The guy's probably a major mobster, and we're trapped inside his citadel. Even if he wouldn't kill us, he's got guys who would. How could I have been so stupid—?

But all Bartolo pulled out was a big white handkerchief. He wiped his brow, stuffed the cloth back into his pocket, and glowered at Mary Beth.

"Turn off the recorder," he said.

I was slightly surprised that Mary Beth immediately obeyed.

"Okay, done," she said. "Now, let's hear your side of the story."

"I don't have to tell you a goddamn thing, and you know it," Bartolo growled. "And I'd strongly suggest that you carefully consider the ramifications before you start writing lies about me."

He and Mary Beth faced off again, and I struggled to my feet.

"We're actually interested in the truth, Mr. Bartolo," I said. "I'm sure you'll agree that it's better—"

"O'Sullivan and Fleming don't work for me—"

As soon as those words escaped his lips, Bartolo's mouth slammed shut. His eyebrows drew together into one long furry caterpillar. For a second, I thought steam might start shooting out his ears.

"Caleb!" Bartolo bellowed. As he moved to the hall door, another guy in a tux swung around the corner, bumping into him. This one looked like a high school kid, in spite of his shaggy mustache and jaw-length sideburns.

"Escort these two—er—*ladies*—to their cars," Bartolo ordered, jabbing a thumb over his shoulder. "The younger one claims to be injured, so—"

"Not so fast, Mr. Bartolo," Mary Beth began, but the casino magnate had snapped back into king-of-the-castle mode. Within seconds, the three huge security thugs had reappeared. No more than a minute later, Mary Beth and I were back in the foyer where I'd made my dramatic entrance.

"Find my escort," Mary Beth commanded. "Phil Newcomb from Cincinnati. He's short and fat. He's got a mousy gray comb-over, bottle-bottom glasses, and a loud paisley tie."

I stared at Mary Beth. While her description of her friend was remarkably accurate, it was also remarkably harsh. Hope I never hear how she'd sum me up, I thought.

"We'll wait here," Mary Beth added, as though we had a choice.

Our guards grunted, and one of them headed into the nightclub. I could see that the party was in full swing in there—thumping music, legions of babes, flowing booze. I watched through the archway as strobe lights lit up the revelers' faces like sunlight every few seconds, and the heavy techno beat vibrated my whole body. Then—flash!

Sean DuBois!

I blinked. Had my eyes deceived me? The next lightning flash revealed that my vision was fine. It was Sean, all right. Bookended by two blondes in bustiers, he was lounging against the bar, a martini glass in one hand and a cigar in the other.

Despite Detective Booth's assurance just three hours before that my would-be murderer was still locked up, there he was, a carefree playboy. My knees wobbled, my heart revved up, and I started gulping air like a drowning person. When the strobe flashed again, Sean's eyes met mine. It was only for a split second, but it was long enough for me to know that he'd seen me.

"You okay?" Mary Beth asked, laying her hand on my shoulder.

"Yeah," I managed to gasp, hoping I wasn't about to keel over again. The last thing I needed was another trip into Frank Bartolo's lair.

"Just get me out of here," I said.

Fortunately, her friend from Cincinnati showed up just then, and the elevator doors opened.

"Sorry about the quick exit," Mary Beth said.

"What's going on?" Phil asked as we rode back down to ground level with our ever-present bodyguards. When the only response he got was a raised eyebrow from Mary Beth, he joined the silence.

The bouncers stuck with us until we were outside under the porte cochere and the parking valets had run off to fetch our cars.

"Are you sure you can drive all right?" Mary Beth asked. "We'd be happy to give you a ride somewhere."

"Thanks, but—"

Her offer actually sounded pretty attractive, if only because I didn't like the idea of driving off alone now that I knew Sean was on the loose. He'd seen me—there was no doubt about that. Would he follow me? But even though that thought was keeping me sweaty, hanging around with Mary Beth wouldn't be uneventful, either. It was only a matter of time before she began asking—

"Copper, how did you know that Bartolo was connected to the Morningthunder shooting?"

Damn! Exactly the question I had been hoping to avoid.

"A hunch," I lied.

Mary Beth squinted at me. "Awfully good hunch," she said.

Just then, my borrowed Chrysler rolled up.

"That's *your* car?" Mary Beth said.

"Yeah," I said. "Cool, huh?" But I didn't pause for a reply. "Thanks for all your help, Mary Beth," I said, "and it was nice to meet you, Phil. I hope the rest of your stay in Las Vegas is more fun than this party was."

"This is what I'll remember," Phil said. "High intrigue on the Las Vegas Strip. I can dine out on that for months back home."

It might be a party anecdote in Cincinnati, but it was something else entirely at home in Las Vegas. Detective Booth better have a stellar explanation for why a homicidal maniac was back on the loose.

Chapter 29

I tipped the valet, slipped behind the wheel, and pulled away before Mary Beth could ask me any more questions. I'll get her a box of chocolates, I told myself. She had my gratitude, but I wasn't about to give her my story. And I also wanted to put some distance between me and Sean.

Fortunately, the Monaco is only a couple of resorts south of Caesars Palace. I glanced at the clock on the dashboard as I turned left out of the Monaco onto Las Vegas Boulevard. With a little luck, I'd make it to the buffet line before any of my family members arrived. With a little more, David would be there waiting for me. Sure, I could call Booth, but I sure could use a little backup.

Luck, however, kept its distance on my short journey up the Strip. As I pulled to a stop at a red light at Flamingo Road, a couple in a motorized go-cart that said "Rent Me!" in huge letters on the back smacked into a bicycle. No one seemed to be hurt, but the rider of the bike was a cop. Forty-five minutes and a fleet of patrol cars later, I was once again making progress toward Caesars. By the time I had parked, hobbled into the casino, and found the seafood buffet, my family had already helped itself to plates piled with jumbo shrimp and king crab.

"Copper, darling!"

My mother jumped up as soon as she saw me. "We were getting worried!" I tried not to wince as she hugged me, then held me at arm's length. "Good gracious! Where have you been?"

"Oh, I forgot to tell you," Sierra said, handing Nicky a shrimp. "Copper's been out baptizing a new nightspot."

"Oh! Well, you look—lovely, dear," my mother said, a decided lack of conviction in her voice. "Come sit down. May I bring you a plate?"

Where was David? I wondered. I didn't want to tell my family about seeing Sean, but I sure needed to talk to somebody. A bodyguard might come in handy, too.

The only vacant chair was next to Graham. I wasn't sure whether it was good or bad that he had reappeared, and my father's face didn't make things any clearer.

"Ooh!" Graham said, holding his arm up to my dress as I sat down. "Great minds have similar tastes." Damned if his jacket wasn't made out of a bronzy metallic fabric that almost perfectly matched my dress.

"Yeah," I said, forcing a smile. "What a coincidence."

Where was David?

As I picked at the pile of shellfish my mother set in front of me, I pondered calling Detective Booth. Maybe he could explain why a guy who was supposed to be behind bars in the Clark County Detention Center was feeling up cocktail waitresses at a private party on the Strip. And … had he followed me? I couldn't help glancing around every few seconds.

"Where's David, dear?" my mother asked when we'd moved on to the lobster course. "Didn't you say he'd be joining us?"

"He's running late," I said. "He's—"

The theme from *The Good, the Bad and the Ugly* suddenly blared from my purse.

"I need to take this," I said, pushing my chair back. "I'll be right back."

Easing myself up and limping away from the table, I managed to answer my cell phone before David gave up.

"Where are you?"

"The airport."

"*What?*"

"I'm sorry, Copper, but it's an emergency. Rebecca—"

Rebecca. Not again!

"There's trouble with the pregnancy, and—"

The conversation did not end well, but how could it? David's baby mama needed him, and he was headed to New York to deliver the required support. If a murderer was after me, I'd just have to deal with it on my own. Not to mention my family, the Morningthunder situation, and Marilyn's memorial service.

"I'll be back tomorrow night, Copper," David said. "This is something I have to take care of in person—"

"I need you in person," I said. "Right now. Not tomorrow night."

"I'm sorry, but—"

"Being sorry won't hack it this time. Now is when I need you, and now is when you're gone. I should have known this baby arrangement would never work."

I hung up before either of us could say anything more. Stay away forever, I was thinking.

Somehow I made it through dinner. Mr. Cluff paid for everything, even Graham's multiple margaritas. At least my mother had found a nice upstanding boyfriend, I thought. She was way ahead of Dad and me. Sierra and Michael seemed to do okay, too. They took turns with Nicky and looked out for each other. Why couldn't I find a relationship like that?

As I drove back to my apartment, I sucked air every time I caught sight of a dark blue sedan. Even though Sean had no way of knowing that I was driving a black Chrysler, I couldn't convince my body to let go of the fear that he might be following me. As I reached Maryland Parkway, I knew I was in for a sleepless night unless—damn that David! He should be here with me, not winging his way to Scarsdale. He should be helping me sort things out—

I swung into a strip mall and pulled to a stop next to a fast-food chicken restaurant. As much as I wanted to avoid calling Booth, I couldn't bear the thought of lying awake all night wondering whether Sean was out looking for me. Why had such a monster been set free? Why hadn't anyone warned me?

"Metro Homicide. Booth speaking." He answered on the first ring.

"This is Copper Black. I—"

"I was about to call you."

"About Sean? I already know. I—"

"You know he's been arrested for Marilyn Weaver's murder?"

What? I was too shocked to voice the word.

"He's also being charged with rape, extortion, arson, and grand larceny."

I still hadn't found my voice.

"And attempted murder, of course. Your information—and the file from the Parks Academy you provided—was key."

"He's—he's in jail?" I managed to ask.

"Picked up half an hour ago."

"But I—I saw him at the Monaco—"

"Yep. That's where we nabbed him."

My mind jumped back to the scene at Liqmi. I can't say it wasn't just a bit delightful to imagine a couple of Metro cops relieving Sean of his martini and handcuffing him in front of all those beautiful people.

"No more bail for him," Booth said. "He won't be getting out again for a long, long time."

Suddenly, everything was so obvious. I thought back to the day I'd met Sean. He'd been so eager to take me back to the Weavers' house, and he'd made it ridiculously easy for me to find Marilyn's body. I wondered at the time if I'd been set up. Obviously, my hunch was dead on. The guy was a psychopath, and I was lucky to be alive.

"It's great that Sean's off the streets for good," I said, "but I've got about a thousand questions—"

"I can't take the time now, Ms. Black, but hang tight. We can talk more soon."

"Thanks, Detective Booth," I said. "I'm glad this is finally over."

"Well, I wouldn't go that far," Booth said. "I've been a cop way too long to applaud before the fat lady sings. But you can sleep better now, at least."

As I drove the rest of the way to the vicarage, I suddenly realized I was humming. That realization brought a smile to my face.

Hallelujah!

For the first time in what felt like a century but was really not even two weeks, I felt like my old carefree self. Even the fact that David was off canoodling with his still-not-ex-wife couldn't keep my spirits from rising.

Marilyn Weaver's murder had been solved! My would-be assassin was behind bars for good! In addition, I'd cracked the mystery behind Willie Morningthunder's shooting and saved the girls at the Parks Academy from further abuse. Tomorrow, I'd write the story, and Greg Langenfeld would have no choice but to recognize my brilliance and reward me with a column of my own. Yes, my nose was still broken, and my bruise count was up from yesterday. My boyfriend had let me down, but all in all, things were looking up.

Nice, too, I realized as I pulled into the driveway behind Michael's Jetta, was that Detective Booth would never again direct those unnerving words in my direction: "I've got a few more questions." I could almost like the guy now, or at least respect him. He'd probably suspected all along that Sean was the murderer, but he couldn't do anything without evidence. I just hoped I'd helped him amass enough information to convince twelve jurors beyond a reasonable doubt.

The only thing that dampened my newly restored spirits—besides David's unexpected field trip to New York, of course—was the thought of poor old Oscar the tortoise. Even though I couldn't technically be held responsible for the consequences of Sean's crimes, I couldn't shake the feeling that I'd contributed to Oscar's death. Oddly, I didn't have the slightest compunction about the fate of the Nash house, and only a tiny pang for all the vaporized carnivorous plants.

It's all about living things, I thought as I stepped into the living room at the vicarage, and the ones that have faces rank higher than the ones that have leaves. Even plants with mouths couldn't inspire the wave of sadness I felt for a 50-year-old tortoise with a taste for mangos. I dreaded the day I'd meet Thor, the tortoise guy, again. I had no doubt that in his eyes, I was a killer.

My father was sitting alone on the sofa when I walked in.

"Hi," I said. "Where's—everybody else?"

"Michael's in his study, and Sierra's putting Nicky to bed. Your mother and Patrick are taking in a late show on the Strip somewhere."

What about Graham? I wanted to ask, but something in my father's demeanor held me back. I sat down next to him.

"Are you okay?" I asked.

"I should be asking you that, Copper," my dad said.

"Oh, I'm—" Somehow, for the first time in days, I couldn't bring myself to say "fine."

I sighed. "I'll be okay again one of these days. I really am getting there."

Dad patted my knee. "Your mom and I sure hope so. We worry about you."

"Dad—"

I paused, then let it out. "Where's Graham?"

"He's at the hotel," Dad said. "I dropped him off."

His tone was gloomy, and I had no idea how to respond. I'd never been taught the rules for what to say to your father when he's having a lover's spat with his boyfriend. To fill the void, I slipped off my shoes.

"We—Graham and I—we've broken up," my dad said.

"He *dumped* you?" The words jumped out before I could edit them.

"No, Copper," Dad said. "I told him things weren't working."

"*You* dumped *him*?" Again, the words just popped out.

"Not dumped." He paused, then shook his head and sighed. "Okay, yes. I dumped him."

Our eyes met, and I could swear his were glistening a little more than usual.

"I'm sorry, Dad," I said. "I'm really sorry."

"I'm fine, kiddo," he said. "Or at least I'm getting there."

Damn. That was my line.

"He didn't deserve you." Once again, my mouth acted on its own.

Dad chuckled. "Sounds like the sort of thing I used to say to you when you were going through a rough breakup in high school."

"It's true. You're way too good for him."

"You're way too good for David, too," he said.

I sighed and hung my head. I didn't want to admit it, but David's latest escapade was all too easy to interpret as immoral behavior—

"But then," Dad went on, "you're way too good for any man."

That made me smile in spite of myself.

"You're way too good for any man, too, Daddy-o," I said. I paused, then looked him square in the face before repeating another set of words he'd been so generous with in my youth. "I'm proud of you."

My dad smiled and planted a kiss on my cheek.

"I'm proud of you, too, Copper," he said. "But that doesn't mean I don't worry."

I knew he was referring to my relationship with David again. Even though it had heterosexuality going for it, it still seemed less mainstream than my dad's dalliance with Graham. Could I really share David with Rebecca? I didn't see how. I also didn't see how I had ever been crazy enough to think I could have a relationship with a baby without having to interact with its mother. Love might be able to conquer a lot, but a triangle with a kid in the mix? I had serious doubts. But there was no time to think about David now. I forced my mind to shift gears.

"I do have some good news," I said. Just then Michael walked into the room.

"Willie's better," he said. "Just got off the phone with him. He might even be released from the hospital tomorrow. What's your good news?"

"Sean DuBois has been arrested for Marilyn's murder," I said. "Along with a bunch of other crimes."

"I guess I'm not surprised," Michael said. "It'll be hard on Curtis, but at some point it will at least help him have some closure."

Sierra appeared, and Michael filled her in about Willie and Sean.

"Damn, that's a huge relief," Sierra said, flopping down into the big club chair next to the sofa. "The thought of that murdering maniac masquerading as Marilyn's bereaved son tomorrow at her memorial service—"

"Now, if we only knew who shot Willie," Michael said, "Things would really be—"

"But I *do* know who did it," I said. "And I even know why!"

Chapter 30

Of course, once I revealed that I knew what was fomenting the violence at the homeless center building site, I had no choice but to reveal Jenna Bartolo's scheme and my resulting adventure at Liqmi. By the time I crawled into bed, it was well after midnight. Even so, I set my alarm for five. I needed to get to *The Light* early if I was going to write my story about Frank Bartolo, get all my regular work done, and still make it to the Anna Roberts Parks Academy in time for Marilyn's memorial service.

At least Sierra had invited me for breakfast.

"Michael and I both have early appointments, too," she'd said, "and you still look like you need some TLC." She didn't say anything about David, but I knew she was referring to his absence at least as much as to my fresh crop of bruises. Whatever motivated her concern, the offer of early-morning toast and coffee was comforting.

Breakfast wasn't the only thing waiting in the kitchen when I staggered down my staircase at dawn. *The Light* lay on the table, a screaming headline sprawled across the front page.

"BARTOLO LINKED TO MORNINGTHUNDER SHOOTING"

"You were right," Sierra said, handing me a mug of coffee. "That bastard's got a lot of explaining to do."

He's not the only one, I fumed to myself as I looked at the byline. *Mary Beth Sweeney.*

Damn her! She stole my story!

Still hot, I started reading the article. Without a mention of our little soiree in Frank's secret suite at the Monaco, Mary Beth laid out the facts connecting the casino mogul with the Indian chief. My anger subsided as I marveled at how much she had managed to accomplish between leaving the nightclub party and the final deadline for the morning paper. I'd been stupidly naïve to think that a story this juicy would keep until morning. A picture of Mary Beth hollering "Hold the presses!" flashed across my mind. That sort of thing didn't happen in real life—or did it?

Not that it mattered now. I sighed and set the paper down without turning to the back page to read the rest. At least I didn't have to rush off to work anymore.

"You want to ride to the memorial service with Michael and me?" Sierra asked as she set a plate of toast on the table. "We'll leave here around one. Your dad's coming, and so are your mom and Patrick."

"Everybody's going? Why?"

"Well, they offered to stay home with Nicky, but I told them they'd be missing the event of the decade if they did. There hasn't been a funeral this high-profile since George Khan slipped his wife a lethal dose of strychnine and shot himself with a hunting rifle."

Another Vegas tale I'd never heard, but the details would have to wait.

"I think I'll—"

Just then Michael entered the room carrying Nicky.

"Copper!" Nicky cried, holding his arms out to me.

"Sorry, Nick, but Copper can't hold you yet," Michael said, depositing him in his high chair. "Bruises and little boys don't mix."

"Copper!" Nicky yelled again, but Sierra distracted him with a bowl of Cheerios.

"So, Ms. Newswoman," Michael said, pulling out the chair next to me. "Congratulations on your byline!"

"What are you talking about?"

Michael picked up the paper and flipped it over. Pointing at a spot near the bottom of the page, he held it out to me.

"Okay, maybe that's not called a byline, but—"

Grabbing the paper from his hand, I stared at the italic type at the end of the story.

"Copper Black contributed to this story."

Whoa! She gave me some credit!

"You're right. That's not a byline," I said.

"Well, it's your name in print, connected with the story of the hour," Michael said. "I'm impressed."

"Me, too," Sierra said, setting a bowl of scrambled eggs on the table and sitting down. "You managed to out Frank Bartolo and live to tell about it. You haven't been in Las Vegas long enough to know just how amazing that is."

Even though she was just trying to be colorful, Sierra's words sent a cold current down my spine. Had Jenna Bartolo really put my life in danger by sending me to the Liqmi party? I'd escaped with only bruises to show for it, but Sierra was making it seem as though it was as close a call as my brush with death at the Nash house.

It's at times like these that I always think I should be teaching kindergarten in Connecticut. I have serious doubts that I'm really cut out to be digging into the sordid pasts of people who solve their problems with guns and poison or matches and paint thinner. Why can't I just embrace my inner wimpiness, invest in a denim smock, and lead a safe life among the crayons and paste containers?

I know the answer, of course. I'd go insane in a humdrum job and probably turn into a psycho killer myself. I'm stuck trying to prove myself as a competent journalist, even if it means spending a third of my life feeling like I'm about to wet my pants.

"So, you want a ride to the memorial service?" Sierra asked.

"I'll have to go directly from work," I said. "Thanks anyway, but I'll meet you at the school."

"I don't know what'll be happening afterward, so we'll just play it by ear," Michael said. "The main thing is to be there for Curtis."

Given his dalliance with Jenna Bartolo, I wasn't sure Curtis deserved the consideration Michael was so eager to dish out, but I didn't say anything. If there was going to be a wake at the Weaver house, I figured I'd be able to handle it. I just wouldn't go looking in any closets.

"I can't tell you what a relief it is to know what was behind the violence at the homeless center," Michael said. "I owe you one, Copper."

"It sure is weird that you have Jenna to thank, too," I said.

"I'll be thanking her more if she can guarantee the next installment of our construction loan," he said. "Without it, the homeless center is dead in the water."

"Did you ever find out who those bones belonged to?"

Michael sighed. "No. The only things we know for sure are that the bones belonged to an adult human and were probably buried within the last fifty years."

"Really?" Sierra said. "So it *could* be Jimmy Hoffa."

Michael shrugged. "Homicide's gotten involved, but I have no idea what they think. All I care about is when we can start building again."

Just then, my mind jumped to the bowling ball bag we'd discovered in the wreckage of the Nash house. I wondered if Detective Booth would ever tell me what was inside. I also wondered if he'd be at Marilyn's memorial service. Did cops go to the funerals of victims whose cases they solved? I had no idea. At least Sean wouldn't be there.

And neither would David. That thought saddened me as I kissed Nicky on the top of the head, limped out to my car, and headed toward *The Light*.

Within five minutes of walking inside the building, I realized that Sierra had been right on target in describing Marilyn's memorial service as "high-profile." By the time I reached my cube, I'd been offered three rides.

It was strange, really. I mean, several far more famous people had died in Las Vegas since my arrival. Tony Columbo, for example. Several casinos on the Strip had turned out their lights for sixty seconds when the beloved old crooner fell asleep in his bathtub and never woke up, but I never heard anything about a funeral. The untimely drug-induced death of "celebutante" Magdalena Patrington-Hawes was another headline generator, but if she had a funeral, it must have been a family-only affair.

The open-to-the-public memorial for Marilyn Weaver, on the other hand, seemed to be the social event of the season—or at least a rare opportunity to peek inside the Anna Roberts Parks Academy. As I picked up my mail and made my way to my cube, I was surrounded by coworkers clad in somber hues. Unless half of them had coincidentally decided to wear dressy black ensembles on "casual Friday," *The Light* was going to empty out to ghost town levels around one o'clock.

The exodus actually began around noon. The wind was already whistling through the empty halls when I went to the lunchroom for coffee around twelve fifteen, and I began thinking I might have to hike a mile or two if I didn't hightail it down to Henderson myself and find a decent parking place. My boss, who was wearing regular jeans and a red polo shirt, seemed to have no interest in celebrity funerals, but he also didn't put up any argument when I asked him if I could leave early.

"We're paralyzed around here, anyway, so go ahead," he said. "Have fun!"

I wasn't quite sure how to take that last comment.

"Thanks," I said. "I actually wish I didn't have to go—"

"You're the one person in this place who actually has a good reason to go, Copper. For everyone else, it's just journalistic voyeurism. For you—well, couldn't you use some closure?"

I nodded, even though I suspected I was really just a voyeur like the rest.

"Thanks, Chris," I said. "I promise I'll make up the time."

He waved me off, and I stumped downstairs to my borrowed Chrysler. It still hurt to walk, but I took it as an encouraging sign that my limp was decidedly less pronounced. I felt as though I was already part of a funeral procession as I rolled out of *The Light*'s parking lot and joined the line of cars heading toward the freeway.

As I approached the campus, I began wishing I had taken Sierra up on her offer to give me a ride. Cars lined both sides of Bermuda Street for blocks. From the look of things, I'd have to park up near St. Rose Parkway and hoof it at least half a mile. I glanced at the temperature readout on the dashboard, even though I already knew the depressing information it would provide: 108 degrees. I'd be a steaming, sodden mess by the time I made it to Beeman Hall, if I didn't keel over on my way.

When I neared the corner of Bermuda and Bruner, I saw a couple of guys in Day-Glo vests directing traffic to a vacant lot that was already half full of cars. Parking there would still mean a hike, but at least it was closer to the main entrance than anything available on the street. I pulled in and, following the instructions of a couple more guys in orange vests, I parked next to a black pickup truck. A Volkswagen Beetle pulled in next to me. As I trudged back to the street trying to avoid getting too dusty, I counted the rows of parked vehicles to make sure I could return to my car without any unnecessary detours. My body was still complaining, and every step counted.

By the time I reached the school's entrance gate, I was walking with a throng. Families with little children in sun hats braved the heat next to middle-aged and elderly couples. In spite of the temperature, most of the teenagers in the crowd were clad in navy blue Parks Academy blazers.

The heat was easier to bear on the campus because the trees provided some shade. They were also gaily decorated with colorful banners and garlands. If I hadn't known I was headed to a memorial service, I might well have guessed the school was in celebration mode. The fluttering colors reminded me of a Renaissance fair.

Sticking with the crowd, I arrived not at Beeman Hall, but at a building bearing the sign "Bennett and Bangstrom Gymnasium." I should have realized that the auditorium wouldn't be large enough.

A long black limousine occupied the loading zone in front of the gym's main doors. A placard on the dashboard read "CRAWFORD FAMILY," and a woman with half-inch-long, bleached blonde hair in a sleeveless black dress held a wheelchair ready next to the door. I watched as an elderly lady with a helmet of lacquered silver hair and dark, rhinestone-encrusted glasses struggled out of the limo and into the chair.

"This is so unnecessary," I heard her say as I drew nearer. "I can walk perfectly well, Charlene."

Charlene.

Was her last name Crawford? I realized I had no idea, but it didn't matter. This woman couldn't be the same person. Marilyn's niece had long dark brown hair.

As the woman spun the wheelchair around to enter the gym, I

caught sight of her glasses. Marilyn's niece wore glasses like that, I remembered: narrow with dark tortoise-shell rims. Suddenly, she was glaring straight at me, squinting in the sun.

Damn! What a transformation! Except for the glasses and bright red lipstick, she looked totally different.

"Hello, Copper," Charlene said.

"I—I'm so sorry about your aunt," I managed.

"Thanks *a lot*," she said.

It sounded almost accusatory, but before I could say anything else, she turned and moved away, propelling the wheelchair into the gym.

Two other people emerged from the limo before it drove off. The first was a stylish forty-something woman with a short chestnut bob and a perfect tan. The other was a wiry guy in a cowboy hat. They followed Charlene and the old lady between two enormous floral wreaths and on into the gym. I was about to follow when another limo pulled up. The sign on this one said "WEAVER."

Ah, Curtis is here, I thought, but the first person to emerge was a tall woman in a long blue dress whose face was obscured by a large floppy straw hat and an enormous pair of dark glasses. A shorter, chubbier woman in a pantsuit climbed out after her and unfurled a pink parasol over her curly gray hair.

At last, Curtis emerged from the sleek black car. He looked over-heated in his dark suit, and he squinted in the harsh sunlight.

Because ... no sunglasses. Damn! That was my fault. I still had the pair I'd accidentally swiped from his bathroom. I really should return them, I told myself. They looked expensive, and now that Sean was locked up and the case closed, I had no reason not to return them. Poor Curtis looked like he could use them, too. Not only was the sun blindingly bright, he looked dangerously close to tears. I watched him as he walked past the giant flower arrangements. The two women—his sisters, perhaps?—almost looked as though they were keeping him vertical as they moved into the gym.

"Copper! Copper!"

Nicky had just rolled up in a stroller powered by my mother. Sierra, Mr. Cluff, and my father followed right behind.

"Hi!" I said. "Did you have to walk far?"

"No, thanks to Michael," Sierra said. "We got VIP parking because he's giving the benediction."

"Copper!" Nicky said again, and this time I was close enough to exchange high fives.

"Let's get out of the sun and grab some seats," Sierra said.

After we'd received programs from a polite Asian girl in a school blazer and plaid pleated skirt, we headed inside the gym. The smell of flowers enveloped us in the cool entrance hall, and we walked between two walls of floral wreaths and arrangements toward the gym door.

"Holy cow," Sierra whispered as we moved through the doorway, and I'm not entirely sure a similar expression of amazement didn't slip out of my mouth, too. While the basketball hoops left no doubt we were in a gymnasium, I have never seen such a fabulous decorating job.

Miles of ribbon garlands and scores of colorful banners hung from the rafters, repeating the festive theme from the trees outside. Bleachers stepped down from the sides of the room to surround hundreds of white chairs lined up in rows facing a large dais, which was bedecked with more flower arrangements, several flags in stanchions, and a large portrait of Marilyn projected on a screen suspended overhead. In front of the dais, a small student orchestra was playing "Candle in the Wind."

"Sweet song," my mother said as we moved forward. "Reminds me of Princess Diana."

And Marilyn Monroe, I couldn't help thinking. Were Marilyns always tragic?

More than half the seats were already occupied, and people were streaming in steadily. Several sections were roped off and labeled with signs. "RESERVED FOR BOARD MEMBERS" read one. "RESERVED FOR FACULTY" read another. The first three rows in the center section were labeled "RESERVED FOR FAMILY MEMBERS." Charlene and the other people she'd arrived with were sitting in the third row at one end, where it was easy to park a wheelchair. Curtis and his two female companions had chosen front-row center seats.

"Looks like we can get closer to the front if we sit on the bleachers," Sierra said. As we made our way forward, I noticed that the first row of the bleachers was cordoned off and labeled "RESERVED FOR STUDENT BODY." Fortunately, we found enough room for five adults and a stroller at the end of the second row.

"Perfect," Sierra said. She pointed toward a nearby set of double doors marked "Exit." "We can escape easily if 'his nibs' starts making a commotion."

A portrait of Marilyn—the same one that was on the big screen—was printed in color on the front of the program. "Marilyn Canaday Weaver, 1952 – 2010" read the caption underneath it, followed in smaller letters by "Portrait by Anna Kalajian, Class of 2012." A high school student's work, and Marilyn looked better than George Washington in the hands of Gilbert Stuart.

"That orchestra is really good for a high school," I heard Mr. Cluff whisper to my mom as the ensemble launched into "You'll Never Walk Alone."

I opened the program and glanced down the list of songs, poems, and other tributes. There was even an interpretive dance in the lineup, and a "photo montage." Damn! Mr. Rice hadn't been exaggerating.

School wasn't even in session, and this impressive production had been pulled together in less than a week. I couldn't help thinking that Marilyn would be proud.

Within minutes, nearly every unreserved seat in the gymnasium was occupied.

"We got here not a moment too soon," my mother said.

Just then, the double doors Sierra had identified as a convenient escape route swung open. Mr. Rice, dapper in a black tuxedo, led a long single-file line of teenagers in white robes into the gym. They climbed the stairs onto the dais and took their places on three tiers of risers at the back. When they were all assembled, they looked like a gospel choir.

I scanned the faces. Sure enough, I recognized both Kelly Baskin and Chanel Torres. They were standing next to each other in the middle of the first row.

The final notes of "You'll Never Walk Alone" were still hanging in the air when Mr. Rice raised his baton. The choir began with a hum, a sweet harmony that carried over the gym and instantly silenced all the subdued conversations. The hum swelled, and I could swear the choir was swaying ever so slightly when Chanel's clear soprano filled the room.

It heartened me that Chanel was there. As horrible as her experience with Sean had been, the worst was over. No matter what—even a baby—she'd survive. I just hoped that babies were in her distant future—that her dreams of becoming a professional singer still had a chance.

"*Swing low, sweet chariot,*" she sang, "*Coming for to carry me home.*" Halfway through the first stanza, the other girls in the front row joined in. With the first refrain, the rest of the choir joined the chorus. The doors at the far end of the gymnasium opened, and a double-file line of girls and boys, all clad in their school uniforms, led a procession down the center aisle toward the dais.

Clearly, the entire student body had turned out for the memorial service, which struck me as pretty amazing. If my high school principal had died before Labor Day, would I have cut my vacation short for his funeral? Probably not. I seriously doubted any of my classmates would have, either. The show of support offered concrete evidence that the Parks Academy was a truly remarkable school. Could it survive the loss of its founding personality? I hoped so. The world—and Las Vegas—needed more schools capable of inspiring the kind of loyalty this place engendered so successfully. And more schools should do as good a job of teaching their students how to sing.

As the choir belted out "Swing Low, Sweet Chariot" and the audience joined in, the old spiritual's unifying power washed over me. By the time the students reached the front of the dais, everyone in the gym was swaying and singing. Splitting ranks, the boys and girls filed to their seats on the front row of the bleachers. Still singing and swaying, they remained standing as the faculty walked down the aisle. Clad in academic gowns, hoods, and mortarboards, they, too, sang as they slowly walked to their seats in the center section.

Board members followed the teachers, followed by Michael, a rabbi I'd once met, and—*Willie Morningthunder?*

What was he doing here? The question must have been obvious on my face when I turned to Sierra.

"Oh, I forgot to tell you," she whispered. "Michael was visiting Willie at the hospital when the school called. They wanted clergymen of all faiths represented. Willie was about to be released, so Michael asked if he felt well enough to represent the Native American community."

Willie's left arm was in a sling, but he was still awe-inspiring in his full Indian regalia. Behind him walked a Greek Orthodox priest, a woman in a long black cape, a man in a turban, and a few other people who looked like they had connections with various versions of God. They all seemed to know the words to "Swing Low, Sweet Chariot."

If you get to heaven before I do
Coming for to carry me home
Tell all my friends that I'm coming, too
Coming for to carry me home.

Somehow I'd never realized the ecumenical power of that song. Somehow I'd also forgotten the power of Mr. Cluff's baritone. Hearing it snatched me back to St. Mark's Episcopal Church in New Canaan, where he'd been my Sunday school teacher back when I was nine years old. Everybody always commented at coffee hour that if God hadn't heard our prayers, at least he'd heard Patrick Cluff. Fortunately, his voice wasn't too bad, and most of the time he sang on key.

After we had all finished singing the last "Coming for to carry me home," everyone sat down. Without a cue that I could detect, a boy stood up from his seat on the front row of the bleachers and walked to the dais. He was short—could he really be a high school student?

I looked at my program, but before I could read it, a man in a cap and gown spoke into the microphone.

"Armando Cardenas," he said. "Class of 2014."

An eighth grader. That explained it.

Armando had no notes. He stepped in front of the microphone, and his high, clear voice flew out over the audience like birdsong.

"She was my friend," he said.

"When no one could see me,
She lifted me into the sunlight.
When no one could hear me,
She spoke for me.
Now—too soon—it's my turn to speak for her.

We—her students—must be her voice now.
We must be her hands, her feet, her heart, her spirit.
In us, she will sing, she will dance, she will sculpt and write and paint.
Through us, she lives on.
I love you, Marilyn Weaver.
You are, and always will be, my friend."

He had me at "She was my friend," damn it. I glanced around. I wasn't the only one in need of a tissue.

The photo montage listed in the program turned out to be far more than a slide show. As a black-and-white photo of a bald baby in a long white christening dress faded in, the choir began singing.

"Hail to Seattle, pearl of Puget Sound ... "

One image faded into another: a tiny blonde cowgirl astride a pony, a group of happy children playing on a beach, a smiling girl with blonde pigtails blowing out birthday candles, a Girl Scout receiving an award, a high school prom princess in pink chiffon.

I was still staring at a windblown Marilyn waving from a white convertible when—

"Horseshit!"

The outburst seemed to come from where Charlene was sitting next to the woman in the wheelchair. The choir sang on, but the audience murmured a shocked response.

"Bless you!" I heard someone call out, followed by the sound of chairs scraping and some hissed words I couldn't make out.

"It was only a sneeze," my mother whispered.

"Sure didn't sound like a sneeze to me," Sierra whispered back. "But the 'bless you' was a brilliant save."

As the audience quieted back down, the choir launched into a college song I didn't recognize. I decided it must be Vassar's as photos of

Marilyn on the Vassar campus and at graduation appeared.

Next came "New York, New York," and images of Marilyn in Manhattan. After a montage of pictures taken everywhere from San Francisco and Chicago to Rio, Paris, and Rome, the scenes turned to Las Vegas. To the strains of "Home Means Nevada," the history of the Anna Roberts Parks Academy appeared on the screen in photographs, from ground-breaking and tree-planting ceremonies to classrooms, performances, and visits by celebrities.

The picture show ended with a flurry of recent photos: Marilyn speaking at an assembly, Marilyn at graduation. Marilyn with a senator, the mayor, the governor. Marilyn smiling with students. In the last picture, Marilyn stood alone in front of Beeman Hall. A setting sun bathed her face in gold and caught an arresting, wistful smile. It was the perfect image to end the presentation, especially since Marilyn was gazing at something beyond the photographer's left shoulder. *The things we'll never know,* I thought. That's what she's looking at.

As the screen faded to black, I happened to rest my gaze on the bleachers facing me on the other side of the audience occupying the sea of white chairs.

In the row at the same level as my own—one tier behind the students—was a familiar high flat forehead. Could it be—? Yes! Detective Booth's distinctive visage was instantly recognizable. So he *had* come!

Again I wondered whether it was standard practice for police detectives to attend services for murder victims whose cases they had investigated. Or did Detective Booth just want to pay his respects? Given the local hero status of Marilyn Weaver, it was certainly a possible explanation.

I couldn't tell whether Booth had noticed me. He seemed to be looking at Curtis, or perhaps the other family members in the first three rows. Maybe I should look for him after the ceremony, I thought. Now that the case was all wrapped up, it might be a good idea to thank him for all his hard work. As nerve-racking as the investigation had been for me, I had to give Booth credit for nailing the murderer.

I was still lost in my thoughts about Detective Booth as the president of the board of trustees finished his tribute to Marilyn and the orchestra played the opening bars of "Memories."

Chanel's beautiful voice filled the gym again, but before she could finish the second line—*crash!* Another disturbance from the family section.

I couldn't see what had made the noise, but no one missed what followed. Charlene stood up. Her head bowed and her shoulders heaving, she squeezed past the wheelchair. As she walked by the end of the bleachers, I caught sight of her tear-streaked face. She'd taken her glasses off, and she was mopping her eyes with a tissue.

Oh, poor thing, I thought. She didn't just lose an aunt. Marilyn was more like a mother to her. Charlene pushed through the door and left it to slam shut behind her.

The service ended with words from each of the religious figures. Michael and Willie gave the final benediction, an antiphonal reading of the Twenty-Third Psalm alternating with a Lakota funeral prayer.

The recessional was "You Raise Me Up." As the students filed out singing the words, I could see tears glistening on most faces. Emotion didn't muffle their voices, though. They sang like the professionals they were on the road to becoming. Hell, as trite as it sounds, they sang like angels.

Once again, the entire audience joined in, and Mr. Cluff wasn't even the loudest. As the final notes poured forth, I couldn't help feeling that Marilyn was actually present, as though her students had—for one last moment—called her back.

As the last singer passed through the double doors at the back of the gym, the music stopped. As hot as it was outdoors, a sudden chill rolled across the room. The air conditioning kicking on? If that's all it was, the timing couldn't have been more perfect. If she had returned for one last ethereal visit, Marilyn had definitely left the building now.

Chapter 31

"That was probably the nicest memorial service I've ever attended," my father said as we moved back outside with the exiting crowd. "I can't help wishing I'd known Mrs. Weaver."

"Me, too," my mom said. "Those kids had me in tears."

"Canonized by children," Mr. Cluff said. "That's got to be the highest level of sainthood of all."

My family took off after a quick stop for a cold drink at the long tables set up under the trees in front of Beeman Hall. Michael had another appointment, Sierra said, and Nicky deserved a trip to the dinosaur park for his stellar behavior during the service.

"You were great!" I said, planting a kiss on the top of his head. "Say hi to the stegosaurus for me."

"Copper come too!" he yelled, which made me think about what Mr. Cluff had said about Marilyn. I'll never merit sainthood, but I do enjoy the sincere adoration that only my nephew can provide.

"Give my best to Willie," I said. "I'm glad he's on the road to recovery."

Maybe I should leave, too, I thought as I watched them move off toward their VIP parking place. If I caught up with them, I could get a ride back to my car.

Just then, I caught sight of Detective Booth at the other end of the table closest to me. He'd put on a pair of super-dark aviator sunglasses, but they were hardly a disguise. I headed toward him, weaving through the crowd.

"Copper!"

I turned to find myself face to face with Curtis Weaver, still flanked by the two women he'd arrived with.

"I didn't expect to see you here!" Curtis said. "I thought you were still—are you okay?"

"Oh, I'm fine," I said. "I'm just—how are *you*?"

Hot, if nothing else, I noticed. The man's face was strawberry red, and the light was still bothering his eyes.

"Want some iced tea, Curt?" The woman in blue interrupted.

"Oh! I'd like you to meet my sister Edith," Curtis said.

She frowned, but she held out a hand.

"And this is my sister-in-law, Patricia."

"Trish," the other woman said from under her pink parasol. "Hi."

"I'll get you some tea," Edith said, moving off toward the table.

As she did, she revealed an approaching wheelchair. In it sat the elderly woman with stiff silver hair. Charlene, looking remarkably recovered, was pushing.

"Don't worry, Aunt Rosemary," Curtis said, bending down to peck the old lady's cheek. "We'll get you out of this heat soon."

"I'm not worried, Curt," Aunt Rosemary said. "You're the one who needs some air conditioning. Don't you have a hat—or at least some sunglasses?"

"Oh, my God," I said. "I've actually got your sunglasses in my car."

"What are you talking about?" Curtis shot me a baffled look. "How did you get my glasses?"

"I've been meaning to return them to you," I said, and the words kept tumbling out. "I picked them up by mistake when I was at your house. But then, with everything that happened—"

Curtis squinted at me. "I'm not missing any sunglasses," he said. "Except the ones I left in the limo just now."

"But I'm sure these are yours," I said. "Aviator style—"

Curtis shrugged.

"Well, they must be Marilyn's, then. I'll get them to you."

Just then, Edith returned with a plastic cup of iced tea. As she moved closer to Curtis, I found myself clearly on the outside of a tight family circle. I might as well leave, I told myself. No reason to stand around in the heat any longer.

As I moved back through the crowd, I kept an eye out for Detective Booth. By the time I reached the gym, however, I hadn't spotted him again. It didn't matter, I told myself. I'd have plenty of time later to call him to get the lowdown on the investigations.

As I turned to head for the main gate, I felt a hand on my shoulder. Whipping around, I found myself face to face with—

"Charlene!"

"I'm glad I caught you. Curtis remembered that those *are* his glasses, after all, and he asked me to get them from you. Where are you parked?"

"Not exactly nearby," I said. "I'm in a dirt lot a few blocks away."

"My truck's right behind the gym," Charlene said. "Come on. I'll give you a ride."

She strode off but slowed down as soon as she realized she was in the company of a quasi-invalid.

"I heard about your—accident," she said when I had caught up. "Sounded pretty bad."

Purdy bad. She still talked like the cowgirl she was, even though she no longer looked like one.

"I'm better now," I said. "Couple more days and I'll be fine."

Charlene stopped next to a beefy white pickup and fished keys out of her handbag. She unlocked the driver's door while I walked to the other side. I almost burned my hand opening the door.

"Oh, sorry," Charlene said, referring to the leather jacket occupying the passenger seat. Just before she grabbed it, I saw the back.

WOLLENSKY.

The name was spelled out in big embroidered letters in a half circle over an eagle with outstretched wings.

Wollensky. So that was her last name.

A big shiny belt buckle lay under the jacket. Charlene picked it up and motioned me to climb in. Then, thank God, she turned on the ignition, and the air conditioner roared to life.

"I've still gotta deal with all my horse stuff," she said.

She leaned over and opened the glove compartment in front of me. A small handgun slid forward.

A gun!

I told myself that all cowboys have guns, but it still unnerved me. This was no rifle, and it wasn't a Wild Bill six-shooter, either. This one looked like the sort of sleek little weapon the wife of a mobster might keep in her Hermès purse.

Charlene quickly shoved the gun to the back of the glove compartment and pushed the buckle in behind it.

"My belt buckle," she said as she snapped the compartment closed. "I took first in my division."

"I'm so glad you were able to finish, with everything that happened," I said. "Your aunt would have been so proud. I'm so sorry she never knew."

Ignoring my comment, Charlene twisted her head around and narrowed her eyes against the raking late afternoon rays.

"Damn the sun!"

Charlene backed out, and we followed a line of departing vehicles around the traffic circle toward the gate.

As we passed by the security kiosk, the guard waved. I waved back, but Charlene just gripped the wheel and squinted. We were headed directly into the sun now.

"Which way?" She sounded angry.

"Left," I said.

Charlene grunted and wiped her eyes behind her glasses with her fingertips.

She's just distraught, I told myself. Poor thing.

"Losing someone you were so close to—so suddenly—" I said. "I can't imagine, and I'm so sorry—"

Charlene slammed on the brake as we approached a stop sign, flinging us both forward.

"I know she was like a mother to you," I went on, trying to be comforting. "Some people leave such an impression on the world. You carry on a wonderful legacy—"

Charlene stamped on the gas, and the truck lurched forward with a screech.

"God *damn* it!" As I stared at her, tears sprang to Charlene's eyes.

"I—I'm—" I paused, completely at a loss for words.

"Oh, hell," Charlene said.

"Look," I said, "I didn't mean to—make things worse—"

"God, the sun is so freaking bright. How do you stand it?"

"This is the worst time of day," I said. "Oh—turn left at the next corner."

Slowing abruptly, Charlene made the turn and pulled into the dirt lot. It was already more than three-quarters empty.

"Mine's that black Chrysler," I said. "Or at least it's black under the dust."

"Look, I'm sorry," Charlene said as the truck crunched slowly over the gravel. "I'm just—I'm just—"

"You don't need to apologize," I said. "It's such a tragedy—I'm so sorry—"

Charlene flashed me a fierce look, but she quickly corralled it into a forced smile.

"Yeah, thanks."

"Marilyn asked me to write a story about the school's first graduating class, and I think it's more important than ever that I write the story now," I went on. "The world should know about her amazing work and generosity. She was so much more than a school principal to those kids. She was a genuine mentor."

Charlene let out a grunt that I took for agreement.

"I met two of the seniors the other day," I continued. "I knew they respected her, but I didn't realize until now that it was much more than that. Those kids *loved* her. Anyone who can inspire that kind of devotion in teenagers is very, very special."

Charlene pulled to a stop behind my car and turned her red-rimmed eyes to meet mine. For a split second, we just stared at each other. Then—

"Shut up! Just—shut up!"

What?

"I just can't take the lies anymore, okay? It's all such a huge load of—*horseshit*."

Horseshit.

Sierra was right. That was no sneeze. Damn! This was one weird cowgirl.

"Those assholes at that goddamn school want to make her a saint," Charlene went on, her voice rising and shaking. "Well, she ain't no saint. She's a goddamn murderer. She killed my cousins—"

Charlene broke off. She pulled off her glasses and wiped her eyes before continuing.

"Just get me the sunglasses."

I made no move to open the door.

"Are you talking about the Beeman children?"

Charlene's eyes widened.

"You know about them?"

"Yes, I heard. What a horrible tragedy."

"It was horrible all right. Marilyn kills three kids, and my mother gets the blame."

I tried my best to dredge up the assorted facts I'd heard about the chicken house fire. Charlene's mother was Marilyn's cousin Anita—the older girl who allegedly set the fire. The one who should have known better.

"Marilyn tried to save them," I said. "She ran back—she got burned—"

"She ran back, all right," Charlene said, "but not to let them out. Marilyn ran back to lock them *in*."

I sat there in the breeze of the air conditioner and tried to let her words sink in.

"I need those sunglasses," Charlene said. "I've got to—"

"How do you know?" I said. "You weren't even born yet, and all the stories—"

"My mother told me," Charlene said.

Oh, so that was it. Anita had wanted to look less evil in the eyes of her daughter. I guess I couldn't blame her—

"I'll get the glasses," I said. I reached forward to open the door.

"My mom didn't lock the chicken house door," Charlene said. "She just wedged it with a wood chip. Anybody could have pushed it open."

I didn't say anything. It was one girl's word against another's, and it all happened a long, long time ago.

"My mom went back the next day and looked through the ashes. She found the slide bolt—locked. She wasn't the one who locked it, but it didn't matter. Marilyn was a hero, and my mother—"

"Why didn't she say something?"

"She did, but nobody believed her. It just made everyone hate her even more. So she gave up. She lived her whole life with everybody thinking she was a child-killer. Except Marilyn, of course. It was so unfair, but my mom learned to live with it somehow. She actually forgave Marilyn, if you can believe it."

It was no harder to believe than Charlene's other revelations.

"Well, I'm sorry," I said. "It all sounds terribly sad."

Charlene shrugged.

"I didn't know the whole story until a couple of years ago. Up to then, I thought Marilyn was my fairy godmother. She bought me horses and paid for all my riding lessons. Later on, she totally supported my mom—paid for everything when she got sick." Charlene snuffled and wiped her nose with the back of her hand. "If Mom hadn't gotten cancer, I might never have found out the truth. She told me a week before she died."

Even though she was crying, Charlene seemed to have calmed down. Just as well, I thought. She was more than a little scary when she got worked up.

"So, if you could get those—Curtis's—glasses—"

Opening the door, I eased myself to the ground. Retrieving the key fob from my purse, I clicked the remote. The trunk popped open.

My eyes were still adjusting to the darkness inside as I pulled my backpack toward me. As I unzipped it, I heard the door of the pickup slam shut. A second later, Charlene was at my side.

I rummaged through the assortment of belongings in my backpack and quickly recognized the sunglasses case by feel. As I pulled it out, sunlight caught the little metal plate on top.

CW.

Charlene's hand reached toward it. At the same instant, my mind made the connection.

These weren't Curtis's glasses.

These glasses belonged to Charlene Wollensky.

Which meant—

Charlene had left them in Marilyn's bathroom.

A picture of Marilyn's body flashed across my mind, and another puzzle piece slid sickeningly into place.

The slide bolt.

The image of that piece of hardware protruding from Marilyn's traumatized mouth had etched itself permanently into my brain. I had assumed I'd never make sense of it, but now—

There was no time to second-guess what had transpired in Marilyn's bedroom. Right now, my only task was to preserve the evidence and get the hell away—

"Give me those!" The words turned into a shriek as I reached up and slammed the trunk lid down as hard as I could. It hit Charlene's forearm with a thwack, but that didn't stop her from grabbing my hair with her other hand.

"You tried to break my arm, you crazy bitch!"

But the trunk was closed, and the glasses were still inside. Wrenching myself free and losing a handful of hair in the process, I scrambled toward the front of the car. Opening the door, I slid inside and slammed it. One click, and all the doors were locked. As quickly as I could, I jammed the key into the ignition. In my rearview mirror, I caught sight of Charlene.

What was she doing on the passenger side of her truck?

A moment later, I had my answer. Charlene swiveled around with something black in her right hand. I had just thrown my car into drive when—

Bam!

She'd grabbed her gun! She was shooting at me!

Jesus Christ! Was this really happening?

I stamped my foot on the accelerator. A rooster tail of gravel shot out from under my rear tires as the big Chrysler jumped forward.

Whack! A bullet must have hit my car.

Ducking my head down as far as I could without blocking my view, I struggled to steer toward the street. At least my tires still seemed intact.

I saw no one else in the parking lot as I crashed over the curb and shot out onto Bruner Avenue. A tan sedan swerved to miss me, but otherwise the street was clear. A moment later, I screeched to a stop at St. Rose Parkway. I just couldn't muster the nerve to pull onto a six-lane road of speeding traffic without pausing first. As eager as I was to ditch Charlene and her Saturday night special, it seemed counterproductive to turn myself into roadkill.

No white pickup appeared in my rearview mirror as seconds ticked by. Then, emboldened by a tiny break in the traffic, I stepped on the gas and careened across all six lanes. The air brakes on an eighteen-wheeler screamed their disapproval, and a taxi swerved onto the median, narrowly avoiding my rear fender. But as the chorus of angry honks died behind me, my only regret was that there was no cop around to notice. Where were the police when you wanted them?

I'll get on the freeway, I told myself. With luck, a state trooper would pull me over. And if that didn't happen, I was pretty sure I remembered seeing a police station near the "Welcome to Fabulous Las Vegas" sign. If I got off the freeway at Russell Road, I'd be near it. If Charlene reappeared, I might as well lead her to the cops.

An almost law-abiding right turn put me on the on-ramp to I-15, and I merged into the freeway traffic without raising anybody's blood pressure. Hammering down on the accelerator, I sped up the freeway in the right-hand lane, keeping one eye on my rearview mirror. By the time I passed Silverado Ranch Boulevard, no white pickup had appeared.

Whew.

She must have given up, and now all I had to do was let Detective

Booth know that while he did have a bad guy in jail, there was *another* psychopath he needed to nab. Or maybe I should just call 911. Too bad my phone was in my backpack—

No, it wasn't! How could I have forgotten? I'd transferred it to the small purse I'd carried to the memorial service. The small purse that was sitting next to my right hand, still slung across my chest by its narrow shoulder strap.

Keeping one hand on the wheel, I coaxed the zipper open.

Now I was passing Blue Diamond Road, and Charlene was nowhere in sight. Mostly by feel, I managed to scroll down to Detective Booth's number and hit "Send." I had just heard the first ring, when—

Whump!

Something smacked into me from behind, jolting my neck against the headrest and sending my phone skittering across the seat and onto the floor. As my head jerked forward again, I caught sight of a pickup grille in my mirror.

Charlene! She'd bumped me at seventy miles an hour! If I hadn't been traveling equally fast, I'd now be a bloody splat on the embankment! Amazingly, I was still rolling and still more or less in control of my car.

I glanced in my mirror again. The white pickup was glued to my bumper. Damn! Was she revving up to hit me again? And—oh, my God—did she still have ammo?

Just then, the first sign for Frank Sinatra Drive appeared.

That was it!

I could get off on Frank Sinatra! That would catch Charlene off guard, and she'd be stuck zooming north on the freeway.

Yeah! It could work.

I glanced at my phone, which had skidded to the far side of the floor. There was no way I could reach it while I was driving. Had I reached Detective Booth? I wondered. Had he answered and hung up? Or—had I reached his voice mail, maybe?

"*Help!*" I yelled. "*I'm on I-15! I'm being chased by Marilyn Weaver's killer!*"

It was probably pointless, but it actually felt good to scream.

"*I'm getting off on Frank Sinatra!*"

As I veered off the freeway, Charlene's grille hit my back bumper again. Damn! What was with the bumper car game? This chick was really beginning to irritate me. I had to lose her, once and for all.

I blew down the ramp and onto Frank Sinatra, but—damn her!—Charlene stuck right behind me. For a split second, I considered slamming on my brakes and letting her plow right into me. That would bring an end to the nonsense. The trouble was, it would probably bring an end to me, too, and that would definitely leave the wrong woman standing. No way that was happening, at least not without a fight. I might have felt sorry for the rodeo queen back at the memorial service, but now I'd worked my way through freaked out to totally pissed off. This bitch needed to be neutralized, and there was nobody around but me to get the job done.

Hitting the brake pedal and yanking the wheel, I managed to make a hard right into a narrow driveway without taking another hit. For better or worse, I was headed toward a row of loading docks in the bowels of the Mandalay Bay Convention Center.

I had no idea whether I'd just made a brilliant move or trapped myself in a dead end. On the plus side, I couldn't see Charlene in my mirror as I took another right in front of the loading docks, narrowly missed a metal barricade, and sideswiped a huge dumpster.

Damn! I was going to have a hard time explaining the sorry state of my loaner-mobile to the guys at the Chrysler dealership.

At least I'd ditched Charlene. I slowed down as I passed a row of smaller dumpsters and headed toward what looked like it might be an escape route back to Frank Sinatra. I kept hoping I'd see someone to scream at for help, but I'd apparently turned up at a moment when no trade shows were underway. The place was utterly deserted.

All at once, *vroom!* The roar ricocheted off the concrete walls surrounding me. I hardly needed to look in my mirror to know I had company. Charlene's truck was bearing down on me, tires squealing as she rounded the big dumpster.

I glanced at the driveway that curved around the wall beside me.

Go for it! Get away!

That was all I could think. Charlene wouldn't stop until she killed me, and this might be my last chance to escape.

Except—what if it wasn't an escape route after all? What if I turned the corner and found myself boxed in?

There was no way in hell I was going to become Charlene's next victim without a fight. Like it or not, it was time to beat the bitch at her own game.

Stamping on the gas and jerking my wheel to the right, I skidded around the row of smaller dumpsters. Jamming on the brakes, I spun around, hitting the nearest dumpster with my left fender.

Smash! Smash! Smash! The domino effect sent dumpsters careening in all directions. As they scattered, I saw Charlene take two on the right side. The truck spun to the left, completing an about-turn before skidding into a wall with a reverberating crash.

The noise died down to silence.

Oh, my God! Maybe I'd killed her!

"You fuckin' retard!"

Or maybe not.

"I'm gonna blow your goddamn brains out!"

Crap! She still had ammo!

Taking a deep breath, I accelerated again, steering as well as I could to line my front end up with the broad side of one of the dumpsters I'd hit before.

Then I closed my eyes and jammed the pedal to the floor.

Wham! Screech! Wham!

And then I was dead.

I had to be dead, because everything was white and smelled like hell.

Everything hurt like hell, too.

But wait. Do they have car alarms in hell?

Mine was going off.

I blinked, but I still couldn't see.

Jesus! My chest felt like a cannonball had just gone through it.

Which must mean—*hallelujah!*—I was alive after all. I'd just never had an air bag deploy in my face.

Coughing on whatever fire and brimstone they pack into those things, I managed to—another hallelujah!—open my door. The horn was still honking robotically.

My eyes stung, but as I stepped around the dumpster, I had no trouble seeing one very steamed cowgirl through the windshield of her pickup. The left front tire of her truck was flat, and the wheel was bent. The driver's door was pinned shut by the dumpster, and the other door was smack up against a concrete wall. The bitch was trapped.

I inched forward, still unsure whether Charlene was going to shoot at me. But when I got close enough to see inside the cab, my fears subsided a little. Shoulders heaving, she had both hands on her face.

For whatever reason, my car suddenly fell silent. Now the only sound was Charlene's bawling. I could hear it plainly even though her window was only down half an inch.

Oh, God! She saw me!

Or did she? I couldn't be sure, but one thing was obvious. However angry Charlene had been a minute before, she was all grief now.

"I didn't mean to do it!" she wailed. "I wasn't supposed to kill her.

Marilyn is the killer, not me!"

Whoa! That was practically a confession, wasn't it? And Charlene wasn't finished.

"All I wanted was for her to own up to what she did!" Charlene moaned between racking sobs.

Was she talking to me? I still wasn't sure she knew I was there.

"Copper, I swear—"

She knew, all right.

"I just wanted her to—to clear my mom's name—to be *honest*. But all she did was offer me money."

Her voice dropped off into choking gasps. I just stood there, wondering why the racket hadn't attracted any attention. Didn't all these big resorts have private security forces?

"I didn't want her goddamn money!" Charlene howled. "I was sick of the payoffs! She managed to shut my mother up with money for all those years, but I couldn't—and she wouldn't—"

Just then, a symphony of sirens. A minute later, I was surrounded by three cops in squad cars, two dudes on bikes, a guy on a golf cart, and a young suit in a black Jeep.

Hooray! The law was here!

"She's got a gun!" I yelled as two security guards headed toward Charlene. "Watch out!"

They must have heard me, because one of them pulled out his own gun. I was still watching when a large hand grasped my shoulder.

I turned to find myself reflected in the mirrored sunglasses of a Metro cop.

"I'm so glad you're here," I said. "She tried to kill me!"

"Please turn around, miss."

I turned and—what the hell?—cold metal on my wrists.

Handcuffs?

"I—I'm not the criminal," I said, failing to hold my voice steady.

"It's her." I jerked my chin in Charlene's direction. "The woman in the truck—"

It didn't matter what I said. A moment later, the same big hands that had snapped handcuffs on my wrists were pushing my head into the back of a Metro cruiser. Charlene hadn't killed me, but she was certainly turning my life into hell.

Chapter 32

"Darling, we're just not sure Las Vegas is *good* for you."

My mother. She was trying to manage my life, but all she really accomplished was to make me smile. I laughed, in fact, even though it hurt so bad I almost cried at the same time. Air bags might save lives, but they definitely do some damage in the process. My chest—the last remaining unbattered stretch of skin on my body—now sported a big new purple splotch.

"Don't blame Las Vegas for the actions of a maniac from Montana," I said as I took a sip of strawberry lemonade.

Once again, I was queen of my brother's living room, propped up on pillows on the sofa and enjoying the undivided attention of my assembled family. They had all converged on the police department on Russell Road as soon as Detective Booth, who actually had, thanks to the wonders of voice mail, heard my shouted announcement about getting off on Frank Sinatra. It was Booth who called in the cavalry, and he also called my brother.

Of course, the wonders of voice mail also meant that Booth had my screams on tape, and I had little doubt I'd hear them again someday.

I could only hope it would be in a friendly setting and not in a hostile courtroom. I still hadn't adequately explained why I was in possession of a certain pair of sunglasses, after all. For now, I considered myself fortunate to be wearing my own clothes instead of an orange jumpsuit provided by the Clark County Detention Center.

I was also lucky not to be sporting a hospital gown. After she got a load of my latest injury, my mother was determined to take me to an emergency room. Fortunately, Mr. Cluff cooled her down with an air bag experience of his own.

"It was painful, Jackie," he said, "but the best medical advice I got was to rest. Don't you think Copper would feel better if we took her home and babied her instead of making her sit in a hospital waiting room?"

So there I was, but this time Nicky wasn't nearly as understanding. Pirate sword in hand, he glared at me with the one eye that wasn't covered with a black patch.

"I know you're tired of waiting around for me to able to play again," I said. "I'll be better soon, I promise."

Damn. I *better* be better soon. I was really getting tired of looking like a bad boxer.

Just as a double dose of ibuprofen was helping me drift off to sleep, my phone launched into the theme from *The Good, the Bad and the Ugly*.

David.

I groped around in the darkness and managed to answer before the tune ended.

"I'm back."

Two ordinary words, but David's tone was anything but ordinary.

"Are you okay?"

"I think so," he said. "I mean—no."

"What's wrong?"

"I can't tell you on the phone."

"Come over, then. I'm home—in my apartment. I don't have a car."
I took another breath to explain why, but the words wouldn't form.
All I could manage was, "Just get over here."

David arrived twenty minutes later, which meant he was lucky to
have avoided a speeding ticket on the way. I hobbled over to the door
and opened it.

"Oh, my God, Copper. Are you all ri—"

"No." I had finally overdrawn my allotment of fake "I'm fines."

"I'm not all right. Come on in."

I shut the door. My air conditioner may be terminal, but it still
manages to tamp the temperature down a few degrees. Even though
it was past midnight, the air outdoors was as hot as a hair dryer.

I walked over to my bed.

"This is the coolest spot in the place," I said, "and if you don't mind,
I'm better off horizontal."

I stretched out. David perched on the edge of the bed.

"You first," I said.

"No, *you* first."

Too tired to argue, I filled him in on the day's excitement. David
held his head in both hands while I talked. When I was finished, he
looked up.

"Copper. I don't know what to say. Except—you're here. You're
going to be all right."

No thanks to you. I might be injured and tired, but I was also still
plenty angry.

"So what happened in Scarsdale?"

"There's no baby."

I pulled my head up.

"There never was a baby. Rebecca made the whole thing up."

Neither of us said anything more for a few minutes. What was there to say? Obviously, Rebecca had just used a version of the oldest trick in the book to get her man back.

But it was so stupid! She had to know the truth would come out as soon as a baby failed to appear. She must be crazy.

"My mother saw Rebecca in White Plains the other day. Rebecca and Felix, I should say."

"Felix. Her cat?"

"Her fiancé, as it turns out."

Her fiancé! But that meant—

"They were at an Italian restaurant—both drinking red wine. Mom called me. I called Rebecca, and nothing she said matched with what my mother had seen. That's why I had to go find out for myself." He looked at me, his eyes dark pools of pain.

"So you should feel better now. You're off the hook," I said.

"It was a stupid, cruel trick—she just wanted to hurt me." He shook his head. "I don't feel better. I feel horrible."

His head drooped. His shoulders drooped. As I looked at him, I felt a pang of sadness, too.

The baby we had both allowed into our hearts—the little boy Willie Morningthunder had welcomed and blessed—was gone. Okay, I should say he never was, but that's not quite true. He was as real to David and me as anyone or anything you've never seen but believe exists. He was as real to me as Queen Elizabeth or Angkor Wat.

"You feel sad because in your mind he was alive, and now he's dead," I said. "When I was in fourth grade, a mean boy named Preston Cobb told a second grader that his father shot the Easter Bunny when he was on a hunting trip, and he had the skin to prove it. The second grader didn't say anything, but later I found her crying under a lunch table. I got her to come out and talk to me. 'I don't want to believe in the Easter Bunny,' she said. 'But I just can't help it. And now he's dead.'"

I considered telling David to go home after delivering his watershed news, but I didn't have the energy or the heart. He had treated me badly, but he had been hurt, too. We might not be a couple anymore, but we were two wounded souls.

Clad in the T-shirt and shorts he'd arrived in, David was curled up next to me when I woke up.

Could we really get back together again after all that had happened? It didn't seem likely, but it still felt nice to feel him breathe right next to me. If challenges forge a relationship, maybe we had just added some major structural components. On the other hand—

David stretched and turned toward me.

"Saturday morning breakfast at the vicarage," I said. "You'll be the extra guest Sierra always cooks enough for."

"I better go home. I slept in my clothes."

But I won out, and a few minutes later we headed down the stairs and across the lawn. Too bad if we were rumpled and unshowered and uncoupled. It was Saturday morning, and my family would just have to deal with it.

"Copper, darling!" Mom said. "How *are* you? You look—" She paused.

God, I must look really awful.

"You both look—like you could use mimosas!" Mr. Cluff filled in the silence and clapped David on the back. Then he headed for the kitchen, and we stepped into the living room.

I suppose I shouldn't have been surprised that Willie Morningthunder was sitting on the sofa. Michael and Sierra often invite friends to Saturday morning brunch, and Willie definitely needed some TLC. I could see the cast on his left arm under the sling, and bandages peeked out above the collar of his shirt.

Nicky and Willie were examining something I guessed was a peace pipe, but when Nicky saw me, he ran over and hugged me around the knees. David reached down and ruffled his hair. *At least Nicky is a real boy,* I thought. God, I love that kid.

"Miss Copper, I'm so glad to see you," Willie said from the sofa. "I hear you faced a second challenge."

"I'm just trying to keep up with you," I said, moving toward him. "I hope your shoulder is feeling better."

"Once again, death beckoned," Willie said. "But fortunately, life answered."

I was standing in front of him now, and his piercing eyes scanned my face. Why did it always seem like he could look into my soul?

He gazed straight into my eyes—and probably all the way to the back of my head.

"'Blue Sky Thunder,'" he said at last. "I thought of it last night, when I heard what had happened. Now that I see you, I know I'm right." He stretched his good arm toward me and took my hand in his. "To me, at least, you'll always be Blue Sky Thunder."

I was too surprised to say anything. Had a Lakota chief really just given me a Native American name?

"It's like my name because we share a double brush with death." Willie patted my hand. "But it's all yours, Miss Black. Like thunder on a clear day, you're an unexpected force."

Me? A force? I hardly felt like one, standing there in my T-shirt and Band-Aids.

"Thank you," I said, feeling woefully incapable of saying anything more appropriate.

"It is I who am in your debt," Willie said. "You did a brave thing when you stood up to Mr. Bartolo. And you were courageous again yesterday."

"I had help."

"Of course. An arrow can't fly without shaft and feathers. But you were the arrowhead."

Willie smiled and reached into his pocket.

"Give me your hand." He placed a small object on my palm. I looked down to find an arrowhead, exquisitely chiseled in lustrous pinkish-white stone.

"Lemme see!" Nicky cried, jumping off the sofa. "What is it?"

I looked at Willie and answered my nephew. "It's a beautiful, beautiful gift."

"Brunch is served!" Sierra called from the kitchen.

"Don't get up, Mr. Morningthunder," my mother said. "I'll bring you a plate." She turned to me. "I'll bring you one, too, darling—"

"Thanks, Mom. I can get my own."

We all trooped into the kitchen, where the table groaned under a spread worthy of a casino buffet. The only thing missing was a chef's hat on Michael's head. He was carving a whole turkey at the far end.

Just before I stepped out of earshot, Willie called David back.

"We should talk," he said, but I didn't catch David's reply.

What is that all about? But before I could even think about finding out, Mr. Cluff handed me a mimosa, Sierra handed me a plate, and Michael said, "White or dark?"

A nice pile of turkey, sweet potato casserole, fruit salad, and homemade corn bread on my plate, I sat down next to Dad at the dining room table. He leaned over and pecked me on the forehead.

"You're looking better, kiddo," he said. "I can't tell you how glad I am to be able to say that."

"I really *am* better," I said. "I feel like I can actually imagine the day I won't be black and blue all over." There was definitely something healing about knowing for sure that Marilyn's murder had been solved.

"I've got news about your minivan—"

"What about the loaner car?" I asked. "Was it a total loss? Dad, I'm so sorry—"

My father chuckled.

"Don't worry about a thing, kiddo," he said.

"But, Dad—"

"No, I mean it. That car wasn't a loaner. The guys at the dealership were too cheap. I had to rent it, and in the rush to get the paperwork done, I forgot to check the box that said I have my own insurance. It cost me an extra twenty dollars a day, but that car was covered down to the last penny—against everything, including acts of God."

"Even acts of a flipped-out buckaroo?"

Dad looked at me. "I'd laugh if I hadn't been so worried, Copper."

I kissed him on the cheek.

"And as for your car," he said, "well, we can go pick it up later, if you feel up to it."

"That would be great, Dad."

"And—I'm taking everyone to dinner tonight at—what is it again?—Cilia—?"

"Ciliano?"

"Yes, that's it! Sierra says it's wonderful."

Ciliano. The restaurant where my whole fallout with David began.

"Invite David if you like," Dad said.

"Okay. Thanks."

But I wasn't sure I wanted to.

Later, when the turkey was little more than a skeleton and Mr. Cluff had mixed his last batch of mimosas, David and I climbed the stairs to my apartment. He'd told me he wanted to talk. The last time he'd used that phrase was to tell me that Rebecca was pregnant. Could he come up with anything to top that? I doubted it, so I invited him up.

"What did Willie want to talk to you about?" I asked when we were inside.

"The baby."

The baby that never was.

"He asked me how things were going, and I told him. But it was weird—like he already knew. He said I'd be all right—that you would comfort me."

What? How did Willie know what I'd do? And what business was it of his, anyway?

"He was right, Copper. You've already comforted me."

We were standing just inside my door. David looked me straight in the eyes. "He was right about Blue Sky Thunder, too. You are most definitely an unexpected force."

I gazed into David's eyes, those dark mirrors. The guy was obviously sorry, but he had really screwed up.

"I don't feel like thunder, but I love the name," I said.

"I love you, Copper."

I let the words hang there. What was there to say? I had no idea what the future held for us—whether I could trust him, rely on him, or even like him. Except—damn it—I *did* like him. And I really, really, really wanted to talk to him about everything that had happened while he was in New York.

"Want to have dinner with me and my family tonight at Ciliano? My father wanted me to ask you."

"I'd like that."

"You damn well better show up," I said.

That afternoon, my father drove me over to Jim Ward Chrysler in Henderson, where we'd dropped off my minivan two days earlier. It had "only a few dents," he told me. Oh, and "bring your pink slip and registration—you might need them."

I didn't stop to wonder why, but when a salesman handed me a new set of keys, the light dawned. My dad, bless his generous heart, was treating me to a new car.

Oh, God, I thought as we waited on the sidewalk in front of the showroom. It would probably be another minivan. At this rate, I'd still own a van when my caretaker needed it to haul my walker around.

But it wasn't another maxi pad that rolled around the side of the building and pulled to a stop in front of me. My new wheels, like them or not, were attached to a shiny black monster truck with a menacing silver grille on the front.

"Jeez! It's huge!" I said.

"You didn't think I'd let my little girl drive around in a tin-can death trap, did you?"

Yeah, there was a lot to argue with in that question, but I wasn't in a mood to bicker about whether my daddy was the boss of me.

"What's that thing on the front?" I said. I knew I should know, but I'm just not that up on cars, especially boy toys like this one.

"It's a winch. Never know when you might need one."

"Dad, the truck's so tall … " I said. "I'm not sure I can—"

"No problem, shortcake!" Dad was already sprinting to the driver's side. As he opened the door, two steps magically slid out.

Damn! I could already hear the ribbing I'd get at *The Light*. This thing had a carbon footprint as big as Milwaukee, and it could probably straddle Mount Rushmore with room to spare.

"You like it?" Dad was back at my side.

"Dad—"

"You *don't* like it?"

"It's great, Dad. It's just that—" I looked at him. Was there a more generous man on the face of the earth? If I were a gold-digging gay guy, I'd do my best to snag him.

"It's just that I'm worried about you."

Dad laughed. "That's my line, kiddo."

"No, seriously. Are you going to be all right?"

"I'm leaving Las Vegas with a lot more than I brought, even though I'm going home alone. It's been a real education." He put his arm around my shoulder. Our eyes met. "Mr. Morningthunder told me there's no baby. I'm sorry."

I didn't know what to say.

"Of all the amazing things I watched you do these last few days, your announcement at dinner the other night tops the list. That took real strength, Copper."

I looked at my dad again. Wasn't he really talking about himself? He was the one who'd come out of the closet after six decades locked up inside. What I'd done paled in comparison.

"Tolerance and acceptance," he said. "They require a lot more strength than fighting and bullying."

"This truck looks like it could do some serious fighting and bullying," I said.

Dad laughed. "After what I saw this week, I want you in something tough."

"After what I saw this week," I said, "I want you with someone genuine."

"David doesn't deserve you."

"No guy will *ever* deserve you, Daddy-o."

Driving my new black behemoth was considerably easier than I'd worried it might be. Even though I felt like a poster child for conspicuous consumption, I also liked the amazing visibility the high-riding driver's seat provided. I thought back to how intimidating Charlene's grille had looked in the Max's rearview mirror. Now I'd be the one menacing innocent sedan drivers from behind.

Dinner at Ciliano started off badly. Michael and Sierra were late, and they weren't answering their cell phones. David arrived right on time carrying three long white boxes. Inside were orchid leis for my mother, Sierra, and me.

"Oh, how lovely!" Mom said. "I feel like I'm getting off a plane in Hawaii!"

"Well, you *are* on the ninth island," I said. "That's what Hawaiians call Las Vegas." I turned to David. "Thanks. They're gorgeous."

"I went to Lei Lady Leis." He looked at me, his eyes those of a repentant puppy.

Did he really think three leis would get him laid? The jury was still way, way out.

David sat down, and we all ordered cocktails. I polished off two martinis while everybody speculated about what was holding the two latecomers up. Fortunately, just as my dad was asking whether we should go ahead and order dinner without them, they stepped out of the elevator and bounded over to our table.

"Champagne!" Michael said after David had draped a lei around Sierra's shoulders. "We've got something to celebrate!"

A few minutes later, when we all had flutes poised for a group clink, Michael spoke.

"There's good news, and there's better news," he said.

"No games," Sierra said. "They've been waiting long enough."

"Okay, the cops figured out who the bones at the building site belong to," Michael said. "They're Indian."

What? How was that *good news?*

"They belong to a man named Rajesh Gupta. A taxi driver who disappeared back in 1981. The case was never solved, mostly because his body was never found."

Rajesh Gupta.

Couldn't deny it was an Indian name. Even though I felt sorry for the poor guy, I couldn't help smiling at the irony.

"The great thing is, the cops have arrested his killer—the caretaker of the old motel that used to be on the building site," Sierra said. "He managed to bury poor Rajesh just before a concrete patio was poured. They kind of suspected the guy but never had enough evidence."

"We're going to place a marker in the new peace garden," Michael said, "which brings me to my other announcement." He raised his glass. "Marilyn Weaver's will was read this afternoon."

What did that have to do with anything? Surely her estate would go to her family or the Parks Academy.

Michael looked at Sierra, and they both smiled.

"Go on, tell them," Sierra said. "The champagne's getting flat."

"Marilyn left the Alliance for the Homeless two million dollars, the same amount she also left to the Neon Museum."

Whoa! Who knew she cared about the homeless?

"The Alliance and the Museum are Curtis's two pet projects," Michael said. "She did it for him."

I guess she never knew about Jenna Bartolo, I thought. Maybe it was just as well. The sins of her childhood had been enough of a burden.

And who knew if she had even sinned? Charlene thought so, and perhaps her mother had, too. But the only person who truly knew what happened that day when a little girl ran back to a burning chicken house was now silent forever. Had she really locked the door and consigned her tiny cousins to a fiery death? A closed slide bolt in the ashes suggested the possibility, but it was hardly proof.

Whatever happened, Marilyn had certainly tried to make things better for Anita and Charlene. In fact, she dedicated her life to helping children. Was it atonement or guiltless altruism? Perhaps it made no difference. Las Vegas was a better place because of

Marilyn Weaver. Her premature death was a tragic loss.

As I dug into the best shiitake risotto in the universe, my thoughts turned to my last dinner at Ciliano. My world had turned upside down in the intervening two weeks, but now some of it had flipped back. I could have my boyfriend back if I wanted him, and my brother's building project was up and running again. On the other hand, the Nash house was history and Marilyn Weaver was gone forever.

It was dessert—mango sorbet with kiwi and wild berry confit—that reminded me of one other irreversible truth: a 50-year-old tortoise was gone forever, too.

Even Blue Sky Thunder couldn't bring Oscar back.

Chapter 33

A remarkably good night's sleep left me feeling almost restored when I woke up Sunday morning. I knew the bathroom mirror would tell me otherwise, which is why I wished I could stay in bed all day. But Dad was leaving for New York in the afternoon, and I had promised I'd join one last family gathering: church services at St. Andrew's.

My brother's church is really just a humble mission in an even humbler neighborhood on the north side of Las Vegas. My family's attendance increased the congregation in the small, peeling clapboard building by at least a third. Mr. Cluff's baritone sounded like it might blow out the one stained glass window that hadn't already been replaced with plexiglass.

Even though he is not an admirer of organized religion—and is Jewish to boot—David was sitting in the pew next to me. When Michael had invited everyone to attend the service at dinner the night before, he'd been the first to say, "I'll be there."

Nicky sat on my right, happily sifting through the contents of my backpack. Mom was next to him.

"You're going to make a fantastic mommy one of these days," she whispered as Michael finished reading the epistle. She reached across Nicky and patted my knee. I looked up. For a millisecond, our eyes connected. Then we both looked down at our hymnals.

That was it. No more would ever pass between us about the baby that never was.

I suppose it might seem sad or unfathomable to someone whose family members actually discussed things, but not to me. With that one short comment, my mother had told me she loved me. And in the instant that our eyes met, she knew I understood.

After the service, we all retired to the parish hall, which was really just a used trailer rescued from a construction site. Old Mrs. Kershaw, the head honcho of the altar guild and owner of legions of unruly dachshunds, had fired up the dented percolator on a rickety folding table, and we stood around with Styrofoam cups in our hands waiting for Michael to finish counting the collection plate. It never took long. St. Andrew's is a nickels-and-pennies sort of place, with the odd casino chip showing up now and then.

"Darling, I might as well tell you now," my mother said, patting my cheek. "We've all decided you need—"

She paused and opened her handbag. Reaching inside, she pulled out a pale lavender envelope embossed with a paisley pattern. It smelled like lavender, too, I noticed as she pressed it into my hands. *"Aspadé."*

Aspadé? What the heck was that, a fancy new perfume? I opened the envelope and slid out—

"Oh!" I said, feeling slightly stupid. *"A spa day!"* I was holding a gift certificate for an exotic selection of personal services at the Caesars Palace spa, including procedures involving banana leaves, warm stones, and something from Fiji called dilo oil.

My family. Most of the time it is an ordinary dysfunctional social unit whose main coping mechanisms are silence and denial. But— bless their hearts—they'd somehow managed to communicate long enough to chip in and treat me to ayurvedic emollients in a Vegas pleasure dome.

"I—thank you," I said. "This is so sweet. Thank you all."

"It probably won't do anything for your black eyes," Sierra said, "but we're hoping it'll at least let you forget about them for a few hours."

Right-o, sister-in-law. I can always count on Sierra to get me back on track when I start feeling too sentimental.

As I headed home after seeing my father off at the airport, my cell phone buzzed. Thinking it was my mother or Sierra with plans for dinner, I answered immediately.

"Copper?"

The voice was female, but it wasn't one I could place instantly.

"Yes. Who is this?"

"Oh, good! This is Jenna."

That was it! Jenna Bartolo!

"Oh! Hi!"

"I'm on Grand Cayman."

Grand Cayman. Isn't that one of those islands where people escape at the end of John Grisham novels?

"In the Caribbean," Jenna went on. "I had to—get away."

"Are you all right?"

"I don't think I've ever been better, Copper, and that's why I called. I wanted to thank you."

"Well—you're welcome," I said. "Things are better here now, too." I told her about Marilyn Weaver's bequest.

"I'm so glad," Jenna said. "I was hoping the Alliance would be able to go on without me. But that's not why I called. I feel as though— well, I owe you, Copper. And I think you could use—"

She paused, and for a second I thought I'd lost the connection.

"I set up an account for you at the Monaco spa. Under your name. Any day you choose, you'll get treated like a queen."

A spa day! I almost laughed out loud.

"Jenna—you really don't have to—"

"You could use it, Copper. I heard about what happened, and I really do owe you. Thanks to what you did that night at Liqmi, I call the shots with Frank now, and I've got my whole life in front of me."

Along with a fully charged anonymous offshore bank account, I guessed. My mind's eye filled in the attentive waiter, the bottomless piña colada, and the postcard-perfect view of a turquoise ocean.

"Good luck, Jenna," I said, not that she needed it. "And thanks."

"I'll be back in Vegas someday," Jenna said, "but only on my own terms."

I had no doubt she would be.

My family tried its best to persuade me to spend Monday at the Caesars Palace spa, but I resisted. It wasn't that aromatherapy and exotic massage techniques didn't sound appealing. It was that I couldn't bear missing all the scuttlebutt at *The Light* about Rajesh Gupta's bones, Marilyn Weaver's will, and Jenna Bartolo's escape to Shangri-la. And okay, I can't deny I was curious about what gossip might be circulating about me, too. I figured I'd learn far more with my real-live ear to the wall than by getting a secondhand report on Tuesday.

The gauntlet awaiting me in the main hallway at *The Light* consisted mostly of the same "How *are* you?" chorus I'd experienced after the Nash house blew up. What surprised me were all the whistles, cheers, and shouts of "You go, girl!" that were mixed in. It wasn't quite a tickertape parade, but by the time I reached my mailbox, I did feel a bit like a returning astronaut.

Rounding the partition into my cube, I found Mary Beth Sweeney with one hip on the edge of my desk. Standing next to her was—Greg Langenfeld!

The big boss was paying the lowly calendar girl a personal visit?

"Hi, Copper," Mary Beth said. "Glad to see your black eyes are lightening up."

"Thanks," I said. "You were right about ice packs."

Mary Beth and Greg shared a look.

Oh, yeah! The column. That's why they're here.

"So glad you're on the mend, Copper," Greg said. "Mary Beth and I wanted to make sure we caught you as soon as you arrived."

Go ahead. Get it over with, I thought. Tell me how sorry you are that I'm not the one getting a new writing gig.

"I'm so glad you queried me about a regular column," Greg began. "It was a tough decision—"

Right.

"Here's what we've worked out. Mary Beth's new column will run three times a week. She'll cover local issues, human interest—whatever she wants, really. We're calling it 'All Around the Town.'"

Great. I'm so happy for her. Couldn't you have just sent me an email?

"And we're still thinking about what to call your column."

Wait! My *column?*

"Something that captures a young perspective," Mary Beth said.

"It'll run once a week in 'Dazzle,' at least to begin with," Greg went on. "You'll cover arts, entertainment, local trends, singles stuff—oh, and you'll have a blog, too, of course."

I stared at both of them.

"I—thank you," I managed.

"Don't worry—we'll wait a while to take your picture," Greg said, "but your first piece will run in two weeks. Seven hundred words. Sound okay?"

"It sounds—great," I said. "Really. I'm just—surprised."

"Mary Beth has offered to give you pointers if you need help," Greg said. "She'll be an excellent mentor."

Mary Beth lingered after Greg took off.

"You've got the party at Liqmi to thank for this, Copper," she said.

"No," I said. "You're the one I need to thank, Mary Beth."

"You won't feel so grateful when you're up against a bad deadline," Mary Beth said, "but you're welcome."

It was going to take more than a box of chocolates to show Mary Beth my gratitude. I needed to find something that would not only express my thanks, but also overcome all the awful thoughts I'd harbored about her shoes. Mary Beth was my mentor now, my colleague … Suddenly it hit me.

A spa day! Yeah, that would be just the ticket.

My day would have been nearly perfect if my phone hadn't buzzed ten minutes before I left work.

"Hello, Ms. Black," an all-too-familiar voice said when I answered. "This is Detective Booth."

Crap. A nice day shot to hell.

By the time I hung up, I had agreed to meet Booth at his office first thing in the morning.

Which meant tomorrow was shot to hell, too.

Chapter 34

That night, following well-established Black family tradition, I mentioned nothing about tomorrow's command appearance before the law. For all I knew, I'd be led away in handcuffs after I showed up at Booth's lair in the morning. Even though I'd caught a crazed killer and nailed a rat bastard, I was still guilty of withholding evidence, impeding an investigation, obstruction of justice, lying to the police, reckless driving, destruction of property, and whatever other felonies and misdemeanors could be attached to my unintentional theft and prolonged possession of Charlene Wollensky's sunglasses.

The only precaution I took was to call Chris Farr.

"I might not make it in before noon," I said. "I've got an appointment."

I let him assume it was the medical kind.

"Take all the time you need," he said.

"Thanks, Chris."

"Oh, I almost forgot. I've got a greenhouse."

A greenhouse?

"If it would help, I could take care of those plants you rescued from the Nash house."

Before I hung up, we arranged for Chris to pick the plants up at David's house. He had divulged his interest in indoor horticulture, but he wasn't about to share his address. The greenhouse was one more little factoid to add to the short list of things I knew about my boss. Like the others, it inspired more questions. Like—what else did he grow in that greenhouse? Maybe someday I'd learn a little more about my mysterious boss. For the time being, I was grateful that the green carnivores could move into more pleasant surroundings. The sole survivors of the Nash house conflagration were the only living mementos Kayla Lord would have from her brief reign as owner of the *Hitman's Holiday* house.

Okay, I should have told my relatives that I was in danger of getting hauled off to the clink. I might have, too, if it weren't for my brother's idea of a joke.

"She's here," I heard Sierra call when I was still standing at the front door. The second I stepped inside, "My Way" began blaring from the stereo.

Frank Sinatra.

"You faced it all, and you're still standing tall," Sierra said, handing me a glass of champagne. "Tonight, the party's just for you."

I decided it was better to revel in my blaze of glory and my new byline than to let on that I might be in jail this time tomorrow. I mean—come on!—it might well be my last night as a free woman for a while. Why should I cast a shadow on it?

Of course, one might also accuse me of denial, and one might also be dead right. I didn't even tell David. Sierra had invited him to the party at the vicarage, and when I told him about my new column, I could easily read the pride in his eyes.

"All too soon, you'll be moving back to New York," he said. "Las Vegas is a great launching pad."

Yeah! My whole life was ahead of me! Tomorrow was just an unpleasant hiccup, right? I was a good guy, after all. In fact, I was a goddamn hero, with black eyes and bandages to prove it!

After the party, David invited me to go home with him. He used his superior air conditioning system as bait. The temperature outside was still blistering, but I wasn't ready to sell out.

"I need time," I said.

"Whenever you're ready," David said.

Which might be never, I didn't reply. But who knew how I'd feel after my meeting with Booth tomorrow? It might be nice to have a sympathetic visitor while I was doing time at the Women's Correctional Center.

I got little sleep. Every time I began to drift off, I'd jerk wide awake with visions of chain gangs in my head. Then, staring at the ceiling, I'd imagine myself flying off to Grand Cayman like Jenna Bartolo.

But then I'd flip back to denial mode.

This can't be happening. This can't be happening.

I was still thinking "this can't be happening" when I pulled into the parking lot of police headquarters a few minutes before eight the next morning. I'd expected traffic, but the roads had been surprisingly clear.

Might as well get it over with.

I walked across the parking lot, joining a small cadre of what looked like employees heading into the building. As I approached the entrance, a young man in cargo shorts emerged through the double doors. A few steps more, and—wait! I knew that guy! It was Colby Nash!

"Copper!"

"Colby! What are you doing here?"

"Detective Booth called me. I thought he wanted to question me more about the—what happened—"

He shot me a hangdog look. "God, Copper, I'm glad you're all right."

"Thanks."

"All Booth wanted was to give me this." He lifted his right arm. I hadn't paid attention to the bag he was carrying, but now I found myself staring at a pink bowling ball bag with a big "L" on it.

Which I recognized! It was the bag from the wreckage of the Nash house!

"That's—yours?"

He set it down on the pavement, crouched down, and started unzipping it.

Oh, my God!

I shut my eyes, even though I knew the police would never have let him walk out with a severed head.

Slowly, I opened one eye just as he pulled out—

A sparkly pink bowling ball.

"It's my mom's from high school. She'll be tickled to have it back, especially now that the house is gone."

A pang of guilt rippled through me, but I fought off the urge to apologize. Colby was the one who'd stored gunpowder in the basement, after all. *He* should be apologizing to *me*.

"I'm so sorry for what happened, Copper," he said. "I never meant the gunpowder to hurt anyone. I was just getting ready for an explosion scene I was going to shoot out in the desert. I really hope you're okay."

The remorse in his voice sounded genuine.

"I'm getting there," I said. "I hope you can start over."

"I've decided to go to film school at USC," he said. "I've always kind of resisted that structured sort of thing but, well, sometimes life blows up in your face—"

He paused and stared at me as his cheeks turned candy-apple red. "Gosh, Copper, I'm sorry. I didn't mean—"

"It's okay, Colby. It's an accurate description of what happened. I just wish it hadn't happened to an innocent old tortoise."

"No chance he escaped?"

"I don't see how. The only chance he had was by digging under the fence. He was trying to do that the last time I saw him, but he wasn't making much progress."

Colby and I exchanged email addresses before we parted. I glanced over my shoulder at him as he headed toward his SUV, bowling ball bag in hand. Setting aside his penchant for explosives, he wasn't a bad guy. Maybe someday I'd rent one of his straight-to-video movies and see whether he had any talent for filmmaking.

Inside the police station, I spoke with a grumpy middle-aged woman on the other side of a window of bulletproof glass and signed my name on a clipboard. A few minutes later, a young policewoman opened a door I hadn't noticed and called my name. As I rode with her in an elevator to the third floor and followed her through a maze of cubicles, I couldn't shake the feeling of doom that weighed on me. It would have helped if the policewoman had tried to chat, but she was stonily silent until we entered a small office with a window overlooking the parking lot. I could see my big black *vee*-hicle, and I couldn't help wondering if I'd be the one driving it away.

"Sit here," my escort said, pointing to a steel chair next to the desk. "Detective Booth will be right with you."

While I waited, I scanned the office. Nothing about it divulged the slightest detail of Booth's personality or private life. A row of gray metal filing cabinets filled one wall, and a large map of Las Vegas hung on another. The desk was completely clear except for a blotter, a pencil holder, and—then I saw it. Next to the pencil holder stood a small double-paneled picture frame. Stretching my head around, I made out two photos. One was a faded shot of a fair-haired bride, and the other was an equally washed-out picture of a family group. Mother, two kids, and—I craned my neck. Yes, the daddy was Booth. He had more hair—darker than his current crop—but there was no mistaking that forehead and thin-lipped smile.

Wow. The guy had a family. Why had I never wondered about that before?

Just then, Booth appeared in the doorway, and I snapped back into prim attention.

"Checking things out, I see," he said as he closed the door.

Damn. He'd caught me.

"Hello, Detective Booth," I said.

"Good morning, Ms. Black."

Booth walked around to his desk chair, pulled it out, and sat down. Pulling open a drawer, he extracted a yellow legal pad. He selected a pencil from the cup, wrote something on the pad, and finally looked at me again.

"Do you know why you're here?" he asked.

Typical cop question, but two could play that game.

"You asked me to come," I said.

"So I did." He squinted at me. "We have some unfinished business."

Was my forehead shining? I could feel the sweat. My mind churned, but I decided silence was my best tactic.

"You tampered with a crime scene."

Oh, God. Here it comes.

"You withheld evidence."

Bring on the handcuffs.

"You totaled Charlene Wollensky's truck."

"What? She was trying to kill me!"

Booth smiled. "I figured that would get a rise out of you." He tapped his pencil on his pad. "The thing is, you delayed our ability to identify a murderer. You endangered the public with a high-speed car chase. You damaged and destroyed property."

A cold hand squeezed my heart as Booth started talking again.

"The district attorney has decided—"

I held my breath.

"Not to press charges."

Wait! Was I hearing right? I stared at Booth.

"What you did was illegal, and those glasses would have led us to Ms. Wollensky sooner. On the other hand, your little escapade at Mandalay Bay pulled a full confession out of her. It's all admissible, and prosecutors tell me they're building a good case against Sean DuBois, too. The folder you provided was a big help. Gave us all we needed to follow up at the school and also let us know about Sean's nasty little gambling habit. His mother was covering his markers, and he had signed several personal notes promising to pay her back."

So *that* was why Sean was shredding her files—hoping to destroy evidence of his debts. Good thing he underestimated the omniscience and quick thinking of The Hard Drive.

"You played with fire, but—well, you lucked out." He paused. "There is, however, one other small issue."

Who cares? I was going to walk out of the building and drive away forever. That was all that mattered.

"It involves a tortoise."

Oh, my God. Oscar.

"Did your tortoise have a peace symbol painted on his back? And a hole in his shell?"

"Yes! Did someone find him? Is he alive? Where is he?"

"We got a call about a tortoise like that. Evidently a boy found him down on Gallagher Road a couple of days ago, and word circulated. The family was keeping him—trying to find his owner—"

"That's wonderful!" I said. "I can go pick him up—"

"No, you can't."

"Why not? I can return him to his real owner."

"He's gone. He dug out of their yard yesterday and escaped."

But—he was alive!

"Put the word out, and you might find him. That peace symbol is a real asset."

Booth stood up and moved to his office door. He opened it.

"You're free to go," he said. I stood up and crossed the room.

"Good-bye, Detective Booth."

"You're even luckier than that old tortoise," he said. "And just like him, you don't even know it."

Whatever that was supposed to mean.

I didn't bother to try to find out. I was too eager to be back outside again, and to put the last two weeks behind me.

It wasn't until I was zipping down Dean Martin that it dawned on me. How could I have been so dense? I didn't owe my freedom to a kindly D.A. I owed it to a pit bull of a detective who had decided I was a good guy after all. Booth, and Booth alone, was the reason I could have dinner at home tonight instead of in a detention center mess hall.

Making a right turn at the first available driveway, I pulled to a stop in the parking lot of an industrial park. I pulled out my cell phone and clicked on Booth's number.

Please, oh please, no voice mail …

Click. "You've reached Detective Michael Booth. If this is an emergency, hang up and dial 911—"

Damn. This was an emergency, but not the kind 911 could help me with—

Click. "Hello, this is Detective Mike Booth speaking."

Hooray!

"Hello, Detective Booth. This is Copper Black."

Silence.

"I left without thanking you, and I—well, thank you. For everything."

A pause. "You're welcome, Ms. Black."

Another pause. I took a breath, but before I could say another word, Booth spoke again.

"I do hope you find that tortoise."

I drove directly to *The Light*, where I surprised Chris Farr at the mailboxes.

"Copper! I wasn't expecting you until after lunch!"

"Things went better than I expected," I said. "So here I am."

"Congratulations on your new column." He sounded almost wistful.

"Thanks! I wanted to talk to you about that, actually. If there's ever a show or celebrity or topic you'd like me to cover—"

"Well, now that you mention it—"

Damn. What was I talking myself into?

"*Fresh Kings of Cool*, that new Rat Pack tribute show, is opening at the San Marino next weekend. I'd love to have a young person's perspective on it. The producers claim it's going to create a whole new generation of Sinatra fans, and you're the perfect person to know whether they've succeeded."

He paused. I hesitated, but I wasn't quite sure why. He'd just handed me the exact sort of assignment I'd been wishing for ever since I arrived in Las Vegas. Why is it that when you finally achieve a goal you've been working toward, you suddenly have doubts about whether you really want it? I'll never understand that.

"That sounds great, Chris. Thank you."

And really, I realized as I headed to my cube, it did sound perfect. Who better than cub columnist Copper Black to pontificate about whether children of the new millennium are going to get off on Frank Sinatra?

ACKNOWLEDGMENTS

It would be impossible for me to acknowledge all the people who have—wittingly or otherwise—contributed to the existence of this book. First on my list must be Mark Sedenquist. I can truly say that without him, I would have long ago tossed my pages to the wind. Instead, here they are.

Thanks to Nancy Zerbey for insightful editing and to Jennifer Heuer for brilliant cover art and book design.

If I got anything right about crime scenes and police investigations, credit goes to Mark McNett and Sean Taylor.

For inspiration, example, advice, and encouragement, thanks to Eric Miller, Steve Fey, Tami Cowden, Oksana Marafioti, Holly McKinnis, and Brian Rouff.

For insight into the endlessly fascinating history and evolution of Las Vegas, my thanks to Ruth Mormon and John Tsitouras.

Thanks, too, to Stephen Glass, Sandy Glass, and Margaret Sedenquist. You all, in so many ways, helped make this book happen.

Special gratitude goes to Carolyn Goodman, founder of The Meadows School and champion of educational excellence. As our city's mayor, she shares her wisdom and vision with all who live here. For all you have done to make Las Vegas a better place, my deepest thanks.

In closing, I must mention Las Vegas pioneer businesswoman Anna Roberts Parks. No real school bears her name. You can, however, find it on an exhibit hall at the Clark County Museum in Henderson, where items from her extensive collection of Southwestern art and artifacts are on display.

ABOUT THE AUTHOR

When Megan Edwards arrived in Las Vegas to do some quick research for a novel, she had no idea she was on a blind date with her new hometown. Now, nearly two decades later, she's still in love. As founder and executive editor of Living-Las-Vegas.com, Edwards writes about real life in the shadow of the Strip. Her fiction draws on the city's fascinating history, inhabitants, and ebullient, ever-evolving personality.